Unladylike

Editor: Linda Kay Kurtenbach
Cover Design and Interior Layout: MelindaMartin.me
Publishing Services: April Cox

ISBN: 978-1-7370423-1-0 (paperback), 978-1-7370423-2-7 (hardback)

"Mistakes have the power
to turn you into something
better than you were before."

—Oscar Auliq-Ice

based on a true story of love and adventure

NIKKI FREESTONE SORENSEN

Prologue

This book is based on the life of my grandmother Gladys Irene "Peg" Tarbet, born on the cusp of a new century, July 10, 1901. Many of the events in this book happened and others I created to give the story depth and continuity. Everyone, who met her, loved Grandma Peg, especially her grandchildren whom she inspired with her zeal for life, and enchanted with her cooking, handicrafts, and stories of adventures in far-off Alaska.

The youngest of four boys and four girls, Peg grew up secure in the love of a large successful family. Her parents, John Burt and Mary Luemma Tarbet, homesteaded in Penrith three miles from Newport, Washington. They struggled to clear the land of pine and tamarack trees and hauled them to Spokane's sawmills.

One year later, the railroad rumbled by. Tarbet's homestead provided the perfect place to build a store and post office. It served as the hub of commerce and social activity to about fifty surrounding homes filled with families from the local sawmill and logging operation. Built from local lumber, the store threw out a welcoming front porch that provided ample room to sit and visit for a spell. One could purchase groceries, hardware, lumber, clothing, and even furniture or just gather around the pot belly stove and catch up on world and local news.

Two blocks from the store stood the two-story Tarbet family home with an immense garden, fish hatchery, and orchard. Next to the chicken coop, an oversized weeping willow's low arms beckoned to rest in the chairs sheltered beneath. A stone milk house, well house, and towering barn lay to the west. Cattle and sheep grazed in the pasture behind a split rail fence, and beyond that lay Peg's beloved woods. In the winter, the pond turned skating rink and the steep hill near the house a toboggan run. Peg's dad John loved swimming and dug a swimming hole in the creek running from the pond.

Summer weekends, John laid slabs of wood across the wagon bed, hooked up the horses and the whole family piled in for a day with cousins at the lake. Mary's picnic basket leaked tantalizing smells all the way as Peg's brothers jostled and challenged each other to swimming contests. Peg loved life, her family, and the outdoors. She envisioned a bright future until an event a continent away erupted and destroyed her plans.

Tarbet Family 1899
Left to right
Back row: Inez Vivian, Lela Zoe, Jesse Eugene
Middle row: Father John Burt, George Wilbur, Freda Marie, Mother
Mary Luemma
Front: Edwin Bertelle, baby Lester Meryvn

CHAPTER 1

May 1914

"Peg! Peg! Peg!" Chants reverberating from the stands animated her. *Should I? Oh, why did I wear my best shirtwaist and heels?* The shouting tugged her. She glanced at the scoreboard 0-4. *They need me!* Clack! Clack! Clack! Down the bleachers Peg hopped. Bounding onto the diamond, the heel of her new shoe bent, crippling her. Kicking both shoes off, she sprinted to the field and warmed up her arm.

Peg's classmate Helen minced into the ballpark and sat primly on the bottom row next to Florence. She pulled off white gloves, pushed up her parasol, and hissed, "How unladylike! She'll never catch a man!"

Peg let the ball rip. "Stee-rike!" the umpire bellowed. Two more strikes ended the inning. The home team fell into the dugout, slapping Peg on the back.

"What man wants a girl who can play ball better than he can?" Florence murmured as a group of boys sauntered by.

"Oh, hi, Charlie," Helen cooed as he plopped next to them. "We're just a-maz-ed at Peg!"

"Yeah. She can hit, too," Charlie exclaimed, "plus lettered in baseball *and* discus throwing!" He stood as Peg ran over.

"I mean . . . " Helen fumbled, red-faced.

Charlie rose, slapped Peg's back and tagged alongside her. "Great job!"

Helen and Florence whispered behind Helen's hand.

I know I'm rough and ready, but those simpering, giggling girls send me! Peg fumed. *I won't be a decorative house plant! I crave adventure.*

July 1914

Peg breezed into the family store where several men's heads bent over a newspaper. She slid to a stop upon seeing her father's face. *Something's wrong.*

"What Duke?" asked Walter.

"Ferdinand," responded Peg's dad, John.

"What about him?"

"Got assassinated while visiting Bosnia."

"So?" the crowd leaned closer.

"Folks aren't happy since Austria-Hungary took their land," John explained.

Walter nodded. "Can't say I blame 'em there. Bet them blasted Germans are in on it."

Peg moved near as opinions rose from bent heads.

"You watch. Russia's next. Justa tinderbox over there and the Duke's murder the match. Just like a lightning strike to our forests, be hard to control!"

"Well, fire doesn't spread across oceans."

"And President Wilson won't take us into war."

"I knew it. I knew it! Those damn people was justa itching fer a fight. Just needed a dad-blamed excuse!" declared old Eddie, a fixture at the store.

Biting her bottom lip and squinting to see, Peg moved closer. "Dad, what does this mean?"

He held up his palm. "Hold on. Listen."

Today Archduke Franz Ferdinand, next in line for the Austro-Hungarian throne, and his wife were murdered as their motorcade traveled the streets of Sarajevo while attending military exercises in Bosnia-Herzegovina.

A few years ago, Austria-Hungary annexed those provinces where Serbians make up the majority of the population. Apparently, an assassination had been attempted earlier in the day. As the Archduke's open-topped car drove to city hall, a man hurled a bomb that bounced off the roof and rolled underneath an adjacent vehicle wounding two army officers and several bystanders. The assailant shouted, "I am a Serbian hero!" as he jumped into a dry riverbed where he was apprehended.

The Archduke visited wounded officers in the hospital, and then sped

down an unplanned route. A Serbian
nationalist, Gavrilo Princip, believed
to be part of the Black Hand Society,
happened to be standing on the side
street, and fired two shots from
point-blank range. Both the Archduke
and his wife were hit. Reportedly the
Archduke's last words were "Sophie,
Sophie, don't die—stay alive for
our children." Sadly, both died
minutes later.

Men shook their heads.

An overweight man in a dirty shirt dug his finger in his ear,
"What in tarnation he go back out in the street for?"

"Serves Austria-Hungary right for being so greedy and takin'
over their land," the man next to him proclaimed and launched an
apple core into the wastebasket.

Peg swallowed. *Those poor kids are orphans.*

Winter 1914

The train rattled behind the Tarbet General Store and Post Office.
Neighbors came to shop, collect their mail and gather around the
potbelly stove to discuss the situation in Europe.

"That's a continent away. Let 'em solve their own problems," one
man barked.

"What's Europe ever done for us? We broke free from them for a
reason," spat an old timer as a brown stream hit the spittoon with a *tling*.

A rough lumberjack in worn overalls hooked his thumbs under the straps and rocked back. "Pah! If they think I'm sending my son over there, they got another think coming,"

Nothing for me to worry about, Peg mused while replacing the horehound and peppermint sticks in candy jars lining the countertop. She stewed over Charlie, her best friend since grade school, as she mulled over last Friday's conversation.

"Charlie, what is going on?"

His face reddened "What do you mean?"

"Why'd ya snap at Henry?"

"Oh, he's always bragging about his great football plays."

"Well, he *is* good at football!"

"Why does he always have to tell *you* about it?"

"He was telling *all of us* about it, Charlie!"

Why this sudden moodiness? She untied her apron. *Charlie isn't fun to be around anymore.*

The back door swung open; her brother Gene filled the doorway. "Mom wants you to help with the milk." At the same time, Florence and Helen giggled into the store.

Thank goodness! Peg tried to duck out. *Never thought chores would save me!*

Before she could escape, Helen called, "Paaa-eg! Quite the show you put on for May Day. Who'd of thought a girl could outpitch the boys?" Her sidekick Florence smirked.

Clenching her teeth, Peg hoofed it out the back.

Gene looked over her shoulder. "Boy, they're all dolled up. What was that all about?"

"Never mind. She thinks she's Helen of Troy! Give me one of those." Peg thrust her hand out.

Gene tipped the milk can handle toward her. "Saw Charlie. He's hot to join the war."

Peg stopped and grabbed Gene's arm. "What war? We aren't at war."

"We may be soon enough." He took off his hat and wiped his brow with his sleeve.

"No wonder Charlie's been such a bonehead!"

"What makes you say that?"

"He's so moody. I'm about to call him on the carpet!"

"Well, here comes your chance!" Gene pulled the can of milk back, tee-heeing as he walked to the barn.

Her stomach churned. *I'll pretend I didn't see him.*

"Hey, Peg, wait up," called Charlie as he jogged to catch up.

She quickened her pace. *Not now, please!*

He scampered alongside. "Working in the store today?"

Peg sighed and skirted a mud puddle. "Yes, but first, I've gotta help with milking."

"I'll help!" he volunteered.

She hurried on. "Thanks, but I've got it."

His face fell. "My dad says there'll probably be war in Europe soon," Charlie stated as he threw his shoulders back.

Peg agreed. "Well, that's all the talk at the store."

"I'm going," Charlie declared. "This may be the last chance for such an adventure!"

Peg did an about-face. "Don't be such a goop. Don't you have a lick of sense? Why would you want to go get killed or maimed?"

Deflated by her reaction, he stammered, "Don't you think I should support our country?"

"Our country's not in it," she snapped.

Charlie looked down and kicked at a rock. "You'll see. You'll be sorry."

"Sorry about what?"

"How will you feel when your . . . um friend and . . . uh . . . your brothers go off to war," he ventured.

"Nobody's going anywhere!"

"See you 'round," Charlie muttered and stormed off.

Gene hiked back from the barn. "My, my! Someone's sweet on you."

Peg came to an abrupt stop. *Is that what was wrong with Charlie?*

"Gene, do you really think there'll be a war?"

He caught up and slowed his pace. "Wouldn't be surprised."

"Promise me you won't go," she begged.

"Promises like that aren't possible to keep, Peg."

Why can't things just stay the way they are?

Leaning against the warmth of Bessie's flank, Peg relaxed to the soothing rhythm of milk pinging the bucket. *What if my brothers go to war? What will I do without Mud?* Thinking about his nickname, she smiled and shook her head. *Dad nicknamed Gene Lars because he looked like a Swede with his white-blond hair. Lester detested his nickname Olee and declared, "If I'm going to be a Swede, I'm going to be a dirty one. You'll have to call me Olee Mud!"*

When I was little, I so wanted the name Jasper that I cut off all my curls to resemble that chap who'd remodeled our home. Mom made me some bibbed overalls like Jasper's from blue and white gingham. But now I like my nickname. Peg's much better than when kids teased about my real name Gladys Tarbet and called me Happy Bottom-Black-butt!

She patted ol' Bess's skinny hip bone. *I loved the Chinese pheasants Dad kept in a cage outside our store, especially their bright red breasts, yellow heads, ringed necks and long tail feathers! When Mud and I played Indians, we'd sneak into the cage and pull tail feathers from the cock. For war paint, we crept in the house, took Mother's oils, then hid in the attic and painted our faces and legs in multi-colored stripes. Then we went on the warpath. Even though Mother scrubbed our legs with turpentine, we wore that paint for weeks!*

"You coming?" Mother's voice broke her reverie.

"Yes!" She strained milk through a dishcloth and poured it into their new separator, the cream destined for sale in their store, the extra milk for the hogs.

The next day, Peg paid more attention to the talk around the stove. Newspapers provided topics as old timers discussed every subject. Eventually, the talk turned to war.

"Never trusted them damn Germans," snarled Mr. Cox, an old farmer who suffered from rheumatism. "They pour all their money into weapons!"

"Europe's full of alliances . . . that will bring her down. You'll see," another oldster opined.

"If they'd stay home and mind their own business, but no, they're always land grabbing and pro-vo-kin' people."

Eddie agreed heartily, "Just two things you need to know about history: greed and power!"

John looked up from sorting mail. "Hear what happened Christmas Day?"

All heads turned toward him. "What?"

"Someone started singing Christmas carols. Troops from both sides exchanged greetings. Some even climbed outta the trenches and played soccer with the enemy!"

"War's so stupid!" Peg snarled.

January 1915

The Great War blazed in Europe, but Peg didn't want to think about it. She looked forward to the weekend when a group of kids from high school planned to ice skate. Saturday morning, she rushed through chores, put on the new hat and mittens her mother had just finished knitting and flew to the window, pacing.

"Where are they?"

"You're going to wear a hole in the rug," Mud laughed.

Last night's snowstorm carpeted the landscape. The sun caressed the downy snow blanket which responded by shooting diamonds everywhere. She tasted the magic of the first big storm. *Plop, plop,* the heavy snow slid down branches of the pine tree and landed muffled onto the porch.

Finally, Charlie glided up in his dad's new red cutter filled with teenagers. Peg dashed out and crawled under lap robes, placing her feet on hot rocks. Laughter packed the air as they headed to the lake. The cutter's blades sliced through snow. Horses snorted, painting a cloudy trail in the air. Harness bells jingled, creating a holiday atmosphere. As wind whipped their faces, they scrunched into scratchy woolen scarves.

"Throw us those shovels!" Charlie called as soon as they reached the lake. He and the other boys cleared heavy snow from the ice. When Peg picked up a shovel, the boys didn't realize she'd joined them.

"Thought Helen was coming," complained Henry.

"Can't believe Florence came without her." Albert heaved a shovel of snow to the side. "Those two are joined at the hip!"

"Florence just wants to be a part of the 'in' crowd," Charlie observed, "and Helen's dad is loaded."

"Well, Helen's pretty, too. Not a bad combination, you know," Henry tossed the hair from his eyes. The girls called Henry, Sheik or Handsome Henry. His wavy dark hair, green eyes and cleft chin made them swoon.

Will shook his head. "She's spoiled rotten."

I'm tired of hearing about Helen! "Beat you to the tree!" Peg challenged.

Charlie turned, skated over, grabbed her hand and raced ahead. Skaters whooshed behind, bearing down fast. They kept ahead, flying past a stand of trees. Looking over her shoulder, Peg tipped them off balance. They teetered, tilted and crashed into the nearest tree that dumped its snow. Peg landed on top of Charlie's chest. He reached around and held her close. Embarrassed, she pulled away and sprang up, hiding her discomfort with a hearty laugh.

"I don't know what that was all about, but I'll pretend I didn't notice."

"Hey, you guys had a head start!" called Albert.

Henry dragged his toe to stop. "Yeah, but they got their comeuppance! You okay?"

"We're fine!" Peg offered her hand to Charlie. He ignored it and shook the snow from his mittens and hat.

"Wow! I believe you've got a blinker, Charlie! Your eye's turning black!" Henry roared.

Charlie winced, gently touching his eye. "Peg's elbow got me."

Peg gasped. "Oh, I'm sorry."

"Wow! Charlie, you'll have the best shiner ever seen in a month of Sundays!" crowed Henry.

"And to think a girl gave it to him!" wisecracker Albert guffawed.

A commotion from the south side of the lake drew their attention. "Something's wrong! Hurry!" Charlie urged as he pushed off with his back foot.

The group sped to where girls screamed. Florence had fallen through the ice! Charlie sprang into action. Lying on his stomach, he crawled forward, pushing a tree branch to the sputtering girl.

"Florence!" Charlie shouted, demanding that she remain conscious and focus on him. "Here, grab the end of this limb," he commanded.

"Charlie, don't go any closer, or you'll end up in the drink, too," warned a couple of girls.

Florence bobbed down amidst louder screaming. When she surfaced, she reached for the branch and caught hold.

"Hang on. You can do it. Atta a girl!" Charlie encouraged, trying to sound calm.

He inched backwards and pulled, but Florence whimpered, "I c . . . a . . . an't! I can't."

"You can. Come on now!"

Albert scavenged another limb and crawled parallel to Charlie. "Grab this!"

Florence found strength, and the two boys slowly dragged until Charlie grabbed her wrist and pulled her to safety. He carried her to the fire. Boys turned their backs while the girls stripped off Florence's wet clothes and wrapped her in blankets from the cutter.

"Tha-a-ank yoo-u," Florence chattered to Charlie.

"Albert, hitch up the horses," Peg ordered.

Monday, Charlie was the school hero. Helen made it her business to let everyone know about the rescue, even though she hadn't been there. "He didn't even think about his own safety and saved Florence," she gushed.

Oh, please. Peg shook her head and marched off to biology, disgusted with Helen's theatrics.

Mr. Craig's lecture on parts of the cell fascinated her. *There is a whole unseen universe inside each of us! What other things are out there undiscovered?* The class' laughter brought her back.

"Is it true you gave Charlie his black eye?" Tom smirked. "Helen told us all about it! Punching Peg!"

"Punching Peg! Punching Peg!" a few guys took up the refrain.

"I didn't punch him. I *fell* on him," Peg protested.

"Ooh! She *fell* on top of him?" Tom raised his one eyebrow, nodded sagely and looked over his shoulder at his audience.

Darn Helen, Peg fumed. When the last bell rang, she tromped off for the store.

The earthy smell of apples and wood smoke greeted her. Voices of men mumbled around the stove. Her mother smiled as she entered the warm haven, but Peg's scowl let her know she was in no mood to visit. She strode through and out the back door.

Out of habit, she found herself in the woods, where she relaxed, where she'd spent hours exploring and hunting, where she could be herself and not worry about others. She dropped onto the forest floor and remembered how much she enjoyed studying Thoreau in her English class. She felt connected to him as they both found refuge in the woods. She recited aloud the lines she'd memorized:

"I went to the woods because I wished to live deliberately, to front only the essential facts of life, and see if I could not learn what it had to teach, and not, when I came to die, discover that I had not lived."

A tentative doe stepped into the meadow, followed by two fawns who'd lost spots and sported grayish winter coats. Hooo hoo, hoo! The owl's hoot matched her boo-hoo mood. She put her hands behind her head and reclined on a pile of needles under a towering pine. A six-point buck strutted into the clearing.

"Should've brought my gun!" a deep voice whispered next to her.

Peg jumped. "Landsakes! You spooked me!"

"The deer, too, apparently," laughed Charlie as they watched them disappear.

She stood. "What are you doing here?"

"After the way you shot off from school, I could tell something was wrong."

"Yes, well, I can take a good-natured tease, but that didn't feel like one."

"Don't worry. I like my shiner, even if a girl gave it to me." Charlie puffed out his chest. "I look tough."

"You look lopsided. Maybe I should even out your face."

Charlie laughed and confessed, "I've missed our walks here."

"Me, too," Peg sighed.

"Remember when you ran away from home because your sister Freda wanted to curl your hair?" Charlie's unhurt blue eye twinkled just recalling the event.

"And I went to your house blubbering. You dried my tears and showed me your new gun. Then we popped a few cans off the fence! I have *my* gun," Peg suggested.

Charlie scanned the area. "Come on. Let's find something for a target. You still think you can outdo me, don't you?"

"Prove me wrong," she challenged.

"Be happy to!"

CHAPTER 2

The next day at school, Peg looked up from her history test. Charlie watched. She raised an eyebrow, "What?"

"Meet me after," he mouthed.

After class, Peg waited in the hall for Charlie. "So, what's up?"

He looked at his feet. "Hope you're not mad."

"Why would I be?"

"Florence asked me to the school Christmas dance next week," he whispered.

Peg pursed her lips and swallowed. "Oh, yeah, and what did you say?"

The halls buzzed as students strode by. Charlie stuck his chin out. "Well, seeuns as how I didn't have a better offer, I accepted."

Taken back, Peg tried to hide her disappointment. "Good. Hope you have fun," she lied.

"We're doubling with Helen and Henry."

"Ha! Serves you right! You know Florence is her underling," Peg chortled.

Charlie looked like he'd be hit in the stomach. "You going?"

"How long have you known me? Ever seen me dance?"

He leaned in. "Maybe it's time I did."

Peg snorted in disgust. "You wouldn't like it."

"Let me be the judge."

"See ya. I'm going to be late, and Miss Caldwell will crucify me in front of the whole class!" Peg rushed off. *I don't like it. He's my best friend, and I don't want those mindless girls hanging on him. He'll be miserable.*

After school, Peg climbed next to Tom, an old friend, neighbor and driver of the school wagon.

He scooted over. "Hey, long time since you've ridden up here. I remember a round-faced little girl full of spunk who thought she could teach me a thing or two about driving."

"Tom, that's years ago!" Peg chided.

He flicked reins. "Yeah, and things *do* change."

"I don't like it."

"What don't you like? It's life. It's nature. It's inevitable."

"Things get confusing," sighed Peg.

Tom pushed back his hat exposing a white forehead and thinning gray hair. "Wanna talk?"

"Nah, give me the reins, just for old times' sake? Giddy-up!"

The wagon lurched forward. Kids laughed and screamed, "Faster, Peg! Faster!" Soon the Tarbet Store came into view.

"Thanks, Tom." Peg jumped from the seat, catching her skirt on the wagon wheel. Gathering up the torn hem, she jogged to the store.

"I'm starving!" Peg exclaimed, slamming the door behind her, jangling the bell and shaking the window.

Mary pushed strands from her tired, moist face. "Just brought over warm bread." She motioned to the workstation behind the counter.

"I could smell it before I got here. Thanks, Mom!" She slathered on homemade apple butter.

"Hey there, Peg," ol' Harvey Mann turned toward her. "What ya gonna be when ya grow up?"

"Who knows? But my favorite classes are biology and gym," she answered round a mouthful of bread.

He removed a piece of straw he'd been chewing from his mouth. "Why don't cha be a doctor? Ya gone with your mother to deliver babies?"

"Not yet." *Could I?* She faced her mother. "Any babies due soon?"

Mary added a couple of cans to the shelf and hopped down from the step stool. She pulled her sleeves down and smoothed the wrinkles in her dress. "Yes, Annie Williams', any day now."

"Could I help?"

"I'd have to ask Annie. If she's okay with it, I don't know why not. She's got those four younger ones and could use a hand for sure."

"I don't mean babysit! I want to help with the delivery."

Mary pushed the stepstool under the shelf. "Why the sudden interest?"

"Been thinking. That's all."

"I'll ask her this afternoon. I'm planning to check on her after I see how Mrs. Hunter is getting along with her twins," Mary promised. Her dedication to expectant mothers and their babies was well known.

The next day at school, the idea of being a midwife still knocking about her head, Peg paid extra close attention in biology. When she

looked up, Charlie winked. Across the classroom, Florence's face fell. She whispered to Helen. Peg looked back at her text.

After class, Florence and Helen scurried over to Charlie's desk. "Want to come to my house for a Christmas party?" Helen asked as she fluttered her eyes.

Peg retreated with Helen's high giggle grating on her nerves. *One more week, then blessed Christmas break.* She flew out the door and chewed at her lip as the school wagon jolted down the dirt road home.

Around the bend from home, she noticed Mother's buggy was gone. She ran the last quarter mile and threw open the door. "Where's Mom?" she puffed to Mud.

He looked up, replying, "Mrs. Williams'."

"Why didn't someone tell me?" She sprinted to the barn, threw a saddle on Honey, slapped her rump and tore off. *I'll be so mad if I miss the whole thing!*

Mr. Williams paced in the front yard, but no sign of the children. Peg wheeled the horse to a stop in a spray of snow. "Am I too late?" she yelled, sliding to a standstill when screams poured from the house.

Mr. Williams gritted his teeth and turned his hat in his hands, lines creasing his brow.

Peg rushed over. "Everything okay?"

He looked up, grunted and made for the barn.

Another scream split the air. Peg dashed inside. Mrs. Williams lay in bed, sweat soaked, red-faced, and panting. Mary wiped the mother's wet face and murmured soothingly, "There now. Just a couple more pushes, and you'll have a new little one! Peg, quick! Hand me those clean towels on the table. Peg? Hurry."

Peg washed her hands and grabbed the towels. *This is different from the births I've witnessed in the barn!* Her hands trembled, and she prayed for Mrs. Williams. When the baby cried, tears slid down her cheeks. She brushed at them and moved closer to see the tiny girl.

"Take her to the sink, and we'll clean her up," her mother coached.

The blanket felt weightless, empty. Only the crying verified it contained a person. After mother and baby slept, they tiptoed outside. *The father must still be in the barn. He's missed everything but his wife's screams.* Mr. Williams must have been watching. He slunk back in.

Peg tied her horse behind the buggy, jumped in and took the reins. "Giddup!" The buggy lurched forward. She drove in silence the first mile, pondering the event. "I wasn't a lot of help."

They bounced over a rut and Mary grabbed her hat. "Nonsense, it's nice to have another pair of hands."

A mother quail, her top feather bouncing, led her little ones to the side of the road. Peg pulled the reins hard to avoid them. "You'd have done fine without me."

Mary grabbed the seat and hugged the black doctor bag on her lap. "Well, what did you think? Want to go with me again?"

"Yes!" Peg cried eagerly. "How did you know what to do?"

"Always been interested in medicine, so studied medical books and started just as you did today. I assisted the last midwife for a few years, asked questions and watched. I loved it all until . . ." she stopped, searching for the right words.

"Until what?"

Mary looked off in the distance. "Until I helped with a pair of twins." She swallowed and struggled to keep her voice from trembling. "The second baby died. Thought I'd never go again. Had nightmares . . . so afraid a baby or mother would die under my care. I didn't midwife for over a year."

Peg reached for her mother's hand. "Then what?"

"Well, I missed it, so I started again. But it's scary every time. I just pray and tell myself they are better off with someone there."

"Can I go next time?"

Mary wiped her eyes. "If the mother gives her permission."

"Yes! I'm going to study medicine!" Peg slapped the reins.

Her mother gave a tired smile. "That's wonderful, dear."

CHAPTER 3

April 1917

Snowshoeing through the hushed woods, Peg reveled in her sheltered space. She shivered in the brisk morning breeze, punched her poles down and moved faster. On the floor of the forest, buttercups and grass widows struggled through snow. The branches of towering Ponderosas tried to wave her worries away.

This morning on the radio, President Wilson told Americans that the United States had entered "The Great War." *I'm almost 16. Will it be over before I'm a nurse? Will Charlie go off to war? What about my brothers and my dad? Will they go?* Stories of trench warfare she'd heard in the store rumbled in her head. *What does the future hold for us?*

Moving, working and being active always made her feel better. The crunching snow flushed out wild turkeys. Putts, gobbles, and 'kee run' filled the air. When the tom strutted out, Peg's smile spread along with his tail feathers. Everything out here was uncomplicated. Soundlessly, she headed for the turkeys, watching their bald heads that would color if they got excited. Loud and fast, the posse approached. She raised her rifle, sighted down the barrel, and thought of turkey dinner with all the fixings. *If I don't plug a tom before he joins the flock, I'll miss the shot.* One flew from his roost. Sun danced on the snow, forcing Peg to squint hard.

Ka-boom! The kick upset her footing. She landed on her back-side with a grunt followed by a guffaw. "Well, ol' fellar, I hope you're tasty," she laughed and crawled to her knees.

Tromping up the back steps with turkey in hand, she met Dr. Phillips coming out the back door. "Wow! What a shot! That's a big one!" He grabbed one of its legs and looked it over. "Think you can hit a patient with a needle?" he teased.

Peg froze. "Sure thing!"

He smiled. "We're shorted-handed at the office and your mother told me of your interest in medicine."

Peg's eyes widened. She leaned forward. "I could help! When can I start?" *It feels like my destiny.*

He chuckled. "How about you come in after school?"

"Which day?"

"Can you come every day?"

Peg danced. "Oh, yes!" She dropped the turkey and called out, "Mom! Guess what!"

The next day at school, Peg found Charlie. "Guess where I'm going after school today?"

He raised his eyebrows. "Dunno. Hunting, I guess."

Peg put her hands on her hips. "No! Guess again."

He walked to the trophy case and pretended to study the tro-phies. "To a movie with Helen and Florence," he tormented.

"Fun-ny. Never mind. You'll never guess anyway."

He started walking away. "That's okay."

Peg stomped her foot. "No, it's not!"

He exhaled. "Then tell me."

Her face lit. "I'm working for Dr. Phillips after school!"

"Boy, everyone's interested in nursing since we joined the war."

Peg grabbed his arm. "That's not why I'm doing it. I hate the dumb war!"

"Hating it won't change things. I'm going to join and make a difference!" *Then maybe you'll appreciate me.* He shook her hand from his arm.

"You'll only change *your* life," Peg stalked off. *Never mind. I need to pay close attention in biology. I'm on my way to becoming a doctor!*

Soon as the last school bell rang, Peg rushed the door. Rounding the corner of the building, she crashed into Helen and Florence, knocking Helen to one knee. "Oh, so sorry! You all right?"

Helen winced, "Darn you! You've ruined my new skirt! Why are you tearing around like a bat out of hell?"

"I'm going to my new job at Dr. Phillips'. I didn't see you."

"Ahch!" Helen brushed herself off. "Why would you want to be around sick people?"

Peg's brow furrowed. She took a deep breath and slowly exhaled. "I want to help people. Make a difference!"

"How disgusting! Cleaning up vomit, wounds, and catching diseases!" Florence shivered and shook her head.

"Some people have more to do than primp and preen," Charlie retorted as he came forward from a group of friends who'd witnessed the exchange.

"Well, I never!" Florence fumed as she grabbed Helen's hand and flounced off.

"Thanks, Charlie. You're the best."

"Better hurry off now and save some lives," he winked.

"It might be you who needs medical attention, if you keep it up!" Peg warned as she loped off.

Mrs. Waterman sat behind the front desk in her immaculate nurse's uniform. The picture of efficiency, her starched dress matched her no-nonsense personality. *She looks domineering. Hope I can take it.*

"Hi, I'm Peg."

The nurse finished writing before peering over the top of her glasses. "Yes, Dr. Phillips said you wanted to be a nurse." She greeted Peg as if her territory had been invaded.

"A doctor," Peg quickly corrected.

"Well, you have a lot to learn. Start by cleaning the exam room. We have an appointment in fifteen minutes, so make it snappy."

I came to learn medicine, not housekeeping! Peg bristled. "Where are the cleaning supplies?"

"Under the sink. Be sure to wipe down the table well with the disinfectant. We're here to stop disease, not spread it. I'll be in to look it over after I've finished this paperwork."

Peg found the supplies and just finished when Nurse Waterman pounced. She scanned the room. "Trash needs emptied."

Peg grabbed the can. The rest of the afternoon involved more cleaning and organizing, but no helping patients. Her exuberance dissipated as the hours dragged on. When closing time came, Mrs. Waterman cautioned, "Be a few minutes earlier tomorrow. You doddle on the way?"

Stunned by the nurse's curtness, Peg stammered, "No, I nearly ran the whole way."

Nurse Waterman opened a file cabinet. "Well, you almost didn't have the room cleaned before the patient arrived."

"I'll try to get here sooner tomorrow."

"T-R-Y harder," she spelled.

Peg clenched her teeth.

Her mother, with feet propped on a stool, sat next to the fire, knitting. She noted Peg's subdued countenance as soon as she entered. "Hi, dear. You hungry?" She set her knitting aside.

"No," Peg mumbled.

"Come sit." She patted the chair next to her. "I could use help rolling this yarn." Peg slumped in the chair and held her hands up. Mary placed a skein of yarn over them and began rolling it into a ball.

"What are you making, Mom?"

"More socks for the soldiers. Want to learn?"

Peg sighed. "Might as well feel useful. Wasn't any help at the doctor's office."

"Why not?"

"All they had me do was clean and organize supplies. They didn't teach me a thing!"

"Well, you learned where they kept things, didn't you?"

"I guess I did."

Mary read the disappointment in Peg's face and patted her back. "Give it another shot."

CHAPTER 4

When the school wagon pulled in the next morning, excited students handed around a paper.

"What's going on?" Peg whispered to Florence.

"You of all people should know," Florence huffed. "There's signs in your parents' store. Don't you read?"

"Well, I didn't go to the store yesterday. Perchance, you'd be so kind as to enlighten me?" Peg bit back.

"There's a fighter coming!" One of the younger boys exclaimed. "Signs around town offering $100 to any man who can throw him!"

"My brother Gene could, for sure," Peg bet.

"Maybe Peg could, too!" Helen whispered to Florence who burst into giggles.

"Don't put all your chickens in one basket, Peg," Florence warned.

Florence is such a ding-a-ling. But Helen's comment stung. *I know I'm not a lady, but I don't want to be. So why do I let their comments get my goat?* She jumped from the wagon before it stopped and ran into school. All day, Helen's snide comment kept vexing. Not until biology, did she forget about it.

The day's lab on dissecting a frog captivated her. She completely forgot the girls' stinging remarks. *It has such tiny organs! I won't give up medicine because of Mrs. Waterman!*

After school, she approached Dr. Phillips' office resolved to be cheerful and learn everything she could. "Better time," pronounced Mrs. Waterman after looking at the fob watch pinned to her copious bosom. "Several boxes of bandages needing rolled in the back room. Make sure they're tight and even."

More of the same! "Yes, madam," Peg mumbled.

Dr. Phillips came from the examining room as she trudged back. "How are you today?"

Her face brightened. "Great! Thanks for letting me come."

"How are things going so far?"

"When do you think I can take a temperature or give a shot?"

Mrs. Waterman's hulking advance made Peg wish she hadn't asked.

"Well, perhaps Nurse Waterman can let you observe the next patient while she takes his vitals," the doctor offered.

"I'd like that!" Peg exclaimed.

Dr. Phillips looked over his shoulder at the nurse. "Teach this girl a few things, will you, Nurse?"

Waterman pursed her lips.

Peg strained to hear the door as she patiently wound bandage after bandage in the back. The bell tinkled, and she landed in the waiting area before the nurse.

A towering lumberjack supported by two hulking men looked pale while his buddy called, "We need the doctor!"

Peg hustled back to the examining room and hugged the corner but moved forward when she noticed the wide gash in the man's leg. Nurse Waterman didn't flinch. "Lie back, sir, and we'll have you stitched up in no time. Peg, call Dr. Phillips," she commanded. Peg hurried out, panic swelling when she couldn't find him.

"He's not here," she reported breathlessly.

"OK, hold strong, even pressure on this gauze while I set up a suture tray," she calmly instructed.

When Peg started forward, the nurse barked, "Wash your hands first."

Trying to maintain composure, the lumberjack shut his eyes. When he flinched, Peg reached for his hand. He squeezed back.

Nurse Waterman cleansed and stitched the wound while Peg watched. *I could do that.*

Dr. Phillips returned when the stitching was almost complete. The nurse stepped back in deference, but he waved her forward, observing and nodding his approval. "Women have a natural aptitude for sewing."

Peg beamed. *I actually got to see doctoring!*

Mary knew how Peg's day went by the way she bounced into the kitchen. After an enthusiastic report, Peg turned to Gene, eating pie at the kitchen table. "You hear about the wrestler and the prize money?"

He took a swig of milk. "Yeah, at work."

"You can do it, Gene! What will you do with the prize money?"

"Hold on there, little sister." He pushed his chair back. "Who said I was going to fight?"

"You have to, Gene. I've already told everyone you're going to win it," Peg cajoled.

He took his plate and cup to the sink. "When is it? I have a job, you know."

"Come on!" She grabbed his hand and dragged him to the store.

Inside the door on the public notice board hung the poster:

ALL-STAR WRESTLING FEATURING:
JOE ZIMMER
FROM CHICAGO, ILLINOIS
225 LBS. ONE FALL MATCH
$100 PRIZE TO ANY MAN WHO CAN THROW JOE!
HORACE GRIM
OF NEW YORK CITY
215 LBS. 30-MINUTE LIMIT
$100 PRIZE TO ANYONE STILL STANDING AFTER 30 MIN.
WITH THE "GRIM REAPER."
SATURDAY JUNE 1, 1917 8:00 P.M.
FID'S OPERA HALL, DOWNTOWN NEWPORT
RINGSIDE SEATS $.50
RESERVED SEATS $.25
GENERAL ADMISSION $.10
TICKETS ON SALE:
GREAT NORTHERN RAILWAY DEPOT, FIDELITY SAWMILL

"Please. You wrestle, and I'll cheer you on!" Peg entreated.

"Ladies won't be admitted," Gene warned.

"Why not?"

"There'll be gambling, half-naked men fighting, blood, sweating, yelling, and cursing," he said in an ominous voice.

Peg waved her hand. "Well, I've seen all that."

"Mother will say no."

"Yea! That means you'll do it!"

As they strolled home, Peg threw out ideas for the prize money.

"You could make a down payment on a new car and teach me to drive it! We could go on a big adventure somewhere! I could save my wages from Dr. Phillips to help pay for gas. We could take a ride in an airplane . . . "

When they walked in the back door, the tension was palpable. Gene stopped. "What's going on?"

"Telegram for you, son." John held it out.

ORDER OF INDUCTION INTO MILITARY SERVICE OF THE
UNITED STATES

THE PRESIDENT OF THE UNITED STATES TO:
JESSE EUGENE TARBET

ORDER NUMBER 71 SERIAL NUMBER 133

GREETINGS: HAVING SUBMITTED YOURSELF TO A LOCAL
BOARD COMPOSED OF YOUR NEIGHBORS FOR THE PURPOSE
OF DETERMINING THE PLACE AND TIME IN WHICH YOU
CAN BEST SERVE THE UNITED STATES IN THE PRESENT
EMERGENCY, YOU ARE HEREBY NOTIFIED YOU HAVE BEEN
SELECTED FOR MILITARY SERVICE.

YOU WILL, THEREFORE, REPORT TO THE LOCAL BOARD
NAMED BELOW

AT: PENDOREILLE COUNTY COURT HOUSE AT 2:00 P.M.
ON THE 8TH DAY OF OCTOBER 1917 FOR MILITARY DUTY.

FROM AND AFTER THE DAY AND HOUR JUST NAMED YOU
WILL BE A SOLDIER IN THE MILITARY SERVICE OF THE
UNITED STATES.

MEMBER OF LOCAL BOARD: J. E. MEADE

REPORT TO LOCAL BOARD FOR: PEND OREILLE COUNTY,
WASHINGTON

After reading it, Gene sunk onto the davenport. Peg's gut twisted. "No!" she sobbed and threw herself at Gene. "You can't go! I need you, and we have plans!"

The next day in school, students with concerned faces whispered about drafted men. *I hope no one asks about Gene.* She hurried to class with her eyes down. At lunch, Florence and Helen sat by her. *Drat!* She couldn't think of how to escape before Helen asked, "Why so glum, Peg?"

"Don't pretend you haven't heard," Peg mumbled.

"Don't worry, Peg. Every silver lining has a cloud around it," Florence prattled on. "Gene might have some interesting experiences, and you could write his autobiography!"

"Such a *great* idea," Peg sneered and left the rest of her lunch untouched. She ran home.

Mary's brow furrowed when Peg walked in the back door. "What are you doing home?"

She burst into tears. Mary enveloped her. "What's happened, honey?"

"I don't want Gene to leave. He might get killed! We have plans," Peg wailed.

"I know. I know," Mary murmured between Peg's sobs, although they both knew there was no way to alter the circumstances.

"What about my other brothers? Are they next?"

"I don't know. Possibly," Mary whimpered.

Peg hugged her. "Oh, Mother, I've been selfish. I didn't even think about you or Dad. I've only worried about myself. If they go, I'll help around here. I'll do their chores, too," she promised. "I'm just so afraid, and I know Charlie will volunteer as soon as he graduates!"

Mary sniffled. "We'll need to be brave and support them."

"I'll miss Gene! Charlie, too," Peg groaned. "But at least Gene's going to wrestle."

Mary wiped her face. "What are you talking about?"

Peg swallowed. "Gene's going to wrestle for money next Saturday at the Opera House!"

Mary blanched. "You mean the fight from the poster in our store?"

"Yes, and he'll win, too!"

"He doesn't need that stress on top of preparing for war!" Mary protested.

Peg folded her arms across her chest. "Mom, it's exactly what he needs to prepare him for war, and I'm going to the match."

Mary grabbed her hand. "Oh, no, young lady, you are **not.** That's no place for girls!"

"But I promised I'd cheer him on!" Peg protested.

Crunching gravel announced Gene and Dad coming home for lunch.

John entered, "How's my girls?" When Mary and Peg turned to him, John came to a standstill.

"What's the matter here?"

"Peg tells me Gene's signed up to fight the wrestler coming to town next Saturday," Mary protested.

Shamefaced, both men shrugged. "You're *both* in on this, aren't you?" Mary declared.

Peg rushed over. "Gene, are you going to fight The Grim Reaper or throw Joe?"

Gene beamed with confidence. "Well, the Reaper weighs 210, but I think I can take him!"

Mary shook her head and stalked out of the room.

"Dad, can I go? Can I?" Peg begged persistently.

John shook his head. "Already in the doghouse with your mom. Don't need to make it worse."

"She won't know. I'll be cautious!" Peg promised.

"No, someone would tell your mother."

She didn't argue further but vowed to find a way to witness the fight. She ran where she always did when she was upset—into the woods. Several schemes bounced through her head: *I'll get Charlie to take me to the movie. No, too obvious. I could pretend to go to bed and crawl out my window. No, too early for bed. I'll go to Florence's to help knit socks for the soldiers. But what if Mother wants to come, too? Guess I'll just have to go against Mom's wishes,* she concluded. *I'll have Charlie go with me, to chaperone.*

The night of the wrestling match, Peg waited for the right moment to break the news to Mother but procrastinated until Charlie knocked.

"Hello, Charlie. Good to see you," welcomed Mary.

He took off his hat. "Hello, Mrs. Tarbet, Peg ready?"

"Oh, I didn't know you were going out. Peeeg, Charlie's here," she called. "What do you young folks have planned?"

"Just a night on the town," Peg stated as she hurried out, without looking at her.

As they walked toward the Fid's Opera House, Charlie put his hand on her arm. "Your mother doesn't know, does she?"

"She knows Gene's fighting. That's all," Peg confessed.

"You know she won't like it, don't you?"

"Of course, I do, but I'm not missing this for anything!"

He stopped and looked in her face. "Don't you think she knows where you're going?"

Peg shrugged her shoulders. They continued on in silence.

Long lines snaked in front of the ticket office.

"Oh, no!" Peg moaned, "I was so worried about getting here that I forgot about buying a ticket!"

Charlie beamed and pulled two tickets from his pocket.

"Oh! I could hug you!" Peg cried with relief.

Charlie held his arms out. "Fine with me."

"Come on! We'll be late," Peg tucked her hand under his arm and hurried to the opera house. "Where are we sitting?"

"Ringside seats," he announced. This time Peg stopped and gave Charlie a big hug.

The crowd pressed. Peg wrinkled her nose at the scent of wet wool shirts and unwashed bodies in close quarters. She grabbed Charlie's hand as he threaded through the crowd, looking for their seat numbers. Two tall men had to stand for them to pass. Looking through the sea of hats, Peg caught a glimpse of her father and slunk down.

"Make your bets here!" a robust man bellowed to the crowd. *Oh no! I hadn't thought about that. Most people will bet against Gene because he has no track record.*

"I want to place a bet on Gene, Charlie, but I didn't bring any money," she lamented. Charlie pulled a few dollars from his pocket and handed them over. "Will you do it for me?" Peg asked. Charlie climbed back over the big men next to him.

"Cockeyed kid, make up your mind," one grumbled.

Peg didn't see another female in attendance and wished she'd worn a hat. *Maybe Mother had been right after all,* she considered until The Grim Reaper entered flexing muscles, drawing shouts and jeers. Scars zigzagged across his back; his shorn hair and missing teeth added to Peg's excitement. His trainer followed with towels and water.

Oh! Who will bring Gene water or wipe his face?

CHAPTER 5

"The Grim Reaper will take on our own Gene Tarbet!" the announcer bellowed. Peg shot up dancing from one foot to the other and clenched her fists. Money changed hands on last-minute bets when the audience beheld Gene's size and muscles.

What if he gets hurt? I can't watch! Please, God, keep him alive! Peg prayed.

The audience thundered as Gene crouched and approached Reaper who glanced up to accept his adulation. In that moment, Gene dashed forward. The thud of Reaper's head hitting the floor made Peg's stomach turn. She bowed her head and winced. Dazed and angry, Reaper roared as he rose. Gene danced behind him and threw his arms around Reaper's shoulders, trying to bring him down again. Reaper wavered but held his footing. Gene jumped. For a few minutes, it looked as if Gene was having a piggyback ride, and the crowd hooted.

When Charlie patted Peg's hand, she realized she gripped his arm too tightly. Embarrassed, she let go and twisted her jacket as if she were wringing someone's neck.

"Get em, Gene!" she hollered.

Then Gene's weight on his back caused Reaper's leg to buckle. He toppled with Gene on top and struggled to free himself. The ref ran close and held up his fingers. 1, 2, 3, 4, 5, 6, 7, 8, 9, 10!

"He did it, Charlie, but I want to go home." Her enthusiasm fading, she collapsed in her seat, tears running down her face.

Charlie jumped up. He pulled Peg down the stairs before the next round started.

"He sure did," he confirmed as he hustled her through the crowd and out the door.

Just as they left town, Peg halted. "Hey, what about my bet?"

Charlie winked, "If I recall, it was my money."

"True. You'd better go back and collect." Peg stopped and looked back.

"Not until I see you home."

She exhaled, "Thanks, Charlie. I don't think I'd been able to go without you."

He squeezed her hand. "Remember how you need me."

Peg didn't know how to respond. They walked home in silence. About a block from her house, Peg waved him on.

She eased the back door shut and slipped upstairs. Mary sat reading in front of the fire in the parlor and heard her entrance. *Sure hope my impetuous baby learned a lesson.*

Early the next morning, Gene crept into Peg's room and yanked on her blankets with a playful grin.

"Lookee here, little sister," he waved a wad of bills in her face, anxious to see Peg's reaction.

She opened one eye. "How much is it?"

"Two hundred dollars—200 big ones! One hundred prize money and one hundred from bets!" he chortled. "Enough with the money I've saved to buy us a car. Still want to go on a trip?"

"Of course!" Peg hopped out of bed. "Where are we going?"

"Well, for starters," he rubbed his hands together, "I thought we'd go to the city—Seattle. Then California to the beach or to Idaho to visit cousins, just anywhere we want!"

"Count me in! But Gene," she paused, almost unable to finish her sentence. "Don't wrestle again. I worried about you."

His mouth drew into a straight line, and he bit his lip. "Not to worry. I won't! Guess I'll be wrestling Krauts now," he mumbled.

Monday at school, several guys followed Henry to hash over the big wrestling match with Peg.

"You saw the whole thing?" Henry's mouth dropped open. "My parents wouldn't let me go."

"You might say mine didn't exactly give me permission," Peg confessed.

"How much money did he win?" several clambered to know.

"One hundred in prize money and $100 from bets. He's going to put it with his savings to buy a car! We've planned a trip to Seattle," Peg announced proudly.

"I'd love to go," Florence suggested after eavesdropping. "Seattle has a giant 'apartment' store!"

"Not this time, Florence," Peg replied kindly. "This is kind of a goodbye trip before Gene goes into the army."

"Oh, OK," Florence agreed as her face fell.

"I'll bet C-h-a-r-l-i-e is invited," Helen spelled.

Peg spun away. She couldn't wait to go to biology and use the microscope.

Mr. Craig stood at the podium, pushed his glasses up on his head and squinted at the class as he lectured.

"Louis Pasteur was a chemist, but the local wine industry wanted him to research the science of fermentation, so he concentrated on biological questions. He discovered the process was caused by a living organism which he called ferment. Through his experiments, he found none of the liquids he used would ferment after being boiled, which killed the microorganisms. As a result, he developed a simple way to prevent wine from containing unwanted organisms. He heated the wine to fifty to sixty degrees. This process, known as Pasteurization, is named after him." He continued, but Peg's attention turned to the soft tapping on the back of her desk.

Charlie whispered, "Meet at our favorite spot after school?"

"Why?" she mouthed.

Charlie wiggled his eyebrows.

She grimaced and turned back to the next part of the lecture. *This is fascinating!*

"So, you see, students," Mr. Craig brought his lecture to a close, "the work of Pasteur and Koch led to the discovery of 21 different disease-causing microorganisms. Koch said as soon as the right method was found, discoveries came as easily as ripe apples from a tree."

Now, who's Koch? she puzzled.

CHAPTER 6

After school, Peg realized she couldn't meet Charlie. She had a job. *I hope I see him before it's too late.* As kids poured from school, she looked for him, but to no avail. *If I have to choose between upsetting Charlie or Mrs. Waterman, at least the choice is easy.* Mrs. Waterman had softened some and even given Peg a compliment or two on her work ethic, but she didn't want to vex her.

Charlie sat at their meeting place on a downed tree and checked his watch again. After an hour, he headed to Peg's house. At the knock, Mary looked up from kneading bread dough, wiped her hands, then opened the door. "Oh, hi, Charlie. Come on in."

Charlie glanced over her shoulder while biting his lip. "Hello, Mrs. Tarbet. Peg home?"

"Why no. She works at Dr. Phillips' after school."

He brought the heel of his hand to his forehead. "Oh, I forgot!"

Mary sensed his nervousness. "Can I help you with something? Come on in. Sit down."

He shook his head. "Well, it's just I need to tell Peg something, and she's not going to be happy about it."

Mary waited patiently, peering up from her five-foot frame to Charlie's eyes a foot above her head.

"I've known from the first that I was going to join up, and I've done it. I'll leave soon after graduation."

Mary's hand covered her mouth. "You're right. She won't like to hear that. She's already worried about Gene leaving, and I'm afraid her brother, Mud, will be next. They're close, you know."

"I do. I hate to admit this, but sometimes, I'm a little jealous of him."

Mary understood. "Yes, no one comes between Peg and Mud."

The back door slammed. "Mom!" Peg called, interrupting the conversation.

They both turned. "What's the matter?"

"I don't feel so great," Peg sagged, "so I came home."

Mary put her hand on Peg's forehead. "Did Doc take a look at you first?"

"No, he was busy, and Mrs. Waterman was gone. I poked my head in and told him I needed to leave."

"Go up to your room, and I'll come check on you shortly." She turned to Charlie and whispered, "Better wait until she feels better to drop your news."

Charlie agreed. "Sure. Hope she's okay. I'll come back later."

Mary climbed the stairs to the bedroom. Peg clutched the right side of her stomach with tears in her eyes. "I need to lie down. I'm freezing and about to throw up."

Mary retrieved the thermometer. "You've a low-grade fever." Peg grabbed her side in pain.

"Let me see, dear." Mary pressed on Peg's abdomen. When she let up, Peg groaned.

"Can you get up? We need to go to the hospital." Downstairs, she noticed Charlie out the window, visiting with the hired man. She knocked loudly and motioned him back.

He ran in. "What's wrong?"

"Run down and tell Dr. Phillips to meet us at the hospital. I think Peg might have appendicitis."

CHAPTER 7

Peg clawed her way up from the anesthetic, tears running down her face. "I had the worst dreams!" she explained between sobs. "Gene got his leg blown off in the war and Mud was missing in action."

"It's probably the medicine," her mother soothed. "Lie down and rest."

The nightmare felt too real. Peg didn't want to sleep and tried to sit up. Her incision pinched. "Ouch!" Peg yipped.

Mary gently pushed her back. "Now lie still and rest." She held Peg's hand until she finally dropped off.

Peg woke again at two in the morning to see her mother dozing in the chair next to her. "Mother, go home and go to bed. I'll be okay." But Mary shook her head and tugged the blanket tightly around her shoulders.

"Two weeks! I'll go crazy," Peg blurted after Dr. Phillips left her room.

Mary tried to pacify her. "I'll bring you handwork. You can embroider pillowcases, knit socks for soldiers or crochet. Try to sleep, so your body can heal. We want you home for Thanksgiving."

"It's almost Thanksgiving?" Peg mumbled, rolled over and fell into a fitful slumber.

A week later, Peg felt better. It made staying down even worse. At least she had Charlie's daily visit after school to look forward to. But he made her laugh and that hurt! He came in with his usual grin. "How's my girl today?"

"Bored, bored, bored," Peg groused as she pulled the blanket up for modesty.

"I'll entertain you with stories of high-jinx at Newport High."

Peg plumped the pillow behind her. "I'm all ears!"

Charlie settled in the nearby armchair. "You know, I have World History with Florence and Helen."

"Lucky you!"

"Well, I did learn something from Florence."

"Do tell," Peg urged.

"Did you know those people in *mid-evil* time was *alliterate*?"

Peg giggled. "Poor Florence, she can't get it right, but you know she's not mean-spirited like Helen. I think I could like the girl if she didn't hang on Helen's every word."

"Just lacks confidence. Coming from her family doesn't help. Florence only wants to feel accepted."

"You know . . . I think you're right," Peg acknowledged.

Charlie declared, "Of course, I am!" as a well-aimed pillow hit his head.

CHAPTER 8

Peg loved Thanksgiving and wanted to go home for her favorite holiday. After two weeks in the hospital, she'd grown weak and had to be helped to the bathroom.

"Doctor, I've been so obedient. It's killing me to lie here, day after day. If you let me go home, I'll heal faster, I'm sure. At least, I'll have people around me. I'll go bonkers if you leave me here any longer!"

"Promise you won't overdo?" He made a note on his clipboard. "Don't want my best aide out any longer than necessary."

"I promise! What's going on at the office?"

"Mostly colds. Sore throats, coughs, a little pneumonia, the usual. You haven't missed anything exciting."

"I'll be back soon! I miss it. Don't give my job away, please."

"No worries. Don't know too many people who can work with You Know Who," he winked.

The day before Thanksgiving, Charlie showed up at the hospital and insisted on carrying Peg to the buggy.

"I hope no one sees this," she fussed.

He stopped mid-step. "What are you worried about?"

"I don't like to be the object of gossip."

"There's nothing wrong with me taking you home," Charlie snapped.

Peg struggled onto the wagon seat. "I'm sorry. I do appreciate your help. Guess I'm just a little perturbed that my family's too busy to pick me up."

"Actually, they weren't. I asked if I could come after you because I need to tell you something."

Peg tensed, "What?"

He hesitated. "I've been rolling this around in my head for days and can't come up with a good way to tell you."

"Just say it!"

He flicked the reins. "OK. I joined up and will be leaving for basic training the day after graduation."

Peg wailed. "Oh, Charlie! Why would you do such a thing? I have enough to worry about with Gene leaving, and Mud will probably be next!"

Charlie's eyes widened. "You mean you'll miss me?"

"Of course, I will. You're my best friend!"

"Oh." His mouth set in a hard line.

If I'm honest, I'll have to admit I've known he wants more than friendship for some time. But I'm not ready to have a boyfriend. That ruins friendships.

Charlie pulled up to the Tarbet home and extended a hand but didn't insist on carrying her again. Peg noticed his coolness but pretended not to. "You coming in?"

"No, Dad needs me at home," he lied and hunched his shoulders in disappointment. *Guess she doesn't feel the same as I do .*

"OK. Thanks." Peg inched to the back door. *Maybe I was too honest.* Mary glimpsed her approach and hurried out to help her.

"Leaving already, Charlie?" she called, but he'd already started down the road.

Peg slouched and took her mother's arm.

"He told you, didn't he?"

"Yes. I don't want to discuss it." *I just want to crawl into my own bed and can't believe the walk has almost winded me.*

Mary helped her upstairs and returned to her work in the kitchen. As soon as Peg pulled up her wool blankets, she started to sniff. *Why did this stupid war have to take my loved ones away?*

CHAPTER 9

Charlie didn't come around the whole week of Thanksgiving break. By the time school started, Peg was anxious to return. She met Florence shuffling along, hugging the wall, her head down. "Hi, Flor . . . en . . . ce," Peg stammered when she noticed her black eye.

"Leave me alone," she growled and disappeared around the corner.

When the bell rang, many desks stood empty. "Boy, everyone's running late after the holiday," Peg commented to the girl in the next desk.

"I've heard there's lots of flu. I know Helen's family had it, and she's ill," she reported.

Peg's thoughts wandered. *So that's why Florence looked so lost. I wondered what happened to her eye. What am I going to say to Charlie when I see him?*

"Peg, we're waiting." Mr. Craig brought her back.

"What?" She blinked, ran her hand through her hair and looked around.

"Take your paper and go to the lab," he directed.

What paper? Where was I?

After school, she passed Charlie talking to a red-eyed Florence. Charlie's sympathy reduced Florence to tears, and it all came back.

Florence knew before she walked into her house he'd still be sitting in that stained overstuffed chair with padding peeking out of the worn spots and springs sagging in the seat. His looks and posture mirrored the chair surrounded by empty beer bottles and half-eaten food. Tiptoeing in, she glanced at him with disgust. Lank greasy hair stuck to his forehead, and a three-day stubble on his chin held crumbs. The room reeked of stale beer and vomit.

Her drunken father growled at her from his chair, "Where ya been?"

Florence headed to her room.

"Don't cha dare walk away when I'm talkin to ya," he slurred.

She stopped.

"I axed ya where ya been!"

"Visiting my sick friend Helen."

"Your own father's sick, too, but don't see ya home nursing me. Ever since yer mom left me, you've gotten mighty sassy. Ya think you're better'n us, don't you? Hanging around with Miss Up-pity, never wanting to be home."

Florence bristled. "You know the real reason I don't want to be home, don't you?"

He stood. "Why, ya ungrateful little sow!" he stammered and staggered toward her.

Florence yelled. "I like to be where people care about me, where I don't come home to a mess and a drunk!"

He swung. "Ya better hold ya sassy li'l tongue if ya know what's good fer ya!"

As she turned, he caught the side of her face. Florence gasped and fled outside.

CHAPTER 10

When Peg entered Dr. Phillips' office, every chair in the waiting area was filled, but Mrs. Waterman's desk stood empty. *Looks like a night of it!* She walked past the crowd into the back room. Doors to both examining rooms were shut. She went to the storage room and began straightening up the box of supplies, waiting to be shelved. When a door opened, she peeked out. A patient left, so she went to report in. Dr. Phillips looked surprised. "Didn't you get the message?"

"What message?"

"You weren't to come in today."

Peg's brow furrowed. "Why not? The waiting room is packed."

"I know. A terrible flu's going around, and I don't want you exposed. You've just gotten over an illness."

"But that was three weeks ago!" Peg protested.

Doctor Phillips shook his head. "You don't understand. Reports are that thousands have died already. I'm not taking any chances."

"But I can help."

"You don't need to be at risk. I won't ask you again, Peg."

"OK," Peg slunk to the back room and gathered her things. *Great! Now I'll have nothin' to do after school, and Charlie's in such a funk. But if he's going to war, I'd better spend some time with him. He could be gone a long time.* Thoughts continued to tumble until she found herself at the store, not home.

Florence stood by bolts of cloth fingering them. The bruise on the side of her face had greenish-yellow edges. "Hi, Florence," Peg greeted, trying to be pleasant.

"Hello."

"How's Helen doing?"

"Not so good. Her parents won't let me come see her anymore. They're afraid I'll catch it."

"Dr. Phillips sent me home from work today for the same reason." Peg moved closer, "What are you going to make with that fabric?"

"I need a back for the quilt I pieced."

"Which pattern did you use?"

"No pattern. Just sewed together a bunch of scraps around the house to keep me busy. With Helen ill, I've needed something to do," Florence confessed. She chose some cloth, returned with her selection and tossed money at Peg.

An idea nudged at Peg's conscience, but she pushed it back, slid the coins off the counter into her palm and rang up the till. "I know how you feel. I'm in the same boat."

After Florence left, Peg sighed, shuffled to the stove, picked up the newspaper and slumped in a chair. The headlines brought her to her feet.

Death Toll Growing as
Influenza Claims More Victims

The Spanish Influenza—
New Name for an Old Disease

Volunteer Nurses Needed

She digested each article. *This sounds serious. Is that what Helen has? I'll bet they won't let me be a volunteer nurse.*

"Mom, did you see this?" Peg called as she headed to the back room.

Mary looked up and scanned the paper. "Yes, everyone is talking about how it can turn into pneumonia."

"Doc Phillips' waiting room was full of coughing people, so he sent me home."

"Well, I'll thank him next time I see him!" Mary declared.

Peg overslept the next morning and missed the school wagon. She saddled ol' Blaze and spurred him along. As she approached, several kids walked from the building. She spotted Florence and pulled on the reins. "Where's everyone headed?"

"They've 'evaporated' the school because of the flu."

Peg snickered thinking, *Classic Florence!* "Want a ride home?" she offered. To her surprise, Florence hopped on back. *I don't know for sure where she lives. How can I find out without her knowing?*

When they got to the crossroads, Peg squirmed, but Florence dismounted, "I'll walk from here."

"Sorry if I embarrassed you the other day at school when I asked about your eye."

She didn't turn. "Let dead dogs sleep."

School shut down for two weeks. When December arrived, Peg fell into a slump. Only a few more days until Gene had to report. Mud had received orders from the Navy to leave in January. Every day, newspapers reported the atrocities of war. When someone talked about the war at the store, Peg escaped.

I know I'm hiding my head in the sand, but I'm finding that ignorance is NOT bliss. Time for me to clear my mind. She opened the gun cabinet and grabbed a coat.

Upon her return, her mother looked up from her mending with puffy red eyes. *Now what?* Peg panicked.

"Sit down, dear. There's sad news."

Peg collapsed onto the davenport, not sure she wanted to know.

"Your friend Helen passed away this afternoon."

"From the flu?"

"Yes, everyone's frightened," Mary worried.

Peg sighed, "Oh boy, I wonder how Florence will take it."

CHAPTER 11

Too soon the day came for Gene to leave. Peg rolled over in bed when the light crept under her curtains. She covered her head and tried not to think. At eight o'clock, her mother called, "Time for breakfast!" in a cheery voice. She squeezed her eyes, but it didn't block the murmuring voices, lids on the cook stove clanging, or the thud of someone throwing wood in the wood box. The smell of bacon wafted up. She loved big Saturday morning breakfasts of apple fritters, maple syrup, bacon, eggs, and oatmeal with cream. She wavered in her determination to pout upstairs. *I should spend as much time with Gene as I can before he leaves!*

"Good morning, Sunshine!" Gene teased as Peg stumbled down in her nightgown.

A sob escaped and she covered her face.

Gene melted. "It'll be okay, Sis. Besides, when I leave, you'll get more driving time."

Peg's head popped up. "You didn't!"

"I did. Get dressed, and we'll take her for a spin," he sang out.

Breakfast totally forgotten, she flew upstairs, threw on the clothes she'd left on the floor and pounded back down the stairs, "Ready!"

"Hold on," Gene sputtered with a mouthful. "Can't a guy enjoy his last home-cooked breakfast?"

Peg burst into tears.

"Well, that was the wrong thing to say," he muttered, pushed back his chair, grabbing his coat and hat off the hooks by the back door. "Come on!"

In the backyard sat a new Model T.

Peg walked slowly around it, looking puzzled. "Why did you choose black when your favorite color is blue?"

"Well, Henry Ford told me I could have it in any color I wanted as long as it was black," Gene quipped.

"Show me how to drive!" Peg begged as she climbed in the driver's seat.

Gene pushed her shoulder. "Scoot over and observe."

"See this hand lever? Push it all the way back to set the brakes. Halfway down, it's still in neutral. Then release to put the transmission into high gear . . . " He explained levers and pedals in detail until Peg wondered if she'd be able to remember after he left. ". . . this right foot pedal will hold the car stationary."

This is more complicated than I'd anticipated. "Why don't you drive around for a little while, and I'll watch," she suggested. Even though the sun shone, the frosty December air wormed its way into the car. Peg stamped her feet and blew on her hands, but Gene didn't feel the chill.

They drove past the barn, down to the fish hatchery, turned back toward town, passing Williams' Furniture/Undertaking, Judd's Drugstore, Fid's Opera House, the Northern Hotel, and turned around by The Great Northern Railway Depot at the end of Main. When they passed the Empire Laundry Wagon, the horses spooked, and the driver glared at Gene.

By the time they got back, Peg's lips were blue. "Thanks, Gene!" She jumped from the car and ran for the wood stove. Gene's favorite meal lay on the table: rolls with apple butter, venison roast and gravy, mounds of mashed potatoes, sweet potatoes, cooked carrots, green beans from last summer's garden, and apple and pumpkin pies with heaps of whipped cream, but Peg had no appetite.

Time came to take Gene to the train. "Who wants to send Gene off?" John asked as he pushed away from the table.

Mary dabbed at her face with her apron. "I'll say my goodbyes here. I don't want to make a scene."

"I'm going!" Peg declared.

No one talked as they climbed into the truck. No one dared. Peg sat between John and Gene, her two heroes. She looked straight ahead. The old farm truck lumbered off as Mary stood at the window with her hand over her mouth.

On the way, everyone kept silent until Peg blurted, "Gene, I'm going to miss you so much! You've always treated me kindly, helped with my work, listened and . . . " She started to weep.

"I'll miss you, too, li'l sis." He patted her knee. "You oversee my car and drive to the station to pick me up when I come home. Deal?"

"Deal," Peg blubbered. The rest of the journey continued in silence.

When the depot came into view, Peg's heart pounded. Several families sending off men already crowded the station. Peg sniffled in the truck as the men climbed out. Gene hauled his bag out of the back.

John embraced him in a bear hug and cleared his throat. "Goodbye, son. Proud of you. Come home. You're needed here."

"I'll do it, Dad!" Gene croaked, looked over his shoulder and blew Peg a kiss.

The next morning, a wailing wind roused Peg. She scrunched under the heavy quilts of her warm cocoon. Still groggy, she remembered something was wrong, but her foggy brain couldn't name it. She moaned, "What day is it?" When she remembered, her heart sank. Gene's gone. *Today must be Sunday. At least I won't have to go to school and pretend nothing's wrong.*

Tap, tap, tap. Peg's door opened. "Good morning, Sunshine," Mary whispered as she leaned over the bed. Peg feigned sleep. "Are you playing possum?" Mary cajoled. She crossed to the window and pushed back the curtains. "Better get up soon, or you won't have time."

Pretense gone, Peg sat up, "For what?"

"Don't you remember? Helen's funeral is at nine this morning." Mary replied as she busied herself, picking up Peg's wrinkled dress on the floor.

"Oh. Not going." Peg burrowed back into her bed.

Mary stopped. "Why ever not?"

A muffled answer came from the heap. "She wasn't *my* friend."

"What do you mean? You grew up together," Mary puzzled.

"Doesn't make you friends."

Mary hung Peg's dress in the closet. "Your dad and I are going out of respect for the family."

"Go ahead."

"You're sure?" Mary offered one more time.

"Sure."

Mary shook her head and eased the door shut. When she reached the bottom of the stairs, someone was knocking.

She opened the door wide. "Why, Charlie, haven't seen you for some time. Are you hungry?"

"Starving, but not why I came. Peg up yet?" He snitched a piece of bacon from the sideboard.

"I tried to roust her, and she refused."

He wiped his greasy hand on his pant leg. "Doesn't she remember it's the funeral?"

"I reminded her, but she's not going." Mary pressed her lips tightly.

"Well, they didn't have much in common," Charlie admitted.

Mary gave him a muffin and a napkin. "Did you want her to go with you?"

"No, I didn't think she'd go. Just wondering how she was with Gene leaving and all."

"I'm fine," Peg came down the stairs, tying the belt of her bathrobe.

Mary gasped. "Peg! In a bathrobe is no way to greet visitors."

She ignored the reprimand. "Hi, Charlie."

"If only Helen could see you now," he laughed.

"Children! Don't speak ill of the dead," Mary admonished.

Peg picked up a muffin. "Never mind Helen. I'm a little worried about Florence," she admitted.

Charlie grabbed another piece of bacon. "Guess I'll see her reaction at the funeral."

"Sit down. I'll give you some eggs to go with that," Mary offered.

Peg grabbed a chair. "I'm hungry, too!"

Mary set out muffins with huckleberry jam and cracked eggs into the sizzling skillet.

"I hear you're not going." Charlie spooned jam onto his muffin.

Peg thrust her chin out. "Don't like hypocrites. Why pretend we're friends just because she died?"

"Hey, don't jump on me. I'm not trying to convince you," Charlie muttered through a big bite of muffin.

"Good thing, too."

"Nobody's going to the funeral," John announced as he came in. "Word is all public meetings are canceled until this flu thing plays out."

Mary put another plate of muffins on the table. "Well, how sad for the family!"

"It'll be sad for other families, too, if this thing spreads," John affirmed.

"Looks like your morning just freed up, Charlie." Peg rose. "Wanna go shooting?"

Charlie swallowed the last of his milk. "Depends. That is if you comb your hair."

"If you think that'll help, but bet I'll still outshoot you!" She laughed and scooted upstairs.

Charlie wiped his chin. "Thanks for the food. Better retrieve my gun."

"You can use one of mine," John offered.

"That's okay. I have time. It'll take Peg a while to get her hair under control," he snickered and pushed his chair back.

Peg waited for Charlie at the big granite rock formation north of the house that had been their meeting spot for years. She climbed to the top and surveyed the landscape. An eagle flew overhead to the nest in the top of the tallest pine. "What a view from your home!" she exclaimed aloud.

"What home?" Charlie asked from below.

"The eagle nest. I can see it from my bedroom window. I watch those eaglets, their parents bringing food. One day the babies leave, but I've never seen it."

"Goodbyes aren't easy anyway," Charlie mumbled.

Peg pretended not to hear. They fell into companionable silence as they hiked farther into the forest with Charlie in the lead. While navigating a slippery slope, she bumped into Charlie who'd stopped abruptly. She started to cry out, but he put his finger to his mouth and pulled her down. Startled, Peg's eyes asked, "What?"

"Didn't you see him?" he whispered.

"See who?" Peg strained to see around him.

"A man dragging something shuffled through the trees 100 yards ahead."

Peg's eyes widened. She stooped down. Charlie shook his head, warning her to keep quiet.

They stayed down and quiet for several minutes. Charlie whispered, "We're going back."

"Who was that and what was he dragging?"

"I have no idea."

Peg tugged at his hand. "Let's follow and see what he's up to."

"I don't think so."

"Why not?" she demanded.

Charlie stood. "I'm in charge of your safety."

"Who made you my bodyguard?" She bristled and plunged ahead of him.

CHAPTER 12

When flu symptoms died down, school resumed. Many parents still fearful kept their children home, but Peg begged to return. She'd missed her favorite class and with no work at Dr. Phillips', the days had crawled. Between classes, she spotted Florence. *Strange not to see her trailing Helen.*

"Hi, Florence."

"Hi."

"I was so ready to come back. How about you?"

"Not everyone's back," Florence observed.

Thinking she referred to Helen, Peg started to say, "Sorry to hear about Hel . . ." but Florence continued, "There were eight students in my last class, and half of them were teachers."

Peg almost blurted, "That doesn't even make sense," but took a breath, "Whada ya mean?"

"The principal, vice principal, counselor and teacher were in our class. Some parents came with their kids to check if school's safe."

Peg noted, "The flu's mostly killing young healthy adults. Yet old people and young children often survive. It's strange."

Florence's forehead furrowed, "How do you know that?"

"Listen to talk in the store," Peg replied. "In Seattle, flu masks are mandatory if you leave home."

"Oh, that wouldn't bother me. I don't go anywhere anymore."

"Why not?"

"I used to go to Helen's after school every day and stay as long as possible," Florence divulged.

"How could you stand to be around her holier than thou attitude?"

"You ever heard of 'Don't bite the hand that lays the golden egg'?" Florence spouted.

Flummoxed, Peg muttered, "See you around" and took off for her last class.

At least Miss Shepherd was back. The pretty young home economics teacher had won all their hearts, especially the boys. She blushed so easily that the students couldn't resist trying to embarrass her. Today, someone had written a poem on the board:

> Whistle, Miss Shepherd, just whistle now.
> All the young men will scurry over and bow.
> "Why I've never whistled at a man in my life!"
> So, try it now, and I'll make you my wife.

The poem was written in response to the teacher's comments the day before when one of the students had wolf-whistled as she wrote on the chalkboard. "It's not polite to whistle at a woman," she'd admonished without turning.

"What if a girl whistles at a boy?" Peg had chirped, smiling as the red crept up the back of her teacher's neck.

The students giggled and whispered, hoping for the usual reaction from their beloved teacher. However, the room fell silent as soon as Miss Shepherd entered with swollen red eyes. No one wanted to embarrass her today. Every student sat silent as her lips quivered and her shoulders trembled. She gripped a wet hanky and dabbed at her eyes while trying to gain composure. Then she squeaked, "They'll be no class today."

"What's wrong, Miss Shepherd?" Peg voiced everyone's thoughts.

The teacher closed her eyes and drew a breath before speaking. The words gushed from her lips. "Mmm . . . my brother's missing in action," she finally whispered, then could no longer restrain herself and darted out the door.

Peg's heart froze. *What if that happened to my family?* She stumbled out.

Florence stood talking with Doris. "How bad for you! You mean your birthday falls on Christmas every year?"

Her foolish remark caused Peg to smile in spite of her fear.

CHAPTER 13

With Gene gone, the flu sweeping the country and Mud soon to leave, Christmas lost its magic. The wintry skies reflected Peg's mood. Nothing was going as planned unless she counted her work at Dr. Phillips' office. Mrs. Waterman had finally conceded Peg had a knack for medicine and was a hard worker. While she couldn't honestly say she liked Mrs. Waterman, she respected her skills and her ability to remain calm in a crisis. *No wonder Dr. Phillips puts up with her bossy ways.*

She had to run the last mile and arrived breathless. Mrs. Waterman glanced at the watch riding on her large bosom and grunted, "Supplies in the back room." Peg dragged herself back. Boxes rose from the corner to the ceiling. A few opened ones spilled onto the floor. Peg squatted next to them with a loud sigh as Dr. Phillips passed by and looked in.

"Sorry about the mess. With the flu epidemic, we've been running around in a frenzy!"

His having a little sympathy raised her spirits. "That's okay. Thought I'd be behind after weeks off."

"Good to have you back. Did you hear the Public Health Service is offering classes in first aid? I think you'd benefit from attending."

Peg drew a breath. "I'd love to!"

"Come in with this next patient," he invited.

A little girl sitting on her mother's lap whimpered when the doctor entered. While Dr. Phillips talked with the mother, Peg stood behind, winked at the little one and picked up a wooden tongue depressor from the glass jar on the cupboard. She covered one of her eyes, then the other. The little one giggled. "Look down her throat," Dr. Phillips suggested.

Peg stuck her tongue out and demonstrated. She got another depressor. "Your turn," she encouraged. The patient's tonsils looked inflamed. Tiny red dots like strawberry seeds covered her tongue and the back of her throat.

After Peg looked, the doctor leaned in, "Does it hurt when you swallow?"

Tears gathered in the girl's eyes.

Peg shook the mercury down in the thermometer saying, "Now instead of *on top* of your tongue, I'm going to put this *under* your tongue. It won't hurt." She put it in the child's mouth and tried to distract her. "Do you like kittens?"

The girl nodded.

"Do you have one?" Peg asked. "We have some new kittens in our barn. Ask your mom to come see them when you feel better." She removed the thermometer and showed the result to the doctor—102 degrees.

"Have her gargle with one to three tablespoons of apple cider vinegar in eight ounces of warm water. Get her to drink as much as you can. Keep her warm and rested. Take her temperature every four hours and come back if it gets worse," Dr. Phillips advised.

After the patient left, Peg asked, "Did she have the flu?"

"Maybe, but the red dots and inflamed tonsils make me think strep throat."

"Is that serious?"

"Can be," the doctor said. "Could turn into scarlet fever, inflame the kidneys or even worse, rheumatic fever could permanently damage her heart. It's also contagious, so be sure to wash your hands."

"Will do. I don't want to get sick again!"

"You hear Governor Lister's visiting Newport today?" Dr. Phillips asked.

Peg dried her hands. "Why would he come clear out to these tooley-wads?"

"We need a bridge across the Pend Oreille River to link northern Washington to Idaho's panhandle. He vetoed the idea a few years ago. Hope he doesn't this time," he yawned.

Peg finished straightening the exam room. "Have a long night last night?"

"'Fraid so. Grateful I have my trusty Mitchell auto instead of a horse. Although back then, I could let my team take me home and catch a few winks. Now I worry I'll fall asleep at the wheel!"

CHAPTER 14

Walking home after work, Peg shivered in the cold. The sun peeked through the clouds like a shy child hiding behind her mother's skirts. The moon, a full white saucer, promised a bright night. She hurried on, thinking of the fire and warm dinner waiting; yet, gloomy feelings kept creeping in. *Maybe I'm just tired. I'll go to bed early.*

In bed, she wrestled with the covers, her nightgown tangling up to her waist. The full moon shone through her window. She rose to shut the curtain tighter. A figure darted up the hill behind their house. *Who would be out on such a cold night?*

In the morning, muffled voices downstairs stirred her. The memory of a dream lapped at the edges of her mind. John's loud laughter rolled upstairs, ruining any chance of sleeping. Besides, nature called, and she wanted to know what was so funny. She pulled the chamber pot from beneath her bed, put on her slippers and robe and carried it down carefully.

"Good morning, Merry Sunshine!" Mary called.

"Did you take the cracked corn bag from the chicken coop?" John asked.

"Why would I do that?"

John confessed that he was puzzled. "Don't know. Couldn't find it this morning to feed the chickens. Was almost a full bag when I fed them last night."

"Well, it must have grown legs and walked off," Peg teased.

"Aren't you the funny one?"

"Speaking of funny, what were you laughing about that disturbed my beauty sleep?"

Mary smiled. "Just reminiscing about the time our family got quarantined with diphtheria. Your brother Wib told you if you got sick, you'd have to get a shot, and he would administer it with Dad's shotgun! You and Mud ran over the hill bawling and hid."

"Boy howdy, do I remember! It was right before Christmas, cold and snowy. Mud had grabbed matches and built a small fire we hovered over. When we finally decided we'd have to go home, it was dark. We were wet, cold and sick! Everyone had been out searching for us. Mom put us in a hot bath, filled us with warm soup and put us to bed. The next morning, I had a temperature, a sore throat, and worried about getting shot!"

"Yes, and you fought, the needle broke, and Wib even had to hold you down!"

"I worried so," John recalled. "Your mother, Ed, Wib, and Mud and your sister Freda were deathly ill!"

"Remember Ida, our hired girl, was sick, too," Mary added. "Gene put your names on gunny sacks and hung them in the big ol' apple tree for Santa."

"Yes!" Peg interrupted. "On Christmas Eve, here came a big load of gifts in the sleigh. The snow was so deep they drove over the top of the picket fence and put the gifts in our gunny sacks."

John remembered. "So much snow . . . our fence was at least five feet high! I stayed at the store but made sure the doctor came to see Ed every day. Good we can find something funny to remember about it."

"Remember the time Mud and I went swimming in the skating rink?" Peg laughed.

"I sure do!" John exclaimed. "What made you think you could swim during winter?"

"Well, everyone else was skating, but Mud and I were little and didn't have skates. So we decided to swim instead. We broke a hole in the ice, stripped off and jumped in."

John laughed. "I heard you screaming from the barn and came running."

"Yes, it was always high jinx with Mud and me," Peg giggled, "but we didn't catch pneumonia or even a cold!"

Mary changed the subject. "We were just wondering how our eighteen cows will get milked twice a day when Mud goes to war."

"Why can't I do that?" Peg volunteered.

"Those full five-gallon milk cans are heavy," Mary warned.

Peg's hands rose. "I can manage."

Mary passed the muffins around again. "You slept late today."

"Had a fitful night. A full moon shone bright on my pillow, and I couldn't shut down my mind. Had a bad dream, too. Oh, I just remembered, when I got up to close the curtain, a man crept up the hill behind the house."

"That may explain the lost cracked corn," John concluded, thinking he'd solved that mystery.

Peg set her spoon down. "But, Dad, why would someone want cracked corn?"

"I think he may want to drink it." John wiped his face with his napkin.

"Some people around here make their own hooch, and corn is the main ingredient," Mud explained as he tramped into the kitchen from the barn.

"Leave those shoes outside, Mud!" Mary hollered.

"Sorry. I could hear the laughter clear out in the yard and worried I was missing out! What's for breakfast? I'm so hungry I could eat a horse!"

"Lucky for you, we're eating pig. Now go wash up," Mary ordered, "and bring a load of wood for the stove on your way back, please."

"Hope you've got hotcakes and huckleberry jam!" he called.

Something niggled in Peg's mind. It came with force. "Dad! When Charlie and I went hunting a while back, this strange guy pulled a sack through the forest. I wanted to follow him, but Charlie wouldn't let me."

"Thank goodness for Charlie," Mary sighed.

Mud came back, shoeless. "What did you say? Sounds like my gun and I'd better sleep in the barn tonight."

CHAPTER 15

Peg often tended store on Saturday afternoons after Dr. Phillips' office closed. Usually, several local families milled around waiting for the mail, since the store served as the post office too, but most left disappointed.

Lately, Gene's sporadic letters from Europe made Peg worry even more. Some weeks, none came and some weeks, two or three. Today two arrived! Peg tore open the envelopes and scanned the dates since they didn't always arrive in order. She wanted privacy, so she slipped into the back room.

Feb. 1, 1918

Dear Family,

Life here is either boring or terrifying—long stretches sitting in the trenches interrupted by gunfire and shells. The worst are gas shells—what everyone fears most. I've been here long enough to distinguish their sound. You only have to see one victim to make you vigilant with your gas mask. Trench life is all you've heard. I won't go into details. I'm doing pretty well—made some good friends since there's time to talk between bombings. I haven't had the chance to wrestle any Krauts yet. Peg, have you wrecked my new car? Ha Ha.

Keep me in your prayers.

Love,

Gene

March 30, 1918

Dear Family,

Sorry my last letter was so glum. I heard the poor Russians were sent into war without enough food and clothing. Some even sent without guns and expected to pick ammo and guns off their dead comrades! I've never had to go hungry or without a weapon! Good ol' U.S.A.

General Pershing doesn't want us "doughboys" to be part of the French army's support. Guess he wanted to show the Kaiser what we Americans can do! After the American attack this fall, (can't give details) the Germans are pulling back. Hopefully, I'll be home soon!

Love to all,

Gene

The store bell's jingling brought Peg back. She hurried to the front to see Mrs. Edwards who never missed a mail delivery. Her son John had been one of the first to leave for war. Today, a letter waited. Her trembling hands and grief-stricken face drew all eyes. She opened it, yelped, clutched it to her breast and fell to the floor, wailing.

Mary dashed around the counter, put an arm around her shoulder and patted her arm. Peg stood rooted behind the register, tears trickling down her cheeks. A sob rolled up to her throat. She covered her mouth, stumbled to the back room and slumped onto a bean barrel. Her shoulders shook as she covered her face with her hands. She never heard Charlie until he knelt, and his arms encircled her. She buried her face in his shoulder. When she had no more tears, she raised her swollen face and asked, "Is he dead?"

Charlie hung his head. "No, missing in action."

"That's worse, not knowing!"

He put his hand on her shoulder. "At least there's hope."

"I'll die if that happens to you," she blubbered.

He kissed her forehead and tucked stray hair behind her ear. When she raised her face, he leaned down, lifted her chin gently and kissed her.

In two weeks, Mud and Charlie would leave for war. However, Peg's natural optimism blossomed with spring. With birds darting about collecting twigs, apple blossoms humming with bees, and flowers rising from graves, the world promised hope.

She meant to enjoy every day with Charlie. They rode horses through meadows of purple-eye grass, glacier lilies, and delicate white prairie stars. Peg knew Mother loved Charlie, too, and it was no secret she hoped he'd join their family.

After lunch, Charlie wove a crown of wildflowers. He placed it on Peg's head and proclaimed, "For my Queen." Peg picked up a nearby tree limb and touched his shoulders, "I dub you Sir-Poor-Shot!" and dashed away, giggling. When he caught her, they fell, laughing to the forest floor. She gasped, "Good Sir, I'd advise you to be more respectful of your queen."

"And I challenge you to a contest! My name is Sir Sure Shot!" he objected, "and you have questioned my skill! I do not have my pistol at this time, but—" He picked up two sticks and handed one to Peg challenging her. "On guard!"

CHAPTER 16

*H*ow *can a day look so lovely and go on as usual when my world is crashing? Mud and Charlie leave today and may never return.* She moved as if underwater, pushing through muted sounds and scenes, and wondered how she'd gotten to the railroad depot.

The wooden benches usually empty and laden with grit held somber faces. Some dressed in Sunday best: women in hats and white gloves, men in vests. Others had walked away from the plow and kitchen. Sun-baked fathers looked embarrassed and shifted from one foot to the other. Mothers in house dresses covered with full aprons hung onto the arms of young men in crisp uniforms. The children chased and giggled. Peg wanted to shout, "Be quiet!"

Her parents and Mud stood beside her, but she hadn't spotted Charlie. *I'm afraid of my reaction when they leave.* The ground trembled. A whistle blew. People moved as marionettes rising as one, craning their necks to the noise and shuffling toward the platform. *Where's Charlie?*

An adventurous young man had climbed the ladder of the water tower and shouted, "Here she comes!" The tracks started rattling. The engine roared around the bend. Barking dogs and screaming children raced alongside, waving at the conductor who leaned out the window. Amid the din, Peg didn't notice Charlie a few feet away.

The steaming, hissing monster belched clouds of black smoke and lurched into the depot.

She sensed a presence, turned and moved closer. "Are you alone?"

"Yeah, my parents aren't happy I enlisted. Told me it'd be over soon and should wait 'til I'm drafted. Dad says that I'm leaving him in a lurch at the ranch," Charlie unhappily admitted. Peg squeezed his hand, not trusting herself to speak. He took her hand and moved with the crowd.

Charlie left to place his luggage. She followed puppy-like, then remembered Mud. Torn, she looked back and forth a few times, ran and gave Mud a hug. The tears started. *I don't want to make a spectacle of myself!*

"It will be okay, Sis," Mud whispered. "Go to Charlie."

She didn't see him. *Was he already on the train?* Panic-stricken, she struggled through the throng. "Excuse me. Excuse me."

He's not where I left him. Now what? She scanned faces in a panic. *Surely, he wouldn't board without a final goodbye!* She heard a wail. Florence stood close to Charlie, sobbing. Her little brother sniffled and wiped his nose on a threadbare coat. Apparently, her brother was leaving, too. Charlie leaned down and whispered something to her. When he spotted Peg, he patted Florence's shoulder and came her way.

"All aboard!" the conductor bellowed.

This wasn't how Peg pictured this! No time to speak, to tell Charlie she was sorry for all the times she pushed him aside and pretended not to know his feelings. She lay her cheek on his chest. He pulled her close and kissed the top of her head. She held him so tightly that he had to loosen her arms. He walked to the train, turned and blew a kiss, bent his head and mounted the stairs. All the seats next to the window were taken. Men leaned out, waving.

She strained and spotted Charlie's tall shoulders, but his features blurred. He searched the crowd, found Peg, flashed a hopeful wait-for-me smile and saluted smartly. The train belched, hissed, groaned and lurched forward.

She stood with her fist to her mouth until it was long out of sight.

CHAPTER 17

Peg usually loved summer, but along with her heart, her back ached constantly. However, she'd never admit it. With her brothers at war, she milked eighteen cows. Each took fifteen to twenty minutes which meant six hours of milking each morning and six for Dad in the evening. She shuffled into the kitchen, rubbing the back of her neck.

Mary looked up from the sink, bit her lip and shook her head. "Peg, maybe you should give up nursing for a while," she suggested.

Peg's shoulders shook. Her eyes welled with tears. "Never!" she declared, choking on her own determination as she ran upstairs. *The war's already taken too much! It won't rob me of my dreams!*

"I so hate this war!" she raged. She yearned to crawl under warm covers and take a LONG nap. But the thought of Miss Waterman's disapproving scowl drove her on. *I'll give her no reason to let me go! I love medicine.* The hours at work flew since she was nursing more than cleaning and restocking.

As she rounded the corner, she spotted Howard Law on crutches, making his way to Dr. Phillips'. Hop, scrape, hop, scrape . . . his empty pant leg waved in the breeze. Everyone knew he lost his leg when he stepped on a mine in Europe. People said he was lucky to be alive.

The scene added to her gloomy mood. *I'll bet he doesn't feel too lucky.* Peg doubted and caught up.

"How are you, Howard?"

"Great! What a beautiful day to be out and about!"

"How do you manage to stay so positive?" Peg blurted, then blushed.

Howard stopped.

Now I've done it. Why don't I think? She opened her mouth to apologize, but Howard held up his hand.

"Peg, there's always something to be grateful for. I'm alive. I'm home. I'm free. I've learned what's important. Don't get me wrong. When I first came home, I felt sorry for myself, angry my life had changed. Finally, I realized I was choosing to be unhappy. I've learned I can choose to be happy."

"How true! You don't know how much I needed to hear that this morning," Peg thanked him and opened the door. The bell jangled, and disinfectant assaulted their noses. Polished floors, empty chairs in the waiting room, and Miss Waterman stationed behind the counter made Peg feel maybe the world hadn't turned upside down.

Even so, she had trouble concentrating. *I never thought I'd act like one of those silly girls with their head in the clouds!* She watched the clock, marking the time until she could go to the store to check the mail. Mud, Gene and Charlie filled her dreams and prayers. Getting a letter was better than Christmas.

Mrs. Waterman noticed, "Peg! Pay attention. What's wrong with you? I've asked you twice to bring me a file."

Poor ol' maid would never understand if I told her. "Sorry. Coming."

The hours crawled by until closing.

She sprinted to the store. Before she could ask, Mary gestured, "In the office on the desk."

June 15, 1918

Dear Peg,

I'm here—in the trenches. Don't know why I was so fired up to come. You were right—again. I get through it all by thinking of you, home, and all the things we'll do when I return. I remember all the times we tramped through the forest, teasing and enjoying nature. The bombing's created a wasteland here. Just dirt and mud. I sure miss all the trees and lakes of home, but have fun joshing with the soldiers.

Met a guy from down South, strong accent! Sometimes, I have a hard time understanding; it's so thick. Funny how fast you bond with someone when you're in danger. Petty things aren't important. People drop their masks. I've gotten to know these guys in my unit more in one month than friends from home (except you!) I've loved you for years, but you didn't want to see it.

Take care, my love. I'll be home soon, and we can start building our lives together.

Love,

Charlie

Peg didn't realize tears dripped from her chin until some plopped onto the letter. *I'm glad I came back here to read. Better answer. Be too tired after milking.*

She hurried home, went to Dad's roll top desk in the parlor and found paper and pen.

Dear Charlie,

Got your first letter and bawled like a baby. What have you done to me? I've certainly changed. I do admit I've suspected your feelings for me for a few months but pretended I didn't. You've always been my best friend, and I didn't know how I felt about that changing.

I'm keeping busy with chores and my nursing. I hoped if I didn't have time to think, I wouldn't worry, but it's not working too well.

I didn't know until the day you left that Florence had a brother leaving, too. Have you seen him? Unlike you, I get so caught up in my own cares. That's one thing I do love about you. How do you know who needs your help and exactly what to do and say? I must be so unobservant or self-centered.

Please don't volunteer for something. I know you too well, so I beg you—don't be the hero. Come home.

Love you,

Peg

She yawned and lay her head on her arm. *I'll rest a minute until emotions are under control.*

Her mother shook her shoulder. "Peg, you've been asleep for two hours. You're working too hard!"

"I think I'll tuck in early tonight."

"Your dinner's on the sideboard."

CHAPTER 18

With the war on, the small town embraced the Fourth of July with gusto. Businesses and homes alike flew flags. Word was that by the second of July, two million Americans were in France. Most news reported the Allies' progress. Fid's Opera Hall sported red, white and blue bunting under each window. As Peg walked by it, she reminisced about the fight. *Charlie's always considerate, buying me a ticket, watching out for me. I took so much for granted. Now I see it— after he's gone.* Florence exited the store as Peg reached for the doorknob. She felt a kinship with her. "Florence, I didn't realize until the day the men left that you had a brother joining, too."

"You never cared to know about me," Florence countered.

Taken back, Peg tried to smooth things over. "I know, but since Charlie left, I've realized some things. What do you hear from your brother?"

"Nothing for a month. But Dad's gotta stay sober 'cause Will's not there to take up the slack."

"Oh . . ."

"What about Charlie?"

"Well, he misses home like every soldier."

"You mean he misses YOU." Florence's bitterness was palpable.

"That, too, I guess." Peg backed into the store. "Any mail for me?"

"Not today, honey," Mary reported. "No letters from Europe."

"With the fighting heat'un up, prob-ly don't have no time to write, or can't get 'em mailed," Eddie, one of the old timers, theorized.

Mary scowled. *He shouldn't scare her like that,* but he went on.

"Leastwise, we finally took down ol' Bloody Red Baron! And now us Americans are there. We stopped them dirty Krauts near Paris! Yes siree-bob. Won't be long, girl, 'til your honey'll be coming home." He grinned, revealing a few brown teeth left in his gray whiskery face.

Mary softened and added, "I hope so, Eddie."

CHAPTER 19

July 1918

After she finished at Dr. Phillips' office, Peg always stopped at the store to check mail and news. Lately, the headlines brought hope.

```
German Troops Deserting

German troops being shipped from the
Eastern to Western Front are deserting
from transport trains.
```

Many heads bent over the paper. Peg listened intently. News was vital with Charlie, Gene and Mud fighting. The middle of July brought a shocking headline:

```
Tsar Nicholas II, Wife and Children
            Murdered by Bolsheviks

In the wee hours of July 17, the
family of Tsar Nicholas II was forced
into the cellar of a merchant's
home where they were imprisoned and
murdered by Bolshevik troops.
```

"Who are the Bolsheviks?" Peg asked her father.

John lowered the newspaper. "Lenin-backed Communists fighting in the Russian Civil War. The family was a threat to the takeover because they could be considered the rightful rulers of Russia by other nations."

Peg looked over his shoulder and studied the photo of the family, "But who could kill innocent children?"

John put his arm around her. "When wicked people rule, innocents always suffer. Come on, honey."

Life revolved around the mail. When the first letter from Mud arrived, Peg opened it with trembling fingers.

Dear Mom, Dad and family,

I'm living up to my name—covered in MUD! Trying to keep dry is a daily battle. News of the Allies looks good. Morale's rising, especially for those poor guys who've been fighting for four years. Our troops are fresh and fight-un ready! General "Black Jack" Pershing knows what he's doing by keeping us separated from those beat-down soldiers. I predict those Krauts will be on the run soon, and I'll be back.

Keep me in your prayers.

Love,

Mud

I wish I knew where he is and how he is. What's really going on? I need details and honesty. Peg sighed. "Why're letters always so vague?"

"Well, that there is somethun' you can't reveal," one of the newspaper bunch answered. "We don't want no one to know what we're up ta. If'n that info fell into the wrong hands, well, them things is what ya call top secret."

The ever-present Eddie added, "Ya hear 'bout the Harris boy? His nerves give out and he's in some hospital for lunatics."

"Do you mean Florence's brother?" Peg asked, genuinely concerned.

"I didn't want to tell you yet, Peg," Mary interjected, "not until we heard more."

"What DO you know?"

"There's lotsa men whose nerves give out under them bad conditions," old Eddie continued. "I seen it before. This here one guy hid under his bed all day and another fella had such nervous jerks that . . . "

"That's quite enough!" Mary chided. "Come on, Peg. Let's go home." She grabbed Peg's elbow. "That man never thinks before he speaks!"

"Mother, should we go visit Florence's family?" Peg whispered.

She escorted Peg to the door. "We'll talk later."

"Knowing some about the Harris family makes me think his nerves were stretched thin before he went to war. Maybe that's why he cracked," Peg reasoned. Just then, the clock struck, bong, bong, bong. "Oh, Mom, I can't go home. I'd better get down to the hospital. Doc is going to let me watch a Cesarean today!"

CHAPTER 20

July 1918

"You'll be seventeen next week!" Mary reminded Peg. "What kind of cake do you want for your birthday?"

"I don't care. Celebrations are no fun when we're missing loved ones," Peg muttered as she lugged the five-gallon can of warm milk to the separator.

"No matter. We ARE celebrating, so choose." Mary helped her lift the milk can.

Peg tipped it and spilled milk down the front of her. "So surprise me."

Mary looked her in the eyes. "Peg, I've never seen you like this. I'm worried."

Peg grabbed a rag and wiped her shirt. "I've never been afraid people I love will die before." She threw the cloth onto the floor.

Mary leaned over and picked it up. "We're all worried, dear, but stewing about things you can't change doesn't help."

"I know, Mom. I'm sorry," Peg apologized as she headed to the barn for more milk cans.

As soon as the weather warmed, the stove huggers at the Tarbet Store moved to the front porch to await the arrival of the newspaper. Today's headline caused a stir.

Allies Counterattack in
Second Battle of the Marne

"Lookee here! We tricked them blasted Krauts!" Eddie chortled after reading the top story.

"Let's see." John grabbed a copy of the paper and read aloud:

The Allied deception of creating
false, lightly manned trenches kept
their actual frontline trenches safe
during an early morning attack on July
18. U.S., British, and Italian troops
joined with 24 divisions of the French
army in an attack on German lines.

Mary entered quietly to listen to her husband.

John continued:

By July 20th Germans had retreated
from Chateau-Thierry to Soissons on
the Aisne River. Heavy casualties
reported.

"I wonder if Gene, Mud, or Charlie was there. Don't show this to Peg," she pleaded. "She's got enough on her plate."

John dropped the paper. "What besides milking and nursing?"

Mary motioned him to the back room and whispered, "She came home red-eyed and exhausted last night."

"What happened?"

"She was up all night with Dr. Phillips, trying to save a premature baby. Since Mrs. Glines had toxemia, Doc decided on a C-section for the mother's sake, but neither lived."

"Oh my," John declared as he shook his head.

Mary returned to the front, gathered the newspapers and placed them under the counter. "Don't leave these out. Peg will come here as soon as she wakes up, and I don't want her to see them."

The store bell jangled, and every head turned. "Peg, why aren't you in bed?" John put his hand on her shoulder and guided her out the door.

"I'm too keyed-up to sleep. Thought I'd see if the paper was here," she said with a sigh as she sat on the porch steps and rested her head against the railing.

"Oh, no, you don't. Back to the house and bed. You'll get sick if you keep this up," Mary ordered.

John backed his wife. "Go on, honey."

Peg grabbed the railing, heaved herself up and plodded back to the house. Instead of going upstairs, she slumped onto the davenport, pulled an afghan from the arm over her and fell into an exhausted sleep.

Mud screamed in pain as a bullet ripped through his calf. He stumbled, fell into the nearest foxhole and landed on top of a dead soldier. Rolling off into the mud, a rat ran across his chest. The ground shook from explosions.

"Mud!" Peg cried. Clawing up, Peg realized she'd been dreaming. Tears ran.

John heard the commotion and flew in the house. "What's the matter, honey?" He enfolded Peg in his arms.

She sobbed, soaking his shirt front. "A bad dream. Mud got shot. You don't think it was a premonition, do you?" Peg's eyes begged him to say no.

"It was just a dream, dear. Things will work out."

"You can't know that, Dad. No one knows! We've seen men in our own town come back broken in mind and body!"

He gently pushed her back and looked in her face. "We aren't in charge, are we? Try to stay hopeful. You'll be happier."

September 1918

Days passed in a mindless slur: milking, nursing, sleeping, milking, nursing, sleeping. The nights cooled and leaves began to turn. *I haven't been in the woods all summer! Oh well, it would only make me miss Charlie, his freckles, his blue eyes, his . . . Now quit that!* She admonished herself.

School brought a welcome change. Peg's father took up the morning milking and she returned to Newport High. However, the usual anticipation was missing. Even putting on the new dress her mother had sewn in her favorite robin-egg blue didn't lift the worry always at the back of her mind. Peg walked to the road and waited for the school wagon. The younger boys still jostled with playful punches and bragged about their summer escapades while little girls giggled, checked the ribbons in their hair and smoothed the skirts of their new dresses. But the high school kids sat quietly. They'd had to confront new realities and responsibilities that summer. Peg wasn't the only one who remained lost in her thoughts.

As she walked to class, Peg passed Florence in the hall.

"Hi. Hello?"

"Oh, sorry, Florence. I was a million miles away," Peg apologized. "How was your summer?"

"It's over," Florence replied woodenly.

What did she mean? Worried about saying the wrong thing, Peg walked on. *At least biology's next. That's always a bright spot in my day.*

The day passed without the usual excitement of friends reuniting after summer. *It's so empty without Charlie here.*

After school, Peg passed grade school girls jumping rope and chanting:

> I had a little bird
> And its name was Enza
> I opened the window
> And in-flew-Enza!

She stopped and stared. *Are they saying what I think they are? That flu's no joke!*

She shivered, then hurried on to the store to check the mail before heading to the doctor's office and found a letter from Charlie! She clutched it to her chest and flew into the back office to savor it. After plopping her books down, she shrugged off her sweater and closed the door.

Dear Peg,

Thought you'd be interested in how medicine is practiced here (seeing's how you'll be a doctor soon!) Stretcher bearers are first to the wounded. A brave bunch—often running deep into the battlefield, dodging bullets, and slogging through mud. They carry soldiers to first aid for triage. Many are saved right there! Men suffer from gas, wounds, shellshock, and the less dramatic—but just as deadly—flu or dysentery. I'm sure you've heard of the trench diseases, trench foot, mouth etc., to say nothing of the lice. I never knew that lice could be so many different colors!

From there, ambulances take them to mobile hospitals and the severely wounded to hospitals far from the front lines. It's organized, so don't worry, as there are capable hands. We understand blood transfusions and the new X-ray machines are saving many lives. There are women nurses and volunteers, but DO NOT get any ideas! I don't want you over here in this hell. I mean I want to see you, but not in danger. The nurses work so hard and remind guys of their mothers and girls back home. I think this whole nightmare will be over before you're out of school, so do NOT join!

I've made a good friend Patrick Maguire from Boston, Mass. We tease each other a lot. He calls me Lumberjack, and I named him Leprechaun because he's small and Irish. We're opposites: country boy and city boy, Protestant and Catholic, social and shy. We make a real Mutt and Jeff pair. That little guy is tough! Back in Massachusetts, he boxes at night and drives a milk wagon during the day. He can do a backflip, too! Hope after this is over, he can come up to the Northwest. He's fascinated by my stories of home. Would you like to go with me Back East and see how city folks live?

How's everyone at home? My parents write. I can tell they're worried about me. Anything interesting happened at the doctor's office? Write me a LONG letter! I never want them to end.

All my love,

Charlie aka Lumberjack

Peg tucked the letter in her pocket next to her heart and hurried to work. Mrs. Waterman looked at her watch as soon as Peg entered. A scowl crossed her face, but she held her tongue. Peg scurried back to wash her hands. She wanted to re-read the letter but didn't dare.

Dr. Phillips poked his head in as he walked by. "Hello, Peg. Hear anything from your young man?"

"Got a letter today! He wrote about the medical services."

"Great! Come on in my office a minute." He opened the door, gestured for her to have a seat and gave his full attention. "How interesting. What's his opinion?"

Peg shared the whole letter, hoping that Doc could ease her worries.

"Sounds like they're on top of things. X-ray machines are a real blessing. But what they need is more medical personnel. Heard they're expanding the draft age to forty-five years." Doc rubbed his chin. "Wonder if I'll get drafted."

"Oh, no! You are needed here!" Peg protested and immediately started to figure her father's age. "1918 minus 1863 is what . . . forty-five! No fifty-five." She let out a breath she didn't realize she was holding . . . *If one more of my loved ones goes to war, I don't think I can hold on.*

Routine office calls filled the afternoon: colds, sore throats, and pregnancies. Peg thought about Charlie's letter. *I can get trained in time to join as a nurse, and I will, too, even though Charlie won't like it.*

"Peg?" Dr. Phillips' voice brought her back.

"Yes," she jumped.

"I asked you to bring me the alcohol," he reminded.

She lay the rolled bandage back in the box. "Sorry!" she apologized and hopped up.

As soon as she got home, she headed straight to her desk.

Dear Charlie,

Thanks for your letter. Just keep thinking about those brave medics and all the lives they're saving. You're right! I'm itching to help! I'm studying hard, have an A in biology and am looking at nursing schools in Spokane. Just think—I'll already be there when your flight comes in!

Doc's worried about the new draft rules as he's only 44. I wonder how many fathers that may take from their families. Are things so dire there?

School's hard without you there. Ran into Florence on the first day. She acted mad or something. She doesn't like me, but she likes you!

Enough of that. I'm rambling. I know life in the trenches is miserable and pray for you every day. I try not to think about it, or I'd go crazy. I realized the other day that I haven't gone into the woods all summer. When I remember our times there, I get lonely, so probably it's just as well.

Sorry, I'll be positive now. I have dreams, things I want to do, places I want to go. I realize I've been self-centered. I don't know what your dreams are. Did I ever ask you? You asked me questions all the time, and I answered without returning the favor. I owe you an apology. In your next letter, will you tell me what you want to do with your life?

The more I study medicine, the more I love it! Do you feel that way about anything? Hope this letter is long enough.

Love,

Peg

CHAPTER 21

November 11, 1918

GREAT WAR OVER! ARMISTICE SIGNED!

5:00 a.m. Paris Armistice signed.
War ended 11:00 today!

Official terms of the armistice will
be announced later, but it is assumed
by the military that the terms will
include:

Germany will be disarmed and immobilized.
Release of all Allied prisoners . . .

The whooping, back slapping, and cheers of customers in the store were so loud that no one noticed Mary. She slumped to her knees with tears running down her face, "Thank God!"

The church bell rang. Everyone celebrated. Students bolted from school. Strangers hugged. Men dug out secreted alcohol. People danced in the street. Mothers wept. Tin Lizzies honked their horns. Dogs barked at all the excitement and noise.

When Peg heard the news, she sprinted for home. Huffing, she threw open the back door and collapsed on the davenport, sobbing.

No one was home, so she let it all out. With a throbbing headache, she stumbled upstairs to her room and crawled under the covers until she heard her mother tiptoe into the room. She rolled over, sat up, held out her arms, and they wept together.

"Let's go find something to eat. You'll feel better," Mary suggested.

Peg grimaced. "Don't feel like eating."

"Come on, dear. Something hot will work wonders: A cup of tea? a bowl of soup? I made elk stew."

After warm food worked its magic, Peg fired question after question. "When will they be back? What shall we do to celebrate? Do you think Gene will stay here or go to school?"

"Hold on. We'll figure that out as it comes. Let's relax and enjoy." Mary carried the dishes to the sink.

The celebration mood lasted for weeks. John planned new crops and ordered seeds. Mary started spring cleaning early. Peg practiced driving.

At the store, men crowded the wood stove and coddled hot coffee as they waited for the mail. As soon as the door slammed, Eddie hobbled over and grabbed the paper from the stack in Mary's hands.

"Lookee here! Those German ships we took are being used to transport troops home. Now there's justice!" he crowed.

Mary sorted through the stack of mail. "Letter from Gene!"

Peg dropped her book and scampered to the counter.

Her hands shaking, Mary carefully worked at the seal.

"Just rip open the end!" Peg exclaimed as she hopped from one foot to the other. "Here," she offered, "let me help you!"

Mary handed it over.

Dear Folks,

We made it! It's hard to believe war's over! Thought it was a rumor for a few hours as the shelling got worse, not better. We've been keyed-up and on edge for so long that a lot of guys started sobbing. We all had an emotional release. I laughed and laughed. One guy in my unit had a total breakdown. It's hard to think good news can cause such things.

What have you heard from Mud and Charlie? We'll have to have some big shindig when we're all back! Mom, I want to eat a whole boysenberry pie with tons of whipped cream. Now I'm dreaming about home-cooked food! I hope the cellars are full. I'll never take home for granted ever again. When I receive my discharge orders, I'll let you know the when and where. Get ready for one of my big bear hugs!

Love,

Gene

Charlie's letter arrived a week later:

Dear Peg,

When we heard the war was over, we didn't even cheer, just stood there stunned. My friend Patrick, Little Leprechaun, got killed November 11th at eight in the morning. The damn war ended a few hours later! We'd fought together the whole time. He was the bravest soldier I've ever known. What God lets things like this happen?

Don't know when I'll be home. I'm thinking about stopping in Boston and seeing Patrick's parents. I was the last one to see him alive. We're all waiting for a seat on a ship home. Too many soldiers and not enough ships. May not be home until after the first of the year.

I'm trying to forget some of the awful scenes. Plenty of guys are drinking to cope. Some French factories have been turned into training centers to teach us skills and help with the boredom.

Guess I can tell you now that I'm in France. If that is blacked out, you'll know that I can't.

Charlie

"He sounds so different," Peg commented with worry in her voice. *So melancholy. He didn't say a word about seeing me again.*

"After what he's been through," Mary warned, "you'll have to be understanding and patient when he gets home."

"That's not my best quality," she worried.

"If you love him, it will all work out, dear."

December 1, 1918

Dear Charlie,

Got your letter. So sorry about your friend Patrick. The Walls (who live next to you) lost two sons in the war. Everyone knows someone who isn't coming home. I'm so glad you are! Any word as to when? I so wish you'd be here for Christmas!

We've got almost a foot of snow already, and Dad has spotted a beautiful tree not far from the house. Let's take the sled. We can string popcorn and cranberries, sip hot cider, sit in front of the fire and plan our future together.

Tom Jones got home last week. Haven't seen him but heard he and Emily broke up. Guess Emily spent a lot of time with his family last year and fell for his brother while Tom was gone. Poor guy, what a homecoming! He took off for Seattle the next day. Can't blame him. Emily's already planning the wedding.

I skip school when Dr. Phillips is doing an interesting operation. He lets me observe and sometimes help! I've decided to go to St. Luke's in Spokane and become an obstetrical nurse.

What kind of work do you want to do when you return?

Gotta go. Will write again soon.

Love,

Peg

Dec. 28, 1918

Dear Charlie,

I know it's been a month, but I haven't heard
from you either. When you didn't come home for
Christmas, and I never heard from you, I'll admit
I went into a slump and was angry. Anyway, I have
been busier than a mosquito in a nudist colony!
(Heard that joke the other day). What have you
been doing? You MUST be too busy to write.

   It's late, midnight, but I needed to write.
There's a full moon, and it's beautiful outside—so
bright trees cast shadows. I heard a coyote howl . . .

Peg glimpsed movement out of the corner of her eye. She
dropped the pen and stood for a closer look. Yes, someone moved
behind the trees. He carried a bag. Deja vu flooded. She remembered why! *Should I wake Dad or wait until morning?* She debated as
the shadowy figure slipped into the trees. *Probably be gone by time
Dad got his shoes and coat on,* she reasoned and went back to her
letter.

   Just saw a man out the window with something in
his hands. Remember when I wanted to investigate
a few months ago? What do you think could be going
on? I'll tell Dad tomorrow. In this snow, there's
sure to be tracks. I'll let you know what if anything
we find out.

Still waiting to hear from you,

Peg

CHAPTER 22

Peg groaned when her mother called, "It's six o'clock!" Then she remembered last night's mystery, threw her legs over and groped with shut eyes for her knitted wool slippers. Shuffling down the stairs, she heard her parents' goodbyes and called, "Wait! Dad, I need to talk to you!"

John shut the door. "Hold-er, Newt. What's up?"

"Last night, I saw him again!" Peg exclaimed.

His forehead wrinkled. "Who?"

"Maybe it's the same guy Charlie and I saw. Remember how the cracked corn was missing? I'll see if it's gone again!"

"OK, settle down. I'll look." John left to investigate the barn and chicken coop. "Lo and behold," he whispered. "She was right!"

He met Peg in the yard. "You guessed it. The bag's missing."

"Why would anyone want corn, Dad?"

"Well, one use I can think is makin' moonshine," John admitted as he rubbed his chin.

"Right, Dad! Who would do that?"

"I could name a few possible suspects, but most of them grow their own corn," John thought aloud.

Peg rushed toward the forest. "Let's follow the tracks. I'm sure he left some."

"Wait here. I'll get my gun."

Cold bit their faces. Peg bent her head against the wind when a bullet ricocheted off the tree to her right. John fell to his knees, grabbed the front of Peg's coat and pulled her down. "Stay put!" he growled as he crawled forward. He looked over his shoulder. "I mean it. Don't you follow me!"

Snow had packed down her neck. As it melted against her warm skin, she shivered. Scenarios flooded her mind. *What if something happens to Dad? Should I go for help? What if someone comes after me?* She lifted her head, but the undergrowth hid Dad well. *They can't see me either,* Peg hoped, *but someone looking down may spot me. Better find him, but what if he comes back and I'm gone? He'll panic!*

A shot echoed. She jumped and scrambled through the undergrowth on all fours. In the crusted snow, John's path was clear. Brush scratched her face. Footsteps moved closer; she fell flat. After a minute, she sprang from the path, over the top of shrubs through low branches and sunk deep into a drift behind a fallen tree.

"Over here!" a man bellowed. Peg's heart pounded.

Snow crunched under heavy feet. "Well . . . what have we here? Looks like someone's with him. There's two sets of footprints!"

"Where'd they go?" a raspy voice whispered.

"Dunno."

"Musta turned back when they heard the shot."

"You follow the tracks. I'll take a look-see 'round here."

A hacking cough punctuated the air.

Where's Dad? Did he lay in a pool of blood somewhere? Tears froze her face. A panting man moved closer. She held her breath. *Dear God, don't let him find me.*

A loud *haw-choo* exploded feet away, followed by sniffles and throat clearing.

"George!" A call came from below. "Get down here!"

His partner yelled, "Com-min'!"

She peeked out of the drift. Seeing no one, she eased out on her stomach, rose to her knees and glanced quickly around. *Good thing I know this mountain so well.* She trekked west, picking her way through brush and trees, then slipped, fell and slid, landing with a thump at the feet of two shaggy men in ragged coats and ratty hats.

The hatchet-faced one leaned closer. "Well, lookee here. Now who's this? George, get over here!"

Peg recognized George immediately. "Why, hello, Mr. Harris. How's Florence doing?" She tried to sound nonchalant.

"Waddaya doing up here?" he growled.

"Well, you know I just live below this hill. My big brother Ed spotted a five-point buck up here yesterday, so we came up this morning." Peg chatted cheerfully. "We got separated. I'm headed back for school. You fellas seen a buck? Better be off, or Mom will be out. I promised I'd only be gone an hour. Do you have the time?" Her nerves kept her blabbering.

"Aw shut up and get home," George snapped.

CHAPTER 23

Peg sprinted down the hillside. Wheezing and sobbing, she fell through the back door. Her father and uncle Ben Fox, the local sheriff, came around the side of the house, toting deer rifles.

"Wait!" Mary called, "Peg's home!"

John stormed through the door, his eyes blazing. When he noticed his baby girl, he dropped his gun on the table and slumped next to her. "You okay? Why didn't you stay where I told you? What happened? You see anyone?"

Ben put a hand on his shoulder. "Hold on, John. Let the girl settle down."

"Dad," Peg wheezed, "George Harris and another man followed our tracks down the mountain. I hid in a big drift and came home when the coast was clear. Whadda ya find?"

John's voice shook as he stated, "There's a cave near the top of the mountain. Easy to tell from the smell, they're making moonshine. Opening's covered by brush. No chance to explore as the men started down. I was afraid you'd be discovered, so followed from a distance. When I got to the place I left you, and you weren't there, well . . . "

"What shall we do, Dad?"

"You'll stay here," John ordered. "Uncle Ben and I will take care of it."

"But I wanted . . . "

John's temper rose. "Like I said, you'll stay here! And I mean it!"

Mary put her arm around Peg's shoulder. "Let's get you in a warm bath. The water's heating. Then a hot breakfast and into bed with you."

"But, Mom, what about school?"

"It'll wait. Come along, dear." She herded Peg to the bath.

Crushed lavender blossoms parted as Peg slid into the hot tub. She dipped the washcloth in, wrung it, covered her face and noticed her head, throbbing. Sinking, warmth caressed her whole being.

CHAPTER 24

Peg awoke, shivering in lukewarm water, threw on her robe and
ran downstairs, dripping. "Mom? Dad? Where are you?" Out
the kitchen window, a dark cloud glowered over the mountain. It
felt like evening, but the clock on the mantel chimed four times.
Maybe they've gone to the store. She ran upstairs to dress.

A crowd had gathered in the store. "Anyone seen my parents?"
Peg scanned the room. Mrs. Waterman didn't raise her head from an
intent conversation but gestured to the backroom.

"What's going on, Mom?" Peg insisted. Mary turned her swollen,
tear-stained face and shrugged her shoulders. "Mom! What happened! Where's Dad!"

"I'm not sure," Mary gulped.

"Where's Uncle Ben!" Peg cried in a quivering voice.

Mary, unable to speak for a few seconds, squeaked out, "You
mean you didn't notice him?"

"What?" Peg panicked.

Mary covered her face. "You had to have walked right past him.
Dr. Phillips had him stretched out on the floor and removed the
bullet from his leg."

"A bullet? Who shot him?" Peg strode back into the store.

Mrs. Waterman's formidable presence parted the crowd. "Move
on back, everybody!"

"Is he okay?" Peg's voice trembled when she caught a glimpse of Uncle Ben's pale face.

"He'll be fine if these idiots move!" Waterman barked. "Is the wagon ready for him? Move on back. There's nothing to see here!" She pushed forward and cleft the crowd.

Peg caught the nurse's elbow. "Can I come?"

"No. Go to your mother," Mrs. Waterman ordered.

Peg stumbled backwards into the reassembled crowd. "Excuse me," she repeated, pushing back to her mother.

"Mom! Where's Dad! Is he all right?"

"Calm down. Men are out looking for him. There's nothing to do but wait."

"I'm not sitting around!" Peg started for the door.

Her big brother Ed caught her around the waist. "Oh, yes, you are, my little lady Lassie!"

"Ed, we have to do something!" she pleaded.

"We are. We're waiting—right here."

Peg paced. "What if he needs our help? What if he got shot, too? What if he's bleeding? How can you stand there?"

Ed put his hands on her shoulders. "Men are out there doing all that can be done."

Two hours later, Peg pressed her face to the window. Moonlight shimmered over the snow. Shadows of tall pines danced in the wind. *At least, there's a full moon. He should be easy to find.*

"Let's go home where it's more comfortable," Mary suggested and took Peg firmly by the arm. "Ed, lock up the store, will you?"

"Sure thing, Mom."

CHAPTER 25

E d's pretty wife, Ethel, and her father, Ralph Sparks, sat in the big kitchen, sipping coffee and discussing the event. Ralph pulled a flask from his pocket and poured into his coffee.

Ethel froze when she noticed Peg behind Mary. "Mary! Peg? We came to check on Peg. I thought she was still asleep and started coffee. Where've you been, Peg?"

Peg kicked her shoes off. "You must have come after I left for the store."

"Any news?" Ralph stood concern written on his face.

Mary's quivering voice betrayed her. "None yet."

Ed ran huge fingers through his thick hair. He took her elbow, led her to the davenport and handed her a cup. "Drink this, Mom. Ethel makes the best coffee around."

Mary exhaled at the smell and warmth, blew on the coffee and took a sip.

"I should have gone with the deputies," Ed expressed his regret and worry.

"No! I need you here with me in case . . . " Mary's voice dropped.

Ed patted her knee. "OK, Mom."

"Dad, finish your story," Ethel encouraged, her curls bobbing. She hoped to lighten the mood.

Ralph resumed, "Well, like I was saying. I started cooking for lumber crews a few years ago, and I've seen some funny things. Last week, a small man came looking for work. Didn't look like he could pick up an axe, let alone swing one. Ludvig, our big Swede with the nickname Paul Bunyan, sprang forth with the heaviest axe in the camp. 'Let's see what you can do,' he challenged the little guy, who picked up the axe and headed to the biggest tree in the clearing. Man, oh man, he swung an axe like it wasn't his first time!

"Surprised by the little guy's strength, we all watched. But soon as I yelled, 'Soup's on!' they scrambled for food. Dust flew, men jostled, and we forgot he was still choppin'. 'Bout the time we finished, we heard 'Tim-baa!' The crash brought us to our feet! I'll be dog-gonned if that little fella hadn't brought it down."

"You mean he cut it down by himself in less than an hour?" Ed looked doubtful.

"I know," Ralph continued, smiling at the joy of having a captive audience, "A big cheer went up from the men, but Ludvig went to investigate. He pushed at the fallen tree but couldn't budge it, so called and we ran over, wondering what he'd found. I couldn't tell what he was trying to do, but he lined us up along the tree. We pushed together and rolled it over. Ludvig examined the cut on the opposite side and found it'd been cut almost through!"

"You mean he'd come earlier and nearly cut it through? Wasn't that dangerous to leave a tree?" Peg got so caught up in the story that she temporarily forgot about her dad.

"Yeah. When boss found out, he was livid, but Ludvig laughed and laughed. He thumped the jokester on the back and stuck up for him. Told the boss we should take him on because he obviously wanted the job pretty bad."

"So, did he?" Mary asked.

"Nope. Boss was mad he'd sneaked onto private property. Plus, someone could'a got hurt 'fore he'd had the chance to put on his little show."

"So, what happened to the little man?" Ed asked.

"Spotted him today working for another company west of our timber sale," Ralph giggled. "Wondered if he fooled the other guys."

"Tell us another story," Peg begged.

"Well, once we were sure we spotted a Sasquatch . . . "

The back door opened, and everyone rose expectantly. John dragged in, his face scraped and bleeding.

"John!" Mary ran to him. "What happened?"

"Let him sit down, Mom," Ed suggested.

John hobbled to the davenport.

"Someone, please, get him a hot drink," Mary pleaded. "Are you hurt?"

John laid his head against the back of the davenport. "I'm fine. Ben make it back?"

"He'll be okay," Mary assured him.

"Thank God," John croaked. "When we got separated, I heard gunfire and prayed he wasn't shot."

"He did!" Peg interjected.

John bolted up, "What?"

"He took a bullet to the leg, but Doc Phillips got it out and said he won't have permanent damage," Ed explained.

"Why those dirty . . . "

"Hold your tongue, please, John," Mary quickly interrupted.

Peg moved closer. "What did you find, Dad?"

"Told you 'bout a cave opening covered with brush?"

"Yes, go on," Mary commanded.

"We knew from the smell, some kind of hooch was brewing. Ever since Washington went dry a couple years ago, people've been moonshining. Didn't get a good look in the cave, but recognized George Harris and some low-life friend. They fired, and we skedaddled. Then we separated, hoping to confuse them. Apparently, they followed Ben and shot him. I've been searching for him. How'd he get down? Who found him?"

"I did," Ed humbly revealed. "Peg and I've been tracking a big buck. I had the day off, so thought I'd scout around. When I heard the shot, I followed it and found Ben lying against a tree. I tried to stop the bleeding, took off my shirt and made a tourniquet. Then I packed him out. Came straight to the store. Doc Phillips came to fix him up."

John's gaze darted out the window. "Where's he now?"

Ed patted John's back. "Home. Our Freda's a good nurse, and I'm sure Mrs. Waterman will stay until she's confident any danger has passed."

"Someone needs to arrest those sons a . . . "

Mary stopped him again. "John, you need to rest. Let me clean up those cuts."

Ethel stood and nervously checked her watch. She pulled on Ed's arm. "Time for us to go."

"Thanks for the story!" Peg giggled.

Ralph took off his hat and bowed, enjoying his audience. "Sure thing."

Peg moved to the stairs. "I'm still keyed-up. Think I'll write Charlie."

John winced as Mary cleaned a cut. "Had a letter yet?"

"Not for over a month."

"I'm sure the mail's swamped with all our soldiers making their way home. They've time on their hands. I bet you'll get one soon."

Dear Charlie,

Why haven't you written? Something scary happened tonight. Uncle Ben got shot and we wondered if my dad was dead . . . (Peg retold the whole story.) Probably the most exciting thing that's happened around here in years. I'll let you know how things turn out.

Have you not written or is the mail slow? Dad thinks since soldiers have more time, the mail's flooded. I hope that's why. We got a letter from Gene, and he'll be home in two weeks. I promised I would pick him up in his new car at the train depot. So thankful he's coming home, and life can get back to normal.

Any news about when it's your turn?

Love you,

Peg

She licked the envelope, suddenly exhausted and crawled into bed fully clothed.

CHAPTER 26

P eg pushed the scratchy wool quilt from her face. She inched over onto the cotton pillowcase she'd embroidered with butterflies and flowers and fingered the lace her mother had crocheted around the edge. *How long has it been since I sat by the fireplace doing handwork? Now my brothers are coming back, I can return to womanly arts like Mother wants me to. I'd better check out my hope chest. I'll need those things after Charlie's home. Sure hope marriage fits in with my plans to be a nurse.*

"Letter from Gene!" John called up the stairs.

Peg leapt up and hopped on the chilly floor, not bothering to find her slippers or robe.

"Mail hasn't come yet. Why do we have a letter?"

"Came yesterday. With all the commotion with Uncle Ben, no one got the mail sorted until this morning. Ralph happened by the store and dropped it by."

"Ralph?"

"Yes, Ralph Sparks, Ed's father-in-law." John held the letter aloft.

"Oh, right. He did have some good stories last night," Peg commented. "Hurry! What's it say?"

John read the letter aloud.

Dear Family,

Change of plans. Good ol' army. Everything here moves like cold molasses. Looks like there will be a delay in my return. I'm disappointed but trying to stay busy and keep my mind off heading home. We're still drilling; don't ask me why. Keeps us moving, I guess. When I get my new orders, I'll let you know. How's everything? Peg still working for Doc Phillips? I imagine she is—much as she loved it when I left. Soon I'll be able to catch up on everyone's news. Don't bother to write back as I'll probably be gone by the time it arrives. I may even beat this letter home. (Wishful thinking I'm afraid!)

Love,

Gene

"We'll have a lot to tell him, won't we, Dad? What happened after I went to bed?"

"Yes, we will," John continued. "Men got back 'bout two this morning. As expected, they found a still hidden in the cave along with about fifty jugs of white lightning, but no sign of those vermin. I'm sure they skedaddled after shooting Ben, and they'll stay away if they know what's good for um." John folded the letter back into the envelope. "Well, I'm off to work."

"Headed to the bank?"

"Ya, got a couple meetings, but first, I'm going to check on Ben. Wish I could stay," John apologized as he took his hat from the hook by the back door, kissed Mary on the cheek and blew Peg a kiss.

"Hopefully, you'll have no bank robbers!" Peg teased.

"Don't say that! We've had enough excitement around here." Mary shooed Peg upstairs, "Now hurry! Breakfast's getting cold. School wagon in fifteen minutes!"

CHAPTER 27

School buzzed with news of the previous night's shooting. "Peg's here!" someone called as soon as she walked into the building. Kids swamped her.

Peg pushed a boy back. "Give me some room, please."

"Tell us what happened," another girl begged.

"I don't know much," she admitted.

"Did Florence's dad shoot the sheriff?" a small girl pushed her face forward.

Peg shrugged.

"Let's go find Florence!" a guy suggested. They moved off like a swarm of bees.

When Florence was nowhere to be found, the talk turned to Winter Ball. Peg sat in her desk, groggy from her late night, nodding off during a lecture on the Civil War. Finally, she gave in, put her head on her arms and awoke to laughter.

"You were snoring!" Henry whispered.

"Miss Tarbet, you have a one-page essay due tomorrow on 'Why I Should Not Sleep in Class,'" Miss Berry pronounced.

The class tee-heed. "Settle down or the rest of you will have another assignment, too!" The teacher swished by in her dark skirt. Everyone wanted to laugh as the bun on the top of her head wobbled, but no one dared.

Peg tapped her foot quietly the rest of the hour to stay awake.

Henry walked out with her. "What do you hear from Charlie? He comin' home soon?"

"Don't know. Don't think mail is getting through 'cause I haven't heard from him for some time."

Henry puffed out his chest. "Been asked to Winter Ball yet?"

Peg hesitated before saying, "No, don't expect to be. Everyone knows Charlie and I are together."

"Of course, we do, but with Helen gone and Charlie gone, I thought maybe we old friends should go. You know, to cheer us up and give us something to look forward to." Henry hoped he sounded convincing.

Peg didn't have the heart to disappoint him. "OK, why not? But you know, I'll try to lead and step on your toes," she warned.

"That's okay. Pick you up at seven on Friday," Henry chanted as he ran off.

Strange, Peg mused, *and WHY in heaven's name did I ever agree to go?* She was still pondering the question as she entered Dr. Phillips' office.

CHAPTER 28

M rs. Waterman was NOT at her usual post, and no one was in the waiting room. Peg moved back to Dr. Phillips' office. He sat studying a medical book. "Why, hello, Peg." She plopped in the chair across from the desk. "Where's Mrs. Waterman?"

"Making a house call on your Uncle Ben. I suggested she visit now as we have no patients, and as your doctor, I'm giving you the order to go home and catch up on the sleep you missed last night," he added. "You can see how dead it is around here."

Peg didn't argue. The weather had turned. A sharp wind slapped her face. Hunching down, she pulled her collar up and thought of the roaring fire she knew would be in the kitchen. As she approached, she noticed the backs of two men through the window. One she recognized as Ralph Sparks. The other looked familiar . . . She dashed up the drive, threw open the door and blubbered, "Gene!"

"Hey, there, li'l sis!" He stood and held out his arms.

"Oh, no, I promised to meet you in your new car at the railroad depot! I didn't know!"

"That's okay. Buddy a mine bought a used car, so I jumped in with him as far as Wyoming. Caught the train from there. Got tired of waiting for Uncle Sam's ride. How's my Tin Lizzy? You wrecked it yet?"

Peg slapped his shoulder. "Nope. I haven't driven much. Been too busy. Let's go for a ride!"

"No, you don't." Mary stopped them. "Dinner is cooking, and Peg needs to take a nap."

"Mom told me all about the drama last night. Wish I'd been home a day or two earlier," Gene complained.

"No, I didn't need to worry about anyone else!" Mary insisted. "You two can visit later as Gene's going to start the milking. Dad doesn't know he's home yet. Won't he be surprised to find Gene here and the milking finished!"

Peg started upstairs when she remembered they had a visitor. "Oh, hello, Mr. Sparks."

"Just call me Ralph," he smiled warmly. "Came to return a hammer to Ed. Your mom invited me for dinner, so I decided to stay instead of walking back in this weather."

"Can't say I blame ya!" she commented as she climbed to her room, but excitement had overcome her sleepiness, and she doubted she could nap.

CHAPTER 29

"Peg!" her mother called an hour later.

Peg squinted in the dusk, smelled bread baking and remembered *Gene's home!* She bounced downstairs.

"Set the table, please. Add three more plates as I've invited Ed, Ethel and Ralph to our homecoming dinner," Mary instructed as she wiped her hands on her apron and checked the huckleberry pies in the oven. "Ralph's been a big help tonight. He cooks for logging camps and made the mashed potatoes and carrots."

"Smells wonderful. I'm famished!" Peg declared as she glanced out the window and noticed someone approaching. "Oh! Dad's here!"

Boots kicked against the porch, knocking off mud. Then John opened the back door, hung his hat and coat. "I'm home! Oh, looks like we're having company. Who's coming?"

"It's a surprise." Peg smiled impishly.

"Must be a good one from the looks of ya."

"The best!"

A mix of emotions—surprise, confusion, and joy—flitted over John's face when Gene burst in, stomping the snow from his work boots. He crossed the room in three long steps and embraced his oldest boy, tears streaming down his face.

Peg watched. *I've never seen Dad cry before,* and she joined in.

"Sit down, everyone. Things are getting cold," Mary said, taking charge as she wiped her eyes with her apron.

John choked a little. "Gene, will you say grace? We have a lot to thank God for."

"Sure, Dad," Gene bowed his head. "Thank you, Lord, for the safe return to my family. Please bless our loved ones who haven't arrived yet and those families whose sons will not come home. Amen."

"You didn't bless the food," Peg teased.

"I'll be the first to test and make sure it's okay," Gene declared as he piled a mountain of mashed potatoes on his plate.

"Dad," Peg changed the subject, "why do they call alcohol moonshine?"

"You have to make a fire to distill it. Smoke's easily seen during the day, so moonshiners work at night."

"So why's it illegal?" Peg continued her quest for information.

"Washington became a dry state in 1916 when state legislators passed the law."

"Why?"

"Good to see you haven't changed much," Gene interjected, laughing about Peg's endless questions that never failed to amuse family members.

"Then you tell me, Gene," Peg challenged.

"Because alcohol is dangerous and addictive," Gene joked in an ominous voice.

"Alcohol can cause a lot of heartache in families, too," added Mary.

"Intoxicated people don't think clearly, and it's often a factor in crime," John added. "You can't legislate morality or enforce a law that's unpopular. Sometimes alcohol makes criminals out of people who weren't before."

"So, exactly what did you and Uncle Ben find out, Dad?" Gene asked, wanting more details.

"I've lived this too many times already," Peg protested. "Ralph, can you tell us more stories?"

"Let's move into the front room and let Gene and Dad visit here," Mary suggested.

CHAPTER 30

P eg sat on the rug and backed up next to the fire, her arms wrapped around her legs and her face full of expectation. "Go ahead, Ralph."

"Hmm, what should I spin a yarn about?" He paused. "I grew up on the shores of Lake Michigan, so I have a few fish stories," he proposed. "How does that sound?"

"Yes! I like to fish and LOVE to hunt if you have any of those of stories," Peg declared.

"One time I went fishing. The rain had just ended and a bright rainbow arced over the sky . . . gorgeous day! Been going to the same hole for weeks without success. When I looked at that rainbow, I had a feeling I should be following it to the pot of gold. Well, sir, I did just that. Of course, you can never reach the end, but on the way, an inlet up ahead sparkled in the sun. When I got there, it looked deep and calm. Just knew there was a big one in it. I set up, waited and waited. Was gettin' hungry as I didn't bring lunch. Had jus' decided to pack it in and head home when I felt a big tug on the pole, nearly bent double. By darn, me and ol' fish went the rounds! I'd ease up a little and it'd get away some. Sweat was rolling off me, and I wondered what kind of a monster I'd hooked. When I got it ashore, that big flathead catfish jus' grinned at me—bet it weighed over forty pounds. I'd been so busy landing the thing, I hadn't noticed a man about ten yards behind me. Don't know how long he'd been there.

"'Quite the catch!' he jogged to me, his eyes narrowed, and lips tight.

"'Yes, siree, biggest fish I've ever caught.' I boasted as I held it high.

"'You know you're on my property, right?' the owner lashed out.

"'No, sir, I didn't,' I confessed.

"'Legally, that's my fish,' he claimed. 'I can call the law on ya for trespassing, ya know.'

"'Maybe, but this is my fish!' I told him. "I'm the one who earned it.'

"He held firm. 'Still my fish.'

"'No, sir, this is my pet fish. I brought it here for a swim,' I said.

"Guy stormed over to me, 'Hand it over.'

"'How do I know you're the rightful owner of this property?' I asked.

"'How do I know it's *your* fish?'

"'Because if I throw it in the water, he'll come when I call.'

"'Real fun-nee!' he sneered.

"'Watch if you don't believe me!' I took that fish and threw it back. If I couldn't keep it, he darn sure wasn't going to have it!" Ralph guffawed and slapped his knee.

"What happened?" Peg giggled, totally enthralled by Ralph's skillful storytelling.

"Smoke 'bout poured from his ears! Then he threatened, 'I'll have the law on ya for stealing fish from my property!'

"I said, 'What fish?' and walked away."

Peg leaned in and inquired, "Did he follow you?"

"Nope. Just kept looking inta that deep hole. Probably planning to go home and snag his fishing gear!"

"We've good fishing spots 'round here." All the great fishing spots where she and Charlie fished flashed through her mind. "Have you fished in this area?" Peg asked.

"Nope, I'm mostly cooking on a logging site, and those boys can eat! Soon as one meal's cleaned up, it's time to start the next one. Besides, might land a big one on someone's property and have to throw it back," he teased, giving her a wink.

"Since Gene's home, I'll have more time, and I can show you some spots on our land," Peg offered.

"Now that's one offer any man would accept."

Mary shifted in her rocker and dropped a knitting needle.

"Here, let me, madam." Ralph jumped up. "Well, better get on my way. Those loggers will be looking for breakfast early tomorrow, and I have a drive 'head of me." He yawned. "Thanks for the great dinner."

"Thanks for the story," Peg laughed. *That was fun. This is the first time I've laughed in so long!*

Ralph walked back through the kitchen. "Glad you're home safe, Gene. Thanks again for the meal. Ed, Ethel, you ready ta go?"

"Yeah, Ed has some chores to finish up," Ethel stood, "and I do, too."

John shook Ralph's hand. "Come back anytime. My wife can really cook, can't she?"

"Thanks, Mom," Ed yelled into the front room. "Well, we best be on our way. Come on, Ethel." He reached for her hand.

In the front room, Mary cleared her throat. "Peg, I don't think you should take Ralph fishing."

Peg raised her eyes and shook her head. "Why not? Charlie and I found some great places. That lake near Luce's place always has fish."

"It's not seemly, you alone with a man," Mary cautioned, pressed her lips together and dropped a stitch.

"Mom, don't be ridiculous! He's old enough to be my father!" Peg blustered.

"Still, doesn't look good," Mary stated firmly.

"Oh, Mom, you worry too much," Peg sighed deeply and stalked into the kitchen.

Chapter 31

Mary jumped when someone rapped on the door. A young man waved a telegram through the window. She dove out and tore it open with shaking hands.

Coming home—stop—Feb. 1—stop—10:00 a.m. train—stop

Mud

She bowed her head in thanks, then yelled, "Peg! Come down! We have news!"

Peg poked her head out. "What?"

"Mud's coming home," Mary's voice cracked.

Peg took the stairs two at a time. "When?"

Mary held out the telegram and looked into the distance. "Maybe I'll go by and order a new hat from the Fee Sisters. This is something to really celebrate!""

Peg gave her a bear hug. "You should, Mom. Splurge on yourself for a change."

"Why, that's just a week away! We'll have to deep clean his room and maybe order some new curtains. What should we eat? I'd better contact your dad and Ed . . . " Mary trailed off, lost in her own agenda.

What a wonderful day! Peg kissed the telegram. "Now, if only I'd hear from Charlie!"

"You did," John walked in with a letter, raising it high above her head.

"Dad!" She jumped and grabbed at it. "Give it to me!"

1 Jan. 1919

Dear Peg,

Happy New Year. Sorry I haven't written. Been struggling with Leprechaun's death. This war was so pointless. I'm trying to get my head straightened out. I wanted to feel better before I wrote to you. Hopefully, things will get back to normal now I'm going home. Should be there Feb. 1st.

Charlie

"Well?" John asked, waiting for the news.

Peg offered the letter. He scanned through and gave the letter back with a hug. "It's not unusual for a soldier to go through this, Peg. I wouldn't worry too much."

"Now we'll have *two* homecomings, Mom!" Peg cheered as she ran out.

CHAPTER 32

At school, Peg couldn't concentrate. Waves of emotion rolled over her. When she sidestepped the crowd and headed for the cafeteria, she noticed Florence had returned. Emotions from anger to pity assailed her. Tears of frustration welled in her eyes.

I do NOT *need this today!* Peg ducked out the first door she came to and took off running. She skidded to a stop in front of Cottage House, Mrs. Scott's well-kept boarding house, next to the train depot. Green striped awnings flapped in the sharp wind. The smell of hot bread floated out as a customer left. *I'm famished,* she realized and decided to treat herself to lunch. *I'll celebrate Mud and Charlie's return.* The thought immediately cheered her. Nearby, an approaching train whistle screamed. Two long blasts signaled they were near the station, followed by a short blast for each commuter wanting a meal at the boarding house.

Ben Brown, Mrs. Scott's sharply dressed black waiter, stood on the wrap-around porch, listening attentively. *Wah-wooooooooooo! Wah-wooooooooooo, woo, woo!* was followed by rumbling, hissing, screeching brakes and the train arrived in a cloud of steam. "Two for lunch!" Ben called out. The train gasped and exhaled.

"Make that three, please," Peg requested. She plunged into the warmth of the dining room, one of the few places to dine out in

Newport. Prize fish mounted and hung high on the walls, gazed from glass eyes.

Mr. Brown escorted her to a table and smoothed a wrinkle from the red and white checkered tablecloth. "How are you today, Miss Tarbet?" he asked with a little bow.

"Starving!"

"You've come to the right place," he announced as he pulled a chair out and handed her a menu.

"Don't need one. Thank you. I want the famous meatloaf plate followed by apple pie with cheese and ice cream, please."

It didn't take long as Mrs. Scott made meatloaf, mashed potatoes and gravy every morning. Peg knew if you came in late, you missed out because the special was a town favorite. She tucked in.

"Don't you have a hearty appetite?" a familiar voice snickered.

She looked up into Ralph Sparks' wide smile. *He's full of charisma.* "You're not working today?"

"You're not going to school today?" he quipped.

"Guess not," they said at the same time, laughing.

He pulled out a chair and sat across from her. "May I join you?"

"Sure, but not staying long," Peg apologized. "Got to work soon, and I'm afoot." She took a big bite of roll.

Ralph sat down and picked up the menu. "You usually eat lunch here?"

"No, I'm sort of celebrating."

"News good enough to share?"

"Yes! Mud and Charlie will BOTH be home, the first of February!" The words danced off her tongue. Until she shared the news with someone besides her family, it hadn't felt real.

Ralph put down the menu. "I know Mud's your brother, but who's Charlie?"

Mr. Scott brought Peg's order. She stared down at the plate. "He's . . . a . . . friend, my best friend from childhood." A blush crawled up her neck as she took a bite.

"Your boyfriend?" Ralph guessed.

Peg dabbed at her mouth with the napkin. "Guess so . . . ." Uncomfortable now, she lowered her head and devoured the rest of her meal.

Ralph leaned forward as the corners of his eyes crinkled in a smile. "Two men coming home. My, that *is* good news!"

Peg glanced out the window. "You get off the train?"

He lowered the menu. "Been to Spokane, looking into a new job."

"Well, good luck. I'd like to stay and celebrate Mud and Charlie's homecoming," Peg beamed, "but if I'm late, Mrs. Waterman gets her ire up. Excuse me."

CHAPTER 33

D r. Phillips sat at the front desk of the waiting room. "Where's Mrs. Waterman?" Peg wondered.

He looked up from paperwork. "She's not feeling well today."

Peg removed her coat and unwound her scarf. "Huh, can't imagine her ill or weak in any way."

"It's unusual. I can count on one hand the times she's missed work the last ten years. Must be in bed. I think I'll make a house call since it's a slow day," he decided. "Think you'll be okay for an hour?"

"Of course," Peg replied, putting down her schoolbooks.

"If you have any homework, you can do it," he suggested. "She has everything spic and span around here."

"Good. May I study some of your medical books?"

"Go right ahead." He grabbed his black leather bag, and shrugged into his coat, "Be back soon."

The wooden office chair squeaked under her weight and rolled to the side. It was unthinkable she'd have sat in this chair in the nurse's presence. Peg grabbed the chair arms and looked down. *Mrs. Waterman's bulk must spill out the sides of this.* The wheels wobbled. She pushed off the top of the desk with her feet. The chair rolled back and bumped the shelf behind, sending a pile of paper to the floor. "Well, now I have something to do," she grumbled, getting on her hands and knees to sort the mess. A blue letter addressed to Agatha Waterman fell from the jumble. Peg could tell from the envelope that it was a personal letter. She turned it over, but the return address was missing. Curiosity overcame integrity as she pulled the worn letter out and slowly opened it.

Dear Agatha,

I know you've given me an answer, more than once, but I still feel we're meant to be together. I understand your concerns, but haven't you heard love conquers all?

Peg blinked. *A love letter to Mrs. Waterman? No! I* **have** *to read the rest!*

I don't intend, or even think I could fill your late husband's shoes, but we both deserve some happiness, even if the bloom is off the rose. I know we could be good company and a comfort to each other. I'm not handsome, I know, but I'm handy around the house. You like to cook, and I love to eat! We could live in my house or yours, whichever you'd prefer. I'm lonely and know you are, too. We'll both benefit greatly.

Please reconsider,

Arthur

Peg giggled. *Oh! Who's on the make with Agatha?* Gravel crunched outside the office window. She jumped and shoved the letter back under the pile of papers still on the floor. When the door opened, she hoped the person wouldn't notice her discombobulation.

"Oh! Dr. Phillips, back already?" Peg spoke a little too loudly.

"Yes. She had company. Her neighbor Arthur Sims was visiting and brought over some soup. She asked if I could stop by on my way home. You hold down the fort?"

At the mention of Arthur, Peg blushed. "I ran into this shelf . . . so clumsy . . . of me and made a job for myself. Didn't have a chance to crack open one of your books," Peg admitted.

"Need some help?" Dr. Phillips offered.

"No, thanks," Peg stumbled backwards over a book, "just about got it."

"Since I was out and about, I checked on your Uncle Ben. He's almost back on his feet."

"I know. Mother checks on him daily. He say anything about catching the culprits?"

"They must've taken off before the news got to the neighboring sheriff 'cause no reports have come back yet. Too bad." He shook his head. "Doesn't Harris have a girl about your age?"

"Yes, Florence. I feel bad for her. She didn't come to school for some time, but now she's back. I figure she decided everyone knows anyway, so why try to hide?" Peg continued cleaning up papers, careful not to let the secret letter fall out of the pile.

"When you're finished there, might as well go on home. Nothing stirring here." He headed into his office.

"OK, thanks," Peg chimed happily as she straightened the papers and wondered how to place the letter, so Mrs. Waterman wouldn't notice it'd been moved. *If only I'd been watching when I ran into the shelf!* She pushed the letter into the middle of the pile, retrieved her coat and headed home.

CHAPTER 34

Feb. 1, 1919

Peg spent the night trying to sleep. When the alarm went off, she was ready to give up the fight. *This should be one of the happiest days of my life, so why am I not feeling it?* She put on the clothes she'd set out the night before, wound her thick brown hair up and looked in the mirror. She'd never been one to spend time grooming, but today she wanted to look her best. *If I'm honest, I'll have to say I'm nervous about meeting Charlie,* she admitted. *He's changed. But I've changed, too. On the other hand, I can't wait to see Mud!*

Her mother wasn't in the kitchen, evidence today was unusual. She crossed to the sideboard and started setting the table. Mary rushed in, dressed in her Sunday best and a new rust colored wool cloche hat. "Peg, don't bother. Your dad's taking us to Cottage House for breakfast—a little celebration."

"Mom, the hat looks great on you! I'm glad you got it!"

"Thanks, dear. You look lovely yourself." Mary patted her hair. "We're ready, John," she called, pacing over the wooden floorboards. "Where is that man?"

John's cheerful whistling announced his entrance before his frame filled the door. Mary's face brightened. *He's still handsome.* John stood six feet with a muscular build. She just fit under his chin. His eyes usually held a tease; hers were warm and calm. His face, still tanned from summer, showed white lines around the eyes. Her face was pink with excitement. Under a strong nose, a horse-shoe mustache hid his upper lip. Her round face topped by a gray streaked bun held a sweet smile. For as long as she could remember, John's goal was to reach 200 pounds, but he always came up a few pounds shy. After eight children, her girlish figure was long gone.

"You girls aren't ready, are you?" he teased.

Peg pulled her coat from the hook. "Let's go, Dad!"

"Lemme wash up a little first." He started to the sink. "Hope Mrs. Scott's got the stove hot! I'm hungry."

Mary picked up her handbag. "I think I'm too excited to eat anything."

Peg struck out for the barn. "'I'll get Gene's car!" she shouted over her shoulder. "I hope I remember how to drive this," she fretted aloud as she climbed in. *Now let's see . . . The hand lever needs to be all the way back, so I don't run over myself before I crank it. I need spark adjust in the retard position.* She pulled the wire ring at the lower corner of the radiator to choke the engine, stood on her tip-toes and cranked. "Chook, Chook, Chook Chook," it started right up. "What a beaut!" Peg slapped the hood. *Center pedal is reverse . . .*

She eased the car to a stop in front of the house. She'd spent the day before giving the Tin Lizzy a spit polish. It gleamed in the early morning sun.

John opened the passenger door, hopped in and grabbed Mary's hand, "Hop on up here, sweetheart. You're on my lap! You sure look pretty in that hat." Mary giggled and climbed aboard.

"I don't know of a day when I felt happier," she sighed. "I don't even care if I sob in public!"

"You mean WHEN you sob." John's rebuttal made her smile as he kissed the back of her neck.

The Cottage House stood empty as the train commuters had yet to arrive. "Take your pick of seats," Mr. Brown stated as he escorted them into the dining room. "I hear your son's a comin' in today. That's wonderful." He handed them menus.

Mary flipped the menu back and forth. "Coffee and toast, please."

Peg ordered as she handed her menu back, "A waffle with huckleberry syrup and whipped cream for me."

John didn't look at his menu. "I'll have the large stack of blueberry pancakes, a slab of ham, hash browns, two eggs over easy, orange juice and a big glass of milk."

"Think you'll have time to finish before the train comes, Dad?" Peg looked at the clock above the fireplace.

"Have no doubt." He leaned over and squeezed Mary's hand.

Peg and Mary finished before John was through half his meal. Peg rose. "I think I'll walk outside awhile."

Once she'd left the restaurant, Mary confided, "She's nervous about Charlie. His last letters have been troubling."

John gulped his juice. "Why?"

"She's let me read some. He sounds so disillusioned," Mary reported as she pulled a hand mirror from her pocketbook and readjusted the angle of her hat.

John dragged his last pancake through the egg yolk. "Once he's home, gets some home cooking and rest, I'll bet he rebounds!"

Wah-wooooooooooo! Wah-wooooooooooo! Woo, woo, woo, woo, woo, woo, woo!

"Sounds like seven for breakfast, Mr. Brown," John pulled out his wallet. "We'll move on and make room."

"Thank you, sir. I'll get your change." The waiter moved to the cash register.

John pushed back the wooden chair with difficulty on the thick rug. "Keep it. Well, Mary, let's go!"

"Peg, you're frozen, dear," Mary declared as they walked toward the depot.

"I've a feeling she'll be thawing out shortly when a certain young man gets 'hold of her!" John laughed, his voice floating in the crisp morning air.

"Oh, Dad!" Peg blushed and ran ahead.

The train's rumble drowned all human voices. Chug a chugga-uga-uga-ug-catshh-tshh-shh. Mud knelt on his seat, waving madly out the window. Peg's heart skipped at the sight of him.

He'll get his big noggin caught! She ran toward his hand, trying to grab it.

"Peg!" Mary warned, "You'll fall under the train!"

Peg jumped, slapped Mud's hand, turned and ran back to the platform. Before the train came to a full stop, Mud bounded down the steps, dropped his duffle bag and held his arms open wide.

Peg flew into them. He swung her around three times before depositing her with a thump. Mary threw herself at him next, tears streaming. John pulled out his handkerchief and blew his nose. He walked slowly forward, waiting his turn, then exchanged a bear hug with his youngest son.

"Did you drive Gene's car?" he asked, winking at Peg.

"Sure 'nuff. Did a mighty fine job of it, too." John bragged. "Where's your bags?"

"You even remember how to drive?" Peg ribbed him. "Wait! How'll we all fit?" she realized. John put his finger to his lips, took her by the shoulders, and turned her around. "I think you need to greet another fella first, don't you?"

She blushed. "Oh, my gosh! In my excitement . . ."

CHAPTER 35

Charlie slumped against the bench like someone had tossed him there. The train belched, swallowing him in smoke. Peg coughed and squinted.

He waited, watching, watching. The winter day grew dingy as the sun hid behind a passing cloud. Peg's hand covered a gasp. The chilling wind she hadn't taken note of before picked strands of hair from her bun. One hand absently brushed it back as she moved forward. Charlie's once round, red face looked pinched and drawn. His dark red hair matted from a hat curled over his ears. Cinders fell on his rumpled uniform. His vacant stare unnerved her. Her heart sank. "What's happened to you?" she blurted.

"Never one to beat around the bush, were you?" He forced a thin smile.

Peg sunk next to him, picked up his hand and studied his face. She let out a breath she'd not realized she'd been holding. "Oh, Charlie, it is you! You're finally here. Welcome home!" Even to Peg, her trembling voice did not sound like her own.

Charlie stared ahead. Tears trickled over his red cheeks. When Peg covered his cold hand with hers, he jumped and pulled away.

Now what? They sat in silence while people dispersed. Peg glanced back to see her family leaving with Mud at the wheel. The car jerked a little, causing Peg to giggle. She turned to Charlie, "Guess Mud's out of practice."

"What?" he answered woodenly.

"Oh, nothing. Charlie, you ready to go? Are your parents coming? Where's your duffel bag?" She rose and looked around.

"Gave it away," he uttered.

Peg stepped off the platform. "OK, let's go."

"Go? Where?" Charlie questioned as he searched unsuccessfully for his bearings.

Peg tried to conceal her fear. "You're home, Charlie. Come on. I'll walk with you to your house."

He slowly stood, looked over his shoulder a couple of times and followed.

Peg pulled her stocking cap down tighter and hugged herself. "Charlie, you'd better button your coat. We've got a ways to go. Sitting there, I got chilled, didn't you?"

Charlie continued looking at his feet, "I don't think so."

The emptiness about him instilled fear in every fiber of Peg's body. "I'll bet you've been colder over there in the trenches."

Charlie stared off into nowhere as he added, "Sometimes we used frozen bodies to make the trench walls higher."

She winced, clasped her hands and changed the subject. "I'm sorry! You get my letter about Uncle Ben?"

"Lots of people got shot," he replied, still thinking of the war's front lines.

I've done it again! Why do I always say the wrong thing!

"Where are we going?" Charlie puzzled, again revealing his confusion.

"Home. Just another mile," Peg cheerfully replied but swallowed a sob. They walked in strained silence for thirty minutes as Peg kept glancing his way. Finally, she spotted someone.

"There! Your parents are waiting on the porch! Let's hurry!" She took off at a trot.

Charlie stopped in the middle of the road. His eyes darted in a full circle, then squinted as his brain struggled to connect with the view. Finally, a smile slowly spread when his mother ran toward him. Peg trailed behind as his mother led him down the lane. When they didn't look back, she dragged herself home. *Now what do I do?*

CHAPTER 36

Mrs. Waterman sipped the chicken noodle soup and admitted she felt flattered by Arthur's attention. She did feel lonely after work and on weekends. Thinking about having someone to be with and care for had a certain appeal. She and her husband were never blessed by children. After years of dashed hopes, she went to school and became a registered nurse. Over the last forty years, she'd nursed many sick and injured children. It helped ease the sting, and she and George had settled into a comfortable routine. She knew people had called George henpecked, but they'd known each other's limits and respected them. However, she'd been alone for twenty years.

On the other hand, did she want to take care of an old man and put up with the added mess? She ran a tight ship at work and home—not a pin out of place. Arthur's cluttered home made her nervous. But he was thoughtful and obviously cared for her. Marriage might not be so bad. What if she became ill and needed help? She had no family and had never taken time to make a close friend. Her job was her life and if she couldn't work someday . . . then what? *What's wrong with me?* She threw her spoon down. *I've never had trouble making a decision!* She set the empty bowl on the nightstand and tried to sleep. "If I stay away too long, that office will be chaos," she fussed aloud. "I HAVE to get better and soon."

CHAPTER 37

S chool inched on. *I want to talk to Dr. Phillips about Charlie.*
Maybe I'll cut class, but after I left last time, Miss Caldwell dropped
my grade from an A to a B. I need good grades to go onto medical school.
Oh, why does English have to be the last class of the day?

I love reading and can lose myself in a good story but hate studying
grammar rules. So frustrating! There are rules and exceptions to those
rules, so why have the rule in the first place? Science makes more sense!
Wish Florence wasn't in this class. Even before the big fiasco when her
father shot Uncle Ben, we didn't get along. Since Mr. Harris and his
accomplice haven't returned, most people have moved onto other news,
but not Florence.

Miss Caldwell broke into her thoughts, "When you're writing,
what's the difference between showing and telling?"

Florence raised her hand, "Well, for all 'intensive purposes,' it
means the same thing, doesn't it?" Peg choked back a giggle. *She*
means intents and purposes! A flashback popped into her head.
Yesterday, she'd overheard Tom ask Florence about her father. She'd
answered, "He's never been comprehended."

Wonder how Florence's making out alone with her younger siblings.
But when I talk with her, I always end up putting my foot in my mouth.
Anyhow, people with a chip on their shoulder rub me the wrong way.
Peg shot out as soon as the last bell rang.

CHAPTER 38

"Well, speak of the devil," Mud remarked as Peg threw open the back door. "Whadda ya doing home so early?"

"Same to ya!" she retorted.

"Making a habit of early departures?" a man's voice rose from the kitchen table.

"Mr. Sparks! You following me?"

He pushed his hat back, exposing a white scalp. "Came over to talk to your brother about a job opportunity."

"Convince him? He's mighty pig-headed."

"Runs in the family and gets stronger with each successive child," Mud bantered back.

Charlie cracked the door and called, "Knock, knock. Anyone home?"

"Come on in!" Mud opened the door wide and gave him a hearty handshake. "How's it going? Back to work yet?"

"Not yet." Charlie hung his head. "Peg, I dropped by the office, and Dr. Phillips told me you're not working. Can I talk with you for a few minutes?"

Mud shot her a sly look. "Peg, remember—only *talk!*"

"Oh, you!" she slapped his back, took Charlie's hand and led him into the parlor.

Charlie sank back, then leaned forward with his head between his hands. Peg reached out, put a hand under his chin and turned his head to her. "What's goin' on?" He swallowed. Tears filled his eyes. "Charlie! What's the matter?"

He swallowed again, bowed his head and whispered, "That's the problem. I'm not sure."

Peg's thoughts ran the gamut of illnesses he might have. "Are you sick? You should've talked to Dr. Phillips."

He exhaled and slumped over. "I did."

She took both of his hands. "What'd he say?"

Charlie shook his head.

"Don't worry. We'll solve this together." She squeezed his arm.

Charlie dragged his hand through his thick red hair and sighed. "He didn't find anything physically wrong with me."

"Then what?" Peg tried to hide her worry.

"He thinks I need to go to Olympia to the Veterans' Hospital to be treated for shell shock," his voice cracked.

"You should!" Peg agreed. "They'll know what to do." She spoke with more conviction than she felt.

"I'm just a weakling. Some of the officers called us cowards, said we needed more discipline." Another tear leaked out of the corner of his eye. "I'm a mess, Peg. Can't sleep and I'm afraid to because of nightmares. You were right. I should have stayed home. I was all fired-up to go out there and be some big hero, but I found out I'm not," he confessed and hung his head in shame.

Peg knelt in front of him, took his face between her hands and kissed his tears. "You are a hero, Charlie. You're my hero and always will be."

He shook his head, pushed her back and moaned. "I hate having you see me like this!"

"It's okay, Charlie," she pleaded unconvincingly. "You know I'm here for you."

"Well, I AM going to Olympia, Peg. And you don't have to wait around for me," he announced as he made his way toward the door.

"Charlie, wait!" she grabbed the back of his coat.

"Let me go, Peg," he pushed her hand away and walked out.

Sobbing, she sank to her knees. Mud looked in. He knelt beside her, put an arm around her shoulders and let her cry. Ralph stuck his head around the corner. Mud spoke softly, "Can you come back later?"

Ralph gave a thumbs-up and let himself out.

When Peg started to shudder, Mud lifted her to the couch. "Seen my share of guys with shell shock. It's good he's going for help, Peg."

She raised her head. "Were you eavesdropping?"

"A good guesser, and . . . Charlie talked with me earlier," he smiled sheepishly.

Peg started for the door. "I've got to go talk to Dr. Phillips."

Mud checked his watch, "It'll wait 'til tomorrow. He's probably gone home," but Peg had already gone.

CHAPTER 39

Mrs. Waterman had returned to her kingdom, presiding at the front desk. Peg squirmed remembering the love letter. "Hello, Mrs. Waterman. Glad you're feeling better." She watched carefully for any sign she'd been found out, but the nurse didn't look up from her paperwork. Grateful to avoid attention, Peg scurried to the back, looking for Dr. Phillips. He wasn't in his office. The examination room door was shut.

Rats! I need to find a way to talk to him without Mrs. Waterman overhearing. Peg dove into the supply room across the hall, so she could catch the doctor as soon as possible.

She noticed a shipment of supplies that needed organized and dug in. When she looked at her watch, thirty minutes had passed. Mrs. Waterman's starched uniform crackled, the hose rubbing on her thighs scratched like sandpaper, and her white nurse shoes complained with numerous squeaks, signaling her imminent arrival. Peg grabbed the broom and pretended not to notice her filling the doorway. "When you're finished here, come up front." She turned without waiting for a reply.

The door across the hall opened.

"I'm glad you're considering it," Doctor Phillips' voice carried into the hall.

Peg stepped behind the door so as not appear eavesdropping. However, through the crack, she caught a glimpse of red curly hair, immediately turned and resumed sweeping. *What was Charlie doing back here?*

Doctor Phillips heard the swish of the broom and looked in. "Hello, Peg. How are you?"

"Can I talk to you?" she whispered.

He held the door open and motioned to his office. His kind baby face and soft voice almost undid her. Peg followed, wilted in the chair across from the desk and tried to stifle rising tears.

"Saw Charlie, didn't you?"

"Yes," she admitted. "What did he want?"

He used his professional voice as he shook his head. "Peg, you know that's private."

"But I already know you recommended he be treated for shell shock," Peg pleaded.

He folded his arms. "Charlie can tell you whatever he likes, but I keep patients' information confidential. You know that."

Peg moved to the edge of her chair. "What kind of treatment do they give for shell shock?"

"There's not much research published yet, but I understand some doctors are trying shock treatments . . . "

"What!" Peg interrupted in disbelief. "Haven't they had enough shock!"

Dr. Phillips continued, "Let me start over. Been researching this to help Charlie. Many of the symptoms: dizziness, amnesia, tremors, headaches are the same symptoms you'd expect from a physical injury to the brain. Often, there's been no physical injury, so others believe it's an emotional injury. Nightmares and depression are common. Someone aptly described it as shaking limbs and shaking minds." His sympathetic look almost undid Peg. He continued, "Unfortunately, it's not unusual for soldiers to be thought weak or even reprimanded. Some were even put in solitary confinement, which I think is shameful! It takes time to recover . . . but back to shock treatments. The shock causes a brief seizure in the brain which I assume creates chemical changes or changes the wiring in the brain. I'm not an expert. There are cognitive therapies also . . . "

"Will Charlie recover?" Peg interrupted.

"I expect so, if he works at it, but I told you I can't discuss his case with you." He stood to signal the conversation was over.

"Thanks, Doc."

"Give it time," he reassured.

"Yea, that's what I've heard," she muttered. *I don't know if I feel better or worse!*

CHAPTER 40

After work, she found herself in front of Charlie's house. She stood at the edge of the road for a few minutes, debating whether to go home or walk up to the door and knock. Tired and hungry, she turned toward home. *It's stressful enough to talk with him. I'd better feel better if I . . .*

"Peg!" Charlie called urgently.

She whirled to see him standing on the porch with his hands on his hips.

He looked hurt. "You're not staying?"

"Hi, Charlie. I didn't see you." Peg forced a smile, fighting back nervousness.

He walked over. "That why you decided not to stop?"

She shook her head. "Truthfully, I'm tired and hungry, so thought I'd better go home first."

"Will you come in? I'll find something for you to eat." He looked down and shifted from foot to foot.

"Of course." Peg reached to grasp his hand, but Charlie did not take it. She couldn't tell if he'd seen the gesture but followed as he shuffled toward the house. He led her into the kitchen, cut a couple thick slices of bread and set out the butter and jelly.

"This looks good, Charlie. You turned into a baker?"

He slowly turned the knife over and over. "No."

She slathered on the butter, plopped on a big spoon of jelly and took a big bite. "Well, it's good. Got a drink?"

He pushed back his chair. "Tea, coffee, or milk?"

"Hot tea sounds divine."

The "elephant in the room" trumpeted. Peg squirmed. "Charlie, you know I don't beat around the bush."

He stared out the window.

"We have things we need to discuss," she leaned forward, touched his chin and gently turned his face toward her.

He closed his eyes, clasped his hands and started rocking. "I know. You don't need to stick around, Peg." His voice began to shake. "I'm sure you don't want a broken man."

"If you're broken, Charlie, let's get help," she choked out.

"I'll never be the same person you loved, Peg. I've seen some awful things. When I was in the hospital . . . "

"What? Oh, Charlie, you *never* told me that you were in a hospital," Peg whispered.

"I know. Didn't want you to know how weak I am." He held up his hand. "Let me finish. Some men with shell shock had tremors so badly they couldn't walk. They jerked and screamed and howled. One guy went mute and wouldn't respond to any word except 'Bomb!' Then he dove under his bed and shook, another . . . "

Peg covered her ears, refusing to listen. "Stop! Those guys are NOT you!"

"No, but some of our Allies . . . those guys they'd been treating for years with no success. I can't promise you I'll ever be okay. " He looked out the window. "You haven't even seen me at my worst. Sometimes," he paused, "I feel so angry . . . can't control it. I'm moody and bitter."

Peg's hands covered her cheeks. "You'll get better, Charlie. I know you will," Peg implored, wanting to believe her own words.

He swallowed, then spoke stiffly, "Go off to school, Peg. I don't want you here to worry, watch me and feel sorry for me. I don't want to hold you back, to make you feel . . . obligated." He lifted his head. His face held a haunting expression, a part of Charlie that Peg had never seen before.

Peg shrank back. "Charlie . . . " she stammered.

He shot up. "Time for you to go."

Peg dropped the slice of bread and backed out the door, leapt from the porch and ran for home. She didn't hear the car until it slowed. She wiped her eyes on her sleeve and frantically dug in her coat pocket for a handkerchief, though her mottled face and red eyes betrayed her.

"On your way to a fire? Hop in. I'll give you a ride. You okay?"

Peg shrugged. "I'm okay."

His face softened. "Really, it's freezing. I promise not to pepper you with questions."

Peg opened the door, climbed in and kept her face turned to the window. When the car slowed at her house, she murmured, "Thanks," opened the door and scurried in. Thank goodness no one was in the kitchen. She dragged herself upstairs, flopped onto her bed, buried her face in her pillow and sobbed until she got the hiccups. Her feelings alternated between pity for Charlie and anger. "Fine. I'll leave him alone like he wants!" She punched her pillow, scrunched down under a pile of blankets and fell into a fitful sleep.

"There you are!" Mary stood in the bedroom doorway. "Dinner's on. Hurry down. We have company."

Just what I don't need, Peg grumbled, but her good appetite propelled her up. She looked in the dresser mirror, pinned back the frazzled hair, poured water into the bowl and splashed her face. She hoped one of her mother's favorite sayings: "Put on a big smile and no one will notice" would work!

Laughter rolled up the stairs. She eased toward it. Peeking into the kitchen, she found she didn't have to force that smile. Seeing her dad with his head thrown back guffawing drew her in. "Tell us another story, Ralph," he requested.

"Hi, honey," John noticed Peg. "Come on in. Ralph's entertaining us with funny stories from the logging camp again."

Please, don't tell my parents about this afternoon. "Hello. Nice to see you again."

He understood. "Hello, Peg."

"Go on, Ralph," John urged.

Mary set down a platter of roast beef. "Let's pray and let him finish his dinner first, John."

"OK, long as he promises to finish the squirrel story afterwards." John tucked into his meal.

Everyone dug in, and silence reigned as full mouths doused the conversation.

"Hold the pie, Mary?" John asked. "Need time to make room. You ready, Ralph?"

Ralph wiped his mouth and began: "New guys on the job are easy marks for practical jokes. Makes for an entertaining workplace. Bob started this week, and he did somethun he never shoulda! While standing in line for food, he admitted to the guy behind him he hates squirrels. I guess he got bit as a kid and hasn't liked 'em since. You could see the wheels churning in those loggers' brains by the smirks on their faces. 'Course, I pretended not to hear the conversation and kept on filling their bowls. After everyone was eatun, I strolled down the tables, asking how they liked the soup.

Got nods, grunts, and thumbs-up. 'Well,' says I, 'That's good. Took me most of the morn-un to catch enough squirrels—sure fast little critters!' Bob stood, spewed out the soup. When the men started hee-hawing, he realized he'd been tricked. But the best part of story is how he got back at 'em."

Peg forgot her troubles. "What did they do?"

"Well . . . Bob waited a few days. Then he came into camp, all excited. 'Hey, guys! I figgered out how to tame them squirrels!'

"'How?' the men chorused.

"'They like liquor! I put out a cupful for the last few days, and I'll be giggered if he don't drink all of it. Regular little drunk!'

"'Right . . . ' no one moved from their dinner.

"'Come on. I'll prove it to ya!' he coaxed. Still, no one moved.

"Well, 'cause I was the one who started it all, I felt for the guy, so followed him down the trail, and he got me back!

"He'd killed a big ol' fat gray squirrel and propped it up against a tree, put a stocking cap on his head and an empty bottle between his paws! I laughed so hard some of 'em beat a path to see what was goin on!

"Another guy took the squirrel that night. The next day during lunch, he pulled on some fish-un line attached to a roller skate. Who do ya think was perched atop the skate?"

"The squirrel!" Peg laughed.

"'Nother time we had a guy who was fraid a bears. He was slower than a one-armed granny with a pocketknife at cutting down trees! Always look-un over his shoulder for a bear. One night, someone nailed his shoes to the wooden floor, then hollered, 'Bear! Help me! Help me!' The poor guy was sa flustered and couldn't figger out why he couldn't pull his boots up. Finally, he stuck his foot in, laced it up and tried to pull it with brute strength. The whole camp was rolling with laughter!"

"Sounds like a fun place to work!" Peg interjected.

"Well, matter a fact, I'm lookun for some help with the cookun. You folks know of anyone who'd be interested?"

"I am!" Peg declared.

"Peg, you've got enough going on with school and your work for Dr. Phillips," Mary reminded her in an attempt to squelch Peg's interest in working in a camp mostly made up of men. She shook her head.

"But Mom, I **AM** interested," Peg insisted.

John stopped the conversation. "We'll discuss this later."

"Speaking a bears," Ralph drew back the attention. "I didn't witness this one, but it's one of the best pranks. 'Nother guy was deathly afraid of bears. Guess his brother'd been mauled by one . . . and like I said, you **NEVER** tell a bunch of loggers what you're 'fraid of. One of the men had a bear skin and fixed it up on the outhouse seat. Everyone had to be in on the plan, so's they wouldn't use the outhouse until the victim had a chance. Before dinner, nature called, and the victim left for the outhouse. The men poked each other, waiting for a good laugh. They got one, too, when the guy screamed, did a dance and wet his pants!"

John wiped his eyes. "Time for the pie, Mary. I've laughed enough to make room."

"Well, folks, I've got another early morning. Could I take a piece with me?" Ralph asked.

"Sure thing. I'll wrap it up for you," Mary offered, "and thanks for the entertainment."

CHAPTER 41

As soon as Ralph left, Peg began her campaign. "Dad, I need something to do on the weekends. Charlie told me today he doesn't want to see me anymore," she sniffled.

John's voice rose. "What? What's wrong with that boy?"

Peg slumped in her chair. "He said he hates me seeing him like he is," she confessed.

John agreed, "I'm sure that's the problem, darling. A man's pride is fragile."

Mary dropped a dish. "But logging camps are not the place for ladies! Why, the cursing alone . . . we need to talk about this."

Peg began begging, "But I love to cook, and Ralph would be there to protect me. I don't want to sit home, and I don't feel like dating other guys. I'm almost eighteen, and I'll graduate in a couple of months anyway. I'll save all the money for nursing school."

"Let your mom and me think about it, honey," John appeased her for the time being.

Peg thundered up the stairs to her room.

Mary put her hands on her hips. "John, you're not considering letting her work with all those rough men, are you?"

"Well, I can see her point about not wanting to hang around here moping."

"There's plenty to do. I can keep her busy," Mary declared, clearing the table. "She can always work in our store."

John came to his daughter's defense. "And have people questioning her about Charlie all the time? Nah, I don't think that's the answer. Going away may be just the ticket to get her mind off her troubles. Ralph'd watch out for her," John ventured.

Mary crossed her arms. "I'm 100% against her going, John."

"I know she's our baby girl, Mary, but she's grown up. We have to let her make her own choices. I'm off to check the cows. Might get a new calf tonight." He escaped outside. *I'll let her cool down a while.*

The more Peg thought about it, the more the cooking job felt like the perfect answer. *Charlie will realize how he misses me. I won't be asked to weekend parties and have to make excuses. Only gotta get through this year. I could use the money for housing and books at school . . .*

She knew better than to broach the subject with Mother the next morning when she witnessed her slamming the stove lids and scrubbing dishes with a vengeance.

"Where's Dad?"

"Gone to the bank." Mary plunged her hands in the soapy water and flung the dish towel over her shoulder.

Peg grabbed a muffin. "I'll eat this on my way. See you after work." *Not too sure from the look of things I'll be going. Wonder if Mom and Dad had words about it this morning. One more month until graduation. I can do this . . .*

During biology, she felt a spit wad hit the back of her neck. When she turned, Henry smirked. "Yuck!" she mouthed to him. *What a juvenile thing to do!* Ever since their date to Winter Ball, Henry paid more attention to her. *Another reason to go to the logging camp this summer. I don't need any more complications in my life.*

Peg finished her assignment just before the bell rang. She scooped up her books and nearly ran over Henry. "Oh!"

He picked up a book she'd dropped. "You were somewhere far away."

"Yeah, have a lot on my mind. Excuse me. Off to work."

The girls in the hall all watched as Henry moved back.

CHAPTER 42

As soon as Peg walked into the office, she knew something had changed. Mrs. Waterman had moved everything from the shelves behind her desk. Peg hurried to the back room. *Hope she doesn't confront me! Does she know I've read her letter? How would she know? Just my guilty conscience. Act normal.*

When the nurse walked by humming, Peg stuck her head out to make sure it was Mrs. Waterman. "Hello, Peg, how are you?"

Peg took a step back. "Fine, how are you?"

"Wonderful," the nurse stepped lightly to the front office. Peg gaped.

Dr. Phillips looked amused as he came down the hall. "Quite a change, isn't it?"

Peg's mouth dropped. "Whatever happened?"

"Mrs. Waterman is *engaged*," he winked, and a knowing grin spread across his face.

"Love does strange things to you," she giggled. "Who's the lucky man?" She tried to look blank.

"Arthur Sims, her neighbor. I had a feeling when I stopped by to check on her and he'd brought over dinner."

"When's the big day?"

"They haven't set a date yet. Probably too new," he added.

"Should I pretend I don't know?"

"She didn't tell me not to say anything. I don't think she'd mind you knowing."

Peg returned to cleaning; her worries pressed. *Am I not in love with Charlie anymore? I certainly don't feel like humming when I think about him. Am I so shallow my love evaporates when things get rough?*

"Peg? You in there?" Mrs. Waterman sounded like this wasn't her first summons.

"Sorry. I was a million miles away. What did you say?"

"Are you all right?"

The nurse's kind tone made Peg tear up. "I'm okay. What did you need?" her voice cracked.

"You don't sound okay."

"Got a problem on my mind," Peg confessed.

"If it's your young man, I understand."

Peg's eyes widened. "You do?"

She pursed her lips. "Yes, it's difficult to decide if you want to tie your life up with someone else's. You have to sacrifice to make marriage work."

Peg couldn't believe they were having this conversation. "So how do you decide?"

"Give it time. It will come to you," she shared before turning back to the office.

Huh, she forgot what she wanted me to do.

CHAPTER 43

As soon as she walked through the door, her mother confronted her. "You need to think this through, Peg."

"I *have* thought it through, and I want to cook with Mr. Sparks on the weekends!" She slammed the door, flew outside and headed to the woods.

John came home to Mary, sitting at the kitchen table, head down, her eyes red. "What's the matter?" he asked.

"Peg's so bull-headed. She's insisting on going to that old logging camp!" Mary worried.

"Maybe the best thing is to let her have a go at it. She'll find out sloshing through mud and cold and serving rough, stinky men isn't what she anticipated," John thought aloud. "We could let her go on a trial basis. I have friends on the crew that'll look out for her. I'll ask Ralph to report to me."

Peg formed a plan as she stomped through the woods. *Only one month to go until graduation. If Mom and Dad won't let me help Mr. Sparks, I'll go to Spokane for the summer, find a job and settle in for school this fall.* She heard a rustle off to the right, hunkered down behind a tree and held her breath. Her heart raced at the thought of meeting Mr. Harris and his accomplice again. As footsteps moved closer, she wished she'd brought her gun. *What a little fool I am!* Wind rattled the branches, magnifying every sound. She clutched the forest floor. A bullet whizzed past. She dared not move. A man coughed.

Could be a neighbor. When footfalls stopped, she peered around the tree and up the barrel of a rifle into wild blue eyes.

"Charlie! You scared me to death! What are you doing out here?"

"Ditto!" he exclaimed as he lowered the gun. Sweat dripped from his brow. He trembled and steadied himself on the tree trunk.

"You'd better sit down. I didn't realize what a fright I gave you." Peg put her hand on his arm. "Let's sit on that rock," she suggested, her knees shaking.

Charlie followed as if hypnotized, and Peg tried not to look over her shoulder as the hair on the back of her neck stood up. *Charlie would never shoot me, would he?*

Her heart pounded. "What are you hunting for?"

"Huh?" Charlie stared into the distance.

"Why do you have your gun?"

He looked at her as if she were an idiot. "Protection, of course."

"Right. When I heard someone, I felt the same way. After that incident with the moonshiners, I've been a little spooked. Too bad I don't have mine, and we could target practice like old times, huh?" She talked nonchalantly although she didn't feel it. "Want to come home with me for a warm drink? Mom always has a pie or two in the pie safe."

"Better get back. Parents worry about me when I'm gone." Charlie turned red and left without saying goodbye.

"See you later," Peg called cheerily. A shiver ran down her spine as she hurried home.

CHAPTER 44

Her parents sat discussing her in front of the fireplace. As soon as they heard her enter, all conversation stopped.

"Peg, we're in here. Come in for a minute," her dad called out.

"Coming!" She pulled off her boots, hung her coat and steeled herself for a talk.

"Where've you been?" Mary asked.

"I went into the woods. Charlie came upon me and gave me a real scare!"

"Why was that scary?"

"He's so different. When I heard someone, I hid. He drew his gun on me 'cause I spooked him, too, I guess."

"Well, your mother and I feel it would be best for you to get away for a while and have decided to let you cook at the logging . . ."

"Really?" Peg squealed. *I can't believe it!*

"Yes, but not until summer. I've talked to Ralph. He's agreed to keep an eye on you."

"Oh, thank you! I swear it will be just what I need! Thanks!" she rose and gave Dad a hug. "And thank you, too, Mom." Mary's stiff posture revealed her feelings, so Peg ran out before she could say anything.

Mary sighed. "John, can you assure me Peg will be bunking with other women, and there are families there?"

"Yes, dear. I'm sure she'll be safe. Mark my words, when she finds out about the tough living conditions, she'll come home humble and grateful."

"I hope so," Mary replied.

Peg held up her skirt, sprinted to the pond, hopping from one dry patch of dirt to the next and picked up a rock to skip. She leaned back a little, threw and counted the skips—one—two—three—not good enough. Looking around, she found the perfect flat shape. One—two—three—four—five—six! A smile broke. She ambled over to her favorite weeping willow tree and climbed to her seat, sending an upset bird into flight. *I wonder how many hours I've spent in this place. Charlie and I used this tree for an airplane, Aladdin's cave, and a robbers' hideout. I'm so looking forward to the weekend—no work, no school, and since my brothers' return, no more milking chores. I'm reading that new book everyone's talking about.*

Sunday afternoon, she sprawled on the davenport in an unladylike way—as her mom always cautioned. Her head rested on a plump pillow, her legs covered by the crocheted afghan Mother had thrown over for modesty.

"Peg, what do you want for a graduation dress?" Mary thumbed through the spring catalog. "Have you seen these long collars? They're all the go!"

Peg glanced up from her book. "Oh, Mom, I don't care. You choose, as long as it doesn't have ruffles and lace."

"What about a hat?"

Peg kept reading. "No flowers, feathers instead."

Unlike Peg, Mary loved designing and sewing feminine clothes. For Halloween, she created costumes for the whole family including herself, but always kept her own costume secret. John bet Mary every year that he'd recognize her at the annual dance. Every year, he lost the bet.

She tried again to engage Peg. "What are you reading?"

"*My Antonia.*"

"What's it about?"

Peg sighed and rolled her eyes. "A family of pioneers in Nebraska." She climbed the stairs with her nose in the book. *She probably wants to talk me out of going to the logging camp. I don't want small talk about the book. Besides, she'd be shocked about the part when the protagonist comes home from college pregnant and unmarried!*

Chapter 45

Too soon, Monday came. Seeing a note and a flower on her desk made Peg want to run. *Now what?* She opened the envelope.

Peg,

Would you go to the graduation dance with me?

Henry

Oh, Henry, why do you do this to me? I don't feel like going to any dance. Besides, what would Charlie think? Henry's my friend, though. I don't want to hurt his feelings. Boy, oh boy, can't wait 'til I'm out outta here!

She heard a sarcastic snicker and turned to see Florence sitting a couple rows back. A girl behind Peg handed up a folded sheet of paper.

Do I even want to open this? Peg slipped it inside her desk. A few minutes later, she sneaked it out.

"Peg! Are you trying to break all the boys' hearts in one fowl swoop?"

She knew immediately who'd written the anonymous note.

On the bottom, she scribbled:

"No, Florence, I'm not, and by the way, I think you mean one fell swoop!"

On the front in big letters, she penned FLORENCE and passed it back.

After class, Peg waited outside the door. When Henry walked out, she motioned him over. As soon as Florence came to the door, Peg proclaimed, "Yes, Henry, I'd love to go to the dance with you." Henry's face lit up. She ran out the door.

CHAPTER 46

"Mom!" Peg yelled as she walked in the back door.
"In here, dear," Mary answered from the front room.

Peg slumped in the overstuffed chair. "Guess I'm going to the graduation dance."

Mary set her knitting down. "You don't act too happy about it."

"I'm not! Henry asked me, but I worry what Charlie will think." Peg covered her face with a pillow.

Mary picked up her knitting. "I think you should go. Life goes on, and Charlie needs time."

"I know this sounds selfish," Peg pouted, "but I'm so tired of hearing that he needs time."

Mary sighed. "Once you're in the logging camp, you'll probably be wishing you were home."

"Doubt it." Peg pulled the quilt from the back of the chair and covered her head.

"Well, what kind of dress should we make for the dance?"

"None. I'll wear my graduation dress" came her muffled reply. "I'd probably not wear it again anyway." She threw the quilt back. "If you want to buy me something, I could use some new boots and clothes for the logging camp."

Mary closed her eyes, shook her head and left to start dinner.

An hour later, she shook Peg awake. "Come and set the table, please. Company should be here in a few minutes."

Peg moaned and turned over.

Mary lost patience and snapped, "I mean now!"

Peg dawdled to the cupboard and pulled out the plates. The back door swung open with a flourish. "I'm here, Mom!" Ed looked around. "Ralph and Ethel will be along shortly." He sensed the tension. "Kind of cold in here. Why don't I start a fire?"

"That won't help, Ed," Peg retorted. "Mom and I don't agree on me working at the logging camp."

Ed winked at Peg behind Mary's back. "Aw. That explains it. Mom, you can ask Ralph anything tonight. I'll bet you'll feel better after talking with him."

Peg set out the best dishes. These plates had seen many family gatherings. She loved the dainty little violets dancing around the edges and traced them with her finger. She remembered when she was a little girl drinking from the fancy cups with tiny sips, watching for the flowers to appear on the inside.

Ethel and Ralph knocked. "You needn't knock. You're family!" Mary welcomed.

"Smells wonderful!" Ralph sighed. "It'll be nice to eat someone else's cook-un, surrounded by pretty ladies instead of men, wolfing down food with it dripping from their beards!" He laughed.

Mary cringed at the description and looked at Peg, knowingly.

"Well, Miss, how long until my assistant arrives?" Ralph greeted Peg.

"Graduation's next Friday. I'd come tomorrow if I could!"

"No hurry. Enjoy your last days with your friends," Mary counseled. "Ralph, you sit there. Ethel and Ed, can you squeeze in here? We need to save a place for John. He's been putting in some long days lately. Not sure when he'll show, but we won't wait."

Peg sat across from Ralph. As soon as the blessing ended, she peppered him with questions. "Do I need to bring my own bed-ding? Is there a place there to do laundry? How cold is it there at night? Where will I be sleeping?"

"Hold up there, Missy. I can only answer one question at a time," he countered.

Mary frowned. "Ralph, I'd like to know where she'll be staying, also."

"There're three families. Jokinens have an extra bedroom that Peg will sleep in," Ralph reassured her.

"What time do I report up for work? Will I be helping with three meals? Do I cook? Who cleans up?"

"Ha! Which question do you want me to answer first?" He paused. "We start early. Make a BIG breakfast and serve it at six sharp. Boy! Those men can put away the food! Eat 8,000-10,000 calories a day. We pack lunches, then serve another hot meal for supper. Soon as we've cleaned up the first meal, we begin working on the next one."

Peg wasn't put off. "Good. I want to stay busy, too busy to think."

"No problem there. We fall into bed and don't move," Ralph continued as he helped himself to another mound of potatoes.

"Looks like you can keep up with those loggers' appetites," Ed noticed. "All that work must keep you thin."

"Always had a hearty appetite," Ralph agreed. "Maybe that's why I learned to cook!"

"You'll want to bring something for your hands, Peg." Ralph dug in. "They'll be in water and get chapped and crack if you're not careful."

Peg grabbed a paper and pencil. "Anything else?"

"Cold-weather gear: wool blankets, coat, gloves, hat. Even though it's almost summer, it's cold in the mountains at night. Not much to do after supper's cleaned up. You play cards or cribbage? Some guys read."

Peg hadn't touched her supper. "I love games and reading. Are there books there, or do I need to bring my own?"

"Well, I've been reading stories about Alaska by James Curwood: *Kazan, Baree Son of Kazan, Grizzly King, The Gold Theater, The River's End*. Ever heard of them? There's an Alaskan romance there you might like called *Flower of the North*."

"I'm done with romance, but stories about Alaska sound intriguing," Peg confessed leaning forward.

"Probably more intriguing to read about than to live," Mary picked up the platter. "More meat, anyone? Be sure to leave room for pie."

"Always room for your pie," Ralph buttered a roll. "Please pass those tasty bread and butter pickles."

"Have you been to Alaska, Ralph?" Mary asked.

Ralph's eyes lit. "Not yet, but I'd sure love to go to the last frontier!"

Mary shuddered. "Sounds cold to me."

"Many women in Alaska?" Peg asked.

"Not many 'cept for Eskimo women, of course. Couple of our loggers were there during the Gold Rush and tell stories about driving dog sled teams and the fishing . . . "

"I do love to fish!" Peg interrupted.

Ralph's eyes sparkled. "What about cleaning 'em?"

"No problem. Been doing that since I was seven."

"Maybe you would like it there," he admitted. "Scenery's unbelievable. I've seen photos."

Mary looked at the clock. "Now where is John? It's been over an hour and the food's getting cold."

Ralph pushed his chair back. "Thanks again for the wonderful meal."

"You aren't leaving before you tell us stories?" Peg protested in disappointment.

"Sorry. Got to pick up my food order and get back up to the camp tonight, or I'd love to. See you, Mary, and Peg, I'll be back next week."

CHAPTER 47

The theme of graduation "Til We Meet Again" came from the year's popular song. Peg looked over her dance card when the music started and winced. Those words reminded her of Charlie. The war was over, so why play a song about a guy headed off to fight? Her card indicated this last dance belonged to Henry. *At least he knows I'm not interested in being his girlfriend.*

There's a song in the land of the lily
Each sweetheart has heard with a sigh
Over high garden walls this sweet echo falls
As a soldier boy whispers goodbye

Smile the while you kiss me sad adieu
When the clouds roll by, I'll come to you
Then the skies will seem more blue
Down in Lover's Lane, my dearie

Wedding bells will ring so merrily
Ev'ry tear will be a memory
So wait and pray each night for me
Till we meet again

Though goodbye means the birth of a teardrop
Hello means the birth of a smile
And the smile will erase the tear blighting trace
When we meet in the after a while

Smile the while you kiss me sad adieu
When the clouds roll by, I'll come to you
Then the skies will seem more blue
Down in Lover's Lane, my dearie

Wedding bells will ring so merrily
Ev'ry tear will be a memory
So wait and pray each night for me
Till we meet again

"Til we meet again, huh, Peg?" Henry repeated the refrain.

"I'm sure we will see each other again, Henry. This is a small town."

"But you're off to the logging camp, right?" Henry asked. "You know our childhood's over, and life will never be the same."

"Yes. And thank you for a lovely evening."

Peg awoke lighthearted. She'd dreamed of Alaska. She and Ralph rode on a dogsled in a snowstorm, but she felt no cold, only exhilaration. "Better pack up. I'm off to the next chapter of my life!" She hopped up, pulled the suitcase from under the bed and placed her folded clothes inside. Then, she hefted it from the bed and pulled—thump, thump, thump, down the stairs.

"What's all the racket?" John called from the kitchen. He rose and took the load from Peg. "You still sure you want to do this?"

"I am!" Peg assured him, "The only thing, other than family, that I'll miss is my work."

"No doubt, you'll get the chance to nurse there. There's often an accident in a logging camp. In fact, I talked with one of the regulars at the store last night. He told me given the choice between a logging camp and jail, he'd choose jail every time. Still time to change your mind."

"Not on your life!"

"There are many other places," John suggested.

"Dad, not now, please."

"You're right. What do you want for the last breakfast you won't have to make yourself? Ralph'll be by in a half hour." He picked up the skillet and broke a couple of eggs.

"Where's Mom?"

"She's at the store but will come to see you off."

"She's still upset about me going, isn't she?"

"'Fraid so. Feels it's not the right place for a young lady." John looked in her eyes. "Please, don't prove her right."

"Oh, Dad, I've never been ladylike. You know that. Besides, it's a new era for women. We can do anything. I'll wager we'll be voting soon!"

"Could be worse. At least, you're not becoming a flapper!"

"No worries there. Never did like to dance."

"Order up!" he called as he set a plateful of eggs, ham and fried spuds in front of Peg.

"This looks good. You have hidden talents." Peg dove in with gusto. When she took her dishes to the sink, she caught movement through the window. Mary and Ralph had arrived simultaneously and conversed in the yard. Mary shook her finger at Ralph. He took off his hat and wiped his brow.

"Looks like Mother's giving him what for," Peg giggled.

"Just making sure you'll be safe."

Peg gulped the rest of her milk and grabbed her coat. "Get my bag, Dad? I'm off to rescue him."

CHAPTER 48

Mary heard her approach and turned. A lump rose in Peg's throat. *I regret how we've grown apart over this adventure.* She stepped forward and gave Mary a bear hug. John moved boxes of food to find a spot in the back of the truck and secured the suitcase.

"Come here, baby girl," he beckoned to Peg which nearly undid her.

She swallowed hard and steeled herself not to shed a tear. He swung her around like she was eight again. Peg giggled as he let her down and then climbed aboard the waiting truck. A cloud of dust followed.

"Well, Mary, the last of the litter," John said. Mary burst into tears. He put his arm around her waist and led her back to the house. "Don't worry. She's safe."

Mary clutched his arm declaring, "She'd better be!"

Peg watched out the back window until they faded from sight, then pulled her legs beneath her and turned toward Ralph. "Describe camp. How much longer? What's the first thing we'll do after we arrive?"

He laughed. "Let me get a word in. What do you want to know first?"

"Tell me about the camp."

"It has five wooden buildings. Bunk houses sit on skids, so they can be moved to new sites. Sixteen men sleep in bunk beds. They have cast-iron stoves for heat and kerosene lamps. Don't go in them, if you don't want to encounter lice and bugs."

"Don't worry. I'll steer clear! What time do we start breakfast?"

"I start between 3:30-4:00, but you won't have to report until 4:30. Men eat at six and are on the job by six-thirty."

"So, I sleep in, huh?" she snickered. "What do we make for breakfast?"

"Ham, bacon, eggs, boiled oats, muffins, bread . . . what you'd eat at home, but lots more."

"What about dinner and supper?"

"We pack meat sandwiches, fruit, eggs and desserts for them to take to work. Supper's hot: beef steaks and hamburgers, chicken, oysters, potatoes, vegetables, fresh or canned fruit, berries, bread and jams. We also make desserts: pies, cakes, doughnuts, and puddings."

"Sounds good."

"Company believes in feeding well. Keeps men happy in a tough job. Loggers put in ten hours of hard labor. When food's on, we'll bang a circular saw blade. After we sound it, stand back!"

"How many we feeding?"

"Around one hundred. Our foreman is married and has his own place. Three families live there with around twelve kids between um, but they mostly eat at home. But those loggers will eat like two hundred."

Peg spent the trip interrogating Ralph. Two hours later, he thumbed out the window, "Just around that bend. You'll hear the camp before you see it."

When an axe rang through the forest, Peg poked her head out for a better view.

"Pull your head in! Never know if there's a branch around the next bend; you'll get a good slap-un!"

She moved back. A grey slab building with a shake roof and smoke trailing from a chimney caught her eye. "What is that?"

"The van. It's sort of a store. Got lumberman supplies: medicine, tobacco, clothes. Workers buy what they need. Cost's deducted from their wages. Tell me what you want, and I'll pick it up in town. Store's highway robbery."

Ralph backed up to the door of the cook house. "Great! Here comes straw-boss," he muttered.

"Sparks!" the man yelled.

"Yes?"

"'Bout time you returned. We're outta milk!"

"Got plenty." Ralph lifted out one of the five-gallon cans in the truck's bed.

"Good thing. Men're complaining," he groused and turned on his heel, looking for someone else to order.

"Who was that?" Peg whispered.

He reached for another can of milk. "The straw-boss."

"The what boss?"

"Straw-boss, basically the under supervisor. He's one to avoid."

"So, I gathered." Peg hopped in the bed of the truck, slid out a box of groceries to the tailgate and lugged it into the building.

A sloppy-looking woman in a hairnet and dirty apron called out. "Hey, Ralph, you gotcha a new flunkie?"

"This is Peg. She's going to help with cookun."

Peg's ire rose. As soon as they went for another load, she accosted Ralph. "Why'd she call me a flunkie?"

"Oh, that's only logging talk for waiters and waitresses. Not sure why. Maybe the men, who couldn't hack logging, came to work in the kitchen."

Peg bristled. "Well, I don't like it!" *Even Mrs. Waterman didn't insult me like that!*

"Let it go. It's just part'a working at a camp."

CHAPTER 49

Peg lugged an armload of food. Two young boys ran after a baseball, nearly causing her to trip.

"Whoa there, young fellas!" Ralph grabbed the ball. "Watch where ya going!"

Peg watched them retreat. "Who are those kids?"

"Children whose parents work for the company."

"What about school?"

He threw the ball back. "There's a young woman who teaches. You'll like her. Kinda reminds me of you, but not as curious."

Peg's heart lifted to think there may be a friend her age, if she had any time or energy left over. *You're getting what you wanted,* she reminded herself. Not far away, a tree crashed, and Peg jumped. "That sounded close!"

"It was in the dingle down the hill. Falling trees echo sometimes."

"What's a dingle?"

"Small, wooded valley. Come on. I'll show you the kitchen," he beckoned.

The moist heat enveloped her as she took in scrubbed wooden floors and prep tables, metal pitchers hanging from the ceiling, an army of coffee pots standing ready, and two cast iron stoves with huge ovens for baking. Several long wooden tables, their tops mottled with grease stains, pocks, and carved initials, hid benches pushed underneath.

Supper preparations were already underway. Two women sat hunched over huge pots, peeling potatoes. Another woman, her hair tied in a scarf, had stray wisps stuck to her moist face. She rolled out pie dough while a man stood next to her peeling boxes of apples for pie. Huge vats of water boiled on the stove top. Twenty loaves of rising bread strained at the cloths covering them.

Ralph introduced her, "Hey, everyone, this is Peg, my daughter's sister-in-law. Come from Newport to work in the kitchen."

Heads looked up but returned immediately to work.

Not too friendly!

"You'll have to forgive them," Ralph apologized as he read her mind. "We have to work like the devil to have everything ready."

"I'm ready to work," Peg volunteered.

"Settle in first." Ralph picked up her suitcase and led her to a nearby cabin. Smoke twirled from the chimney, clean clothes danced on a clothesline strung between two trees and a sleeping dog opened one eye as they stepped over him to knock. A tall husky woman, with braided blonde hair circling her head, opened the door, wiping her hands on her apron.

Ralph took off his hat. "Mrs. Jokinen, this is your boarder, Peg Tarbet."

"Hauska tavata! Oh, mean, pleased to meet joo. Come in, come in, pleece." She opened the door wider.

Peg looked at the mud on her shoes and bent to unlace them.

Mrs. Jokinen nodded approvingly and continued, "Yo mother taught yo well. Leave dose boots on es rug." She moved across the room and opened a door. "Joo tings in dair, pleece."

Peg padded across the wooden floor to enter a tiny room, sparse but spotless. The twin bed hugged the wall, leaving just enough room to squeeze by to the rough end table, which held a kerosene lamp, metal pitcher of water and washing bowl.

"Thank you," Peg replied, failing to hide her disappointment. There was no closet or chair. She opened her suitcase, pulled out her coat, nightgown, towel and hung them on the three nails in the wall. Using her foot, she scooted the suitcase under the bed.

"Be back tonight," she called over her shoulder and hurried to catch Ralph.

Hearing her running, Ralph turned and continued his role as tour guide, as if he owned the place, "I'll show you where to wash up. There's a pile of vegetables to cut for stew."

The smell of baking bread reminded her breakfast had been hours ago. "What else we having?"

Ralph strode toward the back door. "We'll grab a sandwich." He washed his hands, found yesterday's bread and sliced four thick pieces. "Want roast or butter and jam?"

"Roast, please."

He brought the sandwiches, a couple of apples, and two glasses of milk. He motioned Peg to one of the long tables and dug in. Peg had questions: "Who sets the tables? When do I cook?"

Ralph held his finger to his mouth. "Shhh, There's NO talking during meals here."

Her eyes squinted. "Seriously? Why?" *Is he just pulling my leg?*

"Seriously. Eating here is strictly business." Ralph took another bite of his sandwich.

"But . . ." Peg started.

Ralph held up his hand and shook his head. *Really? There's no one else eating.* Peg finished and returned to the kitchen. All afternoon she chopped, cleaned and carried until the saw blade gonged.

Soon, thundering boots tramped in, accompanied by shouts of men in suspenders and overalls. She looked up to grimy faces, half hidden by full mustaches and beards, broad shoulders covered by plaid flannel shirts and sweat-stained hats.

Soon as the men lined up for food, the cacophony died. Ralph wasn't kidding about the no talking rule. Only the scraping of spoons, slurping of soup and an occasional "Shoot over the butter" or "pass the bread" broke the silence.

Peg hustled down the rows, pouring milk, refilling bread, and wiping up spills until Ralph tapped her shoulder. "Time for dessert." He led her in the direction of a huge table covered with pies and cakes. She followed, cut and served, amazed at the helpings the loggers took—three slices of pie, a couple servings of cake. Finally, chairs scraping over the wooden floors signaled meal over, and Peg began to clean up. Peaks of dishes waited. The ache in her shoulders and feet made her want to fall into bed, but she pushed on, wanting to make a good impression. After the last dish got wiped and put away, she stumbled toward the back door.

"Hurry back," Ralph called encouragingly. "Time to prep for breakfast."

I think I've made a mistake. My first day and I'm already wishing I'd listened to Mom. She trudged to the outhouse, hoping no one would realize she'd been heading for her cabin. Hidden, she gave herself a pep talk: *You can do this. Remember all those cows you milked. You've loaded hay, hiked for hours . . .* but it didn't take the weariness away. *How will I survive a whole day of this tomorrow?* She angrily swiped at a tear coursing down her cheek, forced a smile and returned.

Ralph hauled in bulging gunny sacks of potatoes. "Need to boil spuds for hash browns, make muffins, and pack lunches they'll pick up at breakfast. Frying bacon, cookun eggs and apple fritters will wait 'til morning."

Peg stood washing potatoes next to the sink. *I miss Charlie already.*

Ralph read the disillusion in her face. "It gets easier," he encouraged.

"I'm okay," Peg denied. She wondered if the no talking rule applied in the kitchen also as the other workers bent to their tasks silently.

Ralph patted her shoulder and hauled in more food from the back room.

After the potatoes were boiled, Peg placed them on the counter to cool. Ralph gave her a thumbs-up. "Loggers gather at the fire pit to visit if you want to come. That's where you'll hear the tall tales."

"I'm bushed," Peg admitted. "Think I'll turn in, but thanks!" She dragged herself to the Jokinen's cabin. Two children sat in front of the fire: a little girl of about seven played with a doll and a cute towheaded boy toddled to his mother at the sight of Peg.

"Velcome home,'" Mrs. Jokinen's broad face lit up. She stooped down and scooped up her son, who hid his face in her shoulder. "Little Apar's shy 'round strangers. This is my dotter, Sofia. Lars is avay 'round da campfire. Had supper?"

"Yes, thanks. Want to brush my teeth and hit the hay."

"Filled da pitcher in ya room. Hot water's in dot teapot."

"Great." Peg shuffled to her room, stripped off her sweaty clothes, poured water into the basin, gave herself a spit bath and fell into bed, without bothering to put on her nightgown. Just before she fell asleep, she sat up with a start when the coyotes began howling outside her window. She looked toward the sound, noticed the alarm clock and set it for four o'clcok.

Brinnnggggg! Peg rubbed her eyes, rolled over and fumbled in the dark. Out the window, the moon shone through trees, giving her enough light to dress and make a trip to the outhouse. She quietly shut the cabin door and remembered water in the teapot. Yes, still warm. Padding into her room, she filled the bowl, splashed her face, washed her hands, dragged a brush through her hair and braided it. Her first full day on the job. *I'm ready!* She tiptoed out the front door and sprinted to the cook house.

She heard the commotion before entering. Workers scurried about; eggs sizzled in huge cast iron frying pans on both stoves. Dutch ovens kept the already-cooked eggs warm. Bacon, fried potatoes and onions sent forth tantalizing smells, making her stomach growl.

"Morning, Peg," Ralph called heartily. "Help Maude pack the lunches, will you?" He indicated which woman with his elbow as one hand turned bacon and the other held a cup of coffee.

Peg trotted to the table beside a masculine-looking woman in her late fifties and joined the assembly line filling metal lunch buckets.

Maude gave directions like a drill sergeant without bothering to look at Peg. "Put in two meat sandwiches and one butter and jam. Push it down the line to Roy. When you're finished, head over to the stove and start frying up the apple fritters."

Peg moved into line. "How long you been here?" she asked Roy and pushed the bucket toward him. He added a piece of fruit, two pieces of last night's pie, looked up at her and smiled. "About thirty minutes."

"Was I late?" Peg worried.

"Nah, Ralph lets newcomers ease in." He stuck his hand out. "I'm Roy. After a while, you can't sleep anyway, so might as well get started. You get used to the schedule."

"Don't you log?" Peg blurted. The pained look on his face made her regret it. "Sorry. None of my business. How long does it take until you wake up on your own?"

"Never mind. Someone will tell you soon enough. I took a back-door furlough from the war when they wouldn't let me come home."

"Whadda ya mean?" Peg asked as she pushed more sandwiches his way.

"Means I couldn't take trench life any longer. Wouldn't let me come home, so I went AWOL," he said without emotion. "Got a dishonorable discharge and spent time in a mental hospital, so you see, I'm not tough enough to be a logger."

"Sorry. My boyfriend came back with shell shock, too," Peg confided, thinking about Charlie again.

"How's he doin'?" Roy whispered.

"Not so well." She didn't feel like discussing it further, so she left to fry apple fritters. Thin slices of apples floated in a large bowl of saltwater to prevent browning. She poured a large circle of batter into the hot fry pan, being careful to leave a hole in the middle. When she placed a few slices of apples on the fritter, hot grease spit at her bare arm, making her jump back. She worked four pans at once, watched them bubble, brown and then lifted them into Dutch ovens.

Peg recognized that the eating frenzy was about to begin, once she heard the men assembling outside. Like the night before, she hopped from table to table, refilling platters and pitchers.

"Need some red lead for this table," a logger with a purple scar on his face demanded.

Peg turned around. "Huh?"

"Catsup for spuds," he explained.

She returned with a tray full of catsup, balancing the slippery glass bottles, never taking her eyes off their sliding. She didn't see the man in front of her tip back in his chair. When her hip hit his chair, the bottles slid. Crash! Smash! Exploding glass flew. Catsup shot everywhere. Her face turned as red as the mess.

Frozen in horror, she stood, her mouth gaping. Ralph touched her shoulder. "It's okay. Happens all the time." He knelt and put glass shards in a bucket. Peg squatted beside him, not daring to talk. Together, they picked up the pieces.

"Grab a bucket of soapy water, and I'll find a mop," he told her quietly.

The loggers glanced at the commotion and silently returned to their forks. After they had the floor clean, Ralph patted Peg's shoulder saying, "See good as new." He winked and returned to his duties.

When she dared look around, Roy caught her eye, and nodded. Peg humbly and carefully picked up dirty dishes.

CHAPTER 50

The first week felt like rewind. Wake up early, cook, clean up, and fall into bed soon as possible. *At least the time's going fast.* The only change came Friday afternoon. Peg stood rolling out cinnamon rolls for breakfast. The smell of sweet bread, cinnamon and sugar seeped from the oven.

"What **IS** that heavenly smell?" a young woman called as she entered.

Peg turned to be greeted by an eager face with sky blue eyes, topped by blonde curls, refusing to be contained.

What a god send! Finally, someone here who's friendly. "Want to taste one?"

"Absolutely! I'd like to do more than taste! My name's Rose. Nice to meet you." She put forth her hand.

Peg reached out, looked at her sticky hand and they both laughed. "Peg. I'm new here." She wiped the dough on her apron.

"Yes, I heard you were coming."

"You did?"

"Are you kidding? When a young woman is coming, men talk."

Peg's hand flew to her chest. "They talked about ME? They haven't said one word to me except when they need something like red lead."

"Yes, I heard about that, too!" she giggled.

"How?"

"'Round the fire last night. There's also tall tales, true stories, and music when Hans brings his harmonica." She bit into the sweet roll. "Mmmm, this is still warm!"

Oh, I hope she's staying. "How long you been here?"

"Two years. I love it," Rose reported as she licked her sticky fingers.

"You're the teacher? Ralph told me there was another girl around my age here, but I've been too busy." Peg washed her hands. "Want icing?"

"On my next one. Got milk to wash it down?" Rose looked toward the icebox.

"Sure." Peg found a big glass and poured it full. "So where do you eat your meals?"

"With the Carlsons. They give me room and board in exchange for teaching their children."

"No wonder I've haven't met you. I pretty much spend all my time here," Peg admitted as she opened the oven to check on the next batch.

"Good thing I don't. With rolls like this, I'd be round as a bear before hibernation," Rose joked as she finished draining her glass. "Could I have more milk? Want to meet me at the campfire tonight?"

Peg's spirits lifted. *I deserve a break!* "Sure. I could use a change."

"Great. I'll be there 'bout nine. And thanks for the rolls! See ya tonight," she called back as she made her way to the door.

"I like her," Peg spoke her thoughts aloud.

Roy walked by. "You like who? Are you talking about me?" he teased.

"I said **HER**."

He laughed. "So, you going to the campfire tonight?"

187

"Did you eavesdrop on our whole conversation?"

"Sure thing. When two pretty, young women are talking, I want to know everything they say!"

He reminds me of Mud! "Do you go to the campfire?"

"Wouldn't miss it. Best part of the day," Roy confessed as he set down a box and went back for another. "I'll save you a spot."

"Thanks." *Maybe it won't be so bad here.* "Oh blast! The bread!" A wave of panic washed over Peg's entire body. She opened the oven to dark brown rolls. "At least they're not burned."

When Roy returned with the next box, he took one look at the extra-brown rolls and suggested, "Just put a little extra icing on those."

"Good idea." Peg hummed as she slathered icing.

By the end of her shift, she had second thoughts. Crawling into bed sounded divine. But she'd promised Rose and Roy, so she washed up, redid her hair and grabbed her coat.

"Vere ya off to?" Mrs. Jokinen asked, looking up from the sock she was darning.

"Meeting some friends at the campfire. Won't be too late," Peg promised, stooping to put her shoes on. *I'm looking forward to some fun. All I've done is work.*

CHAPTER 51

A crowd had gathered, some perching on tree stumps, others on the ground. Peg spotted Roy in a clean shirt and pants, his dark hair slicked down. He motioned her over. "Seen Rose?" She folded a red wool blanket she'd brought for warmth to pad the stump.

"Not yet. She has to help her landlady with dinner dishes. Saved her a spot, too," he proclaimed, patting the stump on the other side of him. "I'll be surrounded by pretty young ladies."

Peg's hearty laugh caused several heads to turn. Ralph smiled at her.

"Getting in good with the boss?" Roy teased.

"Already am," Peg boasted. "He's practically family."

"How so?"

"His daughter is married to my big brother, Ed. He stays with them when he comes to town for supplies and comes to our home for dinner sometimes. He sure can spin a tale."

"Oh, I know. I've heard a few from him myself." Roy spotted Rose, waved her over and shared, "You know he's headed to Alaska in July?"

What? Alaska? Why didn't he say something! Peg's eyebrows rose. "Really? I thought he'd work here all summer."

"Dunno. Overheard some guys talking." Roy jumped up and gave his seat to Rose.

"How sweet of you, Roy," Rose's dimple flashed.

Roy beamed.

Oh, so he's sweet on Rose, Peg understood, *and who wouldn't be? Unlike Helen, Rose is genuine.* Rose's blonde curly hair, blue eyes, rosebud mouth, hourglass shape and confident nature caught men's attention.

The fire crackled and popped, shooting sparks skyward. Peg shielded her face as the breeze shifted, throwing smoke her way. Someone stood and pushed a half-burned log into the center of the fire.

Rose leaned over Roy. "Hi, Peg! Glad you came. Want to share my blanket?"

"Hey, I'm cold," Roy protested.

"OK," Rose covered them all.

Peg tucked the blanket around her legs. "When does it start?"

"When someone stands up, the crowd quiets." Rose smiled at Roy who perked up.

"Have you ever stood up?" Peg asked them.

Roy squirmed, scraped a hand through his hair and shook his head.

"Sometimes I sing," Rose admitted.

"A solo?"

"Yes, or with anyone else who wants to. I love to sing."

"Beauty and talent, too? Not fair!" Peg protested.

Talking ceased as a tall thin man rose and cleared his throat. He hooked his thumbs in his pockets, rocked back on his heels and cleared his throat. "Always loved Paul Bunyan and his Blue Ox, Babe. You mighta heard this here story afore, but here goes . . .

"Paul's parents got a shock when five storks delivered a baby to 'em. He was nigh unto 100 pounds! Had to milk ten cows to keep his bottle filled and when he got old nuff to eat—50 eggs, 10 pounds a bacon, and 30 pounds a taters for breakfast."

Across the campfire from Peg, Roy and Rose, Ralph called out, "Sounds like your appetite!" The man next to him guffawed, and snickers rippled around the circle.

"Got sa big when Paul rolled over in bed, it caused earthquakes. That made the townspeople angry, so his parents took him inta the woods."

"Best place to be!" another man bellowed.

"His pa took Paul with him ever' day an' taught um to cut trees. One day, Paul found a baby ox in the snow. It was so cold the little guy was blue. Paul took um home, warmed um by the fire, but he stayed blue. Put um in the barn with the other animals. When he got up next morning, barn was gone! Looked 'round and the dad gummed thing was setting atop a Babe's back whilst he was jus' eatin grass down in the valley. He'd growed huge overnight!

"Back in them days, America was covered with timber. Paul cut down acres a day, swinging his mighty axe. He trained Babe to help. There warn't no straight roads—only trails—made it tough to get felled trees out, sos Paul tied one end a rope to Babe's tail and the other to a log. Babe took off a trottun, trees a thunder-un ba'hint hem.

"Paul knowed he was headed straight ta the river, so he yelled out, 'Gee, Gee!' Babe turned ta tha right and circled back round. When he got 'bout a mile away, Paul hollered, 'Whoa there, Babe!' By the time Babe got er shut down, he'd made a complete circle ten miles long and 50 foot wide—a great loggin' road."

"Hey, I know what they did up in my stretch of the woods," Ralph joined in. "Paul dug the Great Lakes so's to make a watering hole for Babe. Ya know, gets real cold up there by those lakes. In winter, loggers' words froze in the air as soon as they spoke and hung there frozen until spring!"

"He was up in our area, too. He took his axe and dug out Puget Sound right here in Washington," Ole reported.

"I hear Paul and Babe are headed for the Last Frontier, Alaska, and I aim to follow 'em," Ralph declared, spitting tobacco juice to the side, making a bystander jump backwards.

"So, what's in Alaska? Hear the gold's played out up there," a stocky man purported.

Ralph looked into the distance. "Been visiting a guy in Spokane. Looking into a fishing job. So many fish up there in Alaska, you can't stir 'em with a stick. Money to be made just by casting out a line."

"If'n mosquitoes don't kill ya off first." Ole laughed. "Size'a hummingbirds up there!"

Ralph sighed wistfully. "Well, there's work . . . commercial salteries. I love to fish. Just think. Living in one of those houses on pilings . . . sitting on your porch and fishing."

"How'd ya get there?" another curious man wondered.

"Only way's boat or plane. Man, it's some beautiful country— glacier-covered mountains and wildlife! Black bear and grizzlies, an' north, polar bears, tons a wolves, moose, caribou, mountain goats, Dall sheep, deer . . . hunter's dream."

Peg moved close to him. "What about ocean animals?"

"Whales, sea lions, dolphins, and porpoises, I imagine," Ralph answered.

Oh, I'd love to go there. "Sounds heavenly," she sighed.

"Say, Roy," Ole, who sat next to Ralph, interrupted. "Man sick on my shift. Could use another hand tomorra. You interested? Ralph said he'd do without you for one day."

Roy looked from side to side as loggers watched. "OK," he muttered in defeat.

"Say no if you don't want to," Peg whispered to Roy.

"I'll be there," Roy proclaimed. He rose. "Better get some shut eye. See you in the morning."

"He felt forced into that," Rose commented as she watched him retreat.

"I thought the same," Peg agreed.

"Well, maybe this is a chance for him to prove himself." Rose's voice was filled with hope.

Peg hung around, hoping the talk would turn back to Alaska but started nodding, gave up and left for the cabin.

"Peg, hold up." Ralph ran after her.

"Could you come in at four o'clock tomorrow? I'll need your help with Roy gone for the day."

"Sure. See you."

"We'll change to a simple breakfast of oatmeal, hash, and fruit," Ralph planned as they walked. "You'll need to cut potatoes for hash." He stopped and nodded toward the bunkhouse. "Well, it's payday, and if I don't want to miss the deal in at poker, I'd best be off."

At the campfire, Hans stood, cupped his harmonica with beefy hands, blew into it and swayed. Mournful notes floated into the cool mountain air.

CHAPTER 52

The next morning, Peg worked next to Ralph cutting leftover roast and onions for the hash. He stopped, wiped his eyes from the onions and noticed Peg's eyes running also.

"Whatcha crying 'bout?" he teased.

She bantered right back. "Just so touched by those stories of Alaska you told last night!"

"You saying I've a talent for spinning tales?" He threw onions in the skillet.

"Saying I'd love to explore Alaska. You're going there next month?"

"Who told you?" Ralph questioned Peg like she had violated his trust by listening to someone else.

Peg felt somewhat betrayed herself since he'd not been totally honest with her or her parents. "I don't reveal my sources."

"Yes, I am going. Sounds perfect for a fisherman."

"Someday, I'll go, too, but please don't tell my folks you're leaving. They'd probably make me come home," Peg pleaded.

Ralph tested the waters, "You like it here?"

"I like Roy and Rosie. We plan to play cards tonight, if Roy's not too tired from logging. Think it was a good idea for him to go?"

Ralph shrugged. "He's a grown man. None of our business."

Peg let it go. "Hash smells good! It oughta wake the guys up!" She finished the potatoes and began packing lunches, missing Roy to trade jibes with. *Hope he does well today.*

That evening, Peg found Rose shuffling cards at one of the long serving tables. "Heard anything from Roy?"

"Nothing," Rose replied while expertly dealing the hand.

"Probably too tired. What are we playing?"

"Spades?"

Peg looked over her cards. "Sure. Remind me of the rules."

Rose gave her a rundown. "Do you think Roy's good looking?" She laid down a card.

"Sure. He's okay," Peg stated as she took the trick.

"Only okay?" Rose probed.

Peg looked up. "Do you?"

"Yes. He's sweet, too, always so polite, and funny."

"He's still dealing with war issues. I'd steer clear," Peg warned, flippantly.

Rose almost shrieked as she put her card down. "What are you talking about?"

Wish I could take that back! "Never mind. Shouldn't have said anything."

"You can't never mind now! What kind of issues?" Rose demanded.

Peg refused to budge. "You'd better ask him. I don't want to carry tales or hurt his reputation. A lot of good men are suffering through no fault of their own."

"How do YOU know?" Rose pouted.

"My old boyfriend for one . . . he came back so changed."

Rose wanted specifics. "How'd he change?"

"He was optimistic, energetic, and fun when he left. When he came home, it was like . . . " she struggled to put it into words, "like he wasn't in our world anymore."

"What did you do?"

Peg shuffled the deck. The truth stuck in her throat, "Took him home to his parents." She shuffled the deck.

"Then what?" Rose asked, leaning forward.

"Not much. He broke up with me—ashamed of his erratic behavior—and I hate to admit it, but I was a little afraid of him."

"How sad! That why you came here to work?"

"Part of the reason. I'm saving money for nursing school, too, but needed to leave town. Plus, one of my high school friends wanted to date. I didn't feel good about that around Charlie." Suddenly home-sick for Newport, Peg slumped in her chair. "I miss my old job."

Rose found this conversation more interesting than the card game. "Where did you work?"

"At our local doctor's office after school. I guess one reason I miss Dr. Phillips is he made made me feel like I really helped people. I could have worked there this summer, but—"

"I understand, and I'm happy you came, so we can be friends."

"Thanks, Rose. Me, too, but I think I'm ready for bed."

Chapter 53

Peg sat up, wondering if it was a dream. She heard men yelling and peeked out the curtain. *Looks like a fight in one of the cabins.* She watched until the cold crept up her legs. Then she jumped back into bed, too awake to sleep. Soon, the uproar died down. She tossed, punched her pillow, and needed the outhouse. Finally, she gave in, slowly opened the bedroom door and tiptoed to the front of the cabin. She stood debating whether to put on her boots or pussy foot it. *I'll put them on outside, so I don't wake anyone.* She eased the door open and sat on the steps. Two men, carrying a stretcher, entered the loggers' cabin. *What's going on? Is someone sick? Maybe I can help.* She threw on her shoes, not bothering to lace them.

Ralph appeared out of nowhere. "What are you doing up?"

"Looked like someone was sick. I thought with my nursing experience I could help."

"Go back to bed," he ordered with irritation. "Nothing you can do here."

"What's the matter?" Peg insisted.

"You'll find out in the morning. Please, go back to bed."

"Fine." Peg pouted and marched back. Then she remembered why she came out and trooped to the outhouse. *I was only trying to help. He needn't act like he's my father!*

She tiptoed back to bed. A dark, foreboding feeling came over her. *What's wrong with me? I need some sleep, or I'll drag tomorrow.* But wide awake, her mind raced on and on. *I wonder who's sick. How's Charlie doing? Did I abandon him when he needed me most? I miss him.* A tear slid down her face into her ear. She turned, sniffled, and plumped the feather pillow to fit her shoulder.

CHAPTER 54

How does my body know the time? Peg woke, pulled her nightgown over her head, splashed her face, and looked out the window. People milled outside the same cabin she'd visited last night. *What's Rose doing there?* She threw on clothes and dashed through the yard. When Rose spotted Peg, her shoulders fell, face crumpled, and a sob escaped her throat.

Peg sprinted over. "Rose, what's the matter?"

"He's dead," she wept uncontrollably. Loggers stumbled from the bunkhouse as news passed from man to man.

"Who's dead?" Last night's image of the body on the stretcher flashed into her mind.

Bugs swarmed the lanterns in the yard. "Roy!" Rose blubbered.

"What happened?"

"A b . . . b . . . b . . . bear!" she covered her face with her hands.

Peg jerked and gasped, "A bear? Where was he?"

Rose shook her head.

"I'll find out!" Peg marched into the crowd of men gathered outside a cabin.

"Who found him?" a bald man asked.

"Ralph Sparks," another reported.

Peg swallowed hard before the shriek rising from her core could escape.

The bald man shook his head. "Those bears are mean S.O.B.s."

"He left in the middle of the night?" Peg asked.

The crew foreman, who often came late to eat, answered, "Wandered off during work yesterday just afore quitting time to take a . . ." He stopped and looked at Peg . . . "a bathroom break . . . and didn't come back . . . happened inta a sow with a cub. I seen the bear but didn't realize 'til I heard her cub a whining. It was close. When a bear starts to woof and chomp their teeth, you know they's mighty upset. They's unpredictable as a woman. I hollered to 'em ta hold still, but I think his head went back inta the war. He took off. So I run fer my rifle and let loose on that ol' sow. She went down for less un a minute, got up, shook her head, all dazed, an took off after Roy agin. I screamed to the fellas ta help, but damn that there bear was off like a freight train. The forest's sa thick in that area, we lost sight of um. We kept yelling and calling out ta Roy, but after an hour with no luck, we sent back to the camp for help. Ralph brung more men. We strung out in a line and combed them woods afore dark set in. When Ralph fired two shots—our signal—we follered the gunshots and helped carry em out. Bloody mess he was, nearly naked and . . ."

"Enough!" Ralph broke into the circle of men. "Peg, go back to your cabin." The men scattered, mumbling that he was just gettin' to the good part.

Peg stumbled to her cabin, relieved Mrs. Jokinen who was hanging out clothes, didn't see her. She dropped on the bed, gulping back sobs.

She heard someone tapping at the window. "Peg, Peg," Rose called. Peg shuffled to the door. Rose fell into her arms. "Can you believe it? Poor Roy! To be killed by a bear! He must've been terrified!"

Peg patted Rose's back as she sniffled, "I closed school because I'm in no shape to teach."

"Let's go for a walk," Peg suggested. She started toward a meadow, but Rose panicked.

"How do we know that bear isn't still around?"

"OK, let's go to the cook house. I'm sure we can find a corner."

CHAPTER 55

All logging ceased as men gathered in groups, discussing the sad news. Peg peered into the kitchen. "No privacy here." A trio of pines grew together fifty yards east of camp, forming a hidden space in the middle. Peg took Rose's hand, pushed aside the branches, and pulled her through the prickliness into the shady green interior.

Rose looked up in wonder. "How'd you know about this?"

"Just found it," Peg whispered. "We can talk here."

"Oh, Peg. I thought I was falling in love with Roy!" Rose confided.

"I know, Rose. It's heartbreaking. These things happen. Maybe he'll be happy now that he's in heaven."

"I could have made him happy," Rose sighed. "He was so sensitive and kind." She wiped her eyes. "He often brought leftover desserts to my students."

Peg squeezed her hand, "Really?"

Rose shuddered. "Will you go with me to his funeral?"

"Sure. You've heard about it?"

"Not yet. But I'd like to meet his family and let them know how much I thought of him," Rose choked out between sobs.

"I'll take time off. Maybe they'll shut things down here."

Rose blew her nose. "Tell me more about your boyfriend, Peg. Think you'll marry him?"

She shook her head. "I used to think so, but not now. He's changed. It's like he doesn't care for me anymore. Just happy to be busy. Maybe if I give him time to heal . . . we'll see."

"What if he doesn't change?" Rose prodded as she pulled a dainty handkerchief from her shapely bosom.

"Oh, Rose, I don't know. Don't want to talk about it now. I need to get to work." Peg tried to dismiss thoughts of Charlie as she parted the branches. Rose reluctantly followed. Peg strode off. Rose stood, looking lost.

"Ralph," Peg called as she entered. *When had he gone from Mr. Sparks to just Ralph?*

He came from the kitchen, wiping his hands on a towel. "Glad you're back. How's Rose doing?"

"Shocked like the rest of us. She had a special fondness for Roy. It's hit her hard."

"Yes, a sad, ugly business, but work's the best thing for it. You ready?"

"One more thing—You think I could go to his funeral with Rose?"

"Sure. We made out without you before you got here. Wash up. There's a mountain of spuds to peel."

"I don't know which day it is," Peg stated, but Ralph had already disappeared into the heat of the kitchen.

Peeling was a mindless job. Peg's thoughts wandered and ended on Charlie. *Maybe I'll take an extra day, go home, and visit him after the funeral. Is it too late? I'll not go begging for his heart again. Why did I let him walk away?*

Chapter 56

Rose hadn't come by for a few days, so Peg took her lunch break and walked to school. She peeked in the windows. Rose stood at the chalkboard, her back to the class, demonstrating how to write a cursive H. The students watched intently and worked to duplicate the letter.

Maybe I'd better come back later. She was about to leave when a curly mop head caught a glance of her at the window, put down his chalk and waved. Charmed, Peg waved back.

"Robert," Rose turned, her full skirt sweeping the floor, "Who are you waving at?"

He looked at Peg. "That lady in the window."

Peg smiled sheepishly.

"OK. Clean up. Time for lunch," Rose announced as she dusted chalk from her hands and found Peg outside.

"Sorry to disturb your class."

Children dashed out the door. "It's okay. What's up?"

"You find out when the funeral is?"

"Saturday in Spokane. 1:00 Methodist Church. Still going?"

"Yes, how will we get there?" Peg wondered.

"I assumed we'd catch a ride with someone from the camp. Can you stay for lunch?"

Peg shrugged. "Didn't bring anything to eat."

"Don't worry. Mrs. Nielson always packs too much. I don't know why she thinks I eat like a horse," Rose laughed.

Students wolfed down their food and ran to the ball field. Peg watched. It felt like years since her carefree days of childhood. The boy who'd waved at her came up to bat. After two strikes and two balls, Peg trotted over. "Wait! Let me show you how to hold the bat, OK?" He held out the bat. She positioned his hands and helped him swing. "Now you'll hit it!"

The pitcher threw; batter swung and . . . missed. He dropped the bat, hung his head, whispered "Sorry" and ran off. The next batter picked it up and jogged to home plate.

"Just a second," Peg called and caught up. "I've done the same thing, you know." She followed him to the school's steps.

"*You* play baseball?" he looked doubtful. The students cheered as the next batter hit a home run, and he watched longingly.

Peg followed his gaze. "Yep, I lettered in baseball along with the boys in high school."

His face lifted. "Can you teach me?"

"Love to. Shake on it?" She offered her hand.

His face lit. "Deal!"

"Thanks, Peg, he needed that," Rose said.

"So did I. I miss sports. See you Saturday. I'll try to find a ride." She jogged back to work.

"Musta been a good break," Ralph stated as he noticed Peg happier than usual.

"It was. You going to Roy's funeral Saturday?"

He wiped down the cupboard. "Planning on it. Boss gave us permission to run a skeleton crew."

"Have room for Rose and me?"

"Sure. Be here at seven o'clock sharp. It's a four-hour drive."

"Thanks! What should I do?"

"Food's ready. Set up for dinner. They'll be here any minute."

Peg grabbed her apron.

Chapter 57

Saturday morning, Peg woke as usual at four o'clock. *Drat! When I can sleep in, I can't!* She untangled her nightgown. After an hour, she gave up, dressed, stole into the chilly morning and wished she remembered her jacket. *A brisk hike will warm me.*

"Where you off to sa early?" A man's voice behind a glowing cigarette made Peg jump.

"Who's there?"

"Sorry to startle you," Ralph stepped out of the shadows. "Don't advise going about alone until they bring that bear in." He tapped ash from his cigarette.

"Couldn't sleep."

"Hang on. I'll walk with you," he offered, threw the cigarette butt and ground it with his boot.

"You're not afraid of bears?"

"'Course, be a fool not to be. But I know better than to run and what to look for." He led the way.

Peg scurried behind. "When you leaving for Alaska? My parents know you're going? How long you staying?"

"Same ol' Peg," Ralph snickered. "Which should I answer first?"

"Did you tell my parents?"

"When would I? Been up here cooking same as you."

Peg bristled. "I don't know. You visited our home a lot."

"Sure, guess I could've. Did discuss me going, but never gave 'em a date. Didn't know for sure myself until last week."

"So you have a date?"

"First week of July." He exhaled as the trail climbed steeply. "Wait 'til you see the sunrise."

They climbed in silence with Peg a few steps behind. Trees blocked noise and light, making it feel dreamlike. When they got to the top, Peg gasped, "Holy Moly!" The sun-gilded clouds melted into fiery shades of orange and red. Wisps of fog nestled among the mountain's cleavage. For fifteen minutes, they quietly witnessed the beauty. Ralph stood and offered Peg his hand. "Better get back. Need to set out cold breakfast 'fore we leave." She allowed him to pull her up. His warm hand felt good. She held on a little longer than necessary.

CHAPTER 58

Rose waited at a kitchen table. Sun shining on her blond head created a halo that puddled on her shoulders. "You look heavenly," Peg exclaimed.

"I wish I were. I could see Roy." She dabbed at her eyes.

Peg winced. "Need to set out breakfast and change. I didn't bring a skirt."

Upon her return, they loaded into Ralph's truck. After an awkward moment, Peg jumped in first. The rough logging roads stifled conversation until they came to the straightaway.

Ralph broke the silence. "Be there in plenty of time."

"Ever met Roy's family?" Peg asked.

"Nope."

Rose stared out the window.

"You know how to find the church? We coming back as soon as the service is over?" Peg wondered aloud.

"Yes, why? What do you want to do?" Ralph laughed.

"I'd like to go to the cemetery. What about you, Rose?" Peg turned to her.

"Doesn't matter," she mumbled so overcome with grief that she couldn't make the simplest decision.

Ralph tapped a rhythm with his fingers on the steering wheel. "That settles it. We'll go."

Cars, trucks, teams and buggies crammed the church lot.

"Good thing we're early. Hope there's seats. Come on, Rose. Open the door," Peg instructed as she nudged her.

They joined the line of people, shuffling into the church. The balcony had a few seats. An usher led them to a narrow staircase. Peg led the way.

"Excuse me. Excuse me." *Why does everyone have to sit on the end of the row instead of scooting in?* A large man stood when they couldn't squeeze by his long legs. Then, his big belly filled the space until he turned toward the aisle. Already, heat from the crowd formed beads of sweat on Peg's forehead. Several women fanned themselves.

Finding room for three people together proved impossible. Ralph headed to a single seat three rows above them. The girls just got settled when Peg let out a gasp.

"What?" Rose came out of her stupor.

Peg's hand covered her mouth; her eyes widened. "What is it?" Rose insisted. Peg shook her head. The preacher rose and welcomed everyone. From that point on, Rose turned her attention to him.

I'd know that head of hair anywhere! What's Charlie doing here and who's with him? The girl sensed Peg's staring and looked over her shoulder. *Florence!*

Peg's teeth and hands clenched. Florence scooted closer to Charlie to make room for another person, then whispered in his ear. He leaned closer. Peg didn't hear a word of the funeral.

Sitting above, Ralph noticed Peg's discomfort, followed her stare, and recognized Charlie. *So that's what's got her so flummoxed. Poor kid.*

After the closing prayer, Peg didn't wait for the bench to empty. Crawling over disgruntled mourners, she glanced down. Charlie and Florence exited the side door. She pounded down the stairs, raced outside, and panicked when she couldn't spot them in the crowd. Then she caught a glance of red hair and rushed forward calling, "Charlie, Charlie!"

Charlie swung around, glanced at Florence and dropped her hand. "Peg? What are you doing here?" His confused look pulled at her heart.

"About to ask you the same thing. Hello, Florence." Florence moved closer to Charlie.

"Roy and I were in basic together," Charlie stammered.

"Oh, and how did YOU know him, Florence?" Peg's voice cracked.

A smirk flitted across Florence's face. "I didn't. I came with Charlie. What about you, Peg?" Florence pretended interest.

"We worked in the camp kitchen," Peg's voice quivered. *Don't you dare cry!*

"You must have been close to him," Florence pried.

As Rose caught up, Peg gained control of her emotions enough to clarify her relationship to Roy: "Actually, no, Florence, I was not close to Roy. This is my friend, Rose. She and Roy were very close." Just as Peg was ready to begin introductions, another whirlwind of emotions swept Rose away. "Excuse us," Peg apologized as she led Rose back toward Ralph's truck. *The nerve of that girl!*

Rose looked back. "Who is she and . . . ?"

Peg cut her off. "A girl I grew up with."

At the cemetery, Florence slipped her hand around Charlie's arm when Peg and Rose arrived. After the burial, the crowd moved to the church for lunch.

"Let's go back to camp," Peg suggested, not wanting to face them again.

"It's a long ride, and I'm hungry," Rose complained. "I couldn't eat this morning."

Ralph looked at Peg with raised eyebrows. "Fine. Let's find food and leave."

Unfortunately, Florence and Charlie also returned for the luncheon.

"I need to find the ladies' room," Rose whispered to Peg. They followed a stream of women with the same idea. Rose moved up the creeping line. "Does your Charlie have a new girlfriend?"

"He's not MY Charlie anymore. We broke up—rather he broke up with me. Oh, that Florence burns me! She's carried a torch for Charlie ever since he pulled her out of the ice," Peg blustered.

"Pulled her out of the ice?"

"Yes, she was dumb enough to skate on thin ice last year and fell through. Charlie threw her a stick and pulled her to safety. She's gone all goo goo over him ever since, but I never thought Charlie would be fool enough to fall for her. She's had a hard life, but I'm so tired of her pity parties."

Florence stepped out of the bathroom stall. Peg's face reddened.

"So sorry to burden you, Peg," Florence retaliated. "You always thought you were too good for Charlie, anyway, so why do you care?"

"I did NOT!" Peg protested, moving toward her.

Rose stepped between them. "Pay her no attention, Peg. Let's go." Florence took to her heels. Peg fumed.

CHAPTER 59

Ralph had a good idea why Peg scowled. "Want to take our plates to the truck? Looks like they're almost out of chairs here," he suggested, realizing the awkwardness of the situation.

Peg followed, thankful he understood. She got food and followed Ralph. Rose would have to fend for herself. The first bite stuck in her throat. She started to choke.

"You okay?"

She swallowed. "Just upset over Florence's gloating," she admitted.

"You still in love with him? Sorry, I spoke before I thought. It's none of my business," he apologized.

"None of that. You know that's my job," Peg snickered. "Good question, though—one I've been asking myself. I don't know. He's been my best friend for years, and I do care about him. He's too good for Florence."

Ralph took another mouthful. "How so?"

"Never been able to stomach people who feel sorry for themselves. Maybe that's why I'm not so attracted to Charlie anymore. He's content to have people do for him. I hate to see him like this." Rose approached, so she scooted next to Ralph.

"So that's where you went. I finally gave up waiting and ate without you." She looked in the truck and noticed the plates of food. "Why'd you eat out here?"

"Too crowded." Ralph passed his plate forward. "Mind taking our plates back?"

"I looked everywhere!" Rose thundered. "OK, but be sure not to leave me again!"

After she left, Ralph changed the subject. "Read any books in the camp library yet?"

"Yes! Devoured ones in Alaska." Peg admitted. "Have to say I'm quite jealous."

"You could come," he offered, testing her.

She fell silent for a few seconds wondering if she'd heard correctly. "How would that work? Think Dad would let me? Who all's going?"

"You never disappoint—always questions, questions, questions, and more questions! We'll talk about it later. Don't say anything about it in front of Rose, OK? Here she comes back already," Ralph cautioned.

"When?" Peg persisted.

"When we're by ourselves."

Rose assumed Peg's silence came from seeing Charlie and dozed. Questions pinged through Peg's head: *Do I want to go to Alaska? What about my schooling? I don't want to go home and see Charlie with Florence! This may be my only chance to see Alaska. But it wouldn't look good for Ralph and me to travel so far together. What would my family say?*

The logging road jolted the truck's occupants. A branch slapped the window, waking Rose. "Penny for your thoughts?"

"What?" Peg asked as if she'd just been awakened from a dream.

"You've been a million miles away. What's on your mind?" Rose wondered aloud.

"Thinking about the future."

"Me, too. I love teaching but want to get married. Start my family."

"Shouldn't be too hard for a pretty girl like you," Ralph interjected.

"Thanks," Rose blushed. "But it's not easy to find the right man. I have standards."

"Well, I hope so," Peg said. "What kinda man you looking for?"

"Funny, kind, thoughtful, a hard worker, and handsome never hurts!" Rose recited the list like she'd been asked that question several times over the past few years.

"Put a good father on the list 'cause I want to have eight big, hungry sons!" Peg added.

Rose blinked. "You want that many?"

"Sure do. Eight kids in my family, and I love having all those siblings."

"Maybe 'cause you're the baby," Ralph suggested.

"What are you saying?" Peg challenged.

He stared ahead. "Nothing. Nothing."

"Maybe he thinks the baby of the family is always spoiled," Rose guessed.

"No, Peg knows how to work. Her dad told me she did a man's work while her brothers were at war. I don't think she's been spoiled, at least not too much," he winked.

"A girl likes to be spoiled some," Rose declared.

The banter continued up the mountain. As they pulled into the camp, men were gathering for supper. "I'm famished!" Peg declared. "It'll be nice to be spoiled a little and eat a meal I didn't prepare!"

Rose slid out of the truck. "Thanks for the ride. See you at supper? Too late to eat with the family."

"Got to change first," Peg waved her on.

Ralph stayed at the wheel and touched Peg's arm. "You really want to go to Alaska?"

Peg surprised herself. "I think I might."

"Meet me after supper in the three trees to discuss it."

Peg's mouth dropped. "You know about that place?"

"Of course, I do." He jumped down and started toward the kitchen.

Am I excited? Afraid? I've been on a roller coaster all day. Maybe after a good night's rest . . .

"Oh, Peg," Mrs. Jokinen looked up as she stirred a pot of venison soup. "Hungry?"

"Yes, but I'll eat with the loggers. Gotta clean up dinner and prepare breakfast anyway, but thanks. Just need to change clothes."

"Oh, vait! You haf a letter!" Mrs. Jokinen handed her an envelope.

She recognized Mud's handwriting with a start. *"What's wrong?"* She fled to her room, shut the door, dropped onto the bed and tore it open.

Dear Peg,

I don't know how to tell you this but think you should know, so you'll be prepared. I've wondered if I should stay out of it, but knowing you, well, I thought you should know. Charlie's dating Florence. I've seen them together a few times. The first time, I thought it was just friends talking at church. Then, I saw them standing in line outside the movie theater. Nearly stopped and accosted him right there but thought better of it. I feel like *a tattletale, but I didn't want you blindsided when you came home.*

When will you be home? Send a letter with Ralph when he comes down for supplies. We're counting on you being here for your nineteenth birthday celebration! Mom's planning it already. She said since it falls on a Saturday, we'd all better be here.

Hope I did the right thing by telling you about Charlie.

Love,

Mud

Huh, I'm not as surprised as Mud thinks. Peg dropped the letter in her lap and looked out the window. *Guess that does it for Charlie. He's made his choice and I'll make mine.* She folded the letter, put it back in the envelope, stuck it in her book, stood determined and struck out for supper.

"Where were . . ." Rose stopped upon seeing Peg's face. "Something's up. What?"

"What do you mean?"

Rose grasped for the right word. "You look mad? Or something . . ."

"I'm not mad," Peg denied, flopping on the chair.

"OK, I get it. If you want to talk, I'm here," Rose continued eating.

"Got a letter," Peg finally disclosed.

Rose put down her fork and moved to the edge of her seat. "From Charlie?"

"No, from my brother, Mud. Apparently, Charlie and Florence are a thing."

"Oh, no! Does it just break your heart?" Rose sympathized.

"No, it doesn't." Peg took a drink of milk. "Now I can move on."

Rose approved. "Good plan. Hope I can say that soon."

"You can, Rose. You'll find your way AND your perfect husband, too. I'm sure of it," Peg promised as she patted her hand, trying to encourage her.

Rose stood. "Thanks. Sorry to run, but I've got papers to correct."

Peg had a lot to think about.

CHAPTER 60

After cleaning up, Peg walked toward the towering trees, waving in a little breeze. *Is this stupid? What if someone sees Ralph and me go in there? They'll have the wrong impression.* Seeing no one in the hidden space among the trees, Peg sat on a close stump. She heard Ralph whistling before he appeared.

"Well, whadda ya know? Maybe you are serious about Alaska." He lit a cigarette.

Peg looked around. "I want to talk out here in the open, not inside the trees."

"Fine with me. Now, hit me with those questions, one at a time, please."

Peg bit her lip. **"IF** I go to Alaska, what kind of work would I be doing?"

"I'm working in the fisheries. Maybe look for some gold in my spare time and explore the place," he stated while leaning back and looking at the stars reaching down. "I'm sure you could find something. You've nursing experience, don't you?"

Do I dare? "Are you going with a group of people?"

"Nope, all by my lonesome. Time to follow my dreams before I get too old." *I won't push her.*

Peg started pacing. "Think my parents would let me go with you?"

"Doubt it." He lit a cigarette.

She stopped short. "So, I'd have to sneak off and not tell anyone?"

Ralph blew a smoke ring, pretending indifference. "You don't *have* to do anything. I offered to take you with me."

"Why?"

"Why don't you have to do anything, or why did I offer to take you with me?"

"Why did you offer to take me?"

"You're the kind'a girl wouldn't be a burden, not like others your age. You know how to work and like adventure."

"I sure do," Peg agreed. "It'd be the trip of a lifetime."

"It wouldn't be a holiday," he warned. "Mean country up there— beautiful, but harsh."

Peg stuck her chin out declaring, "I could take it."

"I'm sure you could, or I wouldn't have offered."

Peg fidgeted. "I got a letter from Mud, and my family's planning a big party for my nineteenth birthday on July 10th. Which day are you headed out?"

"Funny thing. I got a letter, too. Changed my work date from July 1st to July 25th. You can still go to your party if you want." Ralph pulled a flask from his coat and took a swig.

"Maybe it'll work out. Could I think about it some more?"

"Sure thing. I'm going with or without you. Won't change my plans. You need a way home for your party?"

"Oh, hadn't thought! It's a Saturday. You getting supplies?"

"I'll plan on it," Ralph offered.

"Thanks! Better get back."

Peg tried to sleep, but her mind wouldn't shut down. *Maybe if I make a list.*

Go with Ralph	Stay with Charlie
Good friend	WAS best friend
older	young
confident	afraid
Adventurous	cautious
Goals and dreams	Lost his dreams
skillful	Inept?
happy	depressed
fun	woeful
reliable	unsteady
Cares about me	Not anymore?

On paper, the choice looks obvious. I'll miss nursing school. Maybe another list will help.

Going to Alaska

Pros	Cons
Adventure of a lifetime!	Parents won't like it
Learn new things	Miss family
May be only chance	Could be miserable
Get to hunt and fish A LOT	May be no friends
Help me forget Charlie	Miss nursing school
	COLD

Peg jumped at a knock on her window. Her pen fell to the floor. She pulled a blanket around her and peered out. That blonde fuzzy head could only be Rose. She tugged at the window.

"Can't sleep either?" Rose whispered. "Saw your light. Come out, so we can talk?"

Peg glanced at the clock: 2:00. "Why not?" She tiptoed through the front room, eased the door open and slipped around to the back. After her eyes adjusted, she spotted Rose in the shadow of the outhouse.

"You picked a stinky place to wait!" Peg snickered.

"I thought it wouldn't look suspicious if someone came by," Rose explained, "and I could duck in here if I needed to hide."

"Why all the cloak and dagger?"

"Want to be alone. Let's go to the three trees, so we can talk uninterrupted." Rose started off through the forest.

Peg followed in silence. Rose held back an armful of limbs, and Peg ducked in. A couple of cut logs stood on end. "Where did these come from?"

Rose motioned for Peg to take a seat. "I lugged them in a few days ago. This has become my secret thinking spot."

"Not as secret as you think," Peg revealed.

Rose put her finger to her lips to shush Peg's loud voice. "What do you mean?"

"I told Ralph to meet me here, and he knew about it."

"Why were you meeting *HIM* here?" Rose gasped.

Peg shrugged. "He's invited me to go to Alaska with him. I had several questions."

Rose's mouth fell open. "And you're *seriously* considering it?"

"Yes." Peg surprised herself with the answer.

Rose sucked in her breath. "Oh, Peg, don't you realize how would that look? A single girl going off with a man . . . Your reputation would be ruined."

"Honestly, Rose, he's old enough to be my father and a friend of the family! He's just a safe ride there."

"He's still a single man. Aren't you worried about how upset your parents will be?"

"Yes, I am," Peg admitted, "but I'm not going to ask. I had a hard enough time convincing them to let me come here. If I do go, want to be my chaperone?"

"Not me. I'm starting to miss the comforts of the city, and there's no way I want to head to some cold unknown region!" Rose shivered with the thought. "When would you go?"

"Not until after my birthday. Hey, will you come down to my party? Mud said Mother's planning quite a shindig."

Rose grasped the opportunity. "Sure, love to! Need to get my mind off Roy, but what about school? When is it?"

"Saturday, July 10th. Ralph's giving me a ride down, but there's room, I think. I'll ask. Why'd you want to talk to me?"

"Nothing in particular. Feeling lost with Roy gone. Finally looked like my life was working out, and now I'm adrift again," Rose sniffled.

"Oh, Rose, you have your whole life ahead of you. It's a new era. Women can do whatever we want. We're demanding the vote. Then there'll be big changes! But I thought you loved teaching."

"I want to be settled—in my own home—with my own husband and children. I know it's old fashioned, but it's all I've ever wanted," Rose admitted.

"There's nothing wrong with that," Peg assured her. "I do, too, maybe not right away, but someday." She shifted on the hard stump.

"I'm tired, too. Let's go back. Thanks for listening to me."

Peg gave her a hug, apologizing, "I'm afraid I did most of the talking!"

CHAPTER 61

July 9, 1920

Peg thought of home and whistled as she washed dishes. She missed her family. Ralph had arranged for them to leave after supper, so she'd have the whole weekend to celebrate. Rose was as excited as Peg. She arrived with the bag in hand before Peg had finished.

"Ready?" Rose picked up a dish towel and helped wipe the last of the silverware.

Peg put a mixing bowl on the shelf. "I'll run and grab my suitcase. Can't wait for you to meet my family!"

"I'll finish here. Go. Time to agitate the gravel!"

"What?"

"Leave!" Rose laughed as she threw the silverware in the drawer.

Peg hoofed it for the cabin. Mrs. Jokinen squeezed out the front door with a full laundry basket on one hip and her son on the other. "Oh, birthday gal! Vait yust a minute. Got someting for ya." She lowered her load, pivoted and returned with a present wrapped in muslin.

"Oh, how sweet of you! Should I wait?"

Mrs. Jokinen looked pleased. "No! Open," she urged, waiting for Peg's reaction.

Peg removed the string and lifted a set of embroidered pillowcases from the muslin. Tiny, even cross-stitches marched across the hem in a pattern. Above the border, two birds met in the middle with a heart between them.

Peg touched her throat. "They're beautiful! When did you have time to make these?"

Mrs. Jokinen shrugged, dipped her head and her round face blushed. "I vork on dem when da baby sleeps."

Peg inspected the small, perfect stitches and wondered how many hours under poor light it had taken. Touched, she hugged her landlady. Her throat constricted, and tears pushed at her eyes, so she darted into her room.

Ralph and Rose stood next to the truck talking. When they turned, Peg hollered, "Let's go!" and threw her bag in the back. Rose opened the door. Peg hopped in the middle. Ralph started the engine, and they roared off.

"Your parents know I'm coming?" Rose asked, concerned about imposing.

"No, but it won't matter. Mom's unflappable. Everyone feels welcome at our house, and there'll be more than enough food. They'll love to have you. "

"I hope so," Rose murmured. She rolled her jacket under her head, leaned against the window and shut her eyes.

"I don't think you'll be able to sleep on these bumpy roads," Peg warned.

Rose didn't reply.

"She's still having a hard time with Roy's death," Peg whispered to Ralph.

Far away in his own thoughts, he nodded. Peg shut her eyes and leaned her head against the back window. Both girls jerked awake when a big rut bounced them. Peg looked up into Ralph's eyes and lifted her head from his shoulder. He suppressed an impish grin. "Put my arm up to keep your head from banging." He put his hand back on the steering wheel. "You gals must be working too hard," he guessed. They fell asleep again until Ralph spoke. "Well, we're almost there."

The Newport road sign appeared. Peg bolted up in anticipation. "Just wait, Rose. You're going to love it!" She grabbed Rose's hand and craned to see around her. "Look, there's our house, the barn and milk house, the pond where we can fish and . . . "

Rose thought everything looked ordinary, but kindly agreed. "It's lovely."

When Ralph slowed, Peg stretched across Rose and opened the door. "Hold your horses, sister," Ralph ordered. "Can't have fun if you're hurt!"

Mary heard the truck and scurried out the kitchen door. Mud followed with his arms held wide. Peg flew across the yard. "Happy Birthday to you!" he sang as he swung her around.

Ralph and Rose retrieved the luggage. "Oh, Mom, Mud, this is my friend, Rose. I didn't tell you she was coming but knew you wouldn't mind." Peg held her hand toward Rose who timidly came forward. Mary hugged Rose warmly. "So glad you could come."

Mud reached out his hand, "Welcome." He grabbed the luggage and hauled it to the house. "Take it all to my room, please," Peg called after him.

"Oh! My pies!" Mary panicked, remembering and fleeing to the kitchen.

"Your brother's cute," Rose whispered to Peg while smoothing her hair.

Peg bristled. "Thought you were mourning Roy. Come on. I'll get you settled in the spare room next to mine." She led her upstairs, opened the door and bowed, "Your room, madam. What do you want to do before dinner?"

Rose fell onto the bed. "Finish my nap! Wake me twenty minutes before supper so I can freshen up?"

Peg shut the door. She didn't feel like sleeping. Mary stood stirring gravy over the wood stove. Peg stole in, stopped behind, and whispered, "Boo!" Mary jumped and dropped the spoon into the pan. "You stinker!" She laughed, delighted to have Peg safe at home.

"What's the plan for tomorrow?"

"Dad's going to bring the wagon around about nine. We'll pile in and head to the lake for a picnic and swimming," Mary reported while she fished the spoon out with a fork.

"Yea! You know what I love." Peg hugged her. *I'm grateful to have this time with family and friends.* "What are we eating tomorrow?"

"Fried chicken, potato salad, melon, apple, cherry and huckleberry pie, spritz cookies, bread and butter pickles . . . "

Peg interrupted, "Mom, you must have been cooking for days!"

Mary hugged her. "Not every day my baby turns nineteen."

"Who all's coming?"

"Not totally sure. Our family, of course. Ran into Henry in town and asked him to pass the word along."

"Thanks for everything, Mom," Peg croaked. *Why do I feel so melancholy?* She got the dishes down and began setting the table. The back door opened, and John strode in his hands full of papers. Peg squealed, ran and threw her arms around him, sending papers flying.

"Well, if it isn't my baby girl, still as exuberant as ever," he chuckled. They both leaned over to pick up the papers and hit heads. "Ouch! And still as hard headed as ever!"

CHAPTER 62

P eg rose slowly, rubbed her forehead and glanced through the window. "Look! Here they come!" Head forgotten, she bounced out to greet them. First to arrive was her oldest sister Lee, her husband Cliff and their four boys. Peg fiercely loved these first nephews of hers. Since they lived in Newport, she'd grown up with them. They'd contributed to her dream of having a big family of boys. "Aunt Peg!" They all called as they raced to her. "Can we play baseball?" asked Ken, the youngest.

"Yes, of course," she giggled as they mobbed her, stepping on her toes and jostling for attention. She hugged each one.

"Bryon, you're as tall as I am!" she exclaimed to the oldest nephew, only five years younger than herself.

"Hello, Sis," Lee hugged Peg.

Peg asked about her other sister. "Inee coming for dinner, too?"

"No, she'll bring the girls and meet us at the lake in the morning," Lee replied, "but Gene and Marie will be here tonight."

When Gene arrived, she remembered sneaking in with Charlie to see him throw the wrestler. *Feels like years ago.* The deep guffaws of men, giggling, running, screaming children and cackling women echoed through the trees. *When my family gathers, it's noisier than a fox in a henhouse!*

Another sister, Freda, had married Ben Fox, the deputy sheriff of Newport. "Where are the Foxes?" Peg wondered.

"They're coming." Mary moved through the crowd joyfully as all her family gathered for the big event.

Rose stood apart, watching and beginning to understand Peg's deep devotion to family. She longed to belong to a group like this.

"Hey, Rose, come meet Gene," Peg motioned.

CHAPTER 63

The next morning, Peg lay in bed, humming, "Roll out the barrels. We'll have a barrel of fun!" She stretched and nearly purred. Rising to her knees, she squinted out her window. The first soft rays of sun bled through the tops of the trees. Peg looked to the eagle's nest. *Probably too late in the year for babies.* An eagle flew from the nest. *Can't tell if it's a mother, father, or a grown eaglet from this distance. I'll never grow tired of watching it soar over the trees. Well, you're off, my friend, and so am I.*

Out of habit, she fished under the bed for the chamber pot. *No, I'll make the trip outside.* She hopped down the stairs to the back door, slipped on Mud's boots, and tramped to the outhouse. A bluebird darted into the trees. Cows in the barn bellowed for their morning milking. *Everything feels right.* As she approached the house, she glimpsed her parents through the window. John held Mary in his arms as they waltzed around the kitchen to John's off-key voice.

After a hearty breakfast, John and Mud laid boards across the wagon for seats, hitched up the horses and loaded bulging food hampers. Family gathered. Children climbed into the wagon and bounced on the seats, calling, "Let's go! Let's go!" Buggies, horses, and wagon creaked to Diamond Lake. Singing, joking, and visiting made ten miles go fast. John drove the wagon to the best shore. Kids piled out, running for the water. Adults found a shady spot, set planks on sawhorses to create tables and set out chairs.

Peg struck out for water as soon as they'd set up. She hesitated and glanced back. Her parents sat holding hands, surveying the happy scene. *This is the essence of life. Wish I had a camera.* She waded into the brisk water, letting the mud squish between her toes. The older children launched a raft and paddled off. Little ones waded along the edge with their mothers close behind. Some skipped rocks. John threw a stick for a dog. The water shimmered. Peg took a deep breath and dove in. Her strong strokes soon brought her to the raft. She grabbed one edge and rocked it. Squeals and screams split the air as kids moved to the opposite side. One nephew stumbled into the water. "Aunt Peg, stop!" the rest shouted. She laughed and swam off, turning on her back when she got winded. The water cradled her and amplified the sound of oars, splashing closer.

Mud and Gene skimmed their fishing boat along with ease. "Catch a big one for me!" she chimed. They waved, moved to a calm area and threw in lines.

Mary had never learned to swim but wanted to cool off. She floated not far from shore, clinging to a four-foot board.

Peg side-stroked to the beach. More people arrived. One had recognizable red hair. *Charlie!* Her heart missed a beat. She hesitated. *Should I turn back!* Her foot hit the bottom. *Too late. Wish I'd left a towel on the beach!* She rose and waved. He didn't take his eyes off her and waved back.

She sat next to a niece, pretending to be engrossed in making a sandcastle. The sucking sounds of feet came closer. She took a breath, swiveled and pulled her knees to her chest as a shield, "Hello, Charlie." He plopped next to them.

"Happy Birthday, Peg."

"Thanks! Nice of you to join us." Air crackled with unsaid feelings. She let sand fall through her fingers and glanced at his swim trunks. "You swimming?"

He peeked over his shoulder. "Depends."

"On what?"

"Florence's 'fraid of the water. Ever since she fell through the ice, she's . . . "

"She's what?" Florence appeared behind them.

Both Charlie and Peg jerked. "Oh, hello, Florence." Peg pasted on a smile.

"I'm what?" Florence demanded.

Charlie swallowed, took a quick breath, shook the sand from his hands and struggled to finish his sentence: "You . . . don't . . . like water much."

"True," Florence snapped. "Peg's mom sent me to round everyone up." She turned and marched back to the picnic area.

The icy silence between them stabbed at Peg's heart. Memories of them running through forest meadows crowded her thoughts. "You're in trouble," she finally whispered.

His head down, Charlie shrugged, stood and confessed, "I'm used to it."

An image of the two of them racing horses flashed through her mind. "Charlie, wait!"

He whipped around. "Yes?"

Peg's heart ached. "You happy?" she blurted.

His shoulders dropped as he replied, "Sure. Why not?" and trudged silently through the sticky sand toward the picnic.

Peg watched Charlie's retreat until children close by took to their heels screaming when a wet dog shook water on them. She hesitated for a minute, looking at Florence pulling Charlie to the food line. She moved to her clothes, struggling to pull them over her wet suit.

"Over here, Peg! We saved you a spot." Henry called from a picnic table in the shade.

She pasted on a smile and slogged over through the sand, "Hey, everyone."

Rose tossed her hair back, appearing at ease in the middle of the group.

Well, that didn't take long. "Well, you've already met my friend, Rose."

Henry put his arm over Rose's shoulder and tried to impress Rose with his compliment. "Yea, Peg, where ya been hiding this doll?"

"Up in the mountains protected from the likes of you!" Peg retorted, "Come on! Mom's got a feast ready." She led the way to the loaded food table. "Let's eat!"

Hungry little kids descended. Mothers spooned portions onto their plates and helped them carry food and drinks to a table. The teens patiently waited.

Peg moved forward in line. "Corn on the cob!" She took half a piece.

"That *ALL* you're eating?" Mary worried. "Here, take some chicken and a roll."

"Not that hungry." Peg dotted on butter.

Charlie spoke at her elbow. "Hop back in the water. The swim will rekindle your appetite."

Florence swooped in beside him. "Did you hear our news yet, Peg?" She put her arm around Charlie's waist.

Peg braced for the worst. "Guess not."

"We're engaged!" Florence announced proudly.

Peg's eyes widened. She swallowed, "Well, congratulations." Emotions poured through her like hot lava. Not wanting to give Florence the satisfaction of seeing her tears, she searched for an escape.

Charlie cut his eyes at Florence. "I thought we agreed I'd tell her," he hissed.

"Oh, sorry," Florence apologized, feigning innocence, "I guess I just assumed that's what you were talking about earlier."

"Well, it wasn't!" Peg retorted as if Florence had just slapped her across the face. She snatched her plate, stumbled to the table, threw it down, and careened into the woods—no need to stick around and give Florence the satisfaction of seeing her burst into tears. The undergrowth smacked her bare legs. When she reached a clearing, she sank on a fallen log.

"Quite a birthday present, huh?"

Peg whipped around to see Henry with his hands on his hips.

"Well, I shouldn't have been so surprised," she admitted in despair.

Henry sat next to her and placed his arm over her shoulders.

Peg winced, but Henry didn't notice. "Feels like I don't even know Charlie anymore," Peg's voice cracked. "How can a best friend become a stranger?"

"We all change, Peg. We've grown up. World's not simple anymore."

Peg stared down surprised to see blood and dabbed at her scratched legs. "I never thought it was."

Henry took Peg's chin in his hand, turned her head toward him and kissed her forehead. "It'll be okay, kiddo."

At the edge of the clearing, Rose moved slowly through the trees, "Peg?" she called.

Peg stood and waved. "Over here!"

"Where'd ya go?" Rose picked her way closer through the undergrowth.

"Obviously right here." Peg rolled her eyes at Henry.

Rose squinted against the sun. "Who's that with you?"

"Henry. Just stay there. We're on our way back."

"Wait, Peg. I have a birthday gift for you," Henry turned her to face him, gave her a peck on the lips, and ran back, laughing. She shook her head and moved slowly this time, pushing branches back to protect her legs.

Rose waited, her face a question mark. "What were you doing out there?"

"Florence told me she and Charlie are engaged. I needed to get away."

"I'm so sorry, Peg." She held out her hand as they walked back to the table. "Guess what? Henry's so handsome, and I think he's interested in me."

"I'm sure he is," Peg responded cooly while scanning the beach for Charlie and Florence.

"They left," Rose reported, knowing exactly whom Peg searched for.

"Good. I can enjoy my lunch." Peg picked up the cold corn.

Just before sunset, the adults started packing and moved the boards crossing the wagon bed, so children could lie on blankets in the bottom. Tired and sunburned, they watched stars appear. Soon, the rocking wagon lulled them to sleep. Peg climbed up next to her dad.

"Enjoy your birthday?" John asked.

"Yes, thanks to you and Mom. I never realized growing up how much work an outing takes!"

"That's why we'll all sleep well tonight," John confirmed, recalling all the tasks he'd done to make the event a success.

Peg put her arm through his. *Tonight marks the end of an era.*

CHAPTER 64

Peg couldn't believe she'd slept until ten o'clock! She remembered Rose and jumped up.

Mary looked up the stairs. "Well, hello, slug-a-bed."

"Rose up yet?" Peg winced and pulled at her nightgown stuck to sunburned shoulders.

"Up, eaten, and out on a walk with Mud. Your breakfast is in the warming oven," Mary reported, returning to the dishes.

"Great. Now she'll be in love with him, too," Peg muttered sarcastically.

"What?"

"Nothing. Be down in a minute!" Peg shuffled back to bed. Nothing like a slow Sunday morning. Eventually, her stinging shoulders forced her up and downstairs.

"Mom, look at this," she pulled down the neck of her nightgown.

"Ouch! Sit here. Mud just brought in cream." Mary spooned cool cream over Peg's shoulders, took cold oatmeal, and dabbed it on the burn, soaked rags in cold water and laid them on top. "There, now I don't think you'll blister."

"I heard about Charlie and Florence." Mary gave Peg an opening.

"I know. I don't like it. He doesn't act happy—like his Florence's puppet," Peg criticized.

"Probably Florence's insecure with you around," Mary observed. "Maybe she's not so overbearing when it's just the two of them."

"I hope so," Peg sighed. Rose's laugh drew near. "Sounds like Rose's having a good time."

Mary lifted one of the rags and checked the burn. "She is. At breakfast, she told us how she enjoyed meeting your friends and family and how happy she is you're at the camp."

"Thanks, Mom. I'm glad she's there, too. Although I'm so tired by the end of the day, we don't have much time together. Better get ready. Ralph said he'd be by after lunch."

Mary swallowed her objections. "You get any of your birthday cake yesterday?"

"No! Any left? I think I'll have it for breakfast!"

Mary opened the cupboard. "I saved you a piece. There's even leftover boysenberry ice cream." She crossed to the icebox.

"A great birthday breakfast!" Peg laughed.

"What's so funny?" John emerged from the front room. "Well, looks like you are, Peg, with your breakfast sitting on your shoulders and cake for breakfast!"

Mary turned to the window. "Grab some clothes. Here comes someone."

Peg gathered her food and fled upstairs. She finished, crawled back into bed, and was drifting off when John called, "Peg, someone here to see you."

She growled and pulled on her robe. Charlie sat at the kitchen table.

She pulled the sash on her robe tighter. "Hi, Charlie."

Charlie glanced up. A smile chased across his face.

"What's so funny?"

"Had a flashback of another time you came down in your pjs. Can I talk with you a minute?"

"Hold on. Let me dress."

She climbed the stairs. Her shoulders smarted, so she found a loose-fitting dress, slipped it over her head, then noticed her unruly hair in the bureau mirror, and raked a brush through it. By the time she got downstairs, Charlie was gone. "Where he'd go?"

John set down his paper. "Said to meet him at the usual spot."

Peg headed to the granite rock with trepidation. *Whatever did Charlie want to talk about? It was over with them, wasn't it?* He sat at the base of the granite rock, staring at the eagle nest.

"They're still there."

Charlie stood tall and turned to greet her. His countenance lit. "Yes. You keep track of them?"

He looked like her old Charlie, happy, confident. Peg's heart leapt. *Is he getting better?* "What's up?" *Might as well get it in the open.*

Charlie's head bowed, and he kicked at the dirt. "Wanted to apologize for yesterday. Not how I wanted you to find out."

"I'll admit it shocked me but shouldn't have. Already heard about you and Florence."

His head jerked up. "Who told you?"

"Doesn't matter. Look, Charlie, you know you've been my best friend for years. Just want you to be happy." Peg reached for him. "Are you?"

Charlie stared into the distance. "Thought so, 'til you came back."

"What did I do?"

"Nothing." Charlie searched for words and shrugged.

Peg's eyes narrowed. "Hey! *You* changed on us!"

"You're right . . . shouldn't have come over . . . Just wanted . . . "

"Well, you're too late!" Peg stomped off.

She ran for the woods, then looped back to the road. A passing truck slowed, then stopped 100 yards ahead. She paused and edged forward. *Who's that? I don't want to talk to anyone!*

The driver's window rolled down, and Ralph stuck his head out. "Hey, didn't recognize you 'til I was passed. Out for a walk?"

"Something like that," Peg lied.

"Jump in? I'm headed your way." They drove in silence until almost home. He cleared his throat. "Have you decided about Alaska? Need to make plans for the boat. Sleep on it, but I'll need to know by morning so I can make reservations before we leave civilization."

"I'm going," Peg stated without hesitation.

"Great. Told your parents?"

"No, and I'd appreciate it if you didn't."

"Ooo-kay, I'll gather my things, then come back for you and Rose."

Peg hopped out before he could say anything else. "Thanks for the ride."

"Peg, there you are," Mary greeted, "You hungry?"

"No thanks, Mom. Gotta pack and get Rose going. Know where she is?" Peg started up the stairs.

"She left with Henry about an hour ago."

"Great!" Peg growled. "Hope she's back on time." She threw clothes on her bed. *What to take to Alaska? How long until I come home again? Don't think about that!* She threw in a hat, gloves and woolen socks. *My winter coat and boots are at camp . . . what else?*

Gravel crunched in the driveway. Peg moved to the window. Rose stood close to Henry until he gave her a goodbye hug. *Oh boy, Rose's got a new flame!* She slammed her suitcase and lugged it down.

Rose flitted in, humming under her breath. "Oh, already packed? I'll hurry!" She flew to the spare room.

Mary bustled around the kitchen, putting food into a hamper. "Packing a lunch. We have so much left from yesterday. Dad's coming home to see you off."

"Thanks, Mom. Going to take one more walk around before we head out." *I want to commit to memory my home.* She wandered past the milk house, the barn, the big granite rock and climbed into the arms of the weeping willow. A gentle breeze made the limbs sway. A peacock screamed. She closed her eyes, listening to the lowing cattle. Fish splashed in the pond and a horse whinnied. *Wish I had time for a horse ride. I want to say goodbye to everything on the ranch.*

"Peg?" Rose hollered.

"Coming!" Peg slid down the tree trunk. Rose and Mary visited with Ralph. The food hamper sat in the back along with the suitcases.

John stepped forward. "Give us a hug." Peg threw her arms around his neck and hung on. He patted her back and planted a kiss on her cheek. Mary stepped forward and held out her arms. She felt smaller when Peg gathered her into her embrace. Her parents hugged Rose. "You come with Peg next time she comes home!" Mary invited.

They climbed in. Peg turned, waving until they were out of sight. "When can we come back?" Rose asked.

"Anytime you want. I'm sure you'd be welcome," Peg reassured her.

Rose's brow furrowed. "Well, I'm not coming without you."

"Then it'll be a long time."

"What do you mean?" Rose's voice rose.

"I'm going to Alaska with Ralph."

Rose's mouth dropped. "Wow! What did your parents say?"

"They don't know," Peg admitted.

She's sneaking away from wonderful parents and family? Will they forgive her? "Oh, Peg!"

"Don't worry. Someone will need to come down for supplies, and you can catch a ride," Peg suggested.

"I didn't mean that!" Rose pouted.

"Sorry, Rose. I'm worried about their reaction myself. I do care about their feelings, but I know if I told them, they'd try to stop me."

"No one's forcing you," Ralph reminded her.

"I know." Peg lay her head against the back window and closed her eyes.

Ralph glanced at her. "You need to be ready by six Friday morning."

CHAPTER 65

When they arrived back at camp, Rose followed Peg. "Meet me in the three trees after you put your things away?"

Peg agreed though it was the last thing she wanted. She dawdled, kicking a pinecone all the way, then peeked in.

Rose waited on a stump. "Oh, Peg, we've so much to talk about!"

"Really?" Peg waited.

"Yes, I think I'm in love," Rose confessed.

"With Mud or Henry?"

"Well, Henry, of course. Not that I don't like your brother," she backpedaled. "But Henry's so handsome and charming, too. I can't believe I found him!"

Peg sighed. *I really don't care to know all the details, but better be polite.* "So, what happened with Henry?"

"Guess."

"He kissed you?" Peg guessed, raising one eyebrow.

Rose giggled. "How did you know?"

"'Cause, he kissed me, too."

Rose stood and put her hands on her hips. "What!"

"It's not what you think. He kissed me on the forehead—as a friend."

"Why?" Rose worried.

"He was trying to make me feel better about Charlie's engagement. We've known each other our whole lives. He's like a *brother*, Rose."

"Oh, good because the kiss he gave me was NOT brotherly at all. I connected with him right off the bat. That's why I want to visit again and why I'm upset you're going to Alaska."

Peg reached for her hand. "I know, Rose, but you will be welcome at my house whenever you want to visit Henry. My parents love company."

"OK, but it won't be the same without you. They might think I encouraged you to run off!"

"How could you have? I didn't tell you until we were on our way here, remember?"

Rose shook her head. "So, you're going, and you didn't tell them?"

"I am, Rose."

"Traveling alone with an unmarried man? You sure? Do you trust him?"

"You know, I do," Peg realized.

Chapter 66

I won't tell Mrs. Jokinen my plans. She'd disapprove. Peg put her suitcase in Ralph's truck the night before and left at her usual time of 4:30. *Now what will I do until six o'clock? I'll write a note to Rose.* She dug a journal out of her suitcase and tore out a page.

Dear Rose,

Thanks for being such a good friend. Having you at the camp made all the difference. I do hope you stay at my house while I'm gone. I'll write and tell you all about Alaska! I'm excited now I've finally made up my mind. Write back and keep me informed about you and Henry.

Love,

Peg

She folded the note. *Now, how to deliver it without waking anyone? I'll leave it in the three trees.* As she climbed, a cigarette glow winked ahead. Ralph stepped from the shadows of the trees. "You ready?"

Peg jumped. "Yes, just need to leave this note for Rose."

"Sorry to startle you. Meet you at the truck."

A patch of red columbine waved cheerfully. Peg picked a handful and left them with the note.

Ralph waited next to the truck. He took a gulp from a flask, screwed on the lid and poked it under the seat. She hopped in and eased the door shut. Her stomach rolled. *I'm really headed to Alaska with this man.* The truck roared to life. Ralph looked over his shoulder and eased onto the road. "What? No questions?"

"You kidding? Plenty. Ready?" she laughed.

"Fire away!" Ralph lit a cigarette and rolled down his window.

"How we getting there?"

He stared into the distance. "We'll drive to Seattle, stay a night, drive onto British Columbia, find a boat . . . "

Peg interrupted, "Why not go straight to Alaska?"

"This is my dream trip. Always wanted to see B. C. It's on the way." He turned a sharp corner, throwing Peg into the door.

She grabbed the dash. "Oh, what will we do in B.C.?"

Ralph looked away and pulled out another cigarette. Biting his lower lip, he searched his pockets for a match, gave up and picked some lint from his shirt. He blinked rapidly and shifted his weight.

After a few minutes, Peg grew impatient. "So, do you have a plan?"

Ralph stared straight ahead. "I do, but not sure you'll agree."

"Well, what?"

"I want you to know before I tell you, I've been thinking about this for a long time," he paused.

"And . . . ?" Peg prodded as she tapped her hand against her leg.

"I'd have told you earlier, but I was afraid you were still in love with Charlie," he squirmed. "I think highly of you, Peg . . . " he hesitated, "and the only way I can see for us to travel together in Alaska is for us to . . . get married." He explained quickly, "I know I'm old enough to be your father, but I'd take good care of you. We get along well. I dare say we enjoy each other's banter quite a bit." He glanced at her. "Not asking you to give me an answer now. Think about it."

Peg swallowed and squeaked, "Oh." Her heart skipped a beat. *Marry him? Is he crazy? What have I done?* She twisted her jacket and pretended to be interested in the scenery.

"Not too late to turn back, but once a day or two has passed . . . Well, I worry about your reputation. I wouldn't hurt you for anything."

"Thanks," Peg mumbled, still stunned. *I didn't see this coming! Were there signs?*

"I have two rooms reserved in Seattle tonight. It'll give you some time alone. If you want to go home, I'll buy you a train ticket," Ralph offered.

"Thanks." Peg's mind whirred. *I've never considered Ralph in a romantic way. Marry someone as old as my dad?* The rest of the trip silence reigned. *I do enjoy his company and his stories and good sense of humor. I feel safe with him. He doesn't toy with my emotions and is considerate. My family likes him, but . . . would they if I married him? He's not who I imagined marrying, but I didn't spend time imagining marrying anyone, except Charlie. Did I love Charlie that way, or were we just good friends? Is being good friends enough?*

"Wake up, Peg. We're here," Ralph spoke softly as he shook her shoulder.

She rubbed her eyes. "What? Oh. Where are we?" Out the window, a steamer belched smoke in the harbor.

"Seattle. Go sign for our rooms. I'll be in to pay in a minute," Ralph stated, pointing to a hotel across the street. Peg stumbled out, gazing over the gray ocean. Gulls squawked. Thousands of wooden crates labeled Yakima apples, perched on the dock ready to load. An ocean-bound ship left a big wake. She took a deep breath and felt excitement rising, then crossed to the hotel and swung open the heavy door.

"May I help you?" a wizened man with round spectacles asked.

"Yes, two rooms for Ralph Sparks, please."

He placed the registration forms on the counter and turned to pull the keys from one of the wooden cubby holes behind him. The door swooshed. Ralph entered, weighed down with suitcases.

"How many days?" the man peered over his glasses.

"One, maybe two. Can I let you know tomorrow?" Ralph asked as he set down his burden.

He examined the registration. "Tell me before ten tomorrow morning and you should be okay."

Ralph picked up the suitcases. "Get settled. Then we'll go exploring and find food."

"Here, I'll take mine," Peg declared, reaching for the handle of her suitcase.

Ralph led the way. "I'll take 'em. Your room's just down from mine."

Peg stared at the massive chandelier. *I've never stayed in such a nice place. It already feels like an adventure!*

"Meet me in the lobby in an hour. Heard about a great place to eat." Ralph set her luggage by the door. She sunk into the big bed in the middle of the room and slept until Ralph rapped at the door, "Peg? You in there?"

"Coming!" she threw her legs over and wobbled to the door.

"I wake you?" Ralph worried.

"Sorry! Didn't realize I was so exhausted. Give me a minute to freshen up." She splashed cool water on her face and neck. Passing the mirror, she noticed her wrinkled clothes, decided to change, to dress up and unpacked her navy suit and matching hat. She scurried to the lobby and spotted Ralph, reading the newspaper. He'd changed clothes and looked quite distinguished. *Can I see myself married to him?* He sensed her stare, lowered the paper and beamed. Her heart leapt.

He is nice looking. Am I crazy to consider marrying him? My life will totally change.

"You ready?" he asked as he folded the paper, neatly placing it on the end table.

"Yes. Where we off to?"

"Let me surprise you." He held out his hand, took hers and placed it on his arm. "This way, Miss."

Outside stood a horse and buggy; the driver held the reins. Ralph handed her up and climbed in. The horses clopped, clopped, clopped up and up to the top of a hill, bells on the harness jingling. Clanging cable cars whirred past. The setting sun glistened on the white brick and stone exterior of the nearing building. Peg squinted to make out the lettering that ran down one side of the structure: LINCOLN HOTEL CAFÉ.

"Wow! Peg called out. There's trees on top!"

"Yup, a whole garden on the roof," Ralph explained proudly, "and shops. There's a restaurant on the first floor."

"Can we go on the roof?" Peg pleaded.

"Don't see why not."

"I want to see out over the city before dark," Peg announced, leaning out the buggy for a better view. Ralph paid the driver while Peg walked backwards, shading her eyes and gaping.

"Ready?" He held the door.

Corinthian columns paraded through the massive lobby halted by red velvet overstuffed chairs that held down intricate area rugs.

Twinkling chandeliers summoned eyes to vaulted cathedral ceilings. Flowers and potted trees created an outdoor feeling. A curved carpeted stairway beckoned from the side of the room.

"Let's take the stairs," Peg bounced toward them.

"There's nine floors," the desk clerk cautioned. "You'll find an elevator down that hall."

"Thanks, we need to stretch." Ralph took Peg's hand and moved to the stairs.

"Hopefully, you can keep up with your daughter," the clerk teased.

Peg giggled, "Come on."

Ralph didn't hesitate. Peg stopped at every floor and peeked over the rail down the twisting stairs. They caught their breath at the top. A bouquet of fragrances assailed their senses. Multitudes of flowers burgeoned on tables, walkways, and atop the railings. Vines caressed lattices and pergolas. Dozens of trees rose from large decorative pots, and the sunset bathed it all in gold puddling between them.

"Oh my!" Peg gasped. Walking to the edge, they scanned the city and sat in padded wicker chairs, soaking in the view.

Ralph broke the silence. "Hungry yet?"

"I guess I am."

"I'm starving. Let's try the restaurant." Ralph held out his hand.

Peg took it. *This feels natural.* "Let's ride the elevator this time."

The restaurant was as lovely as the garden. "Two for dinner?" the maître d' asked. "This way, please." He took them to a window table. The lights in the city below shimmered.

Peg gazed out the window. "This is fun. Thank you!"

"My pleasure. I like to do for you. Ever eaten lobster?"

Peg held her palms up. "Can't say I have."

"It's mild. I think you'd like it," he suggested.

"Great, I'll try." Peg studied the prices on the menu. "Never mind. Nothing could be that good!"

"You are," Ralph complimented, then turned to the waiter. "Lobster for two and one steak on the hoof, please."

"Tomorrow, we'll drive up to B.C. You'll need to have your mind made up about my proposal before we catch the ship to Alaska. Finding someone to marry us will be harder up there."

"OK, I'll let you know in the morning," Peg promised.

CHAPTER 67

After dinner, Ralph escorted Peg to her room. "I have something I want to give you." He softly kissed her lips. "Hope you'll decide in my favor."

Peg closed the door while the lyrics to a popular song bounced in her head:

> Don't know how it happened quite,
> May have been the summer night.
> May have been, well, who can say?
> Things just happen anyway.
> All I know is I said, "yes!"
> Hesitating more or less,
> And you kissed me where I stood,
> Just like any fellow would.

(from *They Didn't Believe Me* by Herbert Reynolds)

Guess I have my answer. The next morning, Peg threw open the door as soon as Ralph arrived and greeted him with a hearty "Yes!" He hugged her fiercely.

After breakfast, they drove up the coast to New Westminster. Peg scanned the street. "I need to do some shopping. I want something new for my wedding."

"OK, we need a hotel first. After we get settled, I'll drop you in town, find someone to perform the ceremony, buy our tickets to Alaska and see if I can sell this truck."

"Let's meet back at the hotel for lunch," she suggested.

Ralph dug out his wallet. "OK. Need money?"

"Oh no. I'm buying my own wedding clothes. You know I had a high-paying job this summer, right?"

Ralph smirked. "I don't know about the pay, but I heard you had a great boss."

"Just remember, he's not my boss anymore!"

"Oh, I have no doubt." Ralph turned the truck into a hotel parking space. "I'll take the bags in. Did you notice that right across the street is Copp's Shoes and there's another store down the street there? Meet back here at noon?"

Peg entered Copp's Shoes. When the door opened, a middle-age clerk jumped eagerly from his stool. "May I help you?"

"I'm looking for a pair of dress shoes."

"Follow me. Our selection isn't great. We cater to people headed to Alaska since many catch the boat here," he confessed as he led her to the back of the store.

"I'm going to Alaska, too," Peg confided.

"You won't have much use for dress shoes up there, lady. Ol' sourdough came in today on his way back to the states. He said the best thing for warmth was wolfskin boots with moose hide bottoms. Of course, you'll have to buy that from the Natives, but you can purchase a wool scarf from the store down the street."

Peg picked up a pair of black T-straps. "I need shoes for my wedding."

"Those won't look so good with a wedding dress."

"Aren't salesmen supposed to talk you into *buying things?*" Peg chided. "Have these in a size nine?"

He disappeared into the back and reappeared with two boxes. "Only two things in a size nine, so I brought both. Didn't have the one you asked for, but here's a black shoe with a heel that might work."

Peg slipped them on and walked down the aisle. "I'll take them. How much?"

"Six dollars."

"What? I've never paid more than four dollars for a pair of shoes in my life."

"Take it or leave it. We have the best selection around."

"Fine." Peg pulled out her money. *At this rate, my hard-earned cash won't last.* "Where can I buy women's clothes?"

"'Bout half a mile down."

"Just a wonder they're still in business," she muttered to herself as she made her way down the street, but the balmy day lifted her mood immediately. She strolled, observing the business district. *A-hoooo-ga!* The blast from the throat of Model-T made her turn and jump. Bottles in a passing milk wagon rattled in protest as the wheel hit a pothole in the street. Swinging her package, she hummed. The ocean in the distance winked like it realized her great adventure was about to begin. She strolled by a saloon, a drug store and livery, her eyes squinting against the sun when a storefront offered no shady awning. Smoke belched from a ship headed to sea. Transfixed, Peg followed it to the pier. Huge white letters identified the building, straddling pier number two: Alaska Steamship Company. Her heart flipped. She watched the ship until it floated over the horizon. "Waaan-ka!" another ship bellowed, breaking her reverie. She glanced at her watch. *I'd better skedaddle. Almost lunch time!*

Scanning the lobby, she spotted Ralph on his haunches in conversation with a little boy. *He's kind to children. I do care about him.* He stood, patted the boy on the head, turned and caught sight of her. His face brightened as he walked her way.

"Find what you wanted?" He reached for the package. "Didn't buy much."

"Just shoes. Got caught up in watching a ship leave," she admitted. "No matter. Don't want a traditional wedding dress. Brought my navy-blue suit. If you don't mind, I'll wear it." She peeked up hopefully. "Never been a prissy girl."

"Good for me. Had success at the Hudson Bay store, purchased outfitting for Alaska, and bought our tickets. We leave tomorrow at seven in the morning. Guy who sold me the tickets directed me to a justice, too. We're set for five o'clock tonight. That work? Made it late as possible."

Peg's stomach flipped. *Is this really happening?*

"Great. We need to sell our truck after we grab a bite." Ralph steered her toward the hotel cafe. They sat in the back.

OUR truck? We really are becoming partners.

"Penny for your thoughts?"

Peg took a sip of water. "Just thinking this feels like a dream."

"Not a nightmare, I hope?"

"Oh no! I do care about you and can't wait to head up to Alaska. Just hope I don't break my parents' hearts."

"Not too late to change your mind, until five o'clock," he reached across the table and took both her hands.

She shook her head. "I'm not changing my mind."

"Wonderful. Why don't you rest? I'll look into selling the truck," he offered.

"Thanks. I think I will."

After lunch, Ralph escorted Peg to her room, kissed her cheek, and handed her the package of shoes. "See you about 4:30? Justice's office is a couple miles away."

"OK." She turned the knob and set the package on the chair. A hollow feeling filled her chest. Her family meant everything, and they wouldn't be at her wedding. "Better write them." She opened the desk and found paper and pen.

July 20, 1920

Dear Family,

By the time you read this, I'll be Mrs. Sparks. Ralph and I are on our way to Alaska and getting married at 5:00 today.

She lay the pen down. Tears dripped from her chin.

I hope you'll forgive me for keeping it a secret. Try not to worry about me. I'm well and happy. I'll write after we're settled and let you know our address.

I love you,

Peg

She wiped her face and tried to rest, but her mind raced. Finally, she got up, opened her suitcase, dug out her suit, and examined it. *It could use an iron.* She untied the string from the shoe box, set the shoes next to the chair, and gazed in the mirror. *Maybe I should have bought a new dress.* She unpinned her hair and studied her reflection. Thick brown hair hung almost to her shoulders. Brown eyes, clear and full of sparkle, stared back. Her strong nose sat well on a full round face held up by a sturdy neck and shoulders. *I'm stocky. Wonder if I weigh more than Ralph. I bet I couldn't fit into his pants.* Her hearty laugh rang out. *Oh, well, I guess it's true: opposites attract.* She picked up her brush and counted the strokes. Her sister's voice came into her mind: "One hundred strokes a day makes your hair shine." *Forty-eight, forty-nine, fifty . . . enough of that!* Turning sideways, she began pinning her hair up, tried on her hat and studied the effect. *Wish Mother was here to do my hair!*

She carefully pressed her suit and pulled on her hose, only to find a hole. She checked the clock after turning them backwards, positioning the hole in the crease behind her knee. Even with her immaculate grooming, she still had almost two hours until Ralph would be back.

Guess I'll mail my letter. She picked up her pocketbook and headed to the lobby.

The clerk helped a line of people who stood, waiting to check into the hotel. She walked out, scanned the street—no post office in sight—and went in the opposite direction of her last stroll. One store proclaimed Dry Goods and Groceries, but no sign of a post office. After walking for twenty minutes, she decided to ask for directions. A small man turned the corner and came her way.

"Excuse me, sir," she stopped him. "Can you tell me where I could mail a letter?"

He pointed to a large, low squatty building she'd already passed. "There."

"Thanks," she turned back.

The building had no sign posted. *No wonder I didn't recognize it.* She pushed the door open to many government offices. A hand-lettered sign inside had an arrow directing her to the post office. "I need a stamp, please." She dug in her pocketbook for two cents. Seeing the address, John and Mary Tarbet, Newport, Washington, caused her eyes to burn and her hand to shake. She thrust it to the clerk and hurried out. *There's no turning back now. I'll just have to forget Charlie and pray my parents will forgive me.*

As the July sun soaked into her dark navy suit, drops of perspiration formed on her forehead. *There goes the ironing.* Slowing down, she took off her jacket and searched for shade. A table and chairs perched outside a barber shop. *Hope I won't need another bath before my wedding!* she worried, wiping her brow with her handkerchief. The door opened, ejecting a customer. "And don't ever come back!" an irate voice bellowed.

A chill ran up Peg's spine. A disheveled man stumbled out. He wobbled off, obviously drunk. She sat frozen until he turned the corner a couple of blocks away and waited ten minutes to be sure he was gone before returning to her hotel.

Shaped like giant leaves, the lobby fans blew down cool breath. She plopped in one of the overstuffed chairs, leaned her head back, and closed her eyes. The fan's motor hummed a lullaby while people murmured in the background. Twenty minutes later, Ralph leaned over from behind and kissed her cheek.

When she jumped, he threw his head back, laughing, "Gotcha! How was your afternoon?" He pulled the adjacent chair closer.

"Fine. Couldn't rest, so I wrote my family a letter, walked to the post office, and mailed it."

Ralph's eyebrows raised. "What did you say?"

"Not much. Told them we're getting hitched and moving to Seward's Icebox," Peg reported as she twisted her handkerchief.

"Phew! Glad we'll be long gone when they open it."

Peg leaned in. "They know something I don't?"

"No, just don't know how they'll react to me stealing their baby girl."

"Nor do I," Peg confessed.

CHAPTER 68

Newport, Washington, August 1920

Mary stopped sorting the mail when she noticed Peg's large loopy writing on an envelope.

Hum, must be homesick . . . She turned the letter vertical, shook it, held it up to the light until she could see the letter inside, then tore off the end of the envelope and noticed the postmark. *Canada? What's she doing up there?* She unfolded the letter. Her eyes widened. Her hand flew to her heart. "No!" she wailed and ran for home. Mud emerged from the barn. Seeing his mother bawling, he dropped the milk can and loped to her.

"What's the matter?" he called.

She stopped and thrust the letter at him, trembling as if someone had struck her.

He swore. "Why that dirty #*#! I'll throttle him!"

"Find your dad," Mary gulped.

"Let's go. Come on in the house," Mud nudged her forward with clenched fists.

Mary bowed her head and put her hand to her throat. "What was she thinking? What about her nursing school?"

Mud tramped in without removing his boots and eased her toward the rocker in the front room. "You okay?"

"I can't believe it," Mary stated dumbfounded. She rocked and wept. Her thoughts darted from one idea to another. *We'll send her brothers! Is this all because of Charlie? Did Ralph have this planned all along?*

Fifteen minutes later, the door slammed. "Mary?" John called. He stomped into the room, prowling from side to side like a grizzly. "Oh, John!" she passed him the letter now tear-stained in spots.

"What in tarnation's going on?" he sank to his haunches, held her hand and scanned the letter. His eyes tightened, teeth clenched and a vein in his forehead pulsed.

Mary continued weeping, "What will we do? And to think we let her go to that camp with him! I knew it wasn't a good idea, John!" She sprang up. "You'll have to take the boys and bring her home!"

"Whoa there, Mary! We don't even know where she is. Sit down. I'll go talk to Ethel and Ed. They may have insight."

"I'm coming, too! I can't sit here stewing!"

Gene's car sat in front of Ed's house. "Hey, I think there's a pow-wow's already under way," John declared. He opened the door and dove in with Mary in tow. A somber group sat around the kitchen table. Ethel's sodden hankie lay crumpled in her lap. Gene sat with clenched fists, his bouncing leg, making the table jump.

"How could he do this? I'm so sorry," Ethel apologized, her big eyes filled with tears.

Ed put an arm over her shoulder. "It's not your fault, honey. Just because he's your father, doesn't make you guilty."

Gene ground his teeth . . . "I'm for going. I'd like to grab his scrawny neck, ring it and kick his sorry behind to . . ." The anger bubbled up in his cheeks, painting them bright red.

"Calm down, son. We need to keep cool heads to implement a plan," John interrupted.

"Well damn it! We gotta do something!" Gene roared. "If nobody else will, I'll do it myself."

"Agreed. However, remember she chose to marry him. Obviously, he's had some influence on her, and maybe she'll refuse to come home," John warned. "She's spunky and stubborn."

Mary wiped her face. "Oh, why would she do such a thing?"

"Never mind, Mother. She married him, and you can't know until she explains herself. It's done now," Ed rubbed his temples. "We can't do a thing until we know for sure where she is."

"We can follow her trail!" Gene bellowed. "I've gotta do somethun!"

Ta-duk! Taduk! Taduk! They turned to the noise of Mud's horse coming into the yard. It skidded to a stop. Mud slid off, jogged to the house and threw open the door. "Heard Mom's upset. What happened?"

"Sit down, Mud," John directed and related the letter's contents. "We're talking it out."

"I think one of us should ride up to the logging camp, talk to people there, and see what we can find out," Gene suggested.

"Not a bad idea," John agreed.

"I'll go!" Mud volunteered.

"I have the car. I'll go," Gene argued.

John pushed his hands forward. "Both go. Talk to more people."

"What shall I do?" Ed wondered.

Ethel's chin trembled as she spoke. "Talk to the grocer where Dad got his orders. Maybe he knows something."

Mary sobbed. "Let's keep this under our hats. No need to start the rumor mill grinding."

"And don't lose your temper, boys," John advised. "That'll only make things worse."

CHAPTER 69

20 July 1920, New Westminster, Canada

Ralph looked at his watch. "We've got an hour until we have to be there. You hungry?"

"Could we eat afterwards? I have butterflies."

"Got cold feet?"

Peg shrugged. "A little, I guess. It's a big step and not at all what I expected. I need to freshen up a little after my walk."

"Right. Meet me here in fifteen. Could use a splash myself," he admitted as he led Peg to her room.

She studied her reflection in the mirror. Several fuzzy wisps had wrangled themselves from her bun. She took off her hat and jacket and grimaced at the wet spots under her arms. *Should've stayed here in the cool.* She smoothed her hair, took off her blouse, wet a washcloth with cool water and had a spit bath. *Am I truly getting married today?*

Ralph tapped at her door. "Forgot to tell you. I sold the truck. We'll have to hoof it."

"Probably undo my freshening."

"It's all downhill, so should be fine until we walk back."

"Yeah, but I'll be an old married woman, and I won't have to impress you anymore," Peg laughed.

Ralph's eyes crinkled. "Come on. You impress me—always have, always will."

Peg fell silent. *I've never thought of myself as impressive.* After a mile, she limped as her shoes pinched her toes. "My dogs are barking. I hate new shoes."

"It's just round the corner," Ralph sighed, relieved that their destination was near.

Peg hobbled on. She caught their reflection in the window of the door. *I'm dreaming.* Ralph opened it, stood back, took her hand and led her down the hall to the last door.

She didn't hear a word of the ceremony. Ralph nudged her to say I do, leaned in, and kissed her. *Surely, my world couldn't totally change after a few words, could it?*

On the way back, Ralph suggested, "Why don't you take those shoes off?"

"It will ruin my hose."

He raised an eyebrow. "Think you'll need 'em in Alaska?"

"True!" Peg slipped them off, ran down the street, and kicked up her heels. She turned laughing. Ralph bent over, scooped up her shoes, chuckled and jogged to catch up.

"Are you in love with Alaska or me?"

"Not sure. I haven't met Alaska yet," she giggled. "Guess we'll soon see."

He tucked her shoes under one arm and reached for her hand.

CHAPTER 70

P eg awoke with a start. It took a moment to remember who was lying next to her. *Today I'm off to Alaska!* Ralph snored gently, so she slid from bed to find a bathroom. When she returned, he still hadn't risen. She slipped into her clothes, eased the door open and went to check the weather. The sun shone brightly. *A beautiful day for an adventure!* Her spirits rose. *So far, married life agrees with me.*

She whistled toward the docks. A steamship's hoarse voice croaked across the water. Gulls wheeled above, their squawking rupturing the morning calm. A breeze fluttered the leaves. In the distance, the ocean heaved ships forward into a freshly washed sky. She watched until they fell off the edge of the earth. Then she dawdled back to the hotel. Ralph sat smoking under the hotel's awning.

He cracked a smile as Peg approached. "Wondered if ya'd run off after one day of marriage," he teased.

"Didn't act too upset about it."

There was a new aura of confidence about him. "Was pretty sure my magnetic personality would pull you back. Ready for breakfast?"

"Sure am! Shake a leg! I'm packed. Want to leave as soon as possible!"

"Hold yer horses, gal. Alaska will still be there!" He wondered if he admired her fearlessness or her overabundance of enthusiasm more.

Peg stood at the rail on the ship's bow, letting the wind pick her hair from its pins. She inhaled the brisk air, closed her eyes, lifted her face to the sun and almost purred. Ralph stood close, soaking in her vibrant youth. *She's a tonic. I feel more alive, hopeful and excited about the future.* From the stern of the ship, laughter and cheers of a group playing shuffleboard shattered Peg's peaceful moment. She glanced over her shoulder. Ralph followed her gaze.

"Want to play?"

"Maybe later. You know me and sports, but I want to enjoy this and not miss anything!"

Ralph's heart leapt. Her enthusiasm was infectious. He'd dreamed of this trip for a long time, too. After they moved into the open sea with only water and sky, Peg still didn't want to leave her post. She rode a magic carpet in a world of racing clouds. Other passengers had moved below, and Ralph grew tired of standing there.

"Ready to rest?"

"Rest? From what?" Peg puzzled.

"I'm going below to nap."

Peg turned back. "OK, I'm not tired. I'll stay a while."

"Not sure I'll be able to keep up with her," Ralph muttered to himself as he walked to the stairs.

Transfixed by the beauty that unfolded before her, she tried to name her feelings. *I feel at home. There's no other way to describe it.*

Gazing over the ocean, she spotted a whale spout. A pod slipped gracefully through the water! "Ralph!" she called, forgetting he'd gone below. Scurrying to the stern, she strained to see. So mesmerized by the ship's wake, she didn't notice another passenger until cigarette smoke floated by. *Why's Ralph back already?* Turning, she noticed a man with a dirty hat pulled low over his face. A shiver passed through her. *Leave!* She felt more than heard the warning but didn't hesitate and fled downstairs.

Ralph slept in his bunk. *That was strange.* Peg sat. *I guess I am tired.* She kicked off her shoes, lay next to him and didn't move until Ralph touched her shoulder. She jumped.

"Having a bad dream?" he asked.

Peg pushed the hair from her face. "No, why?"

"You were jerking and moaned a couple of times," he reported as he held out his hand. "Time for supper. I'd let you rest, but we may miss it. Come on, Mrs. Sparks." He kissed her cheek.

"Oh, Ralph, you missed the whales!"

"I'm sure we'll have another chance. You'd better see if you can pull a comb through that hair," he teased.

After supper, Peg wanted to return to the deck.

"Pretty cool up there. Sun's down," Ralph warned, but Peg persisted.

"Let's snag our coats. I want to see the stars."

"Why did I pay for a berth?" Ralph chuckled as he followed.

She looked back. "Do you think we'll see the Northern Lights tonight?"

"No," Ralph replied as he dug in his suitcase, looking for his jacket.

Peg's face fell. "Why not?"

"You see them best in winter when it's darkest. Toward the end of September, you'll start to see some."

Peg opened the door. "Drat! I don't want to wait that long!"

"There'll be other things to see." Ralph finally found a sweater, pulled it over his head and grabbed a blanket from the bed.

"Like what?" Peg asked over her shoulder as she led the way to the stairs.

"If you'll let me catch up, I'll tell you . . . BEARS!" he growled as he grabbed her from behind.

She jumped. "Oh, you! But are there a lot of bears?" The memory of Roy still haunted her.

"Yes, and you'd better steer clear of them. They're smart, fearless and unpredictable."

"What kind of bears?"

"Brown, Grizzly, Polar and Kodiak. Kodiak are the biguns. Get up to 12 feet and 1,000 pounds! 'Specially dangerous during mating season or if they've got a cub. Males will kill and eat cubs to gain attention from their mother."

"You're making that up!" Peg protested, knowing Ralph's love for telling stories.

"No, I'm not. If the mother nurses her cubs, she won't go into heat for two years," Ralph continued. "You don't know if they'll charge, run, or chew up everything in sight. If you ever hear snorting, clicking teeth, or something tearing up brush, you're in trouble."

"You're scaring me," Peg protested.

"Good. You'll be careful." Ralph put his arm over her shoulder. "I don't want you hurt."

She snuggled into his warmth. "I'll be careful, but what if I see one?"

"Best to steer clear. Don't walk silently or alone in bear country. Make lotsa noise. They usually avoid people. If you see one, look around. See if it has a cub or is defending a kill. Back out slowly the way you came. Keep your eye on the bear, so you can gauge its reaction. Stand tall. Shout. Look it in the eyes. Wave your arms to make yourself look bigger and **never run**!"

Peg moved closer. "Wow! What if the bear attacks?"

"Play dead. Spread out your arms and legs, so it can't flip you over. Hold still and don't stand until the bear's gone."

Peg's eyes got big. "You mean I just lie there and let it eat me?"

"If it tries to eat you, time to fight back. Kick, punch, use anything around as a weapon. Go for the eyes, face, and nose."

"How do you know so much about bears?" she asked, once again totally caught up in his story.

"Been around them. And remember all those books on Alaska back at the logging camp? Read 'em all . . . some more than once."

The stars gleamed and a near full moon reflected on the undulating sea. "Oh, how beautiful," Peg gasped.

"Makes for a romantic evening." Ralph kissed the top of her head.

"Tell me more about Alaska," Peg begged.

He chose another topic he knew volumes about. "Well, let's see. How about the Gold Rush?"

"Oh, yes. That's exciting. Let's find a place to sit." Peg pulled him toward a couple of chairs. "Go on. What about the Gold Rush?"

"Ya might say the Alaskan Gold Rush started in Canada. Man name'a Carmack, I believe, and his Indian partner were washing their dishes in a tributary of the Klondike River when they spotted gold sandwiched in the river. 'Bout a year later, 'round 1897 er so, bunch a miners from Alaska unloaded in Seattle and San Francisco with boxes, blankets and sacks chocked full a gold, an' herds a people set off for the Klondike. Also found gold in Nome and Fairbanks. Might try my hand at it myself."

"What would you spend it on if you became rich?"

"Never been much for fancy things. Don't need a big house or stuff to take care of. Probably retire, fish, and hunt. How about you?" Ralph spread the blanket over their knees.

Peg stared up at the sky. "Maybe I'd open a clinic. Give free medical help to the poor, especially kids. I do love medicine. It would be a huge log building with gardens, flowers, ponds, a place to heal the spirit as well as the body. Of course, it would be close to a forest. I need to be around trees, guess 'cause I always have," she revealed her now distant dream.

"OK, we have a plan for when we get rich! Ready to go in yet? I'm chilly." Ralph shivered.

"That's 'cause you have no meat on your bones, but I aim to cure that!"

CHAPTER 71

The next morning, Ralph reached for Peg, but found an empty bed. *That girl!* He found her up top, gazing at snowy peaks thrusting brave faces to the wind. Clouds hugged the mountains' shoulders like a shawl. At the base, fuchsia and white splashes adorned green velvet. Water sloshed against the side of the ship. The dull hum of the motor kept Peg from hearing Ralph's quiet approach.

"Oh, good morning! This is stunning!" she gushed. "Wish you could have seen the sunrise."

Ralph shook his head. "What time *did* you get up?"

"Dunno, about five. Too excited to sleep," she confessed. "You know, it's not as cold as I expected."

"Well, it's July. It'll get up to get to 'bout fifty-five. On the bright side, no snakes or reptiles in Alaska. But—it's colder than a polar bear's toenails."

"I do hate snakes! Did you notice how the mountains change colors throughout the day? I wonder if I'll ever tire of watching them."

"I'll never tire of watching you watching them. I feel younger just being with you," Ralph confessed as he took her hand. "I love seeing everything through your eyes."

Self-conscious, Peg squirmed. "There're so many majestic mountains!"

"Yes, Alaska has seventeen of the twenty tallest mountains in the U.S.," Ralph said.

A seagull flew next to the ship. "Do you remember *everything* you read?"

"Not hard, when you're interested in something. Mount McKinley's the highest one. Alaskans call it Denali."

"I have my own personal tour guide!"

He reached for her. "You're chilled. Come on, my cheechako. Time for breakfast." Ralph beckoned, kissing her neck.

"Your what? What's a cheechako?"

Ralph pulled her forward. "A greenhorn. Don't be surprised if a sourdough calls you that."

"A sourdough?"

"A sourdough is someone who's been through at least one winter up in the northern parts. Takes time to earn that title," Ralph explained.

"Good thing I'll have you to interpret. So why sourdough?"

"Not sure. Guess we'll find out."

"Ha! A question you don't know the answer to?"

He started down the stairs. "I could make one up and probably fool you."

Peg hit his shoulder playfully. "I'm sure you could! Let's get packed, so we can be the first ones off the ship."

They entered their cabin. "Wait a minute. I have an idea I want to run by you," Ralph said.

"What?" Peg stopped folding clothes.

"We're close to Stanley Park. How about we stop?"

Peg pursed her lips. "Hmmm, how long?"

"What does it matter? We *are* on our honeymoon. Ships leave for Alaska often."

"But what about our tickets? What about your job?" *Does he really have one?*

"We have time. I promise."

She hesitated, "OK, pretty sure I've heard about the park. If we're this close, we may as well take advantage."

"Great!" he hugged her. "I think you'll love it. We'll find a place to stay for one night . . . unless you want to stay longer."

When the ship pulled into Vancouver, Peg waited up top. After taking the bags to be unloaded, Ralph joined her.

She gazed out. "Isn't it crazy how you travel to a different country but doesn't look different than the one you left?"

"Yes, and when we arrive in Alaska, we'll *feel* like we're in a different country, but won't be!"

Ralph agreed, "Yes, but it's not a state yet."

Peg's hearty laugh rang out. "True. What are we doing first, getting a room?"

"Anxious?" He moved closer with a wolfish grin and put his arms around her.

She cuffed his arm and moved away, "No!"

CHAPTER 72

After they got settled, they walked to Stanley Park. Peg stood transfixed by the beauty. Vibrant floral beds flowed down to the causeway and up to the Park Pavilion where climbing roses and clematis clawed their way up trellises. "Are you sure this isn't the Garden of Eden?"

"It is with you here. Let's find the totem poles. They're past Lumberman's Arch. George had a photo of them at the camp. They fascinate me." Ralph studied the map. "It's a long walk from here, almost to the end of the island."

"Lead on!" Peg quipped. They strolled hand in hand around the edge of the island, stopping to watch squirrels dash about and listen to harbor seals bark. A Great Blue Heron soared overhead, cawing like some prehistoric bird.

When Peg spotted a Bald Eagle land in its nest atop the tallest tree, she called, "Lookee there! I love eagles. I always watched a nest at home."

"You'll see a lot of them in Alaska," Ralph commented as he shaded his eyes with his hand. "Let's stop at Lumberman's Arch and eat our lunch," he suggested. From a distance, the huge tree resting on a V-shaped stand resembled a giant axe. "Paul Bunyan laid down his axe and is taking a rest. Watch out for Babe!" Ralph teased.

"I love it here!" She knelt next to the picnic box and set out sandwiches and water. "I wonder if I'll feel like I'm on vacation all the time in Alaska."

"Don't count on it," Ralph warned. "We'll have to work hard."

"That's okay as long as I'm surrounded by beauty like this." A splash from a nearby pond pulled Peg to her feet. "Come look—a beaver pond!" They watched one swim to the dam, deposit a stick, slap its tail and dive under the water.

"Let's eat. The totem poles are close," Ralph urged.

The pillars towered. Wooden beaks protruded from different levels and giant wings spread out over their heads. Peg ran her hand along the side. "What kind of wood is this? Why did they carve them?"

"Red cedar. Holds up in this wet climate. I think the carvings are symbolic of things, so your guess is as good as mine. George told me some showed clan lineages, memorialized events or something about religion or mythology. Some even have ashes of ancestors in them."

Peg peered up. Menacing eyes glared down over hooked beaks. Bared fangs hung from open mouths. "Guess you had to be there," Peg mused. "Workmanship's amazing. Wonder how long it took to carve and paint. You bring the camera?"

Ralph pulled it from his pack. "Stand next to one."

Peg posed by one with a fierce face, mimicking it. "Maybe this one was meant to scare off enemies." The roar of a cannon made her jump. "What was that?"

Ralph read from a tourist guide.

THE NINE O'CLOCK GUN. A CANNON MADE IN ENGLAND WAS USED TO WARN FISHERMEN AND HELP MARINERS SET THEIR CHRONOMETERS.

"There's so much to see here. Should we spend a few days?"

Peg readily agreed, "May not get this opportunity again."

A few days turned into two weeks. They studied the figurehead of SS Empress of Japan that had transported Vancouver's goods. Peg craned her neck to view the dragon's teeth and claws. "What is it with the ferocious faces?"

"Power," Ralph surmised.

They strolled on, stopping at a rock monument. Peg read:

PROSPECT POINT

HERE ON 26TH JULY 1888, THE STEAMER BEAVER WRECKED.
THE HISTORIC VESSEL WAS BUILT FOR THE
HUDSON'S BAY COMPANY AT BLACKWELL, ENGLAND.
SAILED FOR THE COAST IMMEDIATELY AND WAS THE
PIONEER STEAMSHIP OF THE PACIFIC OCEAN.
THE STORY OF THE BEAVER IS THE STORY OF THE
EARLY DEVELOPMENT OF THE WESTERN COAST OF CANADA.

"Wonder if it got caught in a storm," Peg glanced at Ralph.

He shrugged. "I dunno. Have to ask one of the park employees."

CHAPTER 73

The following day, Ralph stopped by a bike rental shop. "How about it?" He raised his eyebrow. "It'd be faster."

"I always rode a horse."

"Girl, you're a natural." Ralph stepped up and paid the fee.

Peg hiked her skirt and mounted. "Let me practice a few minutes." She wobbled off, picking up speed as the roadway fell. "How do I stop?" she yelled over her shoulder.

Ralph ran behind. "Push the pedals backwards. Backwards! Push backwards!"

Peg stomped the pedal, skidded and crashed. She lay splayed, her skirt over her face. When Ralph reached to pull it down, Peg held on.

"Did anyone see me?" she whispered.

"Just me." Ralph sat on his heels and laughed.

She climbed on, started off slowly, and then picked up speed. "Whee!"

He pedaled hard to catch her. "There's a hollow tree up ahead. Let's stop."

Peg rolled back in front of an information plaque. "This tree is a 700-800-year-old Western Red Cedar tree stump," she read, then stepped inside. "Come on in! Big enough for an elephant!"

He parked his bike. "Good place for a kiss."

Chapter 74

Gene and Mud sped along the dirt road to the logging camp. "Slow down or you'll tear up your car," Mud cautioned. "We're not in a big hurry. They've got a head start. Could be in Alaska."

Trees flew by. Gene grunted, "We'll find Peg's friend. What's her name?"

Mud's head bounced against the roof. "Rose . . . Ow! Thought you were going to slow down."

Gene went faster. "Yeah. If anyone knows anything, she will. Think she knew about this plan when she came down to Peg's party?"

"Who knows? If she did, I'll bet Peg swore her to secrecy. You ever pick up Peg was interested in Ralph?" A deer jumped in front of them. "Watch out!" Mud warned.

Gene veered to the left. "She liked his stories."

"Me, too. He sure had a lot of them. Made Alaska sound fascinating. And, of course, there's the thing with Charlie," Mud reminded.

"I know. They've been best friends long as I can remember." Gene slowed as the road separated. "Which way do I turn?"

"Road to the right looks more used," Mud gestured, "and there's a lotta tree stumps up ahead."

Minutes later, they pulled into the camp and piled out into an empty yard. "Men probably out in the forest." Mud walked toward the first building. "Cooks and families should be around here somewhere. I'll take this building." He waved his hand, "You wanna go that way?"

"OK," Gene strode off. He knocked at the door of the first cabin. No answer. Three cabins later, he heard children laughing and spotted a blond woman next to them that he recognized as Peg's friend, Rose.

Puzzled, she turned at his approach, then walked his way. "Took me a minute to recognize you."

He jogged over and stuck his hand out. "I'm Peg's oldest brother, Gene."

"Of course, I remember you." She hesitated. "You know Peg's not here?"

"That's why we're here." Gene lowered his voice as a couple of little girls, chasing a kitten, came close.

She drew back. "Who's 'we'?"

"Mud and I."

"Mud's here, too? But Peg's not here," she repeated.

"We know. We're trying to find her."

She twisted to see as the thwack of a baseball bat sounded. The boy ran to first base. "But she went to Alaska."

"We know," he sighed.

Rose's brow furrowed. "How?"

"Got a letter," Gene growled.

"It's true then. When she told me, I couldn't believe it!" She shook her head. "I never knew she was interested in Ralph."

"Neither did we. Did you know her plans at her birthday party?" Gene pressed.

"No, but I've wondered if Charlie's engagement pushed her over the edge." Rose turned and called out to a couple of boys, arguing over the baseball bat. "Better go. How long you staying? Food here's wonderful."

"Depends." Gene reached out and touched her arm. "Just a minute. Did she tell you where in Alaska?"

"Sorry, she didn't. Last-minute decision. Told me and left the next day. Didn't have time to talk." Rose looked at her watch. "Recess is over, but if you're still here after school, we can talk more," she offered, then rang the school bell. Children ran over and formed a line in front of her.

Gene tried again. "Know anyone else she might have confided in?"

"No. You might talk to kitchen staff. That's where she spent most of her time."

"Thanks." he stomped off, feeling he'd accomplished nothing.

Mud stood talking to a man, saw Gene and waved him over. "Learn anything?"

"No, how 'bout you?"

"Thanks for your time," Mud stated as he shook hands with the worker. "No leads. Talked to three people." He thumbed toward the kitchen. "That guy's been working with Ralph since he got here, Ralph talked about Alaska a lot, but never mentioned taking Peg."

Gene gritted his teeth. "Anyone notice him flirting with Peg?"

"Nope. Everyone's as surprised as we are," Mud grumbled.

"No one had any idea where in Alaska?" Gene demanded, somewhat overwhelmed.

Mud stepped back. "Don't yell at me. Not my fault!"

"Sorry. Makes me furious. That ol' man taking advantage of Peg!"

"Maybe he didn't. She's no dumb Dora. He spins a good tale. Maybe she wanted to go," Mud surmised.

"Even if she did, he should a told her no!" Gene griped. "Well, if there's no info here, we'd better go. Maybe we can catch up with 'em."

"Really? We have no idea where they are," Mud doubted.

Gene grunted, "Come on. I'd like to get my hands on that ol' bird."

"One guy said he thought Ralph mentioned Ketchikan."

"Well, that's something," Gene groused and cranked the Model T.

Chapter 75

When the ship stopped in Ketchikan, an ol' timer sat on the pier. Gray hair stuck out at odd angles from a stocking cap. Blue eyes struggled to see out of a wrinkled visage covered with hair. His beard hung halfway to his waist. "He a sourdough?" Peg whispered.

"Looks like one," Ralph said.

"Looks like that pot of sourdough bubbled over," she joked as she hoisted her suitcase on her shoulder and started up the ramp.

"Here, let me help you," Ralph offered as they threaded their way through buildings crowding the pier.

Peg forged ahead, then took a minute to stop, breathe in the raw air, and admire the houses clinging to the hillside. "No thanks, I've got it."

Ralph trotted up. "We need a ride to town, a hotel, then directions to the cannery office." He stopped a passerby. "Can you direct me to the office of Pacific American Fisheries?"

The young man stopped. "See that cluster of buildings down there on the water? It's just north of that."

Peg set her suitcase on the wooden sidewalk, hanging over the water. She stood drinking in the tall pines, crowding the mountains backed by majestic peaks. "I can't believe I'm really here!"

"Coming?" Ralph encouraged.

The hike left them both breathless. "Don't leave your suitcase outside," Ralph directed and led on until they found themselves across the desk from a supervisor.

"Ralph Sparks," he held out his hand. "Wrote about a job and told to report here . . . " He pulled a letter from his shirt pocket.

"Have a seat," a middle-age man with salt and pepper hair offered. He pulled over another chair. "This lovely lady your daughter?"

"My *wife*, Peg."

Flummoxed, he cleared his throat and rummaged in his desk. "Yes, well, we have multiple canneries. Have a preference?"

Ralph leaned in. "Where are they?"

"Mouths of rivers. Salmon school there 'fore going upstream to spawn, and salmon spoils fast, so it's handy. Your wife interested in working?"

"Not now. She's an experienced nurse."

"Thank you!" Peg hugged Ralph after they left. "My dreams of Alaska never included working in a stinking fish cannery!"

"Well, mine didn't either, but need a little more money to do my own fishing."

"I know someone who's caught a fish or two and can help," Peg bragged.

"I'm counting on it!"

Peg hung back. "How long will we be here?"

"A couple of weeks. Honeymoon shrank the bank."

Her brow crinkled. "What will I do for two weeks?"

"Oh, I'm sure you'll find something. Need to check things out. May take a while. Don't wait up for me."

When he hadn't returned by ten o'clock, Peg crawled into bed. The next morning, Ralph slithered out of bed early. "See you tonight," he whispered, kissing Peg's forehead. She stirred. A smell wafted into her fuzzy brain—alcohol? Later, she squinted at the clock which read eight o'clock. *A whole day with nothing to do.* Finally, urged by her growling stomach, she surrendered and dressed. *Well, low on money. Better find a grocery store for breakfast.*

She gulped brisk air as eyes flew to magnificent pine-clad mountains. Her shoes beat a hollow staccato down the boardwalk to the harbor. Wooden buildings waded into the ocean on stilts. She passed a laundry advertising baths for two-bits. A slender Oriental man lugged a basket of clean clothes past her, with his long braid swinging behind. A hand-painted sign "CREEK STREET" caught her eye; she turned. One building looked like a bar. *But alcohol's illegal.* She peered in the window; heard a wolf whistle and glared over her shoulder. A scantily dressed woman pulled aside a curtain and peered out a dirty upstairs window. "Move on," she admonished. *This is obviously an unsavory part of town.* Peg backtracked to her hotel to ask directions to a grocery store. The hotel clerk didn't look up. "Two blocks north." He gestured with his thumb.

After the first block, she spotted the store: Sunde & dEvers Co. Groceries, Troller Supplies, Sailmakers. A bell over the door jangled. The smell of apples and wood smoke washed over her, bringing a wave of homesickness. An image of her mother behind the counter and old men gathered around the stove filled her mind. *Better leave before I embarrass myself with tears. In my excitement of traveling, I've not thought much about home. How long has it been? Almost three weeks? Feels like another life.* Her appetite forgotten, she returned to her room and sat at the desk.

Dear Folks,

Please forgive me for eloping. I hadn't planned on it. However, I've enjoyed the travel and sights immensely. We spent several days exploring in Vancouver and are in Ketchikan, hoping to be on a ship soon. It's beautiful country! Don't know when I'll be home but will keep in touch and let you know my permanent address. I'm well and happy. Hope you are also. Miss you all!

She licked the envelope, and her stomach complained again. She returned to the store, mailed the letter, bought an apple, cheese, bread, and nibbled while window shopping. Then, she spied a baseball field. It beckoned; she followed. She found peace as she climbed the wooden grandstand to the top row. She sat and finished her food, watching the ships in the harbor. In the next bay over, wooden poles stood anchored in the ocean with perpendicular logs attached in a rectangular shape. *It resembled the skeleton of a house wall, lying atop the water.* Five of these floated in the ocean, not far from a large building. *Huh, must have something to do with fishing.* She brushed the crumbs from her lap, and leaned back on her hands. She pushed her face to the sun, closed her eyes, listened to the birds, then bounced down the bleachers and looked about for her next adventure. *Think I'll check out those floating logs.*

A trail to the ocean ended short of her destination. She climbed back and followed the road to the center of town, passing a Chinatown and ending up along the coastline. She stood, puzzling over the floating logs when a man meandered by. "Hello, can you tell me what that is?" she motioned toward the ocean.

"That there's fish traps." His toothless mouth caved in on itself and burrowed back into his full beard.

"How do they work?"

"Wire net's hooked ta them logs. Held down by anchors. Fish can't escape 'til they're brailed out."

"Until what?" Peg puzzled.

"Scooped out, dumped in 'ta the scows and taken to the cannery. This here's the canned salmon capital a the world!" he bragged.

"What about local fishermen? Any fish left for them?"

He inclined his head toward the bay. "Them's pirates."

"Pirates?" Peg doubted.

"Yes 'um." He gestured toward a man in a ragged sweater and baggy wool pants with a hat pulled low. "Put them wet burlap sacks over the sides'a their boats, so as ya can't see their letters, then rob tha traps. But ya won't find a jury here 'bouts would convict them!" He smirked. "And them bored and seasick trap watchmen on the Inside Passage is always up for tak'un a bribe."

Peg spotted a flash of silver, glinting in the sun as a boat unloaded fish. "Thanks!" she called over her shoulder and ran for a closer look. Two men in rubber chest waders stood knee deep in a small boat, throwing hundreds of salmon into a wooden container floating next to the dock.

*Well, shiver me timbers! These pirates **ARE** after silver! Thousands of silver.*

She spent the rest of the afternoon exploring the bustling city. At supper time, she headed to the hotel. *I'm bushed.* She flopped onto the bed. *Wonder if Ralph'll be back to eat.*

When Ralph returned, he threw his hat on the chair. "Been abed all day?"

"No! I've walked from one end of this town to the other," she exaggerated. "Lotta people here."

"Yeah. Ketchikan booms in summer. People come to work the fisheries."

"How was work?" Peg stopped. "You stink! Yuck! What's all over you?"

"Fish blood and guts," he advanced with a smile.

"Stay back," she warned, putting her hand up. "That's your job?"

"New help gets the worst: on the slime line. Twelve to eighteen hours of gutting fish. Could drive a fellow to drink," he moved closer.

"Speaking of that, where'd you go last night?"

"A bar," Ralph admitted. "Wanted to talk to some fellas. Get the lay of the land, so to speak."

"So, what'd you learn?"

"Not much but got some leads at work."

"Clean up first. I'll wait in the lobby." She held her nose and inched around him.

"Chicken!" he laughed.

Peg perched on the only chair in the small lobby, a wooden straight back with no cushion, and watched the parade of people: mostly men in woolen work clothes—though one man in a suit and hat strode by as if late for an appointment. A Chinese—or was she Japanese—woman with her head bent down minced quickly by. *This is worlds from Newport where I know most everyone! Wonder what Ralph's news is. How long will we be in town? Maybe I'd better try to find a job.*

A door down the hall slammed. Ralph entered with his brisk, confident step. Below oiled and combed hair, teasing brown eyes lit up his tanned, whiskery face. No one would guess he was fifty-three years old. "Let's grab some grub," he held out his hand and pulled her up from the chair.

Peg contained her questions until after they'd ordered. "What'd you find out?"

"Well, that's why I'm back early. Other poor devils may be there until midnight cleaning fish!"

"And you're not because?"

"It came up that I oversaw the kitchen on a logging camp. Just so happens they need cooks and waitresses. During lunch break, I talked to the supervisor, and we both start tomorrow morning!" He leaned back, folded his arms and beamed. "Boss let me go early as we report at 4:30 tomorrow morning."

"He knows we're not staying long?"

"Didn't ask, and I didn't volunteer. We'll stay until we replace our honeymoon money."

Peg squirmed.

"You still want to, don't you?"

"It's just, well, I didn't plan on extra stops," Peg admitted.

"That's part of the adventure! We have no schedule we have to meet."

Peg bit her lip. "Guess I'm not used to so much freedom."

"Wonderful, though, huh?" He reached for her hand.

CHAPTER 76

At seven o'clock the shrill scream of a steam whistle brought men forth like ants from a stirred pile. Peg watched as workers segregated themselves into different buildings. Dozens of Chinese workers entered a building emanating sweet and sour smells. Alaskan Natives shuffled toward another. Whites entered her mess hall. The rest of the morning reminded her of logging camps. A room bigger than her school gym held long lines of picnic tables. Men filed in and got down to business. They ran Peg ragged, trying to keep the table supplied with copious amounts of bacon, sausage, toast, doughnuts, pancakes and coffee. Food disappeared like her memories with Charlie.

However, unlike the no talking at the logging mess hall, a cacophony of different languages echoed between walls: Spanish, Scandinavian, Italian, and others she didn't recognize. Slurping, burping men and scraping, raking silverware gave birth to a throbbing headache. When the melee finally exited, she slumped into a chair.

"You okay? First mug-up at ten." Ralph swept by, broom in hand.

"Mug-up?" she echoed after him.

He finished sweeping the aisle, worked back and paused in front of her.

"Yep. Mug-up. Ten o'clock, men'll be back for coffee, doughnuts, pastries. We'll serve lunch at noon, afternoon mug-up at three, dinner at five, and final mug-up nine tonight. At the peak of the salmon run, there's a midnight meal, too."

When do they have time to clean fish? Peg wondered as Ralph finished sweeping down the row. *No wonder they needed kitchen help.*

Ralph bent, captured dirt in his dustpan and worked his way back. "You know, the cooks are considered the most important employees as they keep the workers' morale and energy going."

"Why separate mess halls?" Peg wondered.

"China Gang don't speak English and don't eat our kind'a food. Got a lot of tea, rice an' fish there. Heard they got opium to keep 'em happy. Noticed gardens behind the China Gang's quarters, so must grow some of their own food. The Dagos, Chinks an' Natives live with their own kind and aren't paid as much as white workers."

"Not fair!" Peg proclaimed.

"True, but what can we do?" Ralph shrugged. "Got company housing. Tomorrow, we'll leave the hotel. Gotta save money."

CHAPTER 77

G ene and Mud rented a waterfront room in British Columbia. Gene walked the docks, watching passengers and Mud checked hotels. In the evening, they compared notes.

"Any luck?" Mud hoped.

"Nope. Got the schedule of departing ships and made sure I was on the dock for each one. Peg didn't leave today," Gene assured him. "How about you?"

"Same thing. No hotels have a Ralph Sparks registered, but most clerks would only look back a few days. We may need to pretend to be the law," Mud speculated.

Gene shook his head. "No, we don't need more trouble. If we land in jail, we'll never find her. No ships leaving tonight. Let's find some grub, and we'll hit it again tomorrow. Wish we'd brought a photo!"

After three days of searching, Gene decided they'd missed them. "Guess we're lousy detectives," he joked. "Hope she's okay."

"Well, I'm tired of beating my gums. I don't think I've talked this much in my life!" Mud exclaimed. "Wish I'd realized Ralph was carrying a torch for Peg. I can be oblivious, but Peg and I are close, least I thought so." He hung his head.

"Don't worry. She'll get in touch when she can. She promised in her letter. Let's pack up, head home and see if they've heard anything." Gene started throwing clothes in his suitcase.

Mud uprooted himself from the chair. "Wish we had good news for the folks."

Gene slammed his suitcase shut. "Move it, will ya?"

"Don't get yourself in a lather," Mud growled.

"She'll be okay, Mud," Gene softened. "Peg's no milque toast. She can take care of herself."

Chapter 78

No more exploring the city. Drudgery swapped places with adventure. Peg worked long hours now. After ten straight days in the kitchen, she rubbed the back of her neck. *I miss my family, my job with Dr. Phillips, and if I'm honest, sometimes even Charlie. But I'm married and truly admire Ralph's cheerful nature and unflagging energy.*

A week later, Ralph sat figuring their money. "Looks like we can move on soon," he declared with a grin.

Peg perked up. "Really? How soon?"

"How about tomorrow? I gave our supervisor notice last week. Wasn't too happy either. Said we're two of his best workers. Even offered a raise, but I know you're ready for a change, and so am I."

Peg bounced on her tiptoes. "You mean it? We're going tomorrow?"

"Yep, pack your bags, girl. We're off to the Land of the Midnight Sun!"

"Yippee!" Peg kissed his cheek.

She awoke with a feeling of anticipation. From the boarding house, she ran downhill until she spotted Ralph, striding toward her.

"Ho! You ruined my surprise—bringing you breakfast in bed." He handed her a plate.

"Good. I wake up hungry!" She nibbled a piece of bacon as they walked back.

"I got up early and purchased our tickets. Ship leaves in an hour. You be ready?"

"You know it!" Peg started in on a biscuit.

They finished packing, returned the plate to the mess hall and started for the docks. "Oh! A gorgeous morning!" Peg's excitement colored everything. "Isn't it interesting how your life can change so quickly?" She looked back at Ralph. "What's our first stop? Where we staying? How long will it take?"

Ralph threw his head back and guffawed, "Now that's the Peg I know and love!"

CHAPTER 79

M etal walls vibrated the ship's stuffy cabin, keeping time with the engine's steady thumping. Peg threw her suitcase on the bed and scurried up top. Creaking metal groaned as they got underway. Waves of oil filled the air. She faced the wind to escape the stench, bending her knees a little to ride the ocean swells. As before, she stayed on deck as much as possible, drinking in the haunting, lonely landscape. "I belong here," she vowed. Every night, Peg and Ralph stood on deck in awe of the vast sea of stars. Peg rubbed the back of her neck. "You ever wonder if there's people on other planets somewhere, looking at this same scene?"

"Guess I haven't thought much about it. Been too busy with thoughts of this life."

"Wouldn't you love to explore up there?"

Ralph disagreed. "Whadda say we explore Alaska first?"

Five days later, they arrived in Homer. The ship bumped and scraped against pilings. Peg had suitcase in hand before it sloshed to a stop. She scanned the deck for Ralph. Passengers lined to disembark, but Ralph had disappeared. She inched along, thinking he was behind her and would catch up. After stepping off and moving out of the path of other passengers, she still didn't see him. *Should I go back on board? Maybe he got off before me?*

Wooden crates, heaved off the boat by tanned, windswept men passed by her. She moved her things, started up the dock, surveyed the area and trudged toward grey weathered buildings, shuddering in the wind. By the time she got to the top, she worried. *What if Ralph was down there, trying to find her?* The prospect of hauling her load back down and up again gave her pause. At the top of the hill, she set her suitcase on its end and plopped on it to catch her breath. A familiar figure darted out of the Salty Dawg Saloon, cast an eye down at the boat getting unloaded and took off at a trot.

"Ralph!" she called and waved. He turned, lost his balance on loose gravel and careened about. Peg's hearty laugh belted forth. "Loved the dance," she sputtered.

He swept off his hat, slid into his performance role and took a bow. "Sorry! Thought I had a few minutes before you unloaded. You musta nearly beat the crew off!"

"When I noticed you and your suitcase gone, thought I'd better pack up. Where were you?"

"Met a guy on board, Sundsby. Been here a while. Peppered him with questions about work and such. Come to think of it, I sounded 'bout like you," he paused. "Anyway, he's wanting to hustle to Halibut Cove and start his own fishing enterprise. After we talked a while, I offered to go in on it with him!"

Peg pursed her lips. "Without talking to me?"

"Didn't think you'd mind. Thought you'd be happy. After all, it's a great opportunity! Can't believe just ran into him. I've learned from all your questioning!"

Peg folded her arms across her chest. "Don't you think since we're married, I deserve a say in what we'll be doing?"

"Oh," Ralph lowered his chin. "Got so excited. Thought you would, too."

"Maybe, but in the future, I want to be consulted. After all, it's my life and my money, too."

"You're right. Lesson learned," he apologized. "Guess I've been on my own so long I'm not used to asking permission."

"I'm not talking about permission. I'm your wife, not your mother. I mean we should decide these things together."

His face flushed. "OK, so do you want to or not?"

"Guess I'll trust you on this one. Don't know anything about it." She lugged her suitcase toward town. Ralph's boots crunched the gravel behind her. She realized she didn't know where she was going and stopped. "Have you arranged a place for us?"

"There's rooms above the Salty Dawg," he offered timidly, fearing her reaction.

"A saloon?" she raised her eyebrows. "What about there?" She spotted the Driftwood Inn.

"Fine with me. Let's see if they have a place. Want to wait outside with the bags while I check it out?" He set his suitcase next to hers.

A few minutes later, he appeared and cleared his throat. "No rooms tonight. After the boat comes in, they're usually full. Can you stay for a night or two in the Salty Dawg? It's clean, at least downstairs in the saloon, so I'll bet it is upstairs, too." Drained from their first disagreement, Peg followed.

Half a dozen men, a couple still in hip boots, played cards, rubbing stubbly faces while studying their hands. One pulled out a red bandana. "Haw-choo!" They never raised their eyes until Peg spoke. "Ralph, see if they have a room . . . with a view." Peg's voice hesitated when every head in the place looked up. She moved closer to Ralph.

"Scuze 'em, mam," the burly bartender spoke. "Don't see many females up here."

Peg felt eyes burning into her back. She shrugged her shoulders, spun and greeted the crowd, "Hello, I'm Peg Tarbet. I mean Sparks," she stumbled and blushed, pointing to Ralph, "This is *my husband,*

Ralph." *Might as well make that clear from the start.* "And we've come to Alaska from Washington."

Upon hearing she was married—at least claiming to be, changing her name had made some wonder—their heads dropped back to cards. Ralph took her hand and led her upstairs. She glanced over her shoulder and caught all eyes, watching her climb.

"I'm not used to being such a big sensation," she whispered as Ralph opened the door to their room.

"You don't realize how sensational you are!" He took her bag and gave her a hug. "Got a lunch date with Sundsby to discuss our venture. Want to come?"

"Of course. What would I do here? Wouldn't dare go downstairs by myself and cause another commotion! Saw a lighthouse at the end of the spit. Do we have time to go there first?"

"Depends," Ralph leaned in, a slow smile spreading.

"On what?"

"How much time we spend here," he laughed.

She started for the door. "I'm ready. Let's go."

They passed The Cook Inlet Courier, Berry's Trading Post, and streets named Bunnell Avenue, Ohlson Lane, and Jenny Lane. "Must be after former residents," Peg guessed.

"I'm sure," Ralph agreed. "Sundsby told me Homer's named after a man who came here years ago with the Alaska Gold Company. Who knows? Someday there may be a Peg Street in Alaska."

Peg tapped her lips with her forefinger. "Hum, I think Sparks Street has a better ring to it."

They crunched through gravel thrown from the ocean nearly five miles to the end of the spit, along an arm of land jutting out into Kachemak Bay, then toward a whitewashed wooden lighthouse with a red roof. "Think the lighthouse keeper lives there?" Peg asked. "Yes. Bet they're some mighty big waves during a storm surge." Ralph took out his pocket watch. "Better leave soon, so's not to be late for Sundsby. We have a hike back."

Peg took a last look out across the water to dark mountains with fluffy clouds crawling along the top, trailing a gray retinue. "Coming!" She jogged to catch up.

Chapter 80

Ralph spotted Sundsby across the room. Peg followed, surprised to see two men. *Who's that other young man?* Upon seeing Peg, they both stood. The older, bearded man took off his hat, exposing a shock of brown hair and extended his hand, "Sundsby's my name. Glad to meet you, Mrs. Sparks." Peg leaned forward and shook. "This is Malamute Kid, good friend of mine." The Kid's white-blond hair contrasted with his tanned face. Unruly curls danced atop his ears and spiraled over his collar. His smooth cheeks and thinness added to his youthfulness. *He looks like a teenager.*

"Have a seat." Sundsby pulled a chair out for Peg.

"Unusual name," Ralph said to Malamute, "I'm assuming you have dogs."

"Darn right!" Sundsby declared, "Best dogs around."

The Malamute Kid looked pleased.

"Maybe we'll catch a ride after the snow flies," Ralph hinted at the possibility.

The Kid came to life. "Wanna a ride on my sled? Happy to give you one or teach you to mush. It's not hard. My dogs do all the work."

"I'd love to!" Peg jumped at the offer. "Tell me more about your dogs."

At the mention of his dogs, his shyness evaporated. "Well, lead dog's the most important one; that'd be Nugget. There's Akyla which means eagle, Bear and Blizzard, beautiful Bella, Isis after the Egyptian goddess, Nikko and Chinook. Those are my top sled dogs. I've others. I breed them."

"Can I see them sometime?" Peg couldn't contain her curiosity.

"Anytime. Not many roads up here. We use rivers to travel in summer and dog sleds in winter."

"Your dogs are Malamutes?" she asked.

"True and my family. I know them well. I can tell what they need from their bark or howl."

Peg hankered after more information and leaned in for details. "Seriously? Like what?"

"Well, they 'sing' different songs when they're sad, happy, or want food. They even have a rain song and a snow song, too."

"How fascinating. They must be intelligent."

"They are! You should watch them when they see me coming with the harness. They begin barking, yipping, and bellowing. They're made for this place!"

Peg took a drink of water. "Don't they ever get cold?" she asked, continuing her questioning.

"Naw, they're most comfortable at ten to twenty below. Could kill a dog to bring him indoors in his winter coat." The Kid's face beamed. "When the temp falls, I give 'em hot water, so they won't dehydrate. Have to mix it with blood to get 'em to drink it before it freezes again."

Peg grimaced. "Yuck! Hot bloody water?"

"They love it."

"Are they part wolf?"

"Have long snouts like a wolf and howl instead of barking, so lots of people think so. But purebreds are not wolves. If they've interbred, they're called wolf dogs. Malamutes have long snouts to warm the air before it reaches their lungs and a waterproof coat that's double. They use their bushy tails to warm their snouts and their long legs help 'em through the snow," The Kid explained.

"Wow! You know a lot."

He sat taller. "Study everything I can get a hold of. And after working with them for years, you learn things. Malamutes are bred for strength. Depending on the size and training, they can pull up to 3,000 pounds. Siberians are full of energy and small to move cargo fast."

"What do you say, Peg?" Ralph interrupted.

She'd been oblivious to anyone's conversation except hers with Malamute. "About what?"

"Are we able to leave with Sundsby tomorrow?"

"Sorry. Got interested in The Kid's dogs."

Ralph bristled a little. "I noticed. Sundsby and I have a plan. We need a tent and supplies today if we want to travel with him. I made this list of his suggestions. There are no roads to Halibut Cove or in it, 'bout twelve miles across Kachemak Bay from here."

"What will we do there?"

"There's herring salteries, and we can fish for ourselves during time off."

"I'm ready. We'll get after that supply list. Just let me finish my lunch." She picked up her fork.

CHAPTER 81

The boat ride across the bay transfixed Peg. "There's Gull Island," Sundsby yelled over the motor as they passed thousands of seabirds nesting. Snow hugged crevices of rugged mountains that wore a halo of clouds. From their high vantage point, they presided over tree-covered islands. Ralph saw a brown bear with two cubs traversing the base of the forest. "Look!"

Peg shivered involuntarily. Memories of Roy flooded her mind. By the time they entered the mouth of the cove, they'd seen a moose, seals and several eagles. *If it weren't for bears, this would be paradise.*

On arrival, Sundsby showed them where to set up their wall tent in a little clearing close to the beach. He helped Peg and Ralph nail together a wooden floor, attach four-foot walls and set the tent stop. They fit the Yukon stove under the hole for the pipe, set up cots and made a few shelves from leftover wood. "Home Sweet Home!" Ralph declared as they moved their belongings in. Too tired to cook, they ate a cold dinner of sardines and bread and walked down to the beach. They looked out over the moonlit bay and listened to the water, gently slapping the shore.

"Can't wait to reel me in one of those big halibuts." Ralph squeezed Peg's hand.

"Maybe I'll catch one first."

"Probably!" Ralph laughed.

Raucous magpies and chattering squirrels awakened Peg the next morning. The noise, along with the smell of damp canvas and wood smoke, reminded her that she was in Alaska! Both she and Ralph had slept longer than usual. She slipped from bed, pulled on boots and struck out, looking for a bush since they hadn't dug an outhouse. Walking below spruce, birch and alder trees, she strolled down the beach, looking for a secluded place to bathe. Bright spots of color up ahead signaled berry bushes. She stopped, noting a fallen tree, so she could find them again when she had a pail.

A rustle and branches snapping caught her attention. A brown hulk moved among the bushes. She froze. *A bear! What had Ralph taught her?* Her mind went blank, her heart pounded and her breathing quickened. She held still, trying to remember his instructions. Finally, she backed down the beach, never taking her eyes off the trees. Tripping over a rock behind her, she fell on her backside. "Oomph!" Palms stinging and behind smarting, she clambered up, sure the bear would come raging out of the forest. It stood on its hind legs. "Ralph!" She screamed and ran. "Ralph! Ralph!"

Ralph bent over a small fire, slowly poking pieces of driftwood he'd gathered into the center. He heard her panicked cry, dropped the wood, tripped over the coffee pot and loped to her, slid to a stop and held out his arms. She flew into them. "A ba-ba-ba-be-ar," she squeaked out.

He looked over the top of her head. "What did I tell you was the WORST thing to do?"

She shook her head.

"**Run!** Come back to camp, and next time you feel like taking a hike, grab a gun," he warned as he escorted her back to the fire.

She slumped to her knees. "I'm such a ninny! Can't believe I lost control. I'm not usually like this."

"I know, but this state is full of bears, so you'd better be prepared," he counseled, picked up the coffee pot, refilled it and put it back on the fire.

The commotion brought Sundsby jogging down the beach. "You guys all right?" he paused, huffing a little.

"Yeah. A bear. Peg's scared of them since one killed her friend."

"Well, good to have a healthy respect for 'em. You never know what those dirty S.O.B.s will do," Sundsby warned as he spit a stream of tobacco into a bush. "Why, already this year one guy got mauled when . . ."

Ralph shook his head and shot a look that cut him off in mid-sentence.

"Right. See ya later." Sundsby strolled back.

"Why don't you finish unpacking while I do some planning with Sundsby," Ralph suggested, hoping routine deeds would take Peg's mind off the incident.

"Just leave the gun."

"Sure. We'll come on the run if we hear it," Ralph promised her.

I've got to overcome this bear phobia! She wiped sawdust from freshly made shelves and set the tin plates, cups, spoons and forks neatly on the shelf nearest the table. She pulled the clothes from suitcases, putting Ralph's on the top shelf, even though she was almost as tall as he.

An hour later, she had their few possessions organized and wished for a broom to sweep the sand, sawdust and mud from the floor. *Guess I'll have to make one.*

Leaving the tent, she perused the area for the bear. Dark clouds gathered over the mountain. With her pocket knife, she cut long grasses, dried weeds and a pine branch for a handle. Using twine, she lashed the grasses to the branch. Anxious to try it out, she scurried back to the tent surprised to see a Native woman looking in the door.

"Hello?"

The little woman jumped and turned. Her wide grin showed a missing front tooth. Her pungent body odor stopped Peg. "Can I help you with something?" *I don't want to create another scene and yell for Ralph again.*

The woman stood silently.

"I'm Peg," she held out her hand.

The woman stepped forward and silently shook it.

"What's your name?" Peg pressed.

"Amka," she patted her chest.

"Nice to meet you, Amka." Peg scanned the area. "You live around here?"

Amka looked away.

"Where?"

She continued her wide grin but didn't respond.

"She doesn't speak English," Ralph called as he walked toward them.

Peg moved in his direction. "Who is she? How'd she get here? What does she want?"

"Questions, questions, questions!" Ralph replied, shaking his head.

"She's Sam's squaw, but can't say what she wants. You ask her?"

Peg threw her hands up. "How am I supposed to if she can't speak English?"

"I bet you'll think of a way," Ralph teased, mocking Peg's inquisitive nature.

Amka waved goodbye and started down the beach.

"Oh, here comes Sundsby." Ralph beckoned him over with a simple gesture.

"Know what your wife wanted?"

"Wondered who lives here, I imagine," Sundsby replied. "She'll be happy to have another woman on the island."

Peg moved closer. "How are we to communicate?"

"She knows a little English. Just act out whatever you're trying to say."

Ralph looked up. "Looks like it's clearing."

"Naw, probably a sucker hole," Sundsby predicted.

Peg followed his gaze and asked another queston: "A what?"

"A sucker hole. It suckers ya inta believing the weather is clearing, but probably ain't. You'll be seein' more of 'em. July is the best month around here. In August there's lotta what we call 'liquid sunshine,' " he shared.

Raindrops began dropping right on cue as if they'd been listening.

CHAPTER 82

P eg awoke to canvas flapping in the strong wind. Water drizzled into rain barrels at the corners of the tent. *Plop-plop* was punctuated by a steady *plink-plink* against something metal. *Oh, rain.* Her tooth throbbed. The whole side of her face ached. She cradled her face. Her tossing disturbed Ralph.

"You okay?"

"No, my tooth's killing me."

"It's almost light. I'll see if Sundsby's got clove oil. That'll numb it, but you need a dentist," Ralph rose and pulled his pants on.

Peg moaned. "How far's the dentist?"

"Don't know. I'll find out." He slipped out into the dripping semi-dark. Twenty minutes later, she heard the canvas flap open. "A boat's headed to Homer at ten. Get ready and I'll take you."

"You don't need to miss a whole day of work. I'll be fine," Peg protested.

"Sure?"

"I'm sure. Thanks for finding a ride." Peg crawled out of bed and crept from the tent to find a bush. The rain had let up, but a strong wind lifted her nightgown. She fought it down, returned, dressed, and put on a hat rather than deal with her hair. Sensing a presence, she turned around and jumped. Amka stood watching, waiting patiently for Peg to acknowledge her.

"How long you been there? Don't you knock?" Peg growled. When Amka held out a small glass vial, Peg smelled cloves. "Oh, thank you," she apologized. She poured a couple drops on her finger and rubbed it around the gum of the offending tooth. Amka quietly left.

Peg sat on the dock, pulled up her collar and slouched into her wool coat, her back to the wind. The boat's engine growled. She scuttled aboard, hoping for a quick departure. After they got underway, the jarring boat ride compounded her pain.

When they finally tied off, Peg staggered uphill against the bullying wind and dove into the first building available—The Salty Dawg. She cringed remembering the men's reaction last time. However, pain outweighed her embarrassment. She walked straight to the barkeeper. "Can you please direct me to the closest dentist?" All heads turned her way.

The bartender put away the glass he'd been drying, "Yes."

"Well," Peg prodded, "where is it?"

"Anchorage," he answered straight faced, as a chuckle spilled through the room.

"Can't wait," Peg whined, wincing in pain. "Don't you know someone who could help me, a doctor maybe?"

"Nope."

Crestfallen, she turned and started for the door. "Madam," a towering blonde with ice blue eyes stood up and looked down at her. "Ya might want ta try the blacksmith. He pulled a tooth for me once."

"Thank you. Can you direct me, please?"

"Turn right. Go 'bout half a mile same side of the street."

"You're very kind." Peg shoved the door open against the wind, holding tightly to her hat with one hand, her face with the other, and stumbled up the street.

Breathless, she entered the blacksmith's, waiting for her eyes to adjust to the dark. Some rodent scurried across a dirt floor, littered with old horseshoes and ashes. A trail of wood chips led to a rusty iron stove attached to a bent stovepipe, snaking its way out the roof. Red coals winked from the forge on the opposite wall. A wooden workbench cluttered with metal buckets and torturous looking tools held up the third wall. Peg recognized a vise, hand drills, several horseshoes hanging on the walls and the V-shaped harrow someone had brought in for repairs leaning against the forge. A few feet from the forge, the prominent anvil stood atop a stump of wood nailed down with a couple of wide leather straps. Sparks flew as a muscular man in a leather apron pummeled a piece of iron.

Peg stood transfixed by flying sparks. The warm room made her yawn. She rocked to the rhythm like a lullaby. Finally, the blacksmith raised his sooty face and set down his hammer. *What's different about him? Oh, no beard. Maybe for safety reasons around fire.*

With her ears still ringing, she stepped forward, "Hello, I'd like to hire you."

"To do what?" He looked behind her, took a dirty handkerchief from his pocket and wiped his forehead.

"To pull my tooth." Peg hoped.

"Hell, lady! I ain't no dentist!"

"Please, mister. I hurt. A man at the Salty Dawg recommended you."

"Who?"

"I didn't ask his name. A tall blond man." Peg winced as another pain shot through.

"Lars," he grumbled. "Told him to keep it to himself."

"I'll pay you. Please. I know I can't make it all the way to Anchorage," she whimpered.

"It'll hurt like the dickens!"

"I know, but at least it'll heal."

The blacksmith moseyed to the window, picked up a glass, rummaged around on his workbench, found some liquor and poured the glass full. *At least that will numb my pain.* She opened her mouth and touched the offending tooth.

He grabbed heavy pliers. "Open wide!" Then he lifted the glass to his lips, downed it himself, and jerked out the tooth!

Blood ran down her face. She had no rag, so she grabbed her underskirt and tried to rip the fabric. The blacksmith walked to his tool bench and returned with a knife.

"Thanks," she mumbled, cut off the bottom of her skirt and mopped her face. She pulled money from her pocket, "How much?"

"Nuttin," he grunted, "if you promise not to advertise."

She cupped her face, hesitant to return to the stiff wind. *Thank goodness I remember Dr. Phillips' advice for a bad tooth!* She retraced her steps to The Salty Dawg. *How am I to rent a room without advertising the blacksmith? Maybe I should've let Ralph come with me after all.* Tears gathered in the bottom of her eyes. The wind subsided, lifting her spirits as she plodded back to the Salty Dawg.

A couple of men sat in the far corner, drinking. One looked up and stared. She rented a room, trudged up the stairs and fell onto the bed.

Two hours later, a raucous laugh from below brought her from the sleepy fog, trying to remember why her mouth hurt so. Her body ached for water. She struggled to sit up. The throbbing worsened. *That water in the pitcher fit to drink? No cup?* She tipped the pitcher, guzzled and spewed into the bowl, splashing bloody water down her chest. Wiping her hand across her face, she slumped on the bed. *I need to find some salt.* Just then, someone tapped at the door. The doorknob turned. *Did one of those men follow me?* The door cracked open, bringing her to her feet.

"Peg!" Ralph grimaced upon seeing her bloody blouse. "Sit down. Are you all right?" He dashed to her side and grabbed her elbow. "I should've come with you. Felt uneasy all day, so caught a boat over."

"How'd you find me?" she choked back tears.

"Not too many places to check," he assured her, moving her hair from her face. "Lie back. I'll take care of you."

"Need salt to gargle," she groaned in pain.

"Sure thing. Be right back," he promised and exited quietly.

The next day, sunshine streamed through the window, caressing Peg. She awoke ravenous. Ralph looked up from his book. "Well, well, well, look who's coming back."

"I could eat a whale!" she exclaimed.

"Around this country, that could probably be arranged," he laughed.

CHAPTER 83

B ack at camp, Peg paced. A breeze tugged at the tent's canvas, beckoning her out. *I'll go for a walk, find Amka, and make up for my earlier grouchiness. Better grab my gun.*

Far down the beach, someone pushed a canoe into the water as clouds started weeping. She slogged through sucking mud and blinked. *It looks like a harbor seal paddling the rowboat!* The "seal" stood. *Oh! It's someone in a seal skin hat.* Mesmerized by the bobbing hat, she jumped when a shot rang out. The seal lowered a rifle and rowed toward a red spot in the water. Peg drew nearer. *What had been shot?*

The drizzle gave way to a downpour. She scuttled home, clothes soaked, hair dripping, and started a fire in the Yukon stove. Shivering, she lugged in wood, peeled off her wet clothes, crawled under her blankets and snuggled into the warmth.

Charlie waved at her. She ran over. "What are you doing here? He held out his arms."

"I've come for you. I'm better!"

"You didn't hear?"

"Hear what?"

"I'm married."

Charlie swayed and grabbed his stomach.

Peg bolted awake. Shaking her head, she scrambled to find dry clothes. *How long does this rainy season last? I'm tired of liquid sunshine! Guess I'll start a pot of beans.* She left the beans to simmer, slapped at a mosquito buzzing in her ear, then skirted puddles out to the woodpile. *I'll make a sidewalk!* With axe and hatchet, she chopped at fallen logs. She tossed the rotten ones full of ants to the side. *They'll still burn.* After a few hours and multiple mosquito bites, the pile grew.

An appetizing aroma wafted out. *Oh! The beans!* She raced inside, leaving a trail of mud across the floor, added water, grabbed her new broom and swept her way back out.

"Why you've been busy as a little wren building her nest," Ralph said upon seeing the pile of logs. "What ya planning on doing with those?"

Peg scratched a bite on her neck. "Don't you recognize a sidewalk when you see one?"

"Where?" Ralph pretended to scour the area with his eyes.

"Have you no imagination?"

"Yes, I'm imagining myself eating something wonderful." Ralph closed his eyes and inhaled the delectable fumes floating from the pot. "What do I smell?"

Peg held back the tent flap. "Leave those muddy boots outside and follow me."

Ralph put his arms on Peg's shoulders and looked over her face. "Looks like mosquitoes have already eaten!"

"There's so many!"

"I'll find netting to sleep under 'til it gets cold. Sundsby said they're the worst in July and August. We'll need hats with netting, too. He also advised us to keep a green grass fire burning in a pail near the door, and they'll stay outta the tent."

Rain, mud, mosquitoes, rain, mud, mosquitoes—even Peg's cheery disposition began to flag. Huge clouds of the insects eclipsed the sun. Cabin fever struck. After three weeks, Peg approached Ralph.

"Is Alaska all that you hoped it would be?"

"I know this weather's wearing, but it won't last." Ralph removed the netting from his face. "Want to leave?"

"Been considering it," Peg admitted. "Haven't you?"

"Just socking away the money for our fishing enterprise keeps me going, I guess. We could leave and come back later." Ralph searched her face. "I don't want you unhappy. How 'bout a game of pinochle or cribbage," he said, trying to distract her.

Peg shook her head. "I'm sick of cards."

"Tell you what, let's flip for it." Ralph dug out a two-bit coin.

"Really? I'm torn. I've wanted to come here for so long, but not holed up in a tent every day! I can only knit, crochet, and play solitaire for so many hours a day. I'm about ready to join you in the saltery."

Ralph held out his hand. "Want to try? Heads we stay and tails we go?"

Peg exhaled, took the coin, threw it high, and caught it on the back of her hand. "Sure you want to decide this way?" She lifted her hand. "Heads it is. We stay . . . for now."

"Whew! Ya know, I was about ready to leave myself after we lost a man at work today." Ralph wiped his brow.

Peg gasped. "What? Someone got killed? What happened?"

"A horde of mosquitoes carried him off," Ralph deadpanned.

"Oh, you got me!" she laughed.

CHAPTER 84

The *arp, arp, arp* of a seal in the cove let her know the world had come to life. At the sound of water dripping, Peg groaned, then jumped at gushing sounds on the porch and slid into her shoes.

"Ralph?" she called thinking he'd taken a trip to the bushes.

"Amka," a feminine voice answered.

Peg grabbed her coat from the nail, wrestled it on top of her nightgown, and peered out the tent flap.

Amka stood patiently, rain dripping from her sealskin hat.

"So, it was *you* in the boat the other day!"

Amka shrugged her shoulders.

Does she understand me? "Come in, before you drown," Peg motioned. *How do I communicate?*

Amka sloshed in, creating a puddle and thrust forth a bundle wrapped in animal hide.

"For me? Should I open it?"

Amka stood quietly.

Peg struggled with the knotted leather and squeezed the contents. *Whatever's in here is soft.* Out fell fur-lined moccasins the toes beaded with three delicate blue flowers, each with a white inner ring and a yellow center.

"Forget-me-nots!" Peg hugged the gift. "I love this flower."

Amka's eyes lit. She did not know all the words but read Peg's joy and gratitude in her eyes.

"For me? Thank you!" Peg gave the stout little woman a hug. "Can you teach me?"

Amka made no reply.

Peg made sewing motions. "Teach me? How did you know my size?" Peg asked as she slipped them on.

Amka's brow furrowed.

Peg lifted her foot, measured it with her hands, shrugged her shoulders, and turned up her hands.

Amka pointed at the muddy footprint she'd left on the floor.

"You measured one of my tracks! Here, sit. I'll make you a cup of coffee."

Amka sat silently while Peg stoked the stove and filled the coffee pot with water. She retrieved a couple of biscuits from a metal tin, sat next to Amka and noticed the knee-high shoes she wore.

"Did *you* make those, too?" Peg gestured toward Amka's shoes.

"Mukluk," Amka answered.

"Oh, I know the name of them." Peg made the sewing motion again. "I want to make some for Ralph for Christmas," Peg thought aloud. "Can we start today? I need **something** to do during this rain!"

Amka backed out of the tent, beckoning.

"Hold on! I've got to dress!" Peg called after her.

They walked and walked and walked. "Where are we going?" Peg asked, but Amka tramped forward. *At least, we've a break from the rain.*

They traversed mounds, poking above squishy ground and skirted stunted bushes. A couple of hours later, Peg questioned the wisdom of coming. *Ralph doesn't even know where I am, and I have no idea how to get back.* Eventually, they crested a small hill, over-looking a Native village.

Several doorways cut into the side of a hill looked out with blank stares. A few dugouts boasted logs on the front wall. The rest had only a wooden door frame. The remaining walls lay buried.

"Is this where you're from?" Peg asked. *What's winter like shut into a dirt cave with no windows. What do they do when it turns cold? Hang skins over the openings?*

One of the half-naked children spotted them and shouted. People poured from the village. Amka trotted ahead, exchanging greetings. Soon, they gave their attention to Peg. Wide grinning faces looked up, babbling things she could only guess at. She forced a smile, trying not to wince from the smell of unwashed bodies.

Amka talked with an older woman who motioned for Peg to follow inside one of the dugouts. She shook her head. *No way do I want to be in close quarters if their homes smell like they do.* After a few minutes, Amka returned, holding an animal skin up for Peg's inspection. Peg fingered the soft leather, approving the texture. "Nice." Amka struck out.

"Wait!" Peg called. "You forgot to give this back."

Amka motioned Peg on. Baffled, she looked about frantically, not wanting to lose sight of her guide. She dashed forward and held the skin out to a woman who shook her head and pointed at Amka. "Guess it's hers." Peg glanced over her shoulder, making sure Amka was still in sight. "Wait!" she called and trotted off with the skin over her shoulder.

As they retraced their journey, Peg moaned. "What was that about?" she demanded. "You need someone to carry the hide for you!"

Amka thrust the hide at Peg. "Oh, for me?" Humbled, Peg understood. "For the mukluks I want to make? Thank you!"

Amka bowed her head shyly and walked home.

Soon, Ralph arrived. "How was your day?"

"Interesting."

He sat and began tugging at his boot. "How so?"

"I went on a 'walkabout' of sorts."

"By yourself?" Ralph worried.

"No, I went with Amka to some village."

Ralph took off his sock and rubbed his foot. "How was it?"

"A long way! I didn't know where we were going, but by the time I realized I was lost, I had no choice but to follow. Anyway, those poor people live in harsh conditions. I wonder how their little ones survive winter."

Ralph pulled off his other shoe. "It's better here, but farther north, lots of babies don't live 'cause mothers leave the weak ones to die."

Peg pressed her hands against her ears. "What! A mother leaves her baby?"

He peeled off his socks and hung them over the wood box. "If they're born at the wrong time of year, they do. They're nomads. Can't carry all their supplies and a baby, too. The ones born in the winter have a better chance of survival because they move by sled, so they can keep those babies—if they have enough food."

"Oh! That makes me sick." She tilted her head and looked in Ralph's eyes. "You know I planned to be an obstetrical nurse?"

"I know. Hard to understand. Sundsby told me one woman he knew had fifteen babies and only kept three."

"Don't tell me anymore!" Peg covered her ears and stormed outside. She stalked toward Amka's while Ralph watched from the tent door and spotted a bobbing boat. *Amka's fishing, with her gun. Wonder how hard it is to hit something from a wobbly boat.* Peg's ongoing shooting contests with Charlie came to mind, and she wanted to test herself.

CHAPTER 85

I just can't stop thinking of those abandoned babies! Peg scrubbed the floor furiously, trying to scrub the sad images from her head. Then she retrieved the crock of sourdough. She closed her eyes and shook her head, remembering Sundsby's claim as he proudly presented her with the start. "This here sourdough start's old. Been passed down from Gold Rush days!"

I suppose it could be true. She measured the flour into the mixing bowl.

"Peg! Peg!" A panicked call startled her. Dogs yipped and whined. She dropped the dough, rubbed her sticky hands on her apron and fumbled with the ties of the tent. When dogs began howling, she turned back for her gun and thundered down to Amka, screaming at the edge of the forest. A bear yanked a dog into the trees with others, snarling at its heels. Leveling the rifle, she pulled the trigger, but the bear disappeared with its breakfast. She lowered the gun. *Probably the bear that scared me.*

Two dogs loped back. One's ear hung. Blood covered its face. Amka knelt and called it. Peg followed them to Amka's where she disappeared in her tent, appearing a couple of minutes later with a tin full of dried leaves and strips of cloth. She motioned Peg closer, then sat cradling the dog's head in her lap. From her gestures, Peg understood she wanted a poultice of the herbs on the dog's wounds.

Peg picked up the tin and looked inside.

"*Chaithluk,*" Amka whispered.

She'd wrapped wounds at Dr. Phillips', so she bent to her work, trying to keep her hands steady as the dog growled and whined. *Never thought my first patient would be a dog.* A tear slid down Amka's cheek. *Had she left babies to die, too?*

After the dog fiasco, Peg remembered the bread and hurried home. It had overrun the bowl and crawled onto the freshly scrubbed floor. She shook her head, laughed, rolled up her sleeves, cleaned the floor, baked bread and put dinner on the stove. *I'll take bread to Amka, so I can check on her and the wounded dog.* She carefully wrapped a fresh loaf in a dish towel, laced her boots and tied the tent to keep critters out. *Sure wish we could talk. I've never had a close girlfriend, only Charlie.*

When she came near, she called, "Hello! Amka?" and knocked on the wooden frame of the tent. *Amka just came into my house. Should I do the same?* No response, so she walked around back. No one there. "Huh." She looked out in the bay. *Not there. I hoped we could start on Ralph's mukluks today.* She went back to camp, put the bread on a shelf, noticed a pair of Ralph's shoes under the bed and decided to trace the outline for a pattern.

At loose ends, she paced and decided to read one of Ralph's Alaska books. She became fascinated by how Native women made clothing from animal skins that their men had risked lives procuring. They tanned skins, then sewed with sinews to keep the cold and water out. Most men wore the same pair of pants their whole adult life, though some had a couple pairs. *Whew! Bet they stink!*

Chapter 86

After chores the next morning, Peg took the pattern of Ralph's shoe, the bread from yesterday and left early to catch Amka. She found her outside stacking firewood. She held out her pattern and made sewing motions with her hand. Then Peg pitched in stacking wood, delighting in the bright fall morning, the smell of sawdust and ocean. *Now this is the Alaska I dreamed of! Even the mosquitoes have died down.* Fall colors peeked out among the pine trees. She took off her jacket, wiped the moisture from her face and surveyed the pile of neatly stacked wood with satisfaction.

Amka walked to the fire pit and stirred the contents in the metal bucket, hanging from a wooden tripod over coals. Peg followed and peered down into fish stew simmering. Amka licked the wooden spoon, stirred a little more. She beckoned to Peg who pulled the pattern from her pocket, thinking it was time to sew, but Amka led her down a well-used path to a small clearing. *Now where's she taking me? Don't want another long hike.*

They stopped at a tiny white wooden house with the roof painted in red and white stripes. *A doghouse? Why's there a cross on it? Did Amka's dog die?* Peg circled the little house and found "Yura 1918-1919," painted on the back side of the cross. *So it IS a grave . . . for a baby or a dog?*

Amka wandered nearby, picking wild purple iris, yarrow and goldenrod. She lay them at the foot of the small house and started back.

"Wait!" Peg hustled, but Amka pushed on. *For someone with short legs, she sure moves fast!* By the time they got back to the beach, Amka had disappeared again. *That woman could rival Houdini! Guess I'll go home.*

Just then, Amka reappeared, carrying a bundle. She untied the bag, spilling several knives, some in short crescent shapes onto the sand. Peg picked up a metal teardrop tool.

Amka left again, returned with the hide, and spread it on the dirt. From Amka's motions, Peg understood she wanted the pattern of Ralph's boots and pulled it from her pocket. Amka traced two soles onto the hide with a piece of charcoal and picked up one of the knives. "Ulu," she said and bent to cut the first sole.

When finished, she handed Peg the ulu and watched her cut the second one. Then she retrieved a wooden slab, soap, and bucket of water. She sat with the slab between her legs, flipped the hide over and with another tool scraped off fur. After the area was smooth, she handed Peg the scraper and watched closely. Pointing out a spot of oil, she shook her head, "No, off." Peg worked to remove the spot, trying not to leave a hole in the hide. Then she handed it to Amka for inspection.

Amka took it to the bucket where she washed both soles thoroughly, wrapped them in fabric and said, "Tomorrow." She returned to her stew on the tripod, gave it a stir and waved goodbye to Peg.

"Guess lesson's over for today," Peg waved back and went home. While waiting for Ralph, she wrote her family.

25 September 1920

Dear Family,

I learn something new every day in Alaska. Today my neighbor, Amka, a Native woman, helped me start a pair of mukluks for Ralph (soft boots made from sealskin). We worked on the soles. Hope to have them finished by Christmas. Next, I'm going to have her teach me to hunt seals. Natives use their fur, but not bearded seals because its hide is too hard to work with. They use it for their mattresses. I learned this fact from one of the many Alaska books Ralph has collected. I've found things about Native culture to admire and some that shock me like the practice of abandoning babies if food is scarce. They're nomads and only keep babies if it's practical.

Ralph works in a cannery part of the day. Then he and his partner, Sundsby, fish on their own. It's so beautiful here. Mosquitoes have finally died down. Soon, we'll see Northern Lights, if it's a dark clear night. They're visible from just before midnight until three or four in the morning. Can't wait! They stay for about six months. I might have to become a night owl. Ha ha.

We have a bear close that's scared me a couple of times. Yesterday, he stole one of Amka's dogs and wounded another. I don't go far without my gun. Don't worry. I'm careful.

How's everyone? Miss you all terribly. Don't know when we'll see you. Probably won't come to the Lower 48 until after breakup next spring or summer. Please write to me and tell me all the news.

Peg Sparks

Homer, Alaska

They'll keep the letters at the post office until we collect them. When I find someone headed there, I'll send this letter, so this news may be dated.

Love to all,

Peg

Ralph yelled goodbye to Sundsby as she folded the letter in an envelope. *Perfect timing.*

She opened the door. *He looks extra happy.* "Can you mail this for me sometime?"

He took the letter and held it out to read the address. "How was your day?"

"Interesting. I have questions for you." She removed his hat, pecked his cheek and detected alcohol on his breath.

He put his arms around her. "Why am I not surprised?"

"Amka took me to a gravesite today with a house, 'bout the size of a doghouse. At first, I thought the dog that I doctored yesterday died, but it wasn't. You know who or what is buried there?"

"I do." He took off his gloves, blew on his hands, rubbed them together, perched on the edge of the bed and tugged at his boots.

Peg put her hands on her hips. "Well?"

He hiccupped. "And how will you reward me?"

"With a happy wife!" she groaned.

"Deal," he conceded, walked over, lifted the lid of the kettle and peered in.

"*WHEN* are you going to tell me?" Her voice rose a little.

He leaned over, inhaled the fish stew, and replaced the lid. "*WHEN* would you like me to?"

"Brother!" Peg rolled her eyes.

"It's a baby's grave."

Peg blinked. "Was the baby abandoned?"

"No, it's Amka's child. She had a baby before Sundsby."

Peg sank onto the edge of the bed. "What happened to the baby? How did they meet? Are they married?"

Ralph sat on the stump they used for a chair and rocked back and forth. "Not sure, at The Salty Dawg, and depends on who you ask, I guess."

"So where's the baby's father?"

"Dunno. Dinner ready?"

Peg rose and reached for the tin bowls on the shelf, inspected them and blew the sawdust off. "So how did they get together?"

"Put the food on, and I'll tell you everything I know about it," he promised.

She set everything out. "OK, I'm ready."

"For what?" Ralph took a bite.

"The story!" Peg moaned in frustration.

"Oh, that!" He took another bite. "Sundsby said Amka showed up exhausted and begging for food at the Salty Dog one winter. Had a baby strapped to her back . . . baby looked half-dead. Sundsby paid for a meal and a night's stay. He went to check on them the next day. She followed him home and has been with him ever since."

"How strange!" Peg mused, "Any idea why she left her other home?"

"Could be number of things. Sometimes, natives take a second wife, but that's unusual. They've enough trouble taking care of one family. They also trade wives. Could'a been unhappy with her husband. Maybe no food in her village. Maybe she got lost."

"So often I wish I could talk with Amka," Peg lamented. "You know what happened to the baby?"

Ralph tipped his bowl and drank the last bit. "Not really. Assume it didn't recover from the journey." He handed Peg the empty bowl. "More, please."

She ladled it full again. "Why the little house on the grave?"

"Wondered the same thing. Sundsby said they covered the grave with a blanket, then built the house for the departed's spirit to live in. He's the one who painted the baby's name and dates on the cross."

"Natives are Christians?"

"Wouldn't think so, but the Russian Orthodox Church was here years ago."

"Interesting. I'm sure Amka could tell me so many things."

"Why not teach her English?" Ralph suggested. "She's bright."

"Good idea!"

CHAPTER 87

All morning, Peg pondered the idea of teaching Amka English. *She's so hard to read. Either she smiles all the time or wears that poker face. Hope she's willing to learn. I could teach her in exchange for helping me make the mukluks!* Peg brightened. She hurried through housework and headed to Amka's, hoping to find her home.

Halfway there, she stopped. *I forgot pencil and paper!* The rippled beach gave her an idea. *That will make a great chalkboard.* She found a stick. *Which words to teach first? What can't I pantomime? What do I want to ask? That'll help me decide. I need to make an appointment, so I don't come over, and she's gone.* Peg set to work, drawing a clock. *Wait! She doesn't use one!* She drew a rectangle, divided it into fourths, and drew a sun peeking over the mountain, a sun high in the sky, and one setting. She stood back to admire her work, and noticed Amka, standing behind her.

"You're as quiet as a cat!"

Curious, Amka walked around the drawings, studying them.

Peg put her stick on the sunrise, "Morning."

Amka smiled.

"You say it," Peg touched Amka's mouth, "Morning."

"Moor neen," Amka repeated.

"Noon," Peg pointed at the full sun.

"Noooon," Amka said.

Peg pointed at the sun in the sky, "Noon."

Amka's face lit up. "Nooon!"

"Yes!" Peg clapped. She repeated the lesson with evening and night.

Then she pantomimed sewing and scratched a tent in the sand. Amka understood. They walked in silence.

Amka retrieved the mukluk soles along with the bag of tools. Sitting on the ground, she trimmed the soles, checking periodically to make sure they were even on both sides. Next, she cut the soles thinner around the circumference, took a plier tool, and began crimping the toe area. Peg watched closely as she crimped around the heel, then held out her hand. Pinch and crimp, pinch and crimp, pinch and crimp. She frowned as she inspected her work. *Mine's not as even as Amka's.*

Amka bent the sole up a couple of inches around the outside. Then, she put it on the board, and used a teardrop tool, pushing down hard on the inside crease. Finally, she inspected the outside edges and gave them another small trimming.

"It's starting to look like a shoe!" Peg exclaimed and pointed at her foot.

Amka leaned back and blinked rapidly, "Mukluk, mukluk."

"Yes, you're right—mukluk."

Amka rose and disappeared into her house.

Hope I haven't upset her. Ten minutes passed. Peg stretched her legs. *The lesson over?* Amka returned with a tin box and pried off the top. Peg looked in at a collection of bright glass beads.

"Oh, we're going to bead them!"

Amka showed Peg two moccasins and drew a couple of pictures in the sand.

"You want me to choose a design!" Peg exclaimed when she caught onto Amka's message. "OK, I'll go home, draw one and come back tomorrow at noon again?" She drew the full sun in the sand. Amka understood, handed her the box of beads and returned to her tent.

"Thanks!" Peg called after her.

She wanted to have the design finished before Ralph arrived. She hurried home, pulled out her notebook, sat on a rock, looked around for inspiration and started doodling. *I want it to symbolize Alaska—but not flowers, too feminine.*

She drew a moose head with large antlers, a jumping fish, three pinecones on a branch, an eagle head, a bear, the Big Dipper, and a howling wolf. As she drew, the afternoon light seeped into the mountains. Sunset and dropping temperature prompted her to check her watch. *It's nearly eight o'clock and Ralph's not back?* She hurried inside, grabbing her coat and gun. *I'll check with Amka first.* On the way to Amka's, dire scenes played in her mind. Her stomach churned. *What would I do if something's happened to Ralph? Well, I can always go home.*

As she neared Amka's, two men stood in the moonlight under a tree. Something . . . or *someone* hung from the tree. She stepped into the shadows and crept forward, raising her gun. Then one man jovially slapped the other on the back. When he laughed, Peg recognized Ralph's voice. Still unsure, she moved closer. In the moonlight hung the outline of a large fish, swinging from a branch. She released her breath, "Hello!"

Ralph bragged triumphantly. "Look what I caught today, Peg!"

"What kind?" She lowered her gun.

"Halibut! 66 inches!"

She walked closer. "Can we eat it?"

"I want to weigh it first. It's too much for just us unless we smoke it." Ralph ran his hand down the top fin. "But I want a photo of me next to it before we cut into it. We'll have to wait until morning. 'Fraid I'll be sleeping here to protect my catch."

"I'll come down with the camera soon as it's light," Peg promised.

"Here, I'll leave the gun."

"I have some skins you can sleep in," Sundsby offered.

Ralph looked her way. "How 'bout it, Peg?"

"Better than walking home alone without my gun!"

CHAPTER 88

A dog barked. A cool breeze tickled her face. The smell of acrid smoke floated in the air. The cold bit into Peg's backside when Ralph moved. She sat up. *Oh, we slept outside.*

"Brrr!" Ralph declared as he shivered from the blast of cold air. He pulled the skin back down, rolled over, then remembered his catch and jumped up to check on his fish. "You hear anything last night?" he called to Peg.

She stood and stretched. "No. Why?"

"Hell's bells! Something took a hunk outta my fish! Guess I'm not a great watchdog." He peered at tracks. "Looks like a dog or coyote had a midnight meal."

Peg joined him and leaned down to inspect the fish. "Where? Glad they didn't make a meal out of us."

"Now that I'd have woken up for! Take the photo and let's get this thing down before it invites others."

Peg shrugged into her coat. "I'll run home and get the camera while you stand guard?"

"Bring me back a hot cup of coffee, will ya?" Ralph handed the gun to Peg.

"Already thought of that." Sundsby appeared with two cups. "Amka's got sourdoughs frying. Told me to invite you."

"Good deal." Ralph took a sip. "Can you bring me a plate, Peg? Don't wanna to lose any more 'a my fish."

"Sure." Peg followed Sundsby inside.

After breakfast, Peg retrieved the camera and picked up her notebook with her drawings and the beads. Upon her return, Ralph plopped on a rock near his big catch, ran his fingers through his hair, replaced his hat, sat up straight and spun the halibut, so the hole faced away from the camera. Click. Peg wound the film. "Stay there. I'll take another shot." The photo captured his lifelong dream of why he wanted to come to Alaska in the first place. Then, Sundsby helped him cut it down and take it to the fishery to weigh.

"I think I want to bead a fish, especially after today," Peg showed her fish drawing. Amka retrieved a needle and sinew. Using a stump for her table, Peg found a comfortable spot under a tree. She enlarged her drawing, adding bigger fins to make it look more like halibut, traced the drawing onto the mukluk toe and placed beads on it to decide colors. Amka worked close by. She cut paper backing the size of the toe, pulled thread over a piece of wax, poked the needle from the back through the paper and leather into the center of the design and placed six beads on the needle. She held down four beads with her left thumb and sewed two beads down, repeating until all six were secured. Looking up, she raised her eyebrows.

"Got it!" Peg took the needle and loaded beads. Thirty minutes later, she beckoned Amka and held out her bleeding thumb. In response, Amka cut a small piece of leather for her to use as a thimble.

"Thanks!" Peg bent to work. When her thread became tangled, she set it down and stood to stretch. She'd been so engrossed that she hadn't noticed Amka had disappeared. She gathered her supplies and headed home. *Well, Ralph's got his trophy. I'm learning to make mukluks, and we get to live in this magnificent place!* She whistled all the way home.

CHAPTER 89

Her days fell into a routine: Get up, clean up, put something on for dinner, go to Amka's. Peg had almost finished beading but enjoyed Amka's company. After they cut the sole from whale skin and the leg from bearded seal, Amka demonstrated how to sew on the sole and leg piece.

Peg watched the small woman work. Her long black braids swung side to side as she scurried to retrieve a needed tool. Black smiling eyes in a broad, weathered face were hidden by her full cheeks when she squinted at her work. Peg wondered so many things about Amka: *How old is she? Does she had other children besides the one lying beneath the small house in the woods? Is she happy living with Sundsby?*

Amka finished her demonstration, handed Peg the mukluk and stood watching. She leaned close, with her hands clasped behind her back. Her stance reminded Peg of the women in the Native village, carrying children on their backs.

In the early afternoon, Peg's stomach growled loudly. Amka giggled as she trotted off. She returned and handed Peg a slippery gray meat. Peg looked dubious, turned it over and brought it to her nose.

"Muktuk, mmmmm." Amka popped a piece in her mouth and chewed.

Hesitant, Peg tasted. *Not too bad, somewhat of a nutty flavor.* She chewed and chewed. "Which animal?" Amka drew an outline of a whale in the sand, drew another piece of muktuk from her pocket, and held it out.

Peg begged off and returned to sewing. *It's only the end of September, and I have one mukluk finished.* She sat back and inspected her work. *Maybe I'll make me a pair too, or some for Mud and Gene.* Thinking of them brought a wave of homesickness. She'd not gotten a reply to her letter and hoped her family had received hers. *Well, tomorrow I'll take the boat over to Homer to see if the mail has come. May as well write another letter.* She stretched, gathered her supplies and waved goodbye to Amka.

9 October 1920

Dear Folks,

Weather here is cooling, but at least the mosquitoes have died down. I'm wishing I had some of our fall apples and squash right now. Mostly eating fish we catch, beans or something canned. I'll miss Thanksgiving and your great cooking, Mom! My mouth waters to think of your rolls slathered with butter and huckleberry jam.

We're doing fine. Ralph caught a 125-pound halibut! We took a picture. I've made friends with a Native woman who lives down the beach. She's teaching me to make mukluks. We hiked most of a day to a village to get the hide. I'm trying to teach her more English, so we can communicate.

We'll watch the Northern Lights again tonight. They're spectacular! Looks like someone took a knife and slit open the sky, letting green spill through!

The lights are so happy to be released, they dance.
Wish you could come and see them. It's magical.
   How's everyone? I'm hungry for news from
home. Dr. Phillips replaced me? Mud or Gene have
a girlfriend? Dad at the bank? My eagle still
nesting? What's going on at the store?
   Did my friend Rose ever come back for a visit?
She didn't know I was eloping until after we
returned to camp, so don't blame her for not telling
you. She's sweet on Frank—at least she was when
I left. But she changes boyfriends like socks.
   I do love it here. Of course, I've yet to survive
winter, but then I'll be a "sourdough!"

Love to all,

Peg

She sealed the letter, then stirred and tasted the stew. *Needs more salt.* When Ralph hadn't returned by eight again, she wondered if he'd caught another fish and ate without him. By eleven, she decided to go to bed. *Well, Sundsby's with him. What can I do? If something's wrong, they'll contact me, but first, I'll look at the lights.* At one in the morning, she shivered, reconsidered and went to bed. Two hours later, she bolted up when she heard a noise and hurried to the door. "Are you okay? Where've you been?" Smells of alcohol floated in her face. "You've been drinking!"

"Gotta cel-a-brate ma big catch," he slurred.

Peg took his arm. He slumped fully clothed onto the bed and immediately started snoring. She removed his shoes, pulled the blankets over him, and crawled into bed with her misgivings.

CHAPTER 90

P eg hadn't heard Ralph leave. *These late nights watching the Northern Lights have caught up with me.* Then she remembered Ralph's behavior. *I never suspected he was a drunk. I hope it was just to celebrate his big catch. Oh! Better hurry to catch the boat to Homer!* She sprang up. After a quick breakfast of leftover sourdough pancakes, she rushed off until sound in the underbrush made her wish she had her gun. A Ptarmigan burst forth and flapped overhead. *He'd make good soup. Should've told Ralph my plans for the day. Oh, well, serve him right. He worried me last night.*

The only other passenger, an old sourdough, eyed her as she climbed aboard. She ignored him until he smiled shyly and asked, "Where ya'll from?"

"Newport, Washington. Sounds like you're from the South."

"Yip. Mississippi, born and bred. Growed up with Huck Finn," he boasted.

Her curiosity moved her closer. "What brings you to Alaska?"

"Why adventure, of course! What about you?" He pulled a rag from his pocket and blew his nose.

Peg leaned back. "The same. What have you seen up here?"

He coughed. "Easier to tell ya whar I haven't been, madam."

"What's the most interesting thing you've seen here?"

The man stared into the distance as if he hadn't heard.

When she opened her mouth to ask again, he began reciting a poem:

There are strange things done in the midnight sun
  By the men who moil for gold;
The Arctic trails have their secret tales
  That would make your blood run cold;
The Northern Lights have seen queer sights,
  But the queerest they ever did see
Was that night on the marge of Lake Lebarge
  I cremated Sam McGee.

Now Sam McGee was from Tennessee, where the cotton
  blooms and blows.
Why he left his home in the South to roam 'round the Pole,
  God only knows.
He was always cold, but the land of gold seemed to hold
  him like a spell;
Though he'd often say in his homely way that "he'd sooner
  live in hell."

On a Christmas Day we were mushing our way over the
  Dawson Trail.
Talk of your cold! through the parka's fold it stabbed like a
  driven nail.
If our eyes we'd close, then the lashes froze till sometimes
  we couldn't see;
It wasn't much fun, but the only one to whimper was
  Sam McGee.

And that very night, as we lay packed tight in our robes
  beneath the snow,
And the dogs were fed, and the stars o'erhead were dancing
  heel and toe,
He turned to me, and "Cap," says he, "I'll cash in this trip,
  I guess;

And if I do, I'm asking that you won't refuse my last
	request."

Well, he seemed so low that I couldn't say no; then he says
	with a sort of moan:

"It's the cursèd cold, and it's got right hold till I'm chilled
	clean through to the bone.

Yet 'tain't being dead—it's my awful dread of the icy grave
	that pains;

So I want you to swear that, foul or fair, you'll cremate my
	last remains."

A pal's last need is a thing to heed, so I swore I would
	not fail;

And we started on at the streak of dawn; but God! he
	looked ghastly pale.

He crouched on the sleigh, and he raved all day of his
	home in Tennessee;

And before nightfall a corpse was all that was left of
	Sam McGee.

There wasn't a breath in that land of death, and I hurried,
	horror-driven,

With a corpse half hid that I couldn't get rid, because of a
	promise given;

It was lashed to the sleigh, and it seemed to say: "You may
	tax your brawn and brains,

But you promised true, and it's up to you to cremate those
	last remains."

Now a promise made is a debt unpaid, and the trail has its
	own stern code.

In the days to come, though my lips were dumb, in my
	heart how I cursed that load.

In the long, long night, by the lone firelight, while the
  huskies, round in a ring,
Howled out their woes to the homeless snows—O God!
  how I loathed the thing.

And every day that quiet clay seemed to heavy and
  heavier grow;
And on I went, though the dogs were spent and the grub
  was getting low;
The trail was bad, and I felt half mad, but I swore I would
  not give in;
And I'd often sing to the hateful thing, and it hearkened
  with a grin.

Till I came to the marge of Lake Lebarge, and a derelict
  there lay;
It was jammed in the ice, but I saw in a trice it was called
  the "Alice May."
And I looked at it, and I thought a bit, and I looked at my
  frozen chum;
Then "Here," said I, with a sudden cry, "is my
  cre-ma-tor-eum."

Some planks I tore from the cabin floor, and I lit the
  boiler fire;
Some coal I found that was lying around, and I heaped the
  fuel higher;
The flames just soared, and the furnace roared—such a
  blaze you seldom see;
And I burrowed a hole in the glowing coal, and I stuffed in
  Sam McGee.

Then I made a hike, for I didn't like to hear him sizzle so;

And the heavens scowled, and the huskies howled, and the
  wind began to blow.
It was icy cold, but the hot sweat rolled down my cheeks,
  and I don't know why;
And the greasy smoke in an inky cloak went streaking
  down the sky.

I do not know how long in the snow I wrestled with
  grisly fear;
But the stars came out and they danced about ere again
  I ventured near;
I was sick with dread, but I bravely said: "I'll just take a
  peep inside.
I guess he's cooked, and it's time I looked"; . . . then the
  door I opened wide.

And there sat Sam, looking cool and calm, in the heart of
  the furnace roar;
And he wore a smile you could see a mile, and he said:
  "Please close that door.
It's fine in here, but I greatly fear you'll let in the cold
  and storm—
Since I left Plumtree, down in Tennessee, it's the first time
  I've been warm."

There are strange things done in the midnight sun
  By the men who moil for gold;
The Arctic trails have their secret tales
  That would make your blood run cold;
The Northern Lights have seen queer sights,
  But the queerest they ever did see
Was that night on the marge of Lake Lebarge
  I cremated Sam McGee.

Her attitude toward him completely changed. *Impressive memory!* "Did you write that?"

The old sourdough shrugged. "I jus git it. Seeuns as I'm from the South ma-sef."

When a small log cabin on the inlet of the river came into view, Peg stated, "Well, that's where I'm headed—to mail a letter to my folks."

Having completed his performance, the man closed his eyes.

Conversation's over. She watched the approaching shore with anticipation and bounded off the boat before it stopped. Patting her pocket to make sure the letter hadn't fallen out, she marched off to mail it. The morning took her breath away, not the cold air only—but the watercolor scenery. She couldn't call it rain—water suspended in the air—more like looking through glass, and suddenly, she shuddered. *Someone's walking over my grave.* She shook herself and made her way to the post office, keeping to the line of gravel spit up from the ocean to keep her shoes dry. Upon arrival, the rain-swollen door stuck. Peg used hip and shoulder to push her way in.

"Hey, Kid! What are you doing here?" she exclaimed upon seeing the Malamute Kid behind the counter.

"Hey, Peg! I'm minding the place for a couple of days while Eric checks his trap line."

Peg pulled the creased note from her pocket. "I need to mail a letter. Have anything there for me?"

He moved to a desk covered in six inches of stacked mail. Letters dangled from the desk about to join those on the floor. "Lemme check. Nothing came in yesterday, and it's too early for today's boat."

"How do you find anything in there?" Peg puzzled, observing the disarray.

"Secret organizing system," he called over his shoulder.

Delicate gray cobwebs swung in the breeze from the door. "Which is?"

"I told you it's a secret," he teased as he pawed through the pile.

"Why?"

"It's a secret where it is!" Several letters floated to the dusty floor. "Wah la!" he called triumphantly as he waved a letter above his head.

Peg nearly jumped over the counter. "For me?"

The Kid's brow furrowed. "If your name is Peg *Tarbet?*"

"Peg Sparks now." She grabbed the letter, ripped it open and scanned the first few lines. "Oh no!" she screamed and fell to her knees.

The Kid rushed over. "What's the matter?"

Her chin quivered as she thrust the letter to him.

Dear Peg,

I hate to give you this news in a letter, but it's the only way I know to contact you. Dad died yesterday. The funeral is on Saturday, and I doubt you'll get this letter before that. It was a shock to everyone as he was only 58 years old. Poor Mother is beside herself. Dr. Phillips says it was a heart attack. Wish you were here.

Mud

"Geez, Peg. I'm sorry." The Kid helped her up and handed the letter back. He guided her to the only chair and patted her back. "How can I help?"

No! It can't be! Peg shook her head and covered her face with her hands. Her body shook with sobs.

The Kid looked out the window, bit his lip, reached over and tentatively put his hand on her shoulder.

After a long silence interrupted by sniffling, Peg raised her head. "I need to get word to Ralph. I want to go home."

"The next boat back to the Island doesn't leave for a couple of hours. How about some lunch?" The Kid offered his hand.

"Who'd watch the place?" Peg wiped her face on her sleeve. "I'll be okay."

"Where will you go?" he asked. "You can stay here. It's warm. I have paper and pen if you want to write your family."

Peg couldn't remember what she'd planned to do until the boat returned. "Thanks."

"Sit here while I find paper." He shoved the mail to one side of the desk and scrounged through shelves, producing an inkwell, pen and paper.

Peg sat staring out the window. She wanted to go home. Memories of Dad flooded her mind. A strong swimmer who loved water, he'd taught her to swim before she went to school. His large hands cradled her as she practiced floating and tried her first strokes. As she grew, she and Dad competed, but she never won. He'd let her get ahead; then with powerful strokes, he'd catch and pass her.

Much to her mother's dismay, he gave Peg a gun for her eighth birthday and taught her to shoot. As a teen, she'd spent days in the woods, scouting deer and elk with him. *He taught me so much about living in the woods. Now he's gone. I'll never hear him call, "Where's my girls?" when he comes home or see him toss his hat onto the hook behind the door. Did I break his heart by running off?*

She didn't realize tears dripped from her chin until The Kid pulled the scarf from his neck and dabbed her face. He pulled back sheepishly, handed it to her and kept glancing out the window. As soon as the boat came into view, he exhaled and shot up. "Get you anything?"

"No thanks. I'll go down to the dock and wait for the boat."

"Want me to come with you?" he offered. "I can—right after I bring the mail in."

"What time is it?" She looked around for a clock.

He helped her rise. "Almost noon. You shouldn't have to wait long."

"Thanks, Kid. You've been kind. Sure glad that you were the one who was working today," she choked out.

When the boat docked on the island, Peg was surprised to see Amka waiting. *She couldn't have heard my news. Did she plan to catch the boat back to Homer?* She noticed Peg and waved. Peg's tears flowed again.

Looking puzzled, Amka stayed on shore. Peg tried to answer, but a sob crawled up her throat, threatening to burst forth. Amka followed silently until they drew close to home. Peg wanted to explain, but voicing it only made her lose control. She picked up a stick and drew a picture of a family and the father in a grave.

Amka held her hand out for the stick and drew a man hunting seal with two children in a boat. Next, she drew large waves and a capsized boat with the people under the water. *So that's what happened to her first family.* Peg hugged her friend.

Amka followed Peg home, brought in wood, stoked the fire and set a kettle of water on while Peg slumped on the bed. When the water boiled, Amka got down a mug, stirred in tea, set the cup on the table and left.

That evening, Peg awoke with a headache. Ralph sat next to her reading. He heard her stir, looked up and held out his arms. She crawled onto his lap. *Ralph's close to my father's age. Just four years younger. Could he have a heart attack, too?* She hugged him fiercely.

She finally spoke, "I want to go home."

Ralph gently pushed her back and looked into her face. "For good?"

"No, I need to be with my family."

"OK, don't know if we've enough for two tickets, though. Sundsby and I just bought the boat and fishing equipment . . . "

"Do we have enough for me to go?"

"We'll swing it," he assured her.

CHAPTER 91

The boat crept on. Cold forced Peg below where her thoughts lurched with the boat. *Good thing Ralph sent some books with me. No one will be there to greet me.*

As the Dinky chugged through the pines by familiar lakes and landmarks, she thought of her brothers and Charlie's ride home from the war and the old saying: "You can never go home again." *It makes sense now with Charlie and Dad gone.* A gentle snow kissed the tops of the trees as they climbed into the mountains. Lost in a whirlwind of memories, Peg didn't notice how close they were until the familiar *Wah-wooooooooooo woo!* whistle sounded, informing Mrs. Scott of one passenger for lunch.

I do hope the meals at the Cottage House haven't changed. She strained to spot the only employee, Mr. Brown, standing on the porch—and there he was—the lone Negro in town, dressed in his suit, standing ramrod straight and ready to welcome the lunch crowd. Hungry but not looking forward to the condolences or the whispers behind her back (*I'm sure I've been the topic of gossip for some time—running off to Alaska*), she held her head high and stepped off with determination. Mr. Brown—no one *ever* called him by his first name—recognized and greeted her with a little bow. "Welcome home, Miss Tarbet. Sorry to hear about your father."

"Thank you. Will you order me the special?" she forced a smile, slid past to avoid conversation and chose a seat in the corner with her back to the door. Surprised she had an appetite, she ate slowly, watching dead leaves skitter across the road in a gust of wind. They reminded her it was too cold to walk all the way to the store. The school wagon turned the corner.

"Thanks! Keep the change!" She tossed her money and darted out the door. Tom murmured to the horses as children bounced off.

Peg called, "Hey, Tom, need any help?"

He looked over and his face lit. "Sure nuff! Hop up!" He handed her the reins as she climbed aboard.

"I used to think I was such big stuff when you let me do this!" she admitted, recalling those days that seemed centuries ago.

"You were! Never had another girl want or dare to," he teased as he winked.

"Well, you saved me today. I wondered how I was going to get home. Thanks." Peg flicked the reins, and the horses lurched forward.

"You come in on Dinky?"

"Yes, my folks don't know I'm coming, so there was no one to pick me up."

"At your dad's funeral, I wondered where you were. Someone said you'd moved to Alaska. Like it up there?"

"Love it. Didn't get the news about Dad in time to make the funeral."

Tom flipped the reins. "Crazy how life turns out, huh?"

"Sure is." *I'm grateful he didn't ask questions.* They rode in silence until the store came in view. "I'll hop off here. That's where I'll find Mother. Thanks again, Tom!" Peg slowed the horses and swung down.

"Hold up! Don't forget your suitcase." He reached back and handed it down to her.

Seeing the store brought a lump to her throat, so she abandoned her plan to go through the front door and surprise everyone. She lugged her suitcase to the back, eased open the door and dropped it with a thud.

Mary heard the noise, finished sacking a customer's order and went to see what had fallen. Peg perched atop her suitcase. It took a moment to register.

"Peg!" she screeched. They fell upon each other's neck and bawled.

"Oh, Mom!" Peg stood up and wiped her face with her shirt sleeve. "What happened to Dad?"

"He didn't come in for supper, so I sent Mud out to find him. He was lying in the field." She blew her nose before she could continue.

"How horrible for Mud!"

"He'd seen enough in the war to know nothing could be done. Mud and Gene took the wagon down and brought him home."

Peg put her arm around her mother. "I'm sorry I wasn't here."

"You being here would not have changed anything. He had a heart attack."

"Maybe me running off . . . ?"

"No, you don't! You didn't cause this. Don't go blaming yourself." She put her arms around Peg. "Glad you're here. I've been so worried."

"I didn't want you to. Didn't you get my letters?"

"Yes, I didn't know if I believed them. I mean, Peg, he's your father's age. I worried it was a rebound from losing Charlie," Mary confessed.

"I'm sure you're not the only one. I've even asked myself that same question," she admitted for the first time. "But I'm okay, Mom." She paused. "Ralph treats me well and I'm happy," *except for the drinking.* Mary perceived Peg's forced tone. *"*I do love the adventure of living in Alaska," *most of the time.*

"You'll have a hard time convincing your brothers. They were livid. Did he come down with you?"

"No, we only had enough money for one ticket."

"Probably for the best."

"I'm not staying long. I need to return before the weather changes. I want to visit Dad's grave. You have time to go with me?" Peg implored.

The barrier between them fell and Mary's heart rejoiced. "Of course, let me tell the help I'm leaving the store for the day."

Peg walked home, pushed open the heavy barn door and saddled two horses. She and Mary bundled up and rode to the Newport Cemetery. "There's no headstone yet. It's been ordered," Mary explained.

Seeing the mound of fresh dirt and dead flowers caused her heart to ache. She climbed down from the horse and lay her hand on the grave. "Dad, I'm sorry. I miss you." Mary put her hand on Peg's shoulder. "We'll see him in heaven. It's not the end."

The biting wind encouraged them to hurry along. "Race you!" Peg called over her shoulder as she mounted. Mary gave her horse a kick, nearly losing her seat when he lurched forward. She recovered, leaned forward and pushed on past Peg, laughing. They both arrived breathless. "Thanks! I haven't ridden in a long time." Mary's joy burst forth. She was so delighted to have Peg home, even if it was just for a while.

A wave of nostalgia washed over Peg the minute she entered the barn. She swallowed hard as a million memories of her dad flooded her brain. Everything was a trigger, leading to other times she and Dad had been in the barn together. She choked out, "I'll put the horses away."

"Thanks! It's late. Better start supper. I'm sure the family will all want to come over to see you." Mary handed her the reins. A horse whinnied and stomped its hooves. Outside, the whoo, whoo, whoo of a Great Horned Owl echoed through the coming darkness. Peg closed her eyes and breathed in the pungent smell of hay, manure and horse sweat. She strolled past her father's horse, a tall brown Belgian draft horse, paused to stroke its neck and lay her head against his. "You miss him, too, I'll bet. I'll bring you a carrot later." Fearing her brothers' reaction, she puttered in the barn until Mary called, "Yoo hoo! Paaay-egg, dinner's ready."

She looked at her shoes. *Whoops. Should've changed before coming in the barn.* A car rattled into the yard. "Gene!" All trepidation vanished as she ran out. Bewildered, he brought the car to a stop and gaped.

"Peg?" He threw open the door, loped her way, threw his arms around her and choked back a tear.

"I came as soon as I heard about Dad." She linked her arm through his. Gene searched her face. "Are you staying?" *Did you leave that ol' Coot?*

Peg read his mind and his pleading look pulled at her heart. "For a while, but I am going back. You should come with me!"

"Mud and I went to B.C. looking for you," he revealed. "Couldn't find any trace, gave up and came home."

Peg's eyes widened. "Where did you go?"

"We visited the logging camp first and questioned your friend, Rosie. We lost a day there."

"Why'd you follow me?"

"We didn't know, Peg. Why did you marry that old man? I was mad as hops! To think that a guy—Dad's age—ran off with you! How did he talk you into it?"

"He didn't!" Peg pulled her arm from his and jogged ahead.

"Wait! Peg!" Gene swore under his breath, "Now I've done it!"

"Wash up, everyone. Gene, Mud, and Ed's family should be . . ." Mary stopped to watch Peg run up the stairs, " . . . here soon." Her voice trailed off. Gene stomped the mud from his shoes on the porch. "Well, here's someone." Drying her hands on her apron, she hesitated between following Peg or going to the door.

Gene swung the door open. "Where'd Peg go?"

Mary put her hands on her hips. "She ran upstairs. What happened?"

"I asked her why she ran off with Ralph," he admitted.

"She'll tell us more in her own time. Let's just love her and give her some space—please!" Mary begged.

Gene growled.

CHAPTER 92

P eg scanned her bedroom. *Had it only been five months? How could one's life change so quickly?* Out of habit, she looked for the eagles. *They've migrated for the winter* she realized and crossed to her bookshelf. She picked up her dog-eared *The Wonderful Wizard of Oz* with the silly picture of a lion with glasses on the cover. She'd loved that book and remembered how frightened she'd been by the wicked witch and her winged monkeys. Had *The Call of the Wild* lit the fire of exploration in her? Remembering the warm feelings *The Holy Bible* always brought, she realized it had been a long time since she'd read it and placed it inside her suitcase to take to Alaska. She opened her priceless Christmas present from Mud, *Harriet, the Moses of her People.* He knew Peg admired the brave woman. Then she smiled, remembering the plot of *Tarzan of the Apes. Little wonder I grew up craving adventures!*

A soft knock broke her reverie. "Come in." She laid the book down. Mud opened the door slowly and peeked around the corner. "Mud!" She jumped to him.

He caught her in his arms. "It's true then. I thought maybe Gene was funning me!"

She leaned back and looked up into his face. "Yes, I'm back," she smiled sheepishly, "a little too late, I fear."

Mud led her over to sit on the edge of the bed. "No, Peg, you shouldn't feel guilty about not being here for Dad."

"Except I'd not be married?" she twisted the tail of her shirt.

"Well, there's that," he conceded. *Why in the world?* "Gene told you we came lookun for ya?"

Peg stared at her feet. *I'm so sorry I worried everyone.* Her chin started to quiver. "He did. Ralph and I made a couple of stops along the way," she stammered.

"So, how's Alaska?" Mud sat on the bed next to her. *Have you realized your mistake?*

She perked up. "Oh, Mud, you'd love it! The hunting, the fishing, the scenery. It's...indescribable, but I'm not fond of all the bears. You know since Roy's death . . ."

"Yeah."

She cast her eyes down again. *Is Mud still upset with me?* "I feel bad about missing Dad's funeral."

"Well, I'm glad you came back. *Without him!* How long you staying?"

"I can't wait too long, or I won't be able to get back until spring break up."

Mud took her hand and pulled her up. "Let's enjoy what time we have. I'll take time off. Come on. I'm hungry!"

"Some things will never change," she laughed.

When the Tarbet family gathered for a meal, it might last hours. They teased, laughed and someone broke out playing cards while Mary kept bringing more food.

"Oh, Mother, no more," Peg pleaded. "I haven't eaten this much forever! So, what's new around here?" Peg wiped pie crumbs from her face.

"Not much," Mary stated as she reached for the empty plate, "but you *WILL* be interested to know Mrs. Waterman, well, Mrs. Sims now, is expecting."

"What? Isn't she too old?"

"Apparently not. She must be close to fifty, though." *And Ralph's over fifty.*

Peg looked thunderstruck. "I can't imagine her cooing over a baby. She's so brusque and efficient."

"But a baby changes everything," Mary commented while putting another pie on the table. *And if you get pregnant . . .*

"This was a feast, Mom!" Mud patted his stomach and pushed it out. "Did you plan all this for Peg?"

"No, just love to cook. Didn't know she'd be here. It just makes me feel better." Silence reigned as everyone, lost in their own thoughts, polished off the huckleberry pie.

"Well, we all miss him," Gene stood and began to clear the empty dishes from the table. Peg jumped up. "I'll help clean up. You relax, Mom."

Mary stayed seated and dabbed her eyes.

Mud picked up a dish towel. "Here, I'll help, too," he declared as he flicked Peg's bottom with the towel.

"Oh, you!" she dashed after Mud as he ran around the table.

Chapter 93

One week later, Peg and Mary waited for the train. Peg tried to lighten the mood. "I want to be back before Christmas. I've spent days making Ralph some mukluks. Wish you could see them. I can't wait to see his surprise."

But I don't want you to go! Mary squelched her disappointment. "I understand, dear. It just won't be the same without you here. *You've grown up these last few months.* Will you be all right this winter?"

Peg put her suitcase on the train platform and pulled her mother into her arms. "I'll be fine, Mom." Now wasn't the time to share her concerns about Ralph. *Don't make it harder for me. I beg you!* "I'll be back before you know it," she whispered. *I hope.*

"Promise?" Mary pulled back as people began gathering on the platform. *Don't leave, please!*

"Maybe you could come up to visit us this summer? It'd be good for you to get away for a while." *I really need you.*

"Peg! Peg!" A man jogged toward her.

Peg jerked in surprise when she heard her name. Her heart started to pound. "Charlie?" *Oh, please don't reopen my healing heart!*

He jolted to a stop. "Heard you were in town," he exhaled, "went to your house; you're leaving already?"

We can't talk now or here! "Yes." Her heart pounded. She looked for an escape.

"I looked for you at the funeral."

Please, don't give me sympathy now. I'm having a hard enough time! Peg stepped closer to her mother. "I didn't hear until it was too late," she replied, failing to disguise the grief in her voice.

"Well, I wanted to give you my condolences." Charlie ran his fingers through his hair and shifted his weight side to side. *And to see you. I've missed you so!*

"Thank you. It was a shock." The train whistle blew. Peg leaned over and picked up her suitcase. "Sorry, I gotta go. I hope all's well with you."

"Here, let me help." Charlie reached out and put his hand over hers on the suitcase handle.

Peg let go. "Thanks." She gave her mom a desperate hug and climbed aboard, grateful the train was ready to leave. *I don't look forward to the long trip back and fighting to keep Charlie out of my thoughts.*

Mary gave Charlie a forlorn smile. "I'm missing her already."

He squeezed his eyes tightly, swallowed and plodded off.

Chapter 94

P eg holed up in her berth to stay warm and kept her mind busy with two books on the trip home. When the boat finally arrived in Homer, her eyes squinted against the glare of three feet of snow! Stories of snow blindness came to mind. A Native helped unload the cargo. He wore goggles made from hide tied around his head with a leather strap. Peg shaded her eyes and studied them. *Maybe Amka can help me make some of those.*

The cold drilled into her bare hands. She bent her head against the glare, stumbled, and slipped up the path, changing her suitcase from hand to hand. She wished Ralph waited for her, but she hadn't given him a return date. As she reached the top, she ventured to the Salty Dawg, knowing she'd missed the boat to the island until tomorrow. Looking forward to sleeping in a real bed, she pushed on, wishing she'd better prepared for the weather.

At least, it didn't intimidate her now to enter the saloon/hotel. *A few months have changed me.* She pushed open the door. The blast of cold air caused heads to turn. "I need a room for one night, please," she requested, moving to the bar.

"Welcome back, Mrs. Sparks." The bartender smirked at his customers.

"Gonna lose business now?" one of the men asked with a knowing look.

Peg ignored the comments and climbed the stairs but stopped halfway up.

The bartender mumbled. "Yeah, Ralph leaves full as a tick!"

"Can I have dinner in my room, please," she called down.

The bartender looked up. "Starts at six. You'll have to serve yourself."

Before she reached the top, another man's comment reached her: "Yeah, heard he gets ossified."

She climbed to her room and hurled the suitcase on the bed to find her toothbrush and nightgown. On top lay a package wrapped in Christmas paper. "Mom!" Pleased, Peg picked it up and squeezed the softness. *Something warm, no doubt, and I didn't even think to take down something for her!*

The next morning, she stayed in her room until she had just enough time to make the boat. She'd saved a roll from last night's dinner as she didn't want to eat with the men. *Maybe I should open Mom's present.* She debated but decided to save it.

Outside, snow bandaged the ground and frosted the trees. She hurried to the boat and stayed on deck until her numb nose and hands forced her inside. *Ralph will be at work, and I'll surprise him with a hot dinner. Should I stop at Amka's? No, I need time to cook dinner before Ralph arrives.*

As she came within view of home, she noticed smoke rising from their chimney. *Wonderful! It will be warm, and the stove already heated.* She kicked snow from her boots and hopped in with boots in hand. A person inside moaned: she froze and yelped when he sat up in her bed!

"Peg?" a bedraggled man blinked his eyes. A white beard covered his face, but she recognized his voice. "You're back?"

The stench of dirty dishes and alcohol slapped her in the face. "Yes."

"Oh!" He shook his head and covered his eyes. "I thought I was dreaming."

Peg dropped her boots. "What are you doing in bed?"

"I don't feel so good." He sank back.

She dropped her suitcase, taking in empty liquor bottles, littering the floor next to the bed. "What's wrong?" she asked skeptically.

"Had a terrible headache for a week."

She placed her hands on her hips. "Maybe 'cause you're nursing a hangover?"

"It's the only way to numb this pain in my head," he grumbled.

She picked up a couple empty bottles. "Have you eaten anything today?"

"No."

Peg rummaged around and threw food on the stove. Ralph rolled over and started snoring. She didn't try to be quiet, banging pots and pans, sweeping the floor and putting away her things.

Dinner ready, she sunk in a chair, perturbed her homecoming plans failed and left Ralph's food on the stove. Crawling into bed with a man, who looked like he hadn't bathed in over a week, certainly wasn't appealing. She banked the fire, spread blankets in front of the stove and lay down, using her coat for a pillow.

Something walking close to the tent awakened her before light. Not sure if she'd been dreaming, she listened carefully—animal or a human? If it passed over the boardwalk, she'd be able to tell. It brushed against the side of the tent behind her. By the time she'd turned and sat up, it was gone. *Could be anything.* She got up, checked on Ralph who looked as if he hadn't moved, noticed the pot of food she'd left was empty, put more wood in the stove, lay back down and rolled closer to the heat.

The next time she awakened, Ralph was gone. *I can't believe I didn't wake up! Good! He must be feeling better. I can wash the bedclothes and clean up.*

Coming back from the outhouse, she remembered the noise she'd heard in the night and walked to the side of the tent . . . boot marks! *So some PERSON had been nosing around this morning. Can't think of a reason Amka would come by early. Maybe Sundsby came by to check on Ralph. I'll have to ask Ralph about it later.*

The big pot of water finally boiled. She mixed it with cold, retrieved the washboard and broke off a piece of homemade lye soap. Too cold to wash outside, she pushed the table and chairs back and began scrubbing. She strung a rope inside from the tent's support poles, hung the laundry and decided to gather some pine branches for Christmas. She hoped maybe she could even find a small tree to decorate. *I already have two presents to put under it. Now, what can I wrap Ralph's mukluks in?*

Donning warm clothes, she grabbed her hatchet and gun and went in search of a Christmas tree. Seeing one in the distance, she slogged ahead. It didn't look far but breaking a trail through the snow took time. Perspiration ran down her back. She took off her hat, wiped her forehead and stopped to rest. With her arm, she pushed the snow from a fallen tree and perched, looking down at her home. Someone walked toward it. *Rats! Amka's come to visit, and I won't be able to make it down in time!*

The figure didn't approach the door but walked around the tent twice slowly. *That's not Amka! She just walks in. The* footsteps she'd discovered this morning popped in her head. *Who's casing my place!* Angry, she thrust her gun in the air and fired. The person stopped, glanced around and ran off. *There are more creatures than bears to be aware of!* Instead of pursuing the stranger, Peg decided to continue her quest for the perfect tree. She muttered to herself, "I'm almost there."

It stood about four feet and perfectly shaped, so she set to chopping from the uphill side. When almost through the trunk, she gave a kick, toppling it down the mountain. Peg jogged, caught hold of the top and wrestled it home.

While eating lunch, she decided to put the tree outside. She'd planned on using the little bucket, but the tree was too big. *I'll build a stand. Well, I like a project!* She put nails in her pocket, got the hammer and sat down to lace up her boots. Dogs yipping and snow crunching made her hurry outside. The Malamute Kid's team swooshed up as he called out, "Haw, Haw—Easy boys! Whoa!"

Astounded, Peg stared. "What a surprise!" she called as The Kid waved.

She trotted over. "Whatever brings you here?"

"Hey, Peg," the lanky Kid looked up from petting his lead dog. "Thought I'd come out and check on you. Had you in my thoughts after that letter 'bout your dad and heard you're back."

She put her hands on her hips. "You're surprised?"

"No. It's just . . ." he started rubbing one of the dogs.

"What?"

"Well . . . ran into Ralph at the saloon." The Kid squirmed and looked down. "He worried you'd not return." The dogs panted in the background.

He's genuinely concerned. "Well, I did. How 'bout a ride? Or do they need to rest?"

The Kid brightened. "No, they can run for days. Training in a new dog, so thought I'd come for a visit."

"So glad you did! How'd you get the dogs here?" Peg reached down to pet the lead dog.

He thumbed behind him. "Water's frozen across the shallow part. You must have made it back on one of the last boat trips from Homer."

"Really? What do we do if we run out of supplies?" Peg worried.

"Oh, I come out once a month to deliver mail and supplies to the island. You can send back a list with me. I bring people, too. Need to make it back before dark, but we have time for a ride."

"Wonderful! I'm ready. Can I drive?" she pleaded.

He laughed. "This time I'll take you for a ride." He moved to the sled.

"Let me grab my hat," she dashed off.

The dogs strained against the harness, yipping and howling to go. Peg crawled onto the sled. "Hike!" The Kid called and the sled lurched forward.

They flew below the tree line. Ice crystals hit Peg's face. She pulled her scarf up and hat down until she could barely see out. Fog slipped in. Snow-laden pines shivered in the breeze.

"Gee!" The Kid yelled. The dogs entered a clearing. "Gee! Gee!" They circled the clearing and backtracked. An hour later, The Kid called, "Easy! Easy! Whoa! Whoa!" They slid to a stop, just outside Peg's home. The Kid offered his hand. "Gotta beat this storm. We'll have a mushing lesson next time."

On impulse, she gave him a hug. "Thanks for checking on me, and thanks for the ride! Come in for a cup of something hot?"

He hesitated. "Well, just a minute," he said and pounded a stake to hold the sled. He followed and stood with his back to the stove while Peg put the kettle on. "This feels nice!"

"Tea or coffee?"

"Coffee, please."

Peg reached for the mugs. "Have you ever had a sled tip over? Why don't the dogs' feet get cold? What do I need to know to mush?"

The Kid laughed. "You always so full of questions?"

"Yes, guess I am. Ralph teases me about it all the time," she admitted.

"Well, let's see. The dogs have feet like penguins with lotsa blood vessels in the pad and heavy furred webbing between their toes. Sometimes, a sled tips over, but the dogs stop and wait for me to right it. What else?" He rubbed his hands in front of the fire.

She handed him a mug of hot coffee. "How to mush!"

"Oh, yeah. Keep the line taunt, so the dogs don't get tangled. There's a few commands to learn. Then, it's a matter of practice, balancing, and anticipating curves."

"I can't wait to try!" Peg poured herself a drink. "When will you be coming back?"

"Depends on the mail. I have the By-Pass mail contract for this area, or a passenger may hire me. Next time I come, we'll have a lesson," he promised, draining his mug. "Better be off. Thanks for the drink!" He handed it to her.

Hugging herself, she watched until they were out of sight. *Better get that tree stand built.* She looked for the tree. Frowning, she circled the yard. Snow fell in soft flakes. *There's not been enough snow to cover it. Where could it be?* After a thorough search, she exclaimed aloud, "Well, I never! Who'd take a Christmas tree? There's plenty around!" She grabbed an armload of wood and stomped snow from her shoes before going inside. The mystery of the tree baffled her. She greeted Ralph with "Why would someone take a Christmas tree from our yard?"

"What?" he asked, almost acting like he didn't hear her, as he hung his coat over a chair and moved it next to the stove to dry.

"I spent a few hours today finding the perfect Christmas tree, and when I got back from my ride with The Kid, it was gone!"

His head jerked up. "You went with The Kid?"

"Yes, it was exciting! He promised to teach me to mush next time he comes over."

Ralph raised his eyebrows. Peg pretended not to notice.

"So, you feeling better? Hungry? What could have happened to my tree? Does Amka know I'm back?" She set two plates of salmon and potatoes on the table.

"Yes, yes, I have no idea and yes." He picked up his fork. "This looks great!"

She salted and peppered her meal. "You have no ideas about what?"

Steam rose from his wet coat near the fire. Wood in the stove popped and crackled. He poked his fork at her. "See, not even you can keep track of your questions!"

"Guess you're right. The Kid told me I ask a lot of questions, too."

Ralph stuck his jaw out. "So why did he come by?"

Peg shrugged. "Wanted to check on me. Remember I was with him when I got the letter about Dad?"

"Yeah. So, how's your mother doing? You haven't told me about your trip home yet." He changed the subject, hoping to cut the tension.

"She's sad, of course. I invited her to come up next summer. Mud, too. Until I went home, I didn't realize how I'd been missing my family."

"They coming?"

"Don't know. Guess Mud and Gene went to B.C., looking for me after we eloped. Still weren't too happy about it." Peg stirred her coffee.

"Afraid that might be the case. See Ed and Ethel?"

"No, I didn't know if I wanted to. Not sure what Ethel thinks about me marrying her father."

"Yeah, well, there's always talk when there's a May-December wedding."

"But we got married in July!"

Ralph giggled. "It's a saying when one spouse is a lot older than the other. May for the younger one who's in the spring of life and December for the old one who's in the winter of life."

"Well, December, want another piece of fish?"

CHAPTER 95

"I don't know if I have it in me to get another tree," Peg told Ralph as she checked the biscuits in the oven.

"Take the snowshoes this time."

"Oh, yes! I could walk over and visit Amka, too!"

"Maybe you'd better stay for a while. Sundsby told me yesterday she's been puny."

"What's wrong?"

"Dunno. Some kind of stomach flu, puking." He wiped his face and checked his coat by the fire. "Nice and toasty." He slid his arms down the sleeves and picked up the lunch she'd made. "You know I did miss you while you were gone," he confessed as he kissed the back of her neck.

She gritted her teeth. "Why did you drink so much?"

His face clouded. "Told ya I had a bad headache." He jerked on his hat and left without another word.

After preparing supper, she found the snowshoes in a box under the bed. The poles hung on a tent post. *Why didn't I think of them? Funny how you don't see things after a while.* She looked for something to put leftover biscuits in.

As soon as she stepped out on the porch, the sun blinded her. *Wow! Better wait for some cloud cover.* The story of a fisherman who'd come into Dr. Phillips' office came to mind. He'd been blind for three days. Doc said people often didn't realize the damage until it's too late.

Excited about Christmas only ten days away, she decided to wrap Ralph's gift. She pawed through packed boxes and wrapped it in a chintz bathrobe Mary had made her for graduation. The red flowers and green vines looked festive after she'd tied the package with red yarn. With yarn still in hand, the thought came to make Amka slippers for Christmas. *I'm so grateful for my wise mother.* Mary had sent back knitting needles, embroidery floss and hoops, thread, needles, yarn, soft yellow fabric and a crochet hook. She recalled her mother's words: "Something to keep your hands busy on those long winter nights."

By afternoon, she needed to measure Amka's foot. Afternoon clouds filled the sky. She laced on snowshoes, packed biscuits in the canvas rucksack and tramped along quickly to take advantage of cloud cover.

Nearing the woodpile, she looked for Amka's footprints, pulled a piece of string from her pocket, measured and cut it with her pocket knife, smiling at her subterfuge and Amkas's child-sized foot. "Amka," she called out, tapping the doorpost with her pole.

"Peg!" Amka threw the flap open, her eyes vanishing with her grin. Peg dug the biscuits out of the rucksack, hoping they hadn't turned into a pile of crumbs.

"Tank-you." Amka waved her inside. Peg flinched when she noticed a dead seal, lying in the middle of the room. "You shot that?"

Amka beckoned. "Cut time."

"In here?"

"Dog eat," Amka explained and retrieved a couple of knives.

"Oh, you brought it in for the night. Well, I've skinned deer and elk." She grabbed onto the tail and helped Amka drag it outside.

Amka started a fire and put on a pot of water. They rolled the seal on its back. Amka slit it open from chin to tail, exposing a thick layer of white blubber. She proceeded to cut, pull and separate the blubber layer from the meat underneath. She looked up at Peg who started working on the opposite side.

Soon, an oblong piece of skin lay on the ground, connected only along its back. Next, Amka cut open the body cavity and removed all the entrails. The intestines she squeezed out, tied a knot at the top and pulled the rest through, braiding it with her fingers. Peg thought of the knitting she'd done this morning. Amka threw the intestines into the boiling water. They stopped and sharpened their knives on a whetstone while the intestines cooked. Amka used a stick to retrieve them from the water, cut off a piece and offered it to Peg. She popped it in her mouth. Like the muktuk, it took some chewing to swallow the rubbery thing.

Next, they cut the meat from the body until only the spine remained attached and the grey and white mottled pelt lay on the ground to be tanned.

Lastly, Amka cut open the head, saving the brains to be mixed with urine to tan the hide. Peg noticed two drying racks outside. One had a hide stretched on it. She squinted her eyes, looked at the sun and waved goodbye.

"No." Amka held her hand up and went inside. She returned with a pair of wooden goggles carved from driftwood. A slit ran down the middle of each eyepiece. "*Nigaugek,*" she said as she handed them to Peg who tied them on with the leather strap, quite amazed at how well they cut the glare. "Thanks, I'll bring them back," she promised as she strapped on her snowshoes.

After arriving home, she started peeling off layers when she thought she heard whistling. Remembering the man she'd seen earlier, she grabbed her gun and sat, facing the door.

"What the . . . what a welcome!" Ralph sputtered. "What happened today?"

"Not much, skinned a seal, started knitting Amka some slippers and . . . "

"Why the gun?" he interrupted.

"Oh, I heard someone brush against the tent last night. And yesterday when I went for the tree, I noticed someone circling our tent."

He froze. "What . . . why didn't you tell me?"

She shrugged. "Just did," and lowered the gun.

"Coulda been an animal in the night." He took off his mittens and changed the subject. "You find the snowshoes?"

"Wasn't an animal," Peg insisted. "This morning, I found boot prints in the snow."

Ralph looked skeptical. "You sure they weren't mine?"

"Not unless you walked right up against the tent before you left."

"Better keep that gun handy," he warned, wondering who it could be.

Peg patted the gun's stock, "Don't worry. I take it with me everywhere."

"I'll take the day off tomorrow, and we'll go find another Christmas tree," Ralph offered.

Peg clapped. "Oh, yes!"

CHAPTER 96

The frosty air pierced her blankets. Peg moved into Ralph's body heat when something grabbed her hair. Startled, she tried turning her head, but her hair held fast. "Ralph! Ralph!" she croaked as she ran her hand back, trying to loosen its grip. Her panic morphed into giggles, then guffaws as she realized her hair had frozen to the side of the tent. Ralph looked over and joined in.

"Want a haircut?" he reached for his knife.

"No! How you going to release me?"

He grinned mischievously. "What do you propose?"

"Dip a rag in warm water. Free me!"

Still chuckling, he rose. When his feet hit the floor, he drew them back quickly, "Woo, where's my boots? He hobbled to the stove and poked a pot of frozen water."

"Better stoke this fire. You don't want cold water down your neck! Now don't go anywhere," he snickered.

"Hurry, please," Peg pleaded. She pushed her feet into the warm spot he'd left and pulled the covers up.

Soon, the fire roared. The ice melted and began to simmer. He dipped a rag in the water, wrung it out and placed it on Peg's frozen hair. After two good soakings, she pulled it free.

"Well, that's something I'll write home about. They'll certainly get a kick from this story." She pulled her fingers through her hair and scuttled next to the stove. "Let's eat and go tree hunting!"

They ate a leisurely breakfast as the sun wouldn't rise until after ten. Once outside, Peg found six inches of new snow, covering the ground. Ralph had disappeared, so she began shoveling, stopping to admire the morning sunrise as it set the tops of the mountains aflame. Golden rays streamed down mountain sides like molten lava and danced atop waves of the inlet. "You ready?" Ralph hiked to the door, pulling a sled.

"Where did you find that?"

"Brought it home from Sundsby's last night to haul your tree home."

"Yippee!" Peg laughed. She knelt to make a snowball, but the snow fell apart in her hands like sugar.

Ralph watched amused. "The dry cold air does that."

"Lucky for you! You know I'm an experienced snowball warrior," she threatened.

"OK, soldier, grab your gun, and let's get rolling."

She returned with the rucksack full of lunch, handed it to Ralph, and slung the gun over her shoulder. Ralph broke trail, crunching over the hard crust as Peg followed. The muffled grinding of snowshoes and deep breathing were the only sounds in the forest until a bull elk sauntered by. A wide rack rose four feet from its head, making it nine feet tall. Its longer winter mane ruffled in the wind. The stately figure stopped under a tree and reached to nibble some branches. Ralph stopped until Peg came alongside.

"Rather have elk meat or a tree today?" Ralph whispered.

"The meat."

They waited for the animal to move broadside. Ralph signaled Peg. She knelt in the snow, aimed in back of the front leg for his lungs and squeezed the trigger. The elk fell to its knees.

"Good shot!" Ralph praised.

Peg started forward.

"Hold it! Stay back until we're sure it's dead. Let's eat lunch. I'm going to need strength to gut and skin it." He shrugged off the rucksack and sat on the sled.

"I'm not hungry yet," Peg protested, anxious to get started on the task.

He handed her a whetstone. "Sit here and sharpen your knife while I eat."

"I guess we'll have a nice elk roast for Christmas dinner," Peg planned. "Wish I had some potatoes and carrots to go with it."

"You're making me hungry," Ralph replied as he rustled through the rucksack. "What ya got in here?"

"Ralph! Look!" A wary wolf edged from the trees, closing in on the downed elk.

"My turn," Ralph stated, picking up the rifle. A couple of retorts echoed through the air. The wolf yelped and buckled.

After lunch, they slid through a little wash where animal feces still steamed in the snow. Peg stopped at some tracks. "That bear?"

"Yeah, probably took off when it heard the gun," Ralph reassured her. "We'll skin the elk. If we're not too tired, we'll take the wolf hide, too."

Peg scanned the area. "But aren't bears hibernating?"

"Usually, but weather's warm for this time of year. Pregnant sows are hibernating now." He studied the tracks. "Bet that ol' fella will hole up soon now."

Peg anxiously scanned the area. "Where?"

"They look for caves, rock outcrops, dig into hillsides, or tree roots. If there's a dead cottonwood around, they'll even climb down inside it to winter. Keep a lookout. Don't want a bear on our backs while we're skinning this elk."

As they worked, the wind picked up, discouraging all conversation. They rolled the elk on its back. Peg cut the hide from the bottom to the top of the neck. Heat escaped, steaming into the air. A gust of wind sprayed her face with blood. She trailed her sleeve across it and kept cutting, checking over her shoulder for an approaching bear. Ralph gutted the elk, saving the heart, liver and tongue. By the time they'd quartered it, the storm had kicked up.

"Better head for the barn," Ralph yelled over the wind.

"We're leaving the wolf?"

"Maybe the bear will get his belly full and hibernate." He took rope from the rucksack and tied the meat down. With the load, the journey home took longer. By the time they arrived, sweat dripped down Peg's back, and her legs quivered from the hike. They unloaded the meat into the tent and stoked up the fire.

"What now?" Peg sighed.

Ralph looked up from his butchering on the kitchen table. "We'll have to make a cache."

"How?"

"Basically, it's a platform on stilts." He grimaced as he sawed through a bone. "We'll put it about 75 yards away, at least fifteen feet high to keep the critters out. From that distance, we can pick them off."

Peg looked around. "What will we wrap this in?"

"There's extra canvas our tent came in. Here, throw these chops on the stove for tonight." He held forth a wad of meat. "We'd better eat first."

"You mean we'll have to build it tonight?" Peg whimpered.

"Naw. Tonight, we'll string it up high enough to keep the critters out and work on it tomorrow."

Peg flipped the meat into a frying pan on the stove. "Thank goodness. I don't know where you get all your energy!"

"Oh, what about your Christmas tree?" Ralph remembered.

Peg shrugged. "There's still a few days yet." She lifted the meat to see if it had browned.

CHAPTER 97

After hauling their meat up into the newly constructed cache, a howling wind let them know there'd be no Christmas tree hunting today, so Ralph left to fish.

No matter, I need to finish Amka's slippers. Whistling Christmas tunes as her knitting needles flew, Peg stoked the fire and settled next to it. *I think I'll deliver these early in case the weather's worse on Christmas.* She wove in the last tail of yarn, then wound yarn around a flat piece of wood. Next, she tied it in the middle, cut the other side in half and fluffed out a pompom for the toe of the slipper. Then she made another and sewed them on. Digging through their clothing, she found a green flannel shirt with worn collar and cuffs, cut off a sleeve, sewed the end shut, stuffed the slippers in and tied it with a piece of yarn.

Cabin fever struck. She bundled up, threw her gun over her shoulder, strapped on snowshoes and set out. *I think I'll find a dog for company and protection. I'll talk to The Kid about it next time I see him.* She thrust poles through frozen snow and pushed forward.

A trail of smoke rose in the distance. She spotted a figure. *Is that Amka? No—too tall. Maybe Sundsby's home today. Well, where's Ralph?* When Peg got closer, she called, "Yoo-hoo! Amka!" The wind carried her greeting off. She called again. The figure crouched and disappeared into the trees. *Strange!* Peg shivered and took the rifle from her shoulder. She stood and watched for ten minutes, but the person didn't reappear, so she put a shell in the chamber and kept her eye on the edge of the forest. Approaching Amka's door, she tapped on the wooden frame, but didn't call out.

A rifle barrel slipped out the tent door. She gasped, "Amka?"

The little woman answered, "Peg?"

"Yes! It's me. Please let me in before I freeze!" She kept her voice low.

Amka opened the door.

Peg looked over her shoulder. "Did you know there was a person outside?"

Amka looked out the door.

"Who was it?"

Amka shook her head.

"I don't like it. There was someone nosing around my place a couple of days ago." Peg removed her mittens and hung them over a chair. "You seen him before?"

Amka looked at her blankly.

"Oh! I wish you could speak English!" She rubbed the back of her neck and handed Amka her flannel package.

Amka's brow furrowed. "Potlatch?"

"What?"

"Potlatch?" she repeated.

"No, Christmas present. Merry Christmas!"

Amka started to untie the gift.

"No," Peg covered Amka's hand. "Wait until Christmas to open it."

Amka shrugged.

"Ask Sundsby," Peg suggested. "I'd better go before dark." She strapped on snowshoes and shuddered as her eyes followed the tracks from Amka's yard into the forest. *Wonder why Amka's dogs weren't barking. Come to think of it, I don't remember seeing her dogs outside or in the house. Maybe Sundsby's got them.* She snowshoed the mile as fast as possible.

Upon arriving, she set the table in front of the door and put the loaded rifle close by on the bed. It was hard to settle down to anything with the questions running through her mind. *Who has been casing our area? Why would someone steal my Christmas tree?* The most vexing question kept pushing forward: *Am I safe?* With her senses on full alert, she heard Ralph's approach, peeked out the door and moved the table from the door. His countenance told her something was amiss.

"What's wrong?" she moved closer to him.

"Sundsby's dogs are missing. Apparently, someone's been skulking around their place, too."

"I wondered about that. I took Amka a Christmas gift and was greeted by a rifle barrel but didn't realize I hadn't seen her dogs until I was headed home. What do you think's going on?"

"Nothing good," he muttered. "That's for sure."

"Remember I saw someone around our place when I was hunting a Christmas tree. It ended up missing, and there were tracks next to our tent after I heard noises in the night."

"Yes, you'll come with me tomorrow. I'll drop you at Amka's on my way to work. This place is too far from anyone."

Peg agreed. "Good idea. By the way, what does potlatch mean? Amka thought my Christmas gift was potlatch."

"Well, it wasn't potlatch," Ralph informed her.

"What is it?"

"Potlatch is a native custom, usually a feast, where the host gives lavish gifts to guests to show his wealth. Sometimes they even destroy property to demonstrate how well off they are."

"That's crazy. I guess Amka's never encountered Christmas before. Hey, why don't we invite them to our place for Christmas?" Peg planned. "I think it might help me not get homesick."

"Sure. I'll talk to Sundsby about it tomorrow."

Later that night, Peg sat up, her heart pounding. Cold air rushed under the covers. "What's the matter?" Ralph reached for the gun next to the bed.

"Bad dream. I thought someone was staring down at me." Peg pulled the blankets up and moved closer to him.

He lay the gun across his lap. "Did you hear something again?"

"I don't think so. Just spooked from our talk last night. I want to buy a dog from The Kid. I'd feel safer."

"Good idea. Try to sleep," Ralph yawned. Seconds later, he snored softly.

How'd he do that so fast? Too wound up to sleep, she planned Christmas. *I'll take some flour and sugar to Amka's tomorrow. We can bake cookies. I'll bet she never has. We could string popcorn and gather pine branches to decorate. Wonder if her culture has a winter celebration.*

Chapter 98

The sky blew down snowflakes the size of pennies. Peg hummed Christmas songs. *Funny how snow gets you in the Christmas mood.* She tried to catch a few on her tongue. *Maybe I can make a snowman while it's fresh.* She bent and squeezed a ball of snow in her hands. It stuck! She added more and rolled the ball to the door of the tent. The next snowball was almost as big as the bottom, and she struggled to lift it.

"Need some help?" Ralph volunteered as he peeked out.

"How'd you know?"

"Heard you grunting."

"Oh, you!" She threw a handful of snow.

After Ralph placed the head, she stood back. "He needs a hat, scarf and pipe, maybe some rocks for his mouth and buttons as we have no coal."

"I could donate a scarf and a cigarette." He went to fetch them.

"Forget the cigarette!" she called.

He returned with a scarf and a Russian hat.

"I'll dub him Sacha Sparks, our first winter child," Peg decided.

"Oh, speaking of that," Ralph remembered, "Sundsby told me Amka's expecting."

"She is! Why didn't she tell me? When is she due?"

"Dunno. Didn't ask."

"Typical man," Peg muttered. "Wasn't the flu, was it? She must be two, maybe three months along, I'd guess. We'll have a baby here this summer!"

Ralph clomped around, breaking dead limbs off trees and inspecting them.

"Whadda ya doing?" Peg questioned.

"Finding a good gun for Sacha. He can stand guard." He tromped back with a gun-shaped stick and pushed it into the snowman. "Better. How 'bout some grub?" Peg followed him inside, made breakfast and packed a lunch.

Thinking about the coming baby made Peg happy. She couldn't wait to talk to Amka about it. *That soft yellow fabric Mom sent!* She remembered. *I'll make Amka a baby blanket with it!* She dug it out and thought about things she could embroider on it. *Wonder if it is a boy or girl. Much as I'm a tomboy, I'd like to sew little roses on things!* She laughed aloud.

"You ready?" Ralph asked as he reached for his coat.

Peg looked up, her face a question mark.

"Remember you're going with me to Amka's 'til we get this intruder thing sorted out."

"Oh, yeah. Hang on. I want to grab my crochet things. I could make booties for the baby while I'm there." She stuffed the rucksack.

"Don't think Native babies wear many booties," Ralph muttered.

"Goodbye, Sacha. Keep our home safe!" Peg yelled over her shoulder as they snowshoed off. When they settled into an easy rhythm, Peg thoughts wandered:

When the time comes, maybe I can help deliver Amka's baby. Who helped her with her last baby, or did she take care of herself? Boy, I wish we could talk! Wonder if Mom will help Mrs. Waterman when her time comes. Who will be Dr. Phillips' nurse after she has her baby? I could have had her job after I finished my schooling. I'd like to find some nursing books to study. Maybe I can order one from The Kid next time he delivers mail. What will happen if Ralph and I have a baby? Oh well, I won't worry about that now.

They arrived at Sundsby's. Peg's heart fell when she spotted the little building that had sat atop stilts and held all their winter food— their cache—lying in pieces. Jagged pieces of wood stuck out of the snow, pieces of partly eaten meat lay strewn about. Ralph slowed until Peg caught up.

"What happened here?" she gasped.

Ralph scanned the area. "Could be animal or human."

"How could an animal cause this?" Peg doubted.

"You never know. Let's see if they heard anything." He motioned her forward.

Just then, Sundsby appeared from the forest above.

"Did you find him?" Peg called.

"Nope." He hung his head.

Peg peppered him. "Hear anything? Know when it happened? Why would someone do this?"

"Somethun's going on. Never found my two dogs. They'd have alerted us last night. Heard the crash. Shot at a shadow as it ran into the forest but didn't follow. Wasn't sure if there was more of 'em with him."

"Follow the tracks?" Ralph asked, wanting every detail.

"Must a nicked him 'cause there's blood in the snow," Sundsby stated, feeling somewhat avenged.

"One of us ought to stay with the women, and the other go to work to tell 'em we need the day off to figure this out," Ralph suggested.

"Who's the law around here?" Peg asked. "Shouldn't we let them handle this?"

Sundsby laughed. "Why they'd be long gone! If we want to catch 'em, we gotta get right on it."

"I'll go to the fishery. That way, you can both leave," Peg volunteered.

Sundsby looked over his shoulder. "What about Amka?"

"I'll take her with me." Peg snowshoed to the house, tapped her pole at the door and Amka peeked out. "Come," Peg beckoned.

The smell of fish filled the air. Loads of herring, waiting processing, stood on boats. Peg removed her snowshoes, hiked to the office and knocked.

A beefy, red-faced man with a bulbous nose stomped out. She started explaining Ralph's and Sundsby's absence when he interrupted.

"#!#! Lady, I don't want to hear your personal problems," he cussed. "They want a job. Tell 'em to be here and be here on time." He spit tobacco juice at the floor, spun on his heel and left Peg, standing with her mouth open.

"Hey!" she followed, but deafening machinery swallowed her voice. She marched to his back and tapped on his shoulder.

"You still here?" he shouted, perturbed at her insistence.

"Yes, I am. You need a lesson in manners, and I aim to give it to you," she spat. "I tried to explain my situation, but you didn't even listen. I want to talk with the owner." She stood her ground.

He glowered and walked off without a word.

Peg turned to a man on the line, gutting fish. "Can you direct me to the man in charge here?"

"Ya just talked to 'em," he reported.

She stalked to the door, fuming. "Of all the nerve!"

Amka sat on the railing outside, petting a plump cat.

Peg lifted her head. "I'll bet he eats all the fish he wants! Well, Amka, I'm afraid our husbands have lost their jobs,"

Amka looked up blankly for an indicator of their next move.

"Forget it. Let's go home," Peg groused. Then she remembered the baby. "Oh, Amka! Ralph told me."

Amka's raised her eyebrows.

"You're having a baby!" Peg patted her stomach and motioned cradling a baby.

Amka nodded woodenly.

Peg prattled on, "I brought some yarn to your house. I'll crochet some booties, and we can work on a blanket. My mother sent the softest fabric back with me!"

Stoic, Amka followed.

Ralph and Sundsby worked repairing the broken cache. A hammer rung out while a hand saw chewed its way through a log.

"Find anything?" Peg called.

Sundsby stopped hammering. "Someone used my saw to cut most the way through two of the support poles." His words dripped with disgust.

"Able to follow the tracks?"

"Double-backed several times. He must a hopped on fallen logs. We gave up and came back to try to save the food."

"I'm afraid I don't have good news." The men looked up. "Your boss had no sympathy. He didn't even hear me out. Said you'd better be there and on time if you wanted a job. What a cantankerous man! I lost my temper."

"Guess it's time to be on our own. I'm tired of that stink'un place anyway," Ralph declared, looking at Sundsby for confirmation.

"Fine by me! I like being my own boss. Help me move this log, will ya?" Sundsby rolled it toward Ralph. They worked all afternoon, repairing the cache while the women made food. After dinner with their friends, Peg and Ralph started home. When they got within sight of their place, Peg noticed the gun on their snowman had been moved into a position pointing at them.

"Someone doesn't want us here," Ralph observed. "That's pretty obvious."

"Why ever not? We're not bothering anyone!" Peg thundered.

"Apparently, we're bothering someone, but I have no idea how." He moved to the snowman and removed the pretend gun. "I'm gonna catch him, though!"

"How?" Peg wondered aloud.

"Don't know yet, but I will," Ralph promised.

Chapter 99

"What shall we do today?" Ralph asked as soon as Peg opened her eyes.

"Huh?" She tried to think. "What day is it?"

"Monday."

She rubbed her eyes. "Why are you home?"

"You got me fired. Remember?" He started tickling her. "Didn't you? Didn't you?"

"Stop it! Stop, please." She wiggled away.

"Want to go hunting?" he proposed.

Peg popped up. "Yes, I do. Can we?"

"Sure. What do you want to go after—moose? Mountain goat? Dall sheep?"

"Nope."

"OK, what?"

Peg leaned over on her elbow and whispered, "A Christmas tree."

"Fair 'nuff. A tree, it is." He threw his legs over and reached for his boots. "First, I'll make us some breakfast. Ya know, I've kinda missed cooking."

"Good. Call me when it's ready." She pulled the covers up and burrowed in.

"Yes, Mi'lady." He bowed, opened the stove and threw some wood on.

Thirty minutes later, the smell of hot biscuits roused Peg. "Let's celebrate our new business with some of the huckleberry jam Mother sent." She dug under the shelf. "I was saving this for Christmas. Did you return the sled?"

"Not yet. Come and get it."

After breakfast, they insulated the base of their home with snow, packed the rucksack with leftovers and gathered the saw and sled. "I was half expecting the sled to be gone," Ralph admitted, "but that scumbag didn't take it. Which way?"

She held out his snowshoe poles. "Straight up and left's where I found the last one."

"Wait a minute." He went inside. "Here, got some Native sun-glasses from work, and Sundsby gave me his 'cause he had his own at home." Ralph handed her a pair.

"Better! Help me tie them on?" Peg backed up. "Want me to carry the saw or gun?"

Ralph grabbed the sled's rope. "Tie the saw on the sled and carry the gun."

"Oh, Christmas tree, Oh, Christmas tree," Peg sang, but the uphill climb soon robbed her breath. "Look at that one!" She stopped, admiring a tree in the distance.

"They look smaller outside," Ralph warned.

"Could we cut the bottom off? The top's perfectly shaped." Peg stopped and looked over her shoulder when he didn't answer, she said, "Ralph?"

He held his finger to his lips and motioned to boot tracks ten feet away. Peg moved back.

"Looks like I'm hunting something else," he whispered and put a bullet in the chamber. "Here." He handed Peg the rope to the sled. "Have a fun ride down."

"Not on your life! I'm coming with you," she declared and hid the sled under a tree.

"Keep behind me," he ordered.

For minutes, they followed tracks. When they doubled-back on themselves, Ralph stopped to catch his breath. "He's been here this morning."

"Where do you think he is?" Peg looked down the mountain.

Ralph gestured to the right with his pole.

"Let's go!" Peg bounded forward.

"Hold up. Stay behind me." Ralph retrieved the sled. "Might need to bring a body back on this." He handed the rope to Peg, and they followed tracks, leading to an overhang of rock. Snow piled in front of a cave so deep, that they'd never have noticed the opening if the tracks hadn't led them.

"We've found his lair," Ralph whispered. "You stay hidden. If I don't come out in ten minutes, jump on that sled, get down as fast as you can and go for Sundsby."

Peg's jaw jutted out. "I'm not leaving." She took off her mitten and rolled her sleeve to check her watch. "After ten minutes, I'm coming in," she muttered under her breath, wishing they'd brought two guns. A cold wind kicked snow from a branch into her face and down her neck. She took off her mitten and reached to dig it out, then looked up to see Ralph, prodding a man from the cave, his gun in the captive's back. She hurried over.

Ralph spoke sternly, "Stay back. I've got the situation under control."

"But your head," Peg blurted when she noticed blood running next to his ear.

"I'm okay. He's lucky I didn't fill 'em with daylight."

Peg drew a bead on the criminal while Ralph tied his hands. The captive looked at Peg, "You!" he spat, "why'd ya follow me here?"

Stunned, Peg hissed, "Why I don't even know you!"

"Sure ya do," he growled. "Followed me after I shot ya uncle, didn't ya?"

"Mr. Harris?" Peg gasped, not recognizing him even after he'd identified himself.

"What's he talking about?" Ralph interrupted.

"He's the one who shot Uncle Ben in Newport and disappeared. I didn't know he was here."

"Yeah right, ya little #*#," Mr. Harris cursed.

Ralph pushed Harris' face down into the snow. "No one talks to my wife like that."

Harris slowly raised and squinted at Peg. "What? Ya married this grandpa after my girl stole your boyfriend?"

Ralph tore a piece of Harris' shirt and stuffed it into his mouth. "Here ya go 'til you learn to keep your trap shut."

Still in shock, Peg stood staring in unbelief. "So he's the one causing all the mischief?"

"Probably trying to scare us off, but didn't work so well, did it?" Ralph kicked Harris in the pants. The man fell forward, planting his face in the snow again and lay still. "Get yer butt up 'fore I give it a taste of lead. Peg, bring the sled. We'll tie him in it and send 'em down the mountain." Ralph instructed.

Shaken from her daze, she pulled it to Ralph. Harris still hadn't moved.

"He dead?" Peg asked. *That's all we need is to have to explain why he's dead!*

"No, drunk." Ralph rolled the man on his back. "Help me heave 'em onto the sled."

Peg crouched. The stench of alcohol and body odor made her cough.

"Hold your breath and use your legs, not your back," Ralph advised.

Lifting Harris into the basket was no easy task. They tied his feet to the brush bow. Ralph handed Peg the gun. "Stand guard. I want to check out the cave before we leave." He disappeared into a snow wall. Minutes later, two dogs bounded out.

"Sundsby's dogs!" Peg exclaimed. They ran toward her. She bent wincing at the sores around their necks. "Hey, boys, it's okay. We'll get some ointment on that," she promised. One of the dogs walked next to the sled, growling.

"Here, boy. Come here," she beckoned.

Ralph reappeared. "By the looks of 'em, he didn't give them food either. I found several things he'd pilfered from somewhere and a cache of moonshine. Looks like he brought his recipe with him to Alaska."

"You think he's been living there alone?" Peg looked around.

"Only one bed in the cave," Ralph replied. "Let's move this skunk down, so he can pay." He stood on the runners of the sled's foot boards. "Want a ride?"

She waved. "Nope, one sniff convinced me to steer clear."

"OK, follow my trail and don't dally. No tree today. Sorry." He shrugged. "Give me a push?"

"Don't worry. This find beats a tree any day!" Peg grabbed her poles. "Come, boys!" she called the dogs.

Ralph waited at the bottom of the hill. "Still passed out. We'll take him and the dogs to Sundsby's. I don't want you to nurse him. He reeks. Already fed and watered the dogs. I think they can pull him that far. Help me fashion some type of harness from this rope, so we can deliver this package." They made the trek to their friends' home.

When the dogs saw Sundsby, they yipped, sped forward and slid to a stop at his feet.

"Where? What?" Sundsby sputtered.

"It's the guy who ruined your cache and stole your dogs. Got your lead in 'em. Need ta get him in the house," Ralph reported.

"Amka!" Sundsby called. The men moved the unconscious body into the house.

"Let's go," Ralph commanded Peg.

" . . . but I'm a nurse," Peg reminded them.

"Not for him, you're not. After they clean him up, you can take a look at the wound. They know what to do. There's still some daylight. Let's find your tree."

CHAPTER 100

C hristmas morning came, different from any Christmas Peg had ever known, but the smell of a newly cut Christmas tree comforted her. She'd placed her gift for Ralph under the tree after he started snoring. However, with the capture of Harris, the Christmas meal with their neighbors had to be canceled as Sundsby was keeping guard until The Kid came to transport Harris to the authorities.

She lay still, thinking of her family gathering, her excited nieces and nephews running and ice skating with friends, and Mom's big Christmas dinner. But they did have *snow*, lots and lots. She missed the ringing of sleigh bells on the cutter—-sleigh bells. They sounded real. "Am I dreaming?" The faint tinkling floated in again. She sat up. "No, I'm not! Ralph, listen! Do you hear that?"

"Hear what?" he mumbled.

"Bells. I hear sleigh bells." She jumped up, pulled on pants and shirt, grabbed the gun and tiptoed to the door.

Ralph rolled over. "Don't shoot Santa."

Peg peeked out. "Kid! It's the Kid, and he's dressed as Santa!" She laughed, threw on her coat, pushed her hands in mittens and dashed outside.

"Ho! Ho! Ho! Merry Christmas!" The Kid called and waved. "Easy . . . Easy . . . Whoa!" The dogs slowed and stopped in the yard. "You been a good girl?"

"Depends," Peg said. "What are the requirements?"

The Kid stepped from the runners and reached into the sled. "Good enough for a gift?"

"Always!"

Inside the sled, a yipping rose. The Kid retrieved a fluffy malamute puppy with a red bow around its neck.

"For me?" Peg's eyes sparkled like the shimmer of the new fallen snow. She danced around as she held the puppy close to her face. "This is the best Christmas present ever!"

"Merry Christmas, Peg," Ralph emerged. "Thanks, Kid, for the delivery."

"Oh, Ralph! It's the greatest present ever!" She buried her face in the puppy's fur. "Aren't you, buddy? Yes! You're sooo cute!"

"You bring anything else?" Ralph whispered in an aside to the Kid who returned to the sled and pulled out a fur wrapped bundle.

Peg looked up from cuddling her puppy. "Have you had breakfast?"

The Kid pulled off his mittens. "No, and I'm starving."

"Great! We DO have company for Christmas!" Peg chortled.

"It's even better than you think," Ralph put his arm around her. "Sundsby and Amka will come over after The Kid relieves them of Harris."

"Oh, I love Christmas!" Peg handed Ralph the puppy. "Hold him and I'll heat up the stove."

"You'd better take your groceries with you." Ralph followed with the bundle.

"He brought food, too? What's in there?" She unwrapped the fur, spilling potatoes, onions, carrots, apples, and two oranges. "Ralph, you remembered! I wanted an elk roast with the fixings! This is the best Christmas!" She hugged him fiercely. "Oh! I forgot. I have a gift for you."

"I've been eyeing that and wondering." Ralph handed the dog to The Kid and squeezed the package. "Whadda ya think, Kid?"

"No idea." He stroked the puppy. "What will you name him?" He looked up at Peg.

"I'm thinking. Any suggestions?" Peg looked at Ralph.

He opened the present and looked up in wonder. "Who made these?"

Peg looked pleased. "I did. Amka taught me."

Ralph blinked, swallowed and cleared his throat. "This is the best present I've ever received. Thank you," his voice cracked.

"This little guy's a purebred malamute, so give him a good name," The Kid suggested.

Peg stroked the puppy. "How big will he get?"

"About two feet high—85 pounds." The Kid glanced at the stove. "You'd better flip that pancake."

Peg rushed over.

"Here. I'll watch them." Ralph took the turner.

"I'm thinking—Miko. Whadda think, little guy?" She took the puppy's face in her hands. "You like that?"

"Give him a guard dog name," Ralph suggested.

"Well," The Kid interrupted, "malamutes don't make the best guard dogs. They like people too much, but he'll make a good alarm."

"That'll work. Peg's a crack shot and can take care of herself if she has warning," Ralph informed The Kid and set another plate of pancakes on the table.

"These are good!" The Kid took another pile. "After I haul that culprit at Sundsby's off, you shouldn't have to worry anymore."

"Isn't that somethun? A guy from Peg's hometown, and we end up on the same island," Ralph mused.

The Kid turned his full attention to Peg. "What? You know him? That true Peg?"

Peg agreed. "Yes, he shot my uncle who's the sheriff, *and* I went to school with his daughter."

"Well, may as well settle in. Sounds interesting!" The Kid leaned back in his chair as Peg related the story.

CHAPTER 101

"Mom! Did you see this?" Mud dashed into the store, waving a newspaper over his head.

"What is it, son?"

"Read it!" he thrust the paper to her.

THE NEWPORT MINER

Volume VIII Newport, Washington,
Tuesday, December 29, 1920
Number 26

HARRIS APPREHENDED IN ALASKA!

Elmer Harris, native of Newport, has been on the run since shooting Sheriff Ben Fox. Last fall, the sheriff happened upon Harris and his partner's moonshine operation in the mountains above John Tarbet's property. A local search party dispatched at the time of the shooting was unable to locate Harris who had apparently hightailed it to Alaska. Luckily, the sheriff has since fully recovered.

In an interesting twist, John
Tarbet's own daughter (and the
sheriff's niece) Peg Sparks and her
husband Ralph, were instrumental
in bringing Harris to justice.
Harris, who had been vandalizing and
stealing from residents, was shot by
Sparks' neighbor as he fled into the
surrounding woods.

Sparks followed his trail to a
hidden cave where he had secreted
his still and ill-gotten gains. Mr.
Sparks apprehended Harris and took him
to neighbors who nursed him until he
was well enough to transfer to Homer
to face charges. When he's deemed
healthy enough for travel, he will be
extradited to Newport to stand trial.

Mary looked up. "Peg's okay?"

"I'm sure she is, Mom. He's in custody. Man, I'd like to know the rest of the story! Wish I'd been there to drag him in! How do you think Harris ended up in the same area as Peg?" Mud reached for the newspaper. "I'm taking this over to Uncle Ben and see if he has any more info!" He rushed out the door.

"Wait a minute!" Mary called as the door slammed.

"Hey! Got 'nother of them papers?" one of the old timers next to the stove bellowed.

"There's more in the mail bag. Right there on the counter, Eddie," Mary told him.

In a little house a few miles away, Florence put her head in her hands. "I hate this town! I hate my father, and I hate Peg Tarbet!"

Charlie moved next to her. "What's the matter?"

Florence shoved the newspaper at him.

"Settle down. You don't want to upset the baby."

"She's always been a thorn in my side!" Florence stormed.

"Who?" Charlie scanned the article and let out a long whistle. "Wow! I'd like to have seen it."

"Seen what?" Florence demanded.

"The shock when he recognized Peg." He started re-reading the article.

"Humph!" Florence stormed into the next room.

Charlie followed. "What's the matter? Peg did nothing wrong."

Florence sat in the rocker, hands resting on her swollen belly, "She keeps interfering in our lives."

"How?"

"If you don't know, I'm not telling you," she groused.

"Sheeish!" Charlie stalked out of the room.

"I'll bet you'd like polygamy instead of monotony!" Florence yelled after him, making Charlie snicker in spite of the fight. He thought of Peg's usual comment to Florence's blunders, "Typical Florence," and wished for those simpler times.

CHAPTER 102

Peg finished relating Harris' crime to The Kid.

"Interesting. No wonder he was asking about you."

Peg sprung up. "What! Where?"

"Yeah, he was in the Salty Dog not long after you arrived. Came over to my table and asked about you."

Peg couldn't believe it. "Really? What did he say?"

"Wanted to know who you were and where you were going. Didn't think much of it. Always news when a woman comes up from Lower 48. Had I known, I'd a told you," The Kid apologized. "No wonder he tried to spook you outta here."

"Hey, Kid, I need to go to Juneau for some business. How 'bout a ride to Homer?" Ralph interrupted.

"What? That's news to me," Peg protested.

"Was gonna tell you, but just thought of it when The Kid came. Want to come?"

"I'd love it! How long are we staying? What's there to see up there? How will we get there?"

"Fastest way's across the Gulf of Alaska. We'll go by boat. It will take a few days. Maybe fish for herring on the way."

Peg's eyes lit up. "I'm game."

"Yeah, that's why I brought you with me," Ralph chuckled.

"Pack up," The Kid instructed. "Got to leave within the hour."

Peg dashed about, throwing things into a canvas bag. "Wait!" she stopped. "What about the puppy?"

"Amka'll watch him, I'm sure. We'll drop him on the way out." Ralph finished cleaning up breakfast.

The Kid pushed back his chair. "Throw on your warmest things. I'll get the dogs ready,"

Ralph climbed into the sled. Peg handed him the puppy and crawled in. After she settled, he put the puppy on her lap. She leaned against Ralph, pulled up the blanket and tucked the edges in around them.

"Ready?" The Kid questioned from behind.

"Yep!" Ralph answered.

"Hike!" The dogs bounded forward.

"Ralph!" Peg shouted.

"What?" He leaned forward to hear.

"You didn't bring your mukluks!"

He patted her arm. "It's okay."

They glided into a silent blue and white world, the swish of the sled and dogs' panting the only sounds. Miko snuggled into Peg and slept until they pulled up to Sundsby's place. As she struggled from the sled, it yawned and yipped. The wind slashed her face. She lowered her head and scurried to the door, calling for Amka.

Sundsby let them in. He looked at her wriggling coat. "What ya got there, Peg?"

"My Christmas present from Ralph." She squatted. A ball of fur tumbled onto the floor. "Meet Miko!" she chimed in anticipation.

"Aw!" Amka's usual deadpan burst into a crinkled smile. She knelt and scooped the puppy up, stroked his fur and whispered something in her native language to it.

"She'll agree to dog sit," Ralph ventured.

"Where ya off ta?" Sundsby asked.

"That business we talked about in Juneau. Wasn't planning on going until spring, but since I've got no job, and The Kid showed up, looks like a good time to shove off."

"How long ya staying?"

"Well, that depends on Mother Nature," Ralph answered. "You okay with us leaving the dog if we get snowed in?"

Sundsby glanced at Amka, playing with Miko. "Question should be: You think she'll give him back? You'll probably have to go out of Homer to Kodiak, then onto Juneau."

"Starting to snow out there," The Kid announced. "Best be on our way."

"Thanks so much," Peg called to Amka and looked back longingly at her puppy.

A few days later, Sundsby looked up puzzled, "Back already?"

"Yep, big storm came in, so we spent time in Homer until Kid came this way again," Ralph reported.

Outside, Peg played with Miko, then gathered him in her arms, kicked the snow off her boots and followed Ralph inside. The warmth of the tent combined with smells of burning wood and fish stewing on the stove caused a wave of comfort to flow over her.

"Have a seat, Peg," Sundsby offered. "The Kid left something for you."

"He did? What?" Peg let Miko wiggle out of her arms. He sniffed the floor for crumbs.

"Dunno." Sundsby produced a crumpled brown paper package.

Peg tore the package open. A puppy-size harness fell onto the floor. "Look, Miko. The Kid left you a present!" Peg reached for the dog and sensed Ralph standing close behind her.

"You ask him to bring you that?" he bristled.

"No," Peg replied, turning to face him. *Was he jealous of The Kid?*

Sundsby tried to defuse the tension. "That's the first step in training a sled dog, getting him used to wearing a harness."

"Probably wants to make sure I teach a puppy from his kennel correctly. He loves his dogs. Come here, Miko. Let's try it on." Peg picked Miko up and slid the harness over his head. "Oh, it's too big. Well, we'd better not keep The Kid waiting."

Ralph stood his hands on his hips. "No worry. I sent him back."

Peg raised her chin. "I should've thanked him, and I don't know when to have Miko start this." She picked up the harness.

Ralph stalked out the door.

"I know the answer," Sundsby offered. "Wait until he's six months."

"Thanks." Peg slowly gathered her belongings.

Sundsby came forward. "I'll get some snowshoes out for ya. You can return them later."

Ralph paced outside. When Sundsby brought the snowshoes, he held his arms out for Miko while Peg leaned down and strapped them on. They trekked home in silence.

Chapter 103

"Going fishing," Ralph whispered in Peg's ear and slipped out. Miko jumped on the bed and began tugging at the blanket. "Hey, you'll rip it!" Peg sat up. "You little stinker!"

Peg cleaned the tent and put on a pot of soup. She played with Miko for an hour, then decided to return Sundsby's snowshoes, loaded Miko into the knapsack and hung it over her chest.

She arrived out of breath, took her ski pole and knocked on the tent. "Amka, Amka, you home?" When she didn't answer, Peg kicked off snowshoes and went inside. "Amka? You in here?" On the bed, a pile of blankets moved.

"Amka, you okay?" Peg touched her forehead. "You're burning up!" She pulled back the blanket and noticed a red string tied around her leg. A red line streaked from her calf to her foot.

"What happened here?"

"Bite." Amka pulled the covers back and started to shiver.

"Why's this string tied to your leg?" Peg loosened it. "You have an infection spreading. This could be blood poisoning. You need to get to the hospital."

Peg put water on to boil, cooled it and cleaned the wound. She poked around in the kitchen, found a jar of honey and dried garlic and made a poultice and tea from it. *I have turmeric at home, but do I dare leave her for that long?* Peg debated but decided against it, changed the poultice every couple hours and woke Amka every hour to drink the tea. The fire needed tending and the kitchen looked a fright. She went to work but worried. *Is the baby okay? When will the men return? Do I need to go for help?* The work calmed her.

She checked the wound. The red streak hadn't changed. How she wished for Dr. Phillips. *Would they have to take Amka clear to Anchorage?* In the late afternoon, she heard men approaching and flew out.

Ralph rushed forward when he saw her face. "What's up?"

"Amka's sick. Maybe blood poisoning. We need to get her to a doctor."

Sundsby hurried ahead. "She went to bed early last night."

Peg trotted behind. "Why did she have a string tied around her leg?"

"What?"

"She has a wound on her foot. It's infected and she tied a red string around her leg."

"Natives believe that keeps the infection from spreading," Sundsby explained as he dashed inside.

"Wait!" Ralph put his hand on Peg's shoulder. "How bad is she?"

Before Peg could answer, Sundsby threw open the door. "Ralph, grab the sled! We need to make the ferry."

"Sure." Ralph handed Peg his things.

The men lifted Amka on. Sundsby looked back as he put the rope around his waist. "Dogs aren't strong enough yet. Take care of them?"

"Of course! Oh, where's The Kid when you need him?" Peg lamented. She and Ralph watched until they disappeared. They fed and watered the dogs, then took them home with them.

Chapter 104

The next morning, Peg set biscuits and a bowl of oatmeal in front of Ralph. "I'd like to go to Anchorage and visit Amka."

He bit into a biscuit. "How do you propose getting there?"

"That's what I need to know. Can you help me?"

"We'd have to snowshoe out. It's a long way to the ferry."

"I know. Wonder when The Kid's coming back."

"How would I know?" Ralph growled. "Besides, didn't we promise to take care of Sundsby's dogs and watch over things while they were gone?"

"Humph, you're right."

Ralph swallowed his coffee. "Let's check on the neighbors' place. Afterwards, we'll go fishing."

"Ya mean it?" Peg jumped up.

"I do. Could use help with Sundsby gone. Pack a lunch while I bring in the wood and stoke up the fire. I'm hankering for a salmon dinner."

Peg's countenance brightened. "Sounds good!"

After feeding Sundsby's dogs, they decided to take Miko with them. When they got to the shore's edge, Ralph pushed the dory out. Peg grabbed the oars, leaned and rowed out. It felt so good to move that she declined Ralph's offer to spell her. The bracing air, oars dipping, water lapping against the boat and sun creating dancing sequins on the waves revitalized her.

After they rowed far from shore, Ralph tied a heavy cannon-ball-shaped sinker on the line, leaving a foot-long lead. "We'll troll for some halibut, just in case." He attached a dead fish to the hook. The sinker dropped the line to the ocean floor.

"Come here. Bounce this sinker as we move along. It'll attract halibut," he told Peg and moved his pole up and down demonstrating. "I'll try my luck for a King Salmon."

"This time of year?" Peg wondered.

"Winter feeders come north into Kachmemak Bay and Cook Inlet from Canada."

"You're an encyclopedia on Alaska!" Peg shook her head.

"Just read a lot and blessed with a good memory."

An hour later, Ralph felt a tug on the line. "Whoa! Hang on, there big fella. No going anywheres. Now, come on, baby," he crowed and lifted the catch into the dory. "Salmon for dinner it is!"

Miko went crazy, dancing and yipping as the fish flipped in the bottom of the boat. Peg picked him up.

"Well, little buddy, you're not the best fishing partner, are you? You'll scare 'em all away," Ralph scolded. "May as well go back. Not going to work with this puppy." He looked up at steel-colored clouds forming. "'Sides, weather looks to be changing. Here, hand me those oars."

After tying the dory, they trekked to Sundsby's to check on the dogs. A dog and sled sat in the yard. Miko yelped, and the chain of dogs answered, bringing out Sundsby and The Kid.

Peg trotted over. "You're back! How's Amka?"

"Got a bacterial infection and needs to stay in the hospital," Sundsby reported. "Needed to go back to work, so I got The Kid to bring me."

"Hey, Kid, take me to catch the boat to Anchorage? I could stay and help Amka." Peg's eyes lit up.

"We'd have to leave right away. Don't have time to take you home for your things," The Kid warned.

"That's okay." She thrust the puppy to Ralph, declaring, "Surely, I can buy what I need there."

"OK, climb in." The Kid headed to his sled.

Ralph looked from Peg to Sundsby. His lips pursed, and one eyebrow lifted.

"It'd surely ease up my mind some," Sundsby sighed. "That okay with you, Ralph?"

"Sure. Why not?" Ralph fumed. "But how ya gonna buy what ya need?"

Peg's eyes squeezed shut. "Oh! I didn't think. How will I?"

"I've got some money here. Hold on," Sundsby called over his shoulder as he disappeared inside.

Ralph cleared his throat and rubbed his jaw. Peg climbed into the sled. "You'll pay him back for me, right, Ralph?"

When Sundsby returned with the money, Peg jumped out and gave Ralph a peck on the cheek. "We'll be back as soon as we can."

"Hike!" The Kid called, and they disappeared in a swirl of snow.

Ralph sighed and turned to Sundsby. "Well, how 'bout salmon for supper?"

CHAPTER 105

After disembarking, Peg slogged across muddy flats on a half mile of boards laid like railroad track to town. The thriving frontier town of Anchorage spread out farther than she could see, much bigger than Newport! Graded streets joined concrete sidewalks. She asked a man for directions to the hospital.

The Sisters of Providence St. Joseph's Hospital stood higher than any surrounding building. As Peg scurried up the steps, the disinfectant smell made her feel at home. *I hope the Sisters let me stay with Amka.*

"May I help you?" a tall, thin nun in a black habit asked, stopping Peg in her tracks.

"Yes, please. I need to see my friend, Amka. She was brought in a few days ago with an infected leg." The Sister's demeanor reminded her of Mrs. Waterman back home.

"Visiting hours are over."

"But I've traveled such a long way to see her!" Peg pleaded.

"I'm sorry, but the patient's health comes first. You'll have to wait until tomorrow," she held firm.

Peg looked over the nun's shoulder hopefully.

"It's no use. I'm the head nurse."

Peg scowled at the sister and walked toward the door, looking back every few steps. The sister stood guard. *What now?* Her stomach churned. A hulking Native man walked backwards, swiping a mop down the hall. She stopped.

"Hello?" *Surely, he'll stop and go around me?* When he didn't, she stepped to the side, "Well, excuse me," she huffed. When he turned sightless eyes toward her, she realized her mistake and apologized, "I mean I'm sorry."

Outside, she looked up and down the street and started toward the center of town. Many homes sat on skids, waiting to be dragged to their new sites after lots got auctioned. "This is a railroad city," she spoke aloud.

"Yur right, miss," a deep voice responded, making her jump. "Sorry. Didn't mean to give a fright," he apologized.

"I didn't realize I'd voiced my thoughts," she admitted. "Could you direct me to a hotel?"

"Parson's Hotel straight ahead six blocks, but if yur staying long term," he raised his eyebrows, "I'd recommend the boarding house."

"The hotel will be fine. Thanks."

"Accommodations are real uptown. Now when I lived in them muzzleloader bunks . . . "

Peg's interest peaked. "In what?"

"Worker housing with bunks built along the walls. They shoe-horned us in four-foot spaces, but they's eight foot long, so ya could store your duffle bag in the back. But fer big men like me . . ." he grimaced. "A friendly piece of advice: stay away from tha tents and shacks southeast of town," he continued, "or men could get the wrong idea 'bout ya. Can't miss it at night. Must be over a dozen or more phonographs playing down there."

Peg winced. "Thank you." *Wow! I'm out in the real world now.*

"Well, if I can help ya, name's Gustav. Work at the Chickaloon Coal Mine, but ma wife's usually home. Ask for Muriel over on G Street," he offered as he tipped his hat.

She loved exploring and slowed as she passed each place of business: The Lucky Shot Mining Company, J.B. Gottstein Company Wholesale Grocer, Kimball's Dry Goods, Gill's Garage, and Kennedy's Clothing store. Across the street, a broad two-story building divided by three doors gawked at her through two immense picture windows. She crossed, stood contemplating which door to enter and then noticed a sign above the middle door: Hotel Parsons.

The door opened, and a fragrance of something sweet baking invited her in. After registering for the night, she followed her nose to the dining room, hoping the food was as good as Cottage House in Newport. The clock over the cash register showed 4:30. Tables stood empty. She called, "Hello," but when no one answered, she returned to the lobby.

An older man with a gray fringe of hair around his tanned and age-spotted head looked up from the newspaper. "You look a little lost."

"Know what time they serve?"

"In Miss Mac's Lunchroom?" he asked, trying to be helpful.

Peg looked at the dining area, "Is that the name of this one?"

"Guess not." He returned to his reading.

Peg gave a heavy sigh. "Do you know what time that one serves?"

He didn't bother looking up and reported, "5:30."

"So what's that one called?" she persisted.

"Not sure."

"Well, where's Miss Mac's Lunchroom?"

He directed the edge of his newspaper to the same dining room.

"I thought you said that wasn't its name!"

"S'not."

She lost patience for his word games. "That doesn't make sense!"

"Used ta be the name," he confessed as he lowered the paper and grinned at her exasperation. "Us sourdoughs still call it that, though."

Peg sat next to him. "How long have you been here?"

"Came here in '14 when President Wilson ordered Alaska surveyed."

"So you've only been here six years?"

"Yep, but in these parts, that's an old timer," he sniggered.

"You remind me of my teasing brothers!"

"Why, thank you. Had a few sisters of my own to practice on," he warmed to his subject.

"How many?"

"Six, and they nearly mothered me to death. Pa wanted a boy sa bad Ma kept going 'til I finally showed up. Musta been four years old 'fore I knew who my real mother was!"

"There are four boys and four girls in my family."

"Where do ya fit in?"

"The baby."

He nodded knowingly and returned to his paper as the dining room opened.

Chapter 106

The next day, Peg arrived early at the hospital, pacing the lobby until the same nun led visitors to a long room with metal beds, lining two walls. She walked slowly down one row and didn't see Amka. A group of laughing people surrounded a bed on the other side. She stepped around them and continued her search. No Amka! *Where could she be?* Frustrated, Peg returned to the lobby.

"She's still here," the nurse at the desk confirmed. "Did you check every bed?"

"Yes, no . . . Wait a minute," Peg reported and then did an about-face.

The happy group still surrounded the only bed she hadn't checked. *But Amka wouldn't have visitors, would she?* She eased up behind a teenage Native boy and looked over his shoulder. There lay Amka with a little girl, lying on the bed next to her—licking the wound!

"What are you doing!" Peg cried in disgust.

All heads turned, and Amka looked up, "Peg!"

Peg moved to Amka's side. The commotion brought two nuns to the area.

The head nun pushed through. "What's the problem?"

Peg looked at Amka. The previously mirthful group morphed into poker-faced Natives. "Nothing. Glad to see my friend," Peg replied immediately, fearing the nun would ask her to leave.

"Keep it down, or you'll have to leave. There are people trying to rest here," the nun warned and returned to her duties.

"Was she licking the sore?" asked a young man wearing a white coat, standing behind the circle of people. "She must be the little sister," he whispered. "In Native culture, the last child in the family is considered the doctor and able to cure sores by licking them."

Flummoxed, Peg looked from face to face. "This your family, Amka? And who are you?" she asked the tired-looking man who had stepped forward.

"Might ask you the same thing," he replied, surprised to see a white woman visiting Amka.

"I'm Amka's friend and neighbor."

"Dr. Johnson. Glad to meet you," he pushed glasses up on his weary face and held out his hand.

Peg shook it. "You work here?"

"I consult on some cases," he admitted.

"Are you Amka's doctor?"

"No." He turned and spoke to the group in Inuit.

"You know their language!" Peg realized. "Can you interpret for me?"

"I'm awfully busy, but I have a couple of minutes."

"Ask Amka who these people are, please," Peg begged as she scanned the gathered faces.

The doctor conversed for longer than it took to ask the simple question. When he finished, he turned back to Peg, "They're relatives of hers, and just as I thought, the licking girl is her little sister."

"You sure? Amka's old enough to be her mother," Peg doubted.

"Do you know how large Native families are? Women often have babies along with their mothers," the doctor shared as he moved closer to Amka, inspecting her leg.

"I'm her neighbor. I went to visit her and found her in bed. She had tied a red string around her leg, and when I checked her, I noticed the infection," Peg reported.

His head jerked up. His round glasses slid down his long nose, revealing dark circles under his eyes. "You have a medical background?" he asked, sounding hopeful.

"Yes, a little. I've worked in a doctor's office and was headed to nursing school until I came to Alaska."

"Ya, Alaska's derailed many plans," he agreed, his smile hidden under a bushy moustache. "Mine included. Well, if you ever need work, look me up. Got more'n I can handle." He hurried off.

Chapter 107

After the doctor left, the relatives' giggles returned and so did their volume. Peg gave Amka's hand a squeeze. "I'll check on you later. Let you enjoy this time with your family." She returned to the lobby, looked out the window and paced, then pushed open the heavy doors. Noticing a cabin some distance behind the hospital, she slogged through the snow. When no one answered her knock, she stepped to a window and rubbed the frost with her mitten until it melted a peephole. She gasped. Several bodies lay on shelves frozen like marble statues. She looked over her shoulder, shivered and high-tailed it back. The warm waiting room calmed her, but she wanted an explanation and scuttled to the nurses' desk, "Excuse me, please. I was wondering who lives in that small cabin behind the hospital."

The nurse didn't look up from her paperwork. "No one lives there."

"What's it used for?" Peg persisted.

She cast a perturbed look at Peg. "That's the mortuary. We have to wait until the ground thaws to bury them."

"Oh. Do you know how long Amka Sundsby will be here?"

"No," she dismissed Peg, and returned to a stack of papers.

A firetruck peeled into the driveway. Men shouted, gestured and lifted a bloody body out. "Move back! Move back!" the nurse ordered. Those straining to see out the doors, shuffled out of the way.

"Oh! It's the sheriff!" one of the onlookers gasped. "What happened?"

"Someone shot him with his own gun," the red-faced stretcher carrier wheezed.

The nurse pushed back a curtain. "Put him in there."

Finally, the doctor arrived. "Well, where'd ya find this one?"

"Night watchman saw 'em lying in the alley. Thought he was a drunk fell down in the snow. But when he got closer, he heard groans," the stocky ambulance driver reported.

Memories of Uncle Ben's shooting flooded Peg's mind. She sank onto the first available chair.

Minutes later, the nurse stepped out into the hallway, closed her eyes, pursed her lips and shook her head at the men who'd brought the sheriff in.

A middle-age man with a scruffy beard shrugged. "Well, there's 'nothern fer a pine overcoat."

Peg glanced in the room as she walked past on her way to see Amka. A sheet covered the sheriff's face. *This territory's violent!*

CHAPTER 108

D r. Johnson bent his lanky frame over Amka's leg. Peg's delight in seeing him surprised her. "Hello," she stopped a couple of feet from the bed. "How's she doing?"

"Better." He pulled the sheet up.

"Can you tell me when her baby's due? I'm asking because I may help deliver it."

Dr. Johnson looked over the rim of his glasses. "Ever delivered a baby before?"

"Not by myself, but my mom's a midwife, and I've helped the doctor at our hospital in Newport," she exaggerated a little.

"Wonderful. Sure wish you needed a job."

"Can you give me any pointers in case of complications?"

"Most Native women don't come to a doctor. Has she had any other children?"

"One I know of. He's buried on our island, but you'd better ask her. I don't know for sure."

"Have you got any medical books?" Dr. Johnson asked over his shoulder as he moved onto another patient. "You any good at bandaging?"

"Yes," Peg followed, hoping to be of service.

He motioned her closer and handed her scissors.

"Give me a hand here."

Peg cut the bandage from the roll. "Any news on who killed the sheriff?"

"Nope, but I hear the mayor and several of the city council have pledged a reward. Almost up to $2,000, dead or alive. Guess the sheriff was still alive and talking when they found him, but the marshals couldn't answer any questions. Newspaper suggested moonshiners could'a shot him to retaliate for shutting down a dozen stills last week."

Peg handed back the scissors. "Any bounty hunters around here?"

"There is—a native man who can track anything or anyone. Criminals often run to the frontier."

"I know. My husband and I caught one."

The doctor stopped and looked up. "What happened?"

After her story, he warned, "Well, there's still plenty of call for hootch up here, so be careful. Did you know the term hootch actually came from the Tlingit village of Hootchenoo?"

"Really?"

"Yep, soldiers over in Sitka taught the Natives. Too bad, too. Many a Native's life been cursed by the stuff. Recently, the sheriff found five-gallon cans of hooch hidden in bales of hay. Someone even canned it and made labels to make people think it was tomatoes. There's a hefty fine and up to a year in jail."

"I guess when there's money to be made . . . "

"Yep, not only for the moonshiners. Kids who run into stills and report it get a $5.00 reward. One of our more enterprising boys here collects the bottles from the trash in back of the hotel and sells them back to the bootleggers," he chuckled.

CHAPTER 109

O ne week later, Amka still lay in the hospital. Dr. Johnson needed help, and Peg needed something to do between visiting hours. As they worked together, Peg and Dr. Johnson became friends. *I need to contact Ralph, but I love working with a doctor again. I wondered who's taken Mrs. Waterman's place at Dr. Phillips'.* During a slow afternoon, she decided to write to find out.

Anchorage, Alaska March 21, 1920

Dear Family,

I've been in Anchorage for two weeks because my friend Amka is in the hospital with a badly infected bite. She's expecting a baby this summer, and I'm looking forward to that! I ran into a Doctor Johnson at the hospital who's letting me help him while I'm here.

The Northern Lights are the best this month. I love watching them whirl like the skirt of a ballroom dancer. If Dr. Johnson doesn't need help between visiting hours, I spend time watching the ocean. The Humpback whales circle up and create a storm of bubbles that trap herring. Seagulls follow screaming

"Yah! Yah! Yah!" in applause. Boats fill the harbor
and head out. Men can make a year's wages in one
day if they're lucky.

Last week, Doctor sent me out with some of
his Native friends to catch salmon eggs. They cut
branches from hemlock trees and leave them in the
ocean. The salmon come to lay millions of eggs, so
many it changes the color of the water. The next
day, we hauled the branches into the boat. They
were so heavy I could hardly pull one in! The hemlock
branches were frosted thickly with eggs and
sparkled like jewels.

I've been thinking of home more lately,
probably because Ralph and I are apart. Who took
Mrs. Waterman's and my place at the doctor's
office? Has Uncle Ben had any problems from the
shooting? Has Mr. Harris come to trial yet in
Newport? A couple of weeks ago, the sheriff here
got shot with his own gun and died, but they
haven't been able to find out who did it. I guess
that's another thing that caused me to think
of home.

She paused. *Should I take that last sentence out? Mom's already
worried about me. I guess not. It'll give my brothers something exciting
to talk about.*

Mom, how are you doing? Those brothers of mine
taking up the slack around the place? I still think of
Dad often, too.

This is making me homesick! She put the pen down and looked out the window. After two weeks in Anchorage, she wanted to get back to her island. A slight, wiry man in a leather hat walked slowly down the street, looking carefully from side to side.

"Ralph!" Peg ran out.

The startled man looked up. He was a stranger.

CHAPTER 110

Three days later, they released Amka. The trip to Homer went smoothly. They checked into the Salty Dog. Peg walked to the post office, hoping to find The Kid to transport them home. Snow fell lightly on her face. The exercise felt wonderful. She followed the dirty trail, stomped out to the little shack sitting on the water's edge, pushed open the door and peered in. No one was there. A pile of mail dumped on the counter made her wish she'd brought her letter to send. She peeked out the window and began rummaging through the letters. A crumpled envelope with a Washington return address made her squeal. She sat down and tore it open. Three sheets of paper fluttered to the floor. The first letter had a bear, drawn by a child, on the back.

Dear Aunt Peg,

How's Alaska? I'd like to come shoot me a polar bear. Have you seen one? My mom says you won't see a Polar bear. Is she right? This is a bear I saw in the woods last week.

Love,

Wilbur

Dear Aunt Peg,

How much snow do you have? We've had two feet of snow this month, so I wonder how much you have in Alaska. We went sledding Saturday, and I won almost every race. Don't tell the others, but I greased my runners! I'm tired of school. Do you get to hunt and fish all day? What's the biggest fish you've caught so far?

Wish I could live up there with you.

Love,

Cliff

April 23, 1921, Newport, Washington

Dear Peg,

By the time this reaches you, this news will be old, but I trust you'll still be interested. Mrs. Sims (Waterman) had a baby boy last week. She's doing well after having gestational diabetes and a nine-pound baby! He is one doted-on baby, but with her personality, I doubt he'll be spoiled.

Charlie and Florence had a baby girl around Christmas time. They named her Bell, and I helped with the delivery. I ran into them the other day. The baby looks just like Charlie with red hair and freckles. Florence looks happier now that she's not living with her father.

Speaking of her father, he got sentenced, 15 years to life. He's in prison in Spokane. Your brothers and I attended the trial along with Ben and Freda. Such a relief to have that over with!

Spring is here. I've been looking out the window, watching little lambs and calves cavorting. The crocus and tulips are just starting to peek out. This was Dads favorite time of year. The boys help with lambing and calving. I spend most of my time at the store but can't wait to start digging in the flower beds and garden again.

I'm watching Lela's kids today. I got them to write you a letter. Now they're out playing baseball, mostly chasing the ball as there's not enough players. I miss watching you play. Have you had any chances to play ball there?

Had all the family for dinner for Freda's birthday two days ago. Little Wib is running all *over. Hard to believe he's grown so fast. You were missed.*

Write and let us know about all your adventures. We devour your letters.

Love,

Mom

Peg sniffed and returned to the Salty Dawg full of homesickness but determined to finish writing her letter.

CHAPTER 111

Spring finally elbowed her way through winter and burst onto Halibut Cove. Not only did Amka's waistline bulge, but the whole world burst forth with new life. The sun arrived earlier; sap rose in trees, pushing forth buds. The world turning green invigorated everything. Pussy willows' downy heads popped out, and ice melted, exposing rotting leaves full of insects. In April, the caribou started north, so cows could give birth on the North Slope before the snow turned soggy and difficult to walk in. They leapt through rivers as they jockeyed their way forward.

One lazy Sunday afternoon, Peg wandered over to visit her neighbors and stopped to watch a male Willow Ptarmigan repel intruders by stretching his long black neck and flashing his red eyebrows. He warned with machine-gun-like sounds: back, back, back, bbbbbbback. The hen fled to ground, camouflaged by her plumage.

Sundsby strolled over from the beach, sat beside Peg in the sun and started reminiscing, "When I lived in Nenana, whole town placed bets on ice breakup in the Tanana River. Built a big wooden tripod, hauled it to the middle of the frozen river and dug it down into the ice. Banner tied top of a tripod tripped a clock. When it fell, that marked the exact time of breakup. It's when spring officially starts."

Peg petted Miko, half asleep in her lap. "And when is that usually?"

"Anytime from middle of April to the middle of May."

Amka waddled over and sat next to them.

Sundsby moved over to make room. "Ralph and I been thinking. Maybe we should buy us a passenger boat. Know a guy here during the gold rush and paid for his whole boat with one trip up the river."

"But the Gold Rush's over, isn't it?" Peg doubted.

"Yeah, but there's still some prospecting, and there's money to be made mining those miners!"

Peg changed the subject. "Well, it's almost the middle of May. Another month, and you'll have a baby. Have you thought of names yet?"

"I'll name it if it's a boy, and Amka will name it if it's not," Sundsby allowed.

"I'm going to name my first girl, Peggy." Peg waved at Ralph, fishing in the cove.

"Hello!" His voice skipped back over the water.

"Won't that be confus-un?" Sundsby wondered.

"Well, Peg's not my real name."

"Really? What is it?"

"Gladys. Gladys Tarbet. But the kids at school called me 'Happy Bottom Black-butt.'"

"So you won't go by Peg after she's born?"

"No, then I'll be Mom!" Peg laughed.

"'Fore ya know it, yu'll see the fireweed blooming bright. It's my favorite time of year," Sundsby stated, recalling all the springs he'd witnessed in Alaska.

"When will it bloom?"

"Starts in summer—in full bloom by the end of July, first part of August."

"Is that the pink tall flower I saw in the meadows last year? Why do they call it fireweed?"

"Yup. Needs lotsa sunshine. Blooms after fire's cleared an area. Sometimes, they're as tall as you."

"What color?"

"Bright pink or purple."

"I do love having wildflowers for my table."

"I love spring," Sundsby continued. "Ice tinkling, shattering like glass, rivers heaving up blocks of snow and ice and honking geese—hundreds of 'em cummin to breed, grizzly cubs wrestling. Their ma keeps 'em up high, away from the males, feeding in the valleys. They eat young cubs," Sundsby reported.

"Ewwwh!" Peg stood as Ralph beckoned to her.

She walked over. "Any bites?"

"Nope." He cast out again.

Peg was ready to leave. "Let's go home. I'm hungry."

Ralph started reeling in the line. "No one has to call me twice to a meal."

CHAPTER 112

What was that? Someone outside? Peg leaned up on one elbow, held her breath and listened carefully. Yes. Footsteps pounded closer. She shook Ralph. "Wake up!" she whispered urgently. "Someone's coming!"

Ralph reached for his gun. When the footsteps beat a staccato on their wooden walkway, Ralph jumped out of bed and started for the door.

"Ralph! Peg!" Sundsby screamed.

"The baby!" Peg shouted, springing out of bed.

Ralph poked his head out. "It time?"

"Yep. Water's broken." Sundsby leaned over to catch his breath.

"Be right there," Peg announced as she threw her coat on and plopped down to lace boots.

The trio hurried back to Amka. "I'll wait out here," Ralph volunteered, sat and lit up a cigarette.

"You come in and help," Peg ordered when Sundsby hesitated. "Boil some water and find me some clean rags." He looked over his shoulder longingly at Ralph who shook his head.

"Come on! How long's she been in labor?" Peg scurried inside.

Amka squatted in the middle of the floor, holding onto the seat of a chair for support. She grimaced with each pain but didn't make a sound.

"Place a clean sheet under her. I need to wash my hands. Where's your soap?" Peg moved to Amka encouraging her. "You're doing well. Breathe through the pain," she instructed, but Amka was the calmest person in the room.

Peg dried her hands, checked Amka's progress and reported, "The baby's crowning. It shouldn't be long!" She held out her hands, ready to support the little head. "That's right. Push with each contraction."

Peg realized she wasn't needed as Amka serenely proceeded. However, she did catch the baby. When the baby boy cried, so did Peg. "Sundsby, sterilize a knife. We need to cut and tie the cord." She called over her shoulder. After the placenta delivery, she looked around for Sundsby.

He sat with a stunned look, holding the baby. "He's beautiful." A tear ran down his cheek. "Well, little Karl, I'm your papa."

"So his name's Karl?" Peg helped Amka into bed and began to firmly massage her stomach. "Take him over next to the stove. You need to keep him warm. Cover his wet head."

Little Karl started to wail. "Bring him to his mother," Peg suggested. He handed the baby to Amka who bared her breast. The baby nuzzled in and began sucking heartily. Sundsby chortled loudly. "He *is* my son!"

Peg stepped outside and announced, "They have a little boy and they're doing fine."

"I heard him," Ralph stood. "How about some coffee?"

"Good idea." Peg agreed. "I'll start breakfast. Want to come in?"

He threw another log on the outside fire. "Naw, I'll give them some time."

"OK," Peg replied, then bustled back in, put the coffee pot on, finished cleaning and started breakfast.

CHAPTER 113

P eg arrived to find Amka, making breakfast. "You need to relax and let yourself heal," she scolded.

"Natives don't do that," Sundsby explained.

"I don't care. I'm here, and I want to be of help." She took the baby from Sundsby. "Ralph's waiting for you outside." Peg looked into the sweet little face with a head full of black hair and sighed, "I do love babies." By mid-morning, with the housework completed, she got Amka to lie down and feed the baby. When the mother fell asleep, Peg picked up the baby, patted his back until rewarded with a loud burp and wished for a rocking chair.

All week, she returned to help Amka while the men fished. On Saturday, the men returned early. "Stay for dinner?" Sundsby invited.

After eating, the foursome sat outside, enjoying the summer sun. Peg asked Sundsby, "Think you'll ever move to the Lower 48?"

He grimaced and shook his head rapidly. "Never."

"Never? Why not?"

He stood with a determined look. "Got me a son now, half-breed. Don't want 'em called 'siwash'."

"What does siwash mean?" Peg asked, having never heard the term.

"Basically BAD Eskimo. Whites haven't been good to Natives."

Peg couldn't think of an incident she'd witnessed. "How? What do you mean, Sundsby?"

"For one thing, brought in lotta disease—wiped out whole villages. Was here in '18, and flu ran crazy 'mong the Natives. Ya know, they believe if someone dies in their home, they'll be next. Lotta times, they'd run to the neighbors, spreading disease. Finally got a sick house set up, but some believed they were trapped in a death house and hanged themselves."

"Oh no!" Peg gasped.

". . . not the worst . . ." he whispered, "two kids a sitting . . . in a house next to dead parents. Their dogs gnawing frozen bodies. Shot dogs and burned the cabins." He looked off into the distance. "Lotsa abandoned sled dogs roamed . . . feeding on dead in cabins." He lowered his head and shook it.

"What a nightmare!" Peg exclaimed.

"Ja. Mail carriers delivered orders forbidding potlatches and passed the flu from village to village. York wiped out and more 'un half a Wales. Soon as the ground thawed 'nuff, they all got buried in a common grave. Ja, very bad year."

"I'll say!"

"Not all." Sundsby sat, took a deep breath, put his elbows on his knees and rested his head in his hands.

"What else?"

"Same year *Princess Sophia* sank."

"A ship?" Peg asked.

"Ja, steamship from Canada. Hundreds a miners headed south. Bad winter storm . . . 100-mile winds, 30-foot waves, struck a reef . . . sunk," he choked up.

"Any survivors?" Peg asked, completely caught up in his story.

"Nej," he shook his head. A tear dropped from his chin..

"You knew someone on that ship, didn't you?"

He slipped into his native tongue. "Min bror."

"I'm so sorry." Peg put her hand on his arm. "I'll check on dinner. You'll feel better after you eat."

CHAPTER 114

That night in bed, Peg tossed and turned upset by what had happened to her friend. "What's a matter?" Ralph muttered.

"Can't quit thinking about what Sundsby told us. Did you know about his brother?"

"Nope. Told me some about the '18 flu, though. I've heard stories about the Sophia sinking. Rumor is over a million dollars of gold went down with her."

"Really? Have you heard of siwash before?"

"Yeah, think it means savage. People think Natives stink. They have to sit in the back of theaters—things like that."

"Well, they do stink!" Peg admitted. "Don't bathe often and those furs!"

"Yeah, but they're still people."

Peg sighed, "Hard to know if we're hurting or helping them. Used to think they needed our help, like with medicine."

"Yeahhh," Ralph yawned, indicating he wanted to get to sleep.

Peg had something else she wanted to discuss, but Ralph snored lightly. She rolled over. In the distance, a chorus of wolves howled, and Miko joined. Wood crackled in the Yukon stove. A breeze made the tent walls sway to the lullaby.

By the end of June, Peg knew for sure and decided to write to her family.

June 30, 1921

Dear Family,

It's beautiful here. Hummingbirds are coming back from Mexico—one of the first signs of summer. How those little things make it all this way is just a wonder! The red-breasted sap sucker returns when sap starts to flow. I like to watch male ground squirrels fight for turf. The other evening, Ralph and I watched a moose in a pond. We thought it was a big rock until it raised its head. Water ran from his enormous antlers while he chewed pond weed and water lilies.

The whole territory has come back to life. After sixty-five days of darkness, it's so welcome. Someone named winter "The Great Silence." I've decided not to be silent. We're expecting a baby in February! I've enjoyed Amka's little boy so much! Ralph's excited, too. Mom, could you come next spring after breakup to share this beautiful place and happy time?

Any news of Rose? Don't have her address, so am enclosing a letter. Will you see she gets it? Please write soon and give the family all my love.

Peg

She addressed the envelope and wrote another.

Dear Rose,

Won't repeat what I told my family. I'm sure they'll share their letter with you. How's the love life? Why don't you come visit? They have a saying about finding a man in Alaska: "Odds are good, but the goods are odd!" Funny, but not totally true. I've seen many eligible bachelors here. In fact, women are scarce. You'd be a smashing hit. Some men have made a lot of money.

    You could stay with us and use your beautiful voice to sing lullabies to our baby. Yes, I'm having a baby sometime around February. Been sewing a layette. I've knit a couple pairs of booties. Now, I'm making moccasins. My friend, Amka, a native woman who lives close, taught me how to tan and sew hides. She helped me make a pair of mukluks for Ralph. I've always wanted six hungry boys to feed, hunt, and fish with.

    I'd LOVE you to come up. You're the best girlfriend I've ever had. Most of my friends were boys, no surprise!

Love,

Peg

She licked the envelopes. Excitement about the coming baby didn't help with the sickness. Every afternoon, nausea returned. "Not *morning* sickness. I usually do things opposite," she muttered as another wave hit her. She flew outside, bent double and heaved.

Usually she made it behind a bush, not this time. She wiped her face and kicked sand over it.

It's been two months. Should subside soon. It worked best to eat small meals several times a day. Evenings were the worst. Often, she set out dinner for Ralph and crawled into bed. *Should have planned to be sick during the winter, not when I want to be outside!* Every morning she felt better, but by four o'clock, the nausea returned.

One evening, Ralph came home with ginger root. "Wherever did you find this?" Peg wondered.

"Chinese man fishing next to us. Came as a railroad worker. You meet people from all over the world. Here, chew a little." Peg nibbled.

"How 'bout a walk?" Ralph suggested. Strolling down the beach, they rounded a cove to find a whale sunning itself.

"Oh! Wish I had the camera!" she whispered.

Ralph noticed an eagle as it wheeled overhead and flew to his nest in the top of a tree.

Peg thought of her eagle's nest back home when Ralph broke the silence.

"We saw so many terns the other day, thousands. They caused such a racket that Sundsby and I couldn't even hear the ocean."

Peg unconsciously cradled her stomach. "Such a dark, cold and lonely world a few months ago. Now it bursts forth with life."

CHAPTER 115

Peg worked every day with Miko. After harness training, she tied a piece of wood to a towline, hooked it to the harness, ran alongside, encouraging him to pull, then rewarded him with treats. Slowly, she increased the weight behind and taught the command "Hike!"

"Think we could fashion some kind of cart for Miko to pull, so he'll be ready to try a sled this winter," Peg asked Ralph.

"Sure. Maybe he'll be ready for skijoring."

"For what?"

"Skijoring—when a dog pulls a person on skis. But first, he must learn to pull a cart."

"Sounds fun! When can we build it?"

Ralph's eyes twinkled, "How 'bout tomorrow? I'll quit a little early," he promised.

"Yes!" Peg clapped.

"Been thinking. Heard about an ice cave in Juneau. We ought to see some things this summer before the baby comes," Ralph suggested.

"Let's do it! When? How long will it take to get there? How long will we stay? Can we afford to take time from fishing?"

"Sundsby's leaving for a week."

"When's he leaving?"

"Friday."

"I'll be ready! Oh, I should ask Amka to take care of Miko again. I love having things to look forward to!" She gave Ralph a hug.

CHAPTER 116

A s soon as they arrived in Juneau, Peg wanted to go right to the cave. "Let's settle in first," Ralph suggested. "Find a place to stay for a few nights and get some info from one of the locals."

"OK, I'm starving. There a cafe close?"

"Well, you're eating for two, so first order of business—food, right after we find a hotel." Ralph walked briskly, carrying both suitcases while Peg trotted on wooden sidewalks alongside. They passed no-frills storefronts, their flat front walls ascending two stories.

"I love an adventure!" she chirped.

"I know," he chuckled. *That's one of the things I so love about you.*

The Alaskan Hotel and Bar caught Peg's eye as the only building with bay windows. "Let's eat there," she suggested.

After dinner, Ralph asked the morose bartender, "How far to the glacier from here?"

"Which one?"

"The closest."

"That'd be the Mendenall Glacier. 'Spect it's 10-12 miles from here."

"How'd we get there?"

He hesitated as if thinking. "Walk or ride."

"Ride what?"

"Horses."

"Any place here I can rent a couple for a day?"

He replaced a glass on the shelf behind him. "Two blocks north, then a block down, at the livery stable."

"Thank you." Ralph turned and motioned for Peg to follow. "Better wait and get horses tomorrow. We want a full day to explore."

"Think we'll see the glacier calving?"

"Not sure," he replied, shrugging.

A young man at the livery stable spotted them coming and bounded out. "Afternoon, folks! What can I do for ya?" Sunlight behind him illuminated the downy blond hair on his cheeks.

"Looking for couple of horses to ride to the Mendenhall Glacier," Ralph answered.

"Sure 'nuff. Do you want a fast ride or a gentle?" He struck out toward the stables.

Peg stopped him. "Wait. We don't want them until tomorrow."

"Oh, let me check." The boy ducked into a cubbyhole office.

Ralph cocked an eyebrow at Peg. "So, fast or gentle one?"

She put her hands on her waist. "What do you think?"

"A gentle one for the lady," he called out to the boy, then snickered.

The boy returned with a chagrined look on his face, "So sorry. Only one horse's available tomorrow. Do you think your daughter could ride with you?"

"That's okay," Peg giggled. "Now he won't lose a race."

"A girl expecting shouldn't be racing anyway," Ralph stated, making Peg blush. "We'll ride together."

"Good. Let me get your name and a small deposit."

After paying, they meandered through the town until they arrived at the Bergman Hotel, a big boxy building with no decorative architecture. Ralph bought a newspaper and a cigar from the clerk. "I'll stay here and read a few minutes, so this"—he waved the cigar—"won't smoke up our room."

"Thank you. Dad used to smoke one when I had an earache and blow the smoke in my ear. It reminds me of pain," Peg grimaced. "I think I'll have a nice, long, hot bath."

The key jangled in a loose lock, forcing her to work it a couple of times before the door gave in. She unpinned her hair, brushed it for a few minutes and started undressing. *Maybe I'll start the tub filling.* She opened the connecting door.

A large bearded man lay in the tub, half asleep. Long hairy legs draped over the sides. "Oh! Excuse me!" Peg squealed, slammed the door shut, turned the lock and collapsed on the bed in a fit of giggles. She heard a sudden sloshing through the door and water gurgling down the drain. A few minutes later, a knock on the bedroom door caused her to jump.

"Yes?"

"Finished, mam. Your turn," he announced, clearing his throat to subdue laughter.

"Thank you!" *Better wait awhile, just to be sure.*

Another knock and she grabbed her clothes, "Yes?"

"It's me," Ralph spoke from the hall.

"Oh, OK, coming."

"Your hair's not wet," Ralph observed.

"There was a man in the tub."

He looked askance. "How'd ya know it was a man?"

"Walked in on him!"

He walked to the adjoining door and checked the doorknob. "Oh, didn't I mention we share a bathroom?"

She slapped his arm. "No, you didn't!"

CHAPTER 117

The young man at the livery stable had their horse saddled and tied to the hitching post out front. "Got any saddle bags?" Ralph inquired.

"It'll be another dollar."

"Fine. Peg, if you'll pay him, I'll put our food and drink in the bags." He ran his hand over the horse's flank, picked up a leg and inspected its hoof.

"Just put a new set on 'em," the boy proudly announced.

Ralph lowered the hoof. "Did a fine job."

The boy beamed. "You got a canoe?"

Ralph's eyebrows shot up. "What?"

"A canoe."

"What for?"

"Easiest way to the cave's across the lake."

"Thought we could hike in."

"Ya can but be careful. Go to the west side of the glacier. Watch out. It's slippery, and rocks have fallen on people."

They started off easy. The smell of horse, clopping hooves, creaking leather, warm sun on her back and twitter of birds in trees created a sense of peace in Peg. After an hour, she got restless. "If we go at this pace, we won't have time to explore," she whispered in Ralph's ear.

"Giddy up!" he slapped the reins. Peg threw her head back, laughed, and they loped. She peered around Ralph when he called, "Whoa!"

"Why are we stopping?"

"There," he said, looking at the valley of snow unfolding among rock mountains.

"Not what I expected. Thought there'd be a great wall of snow. This looks like winter at home."

Ralph slid off and held up his arms. "Be careful. It's muddy." They hiked up the hill, sliding over ice-covered rocks, scrabbling along until they saw the entrance.

"Hang onto me." Ralph put his hand out. "If you fall into that ice-cold stream, the adventure will be over." They clamored over moss-covered rocks, their feet feeling for purchase. Ralph slipped, landing on his backside. "Umph! This may be too dangerous for you."

"Oh no! I'll be careful," she promised and eased down a steep trail, avoiding an army of jumbled rocks the retreating glacier had heaved behind. The debris varied from boulders the size of a shed to pebbles. She stepped across a small stream, coursing its way to the lake below. Ralph broke a branch from a tree and made a walking stick for her.

Two hours later, they arrived at the opening. Light shimmered on undulating ice blue walls and disappeared into caves carved by melted water. "Listen." Peg stopped. Water, dripping, gurgling, splashing, rushing, beckoned them in. "Oh!" Peg drew in her breath. "It's another world! Look!" She spotted a waterfall ahead. "Like a fantasy!" They crossed an ankle-deep stream. She stopped and ran her hand over a staircase of ice. "Reminds me of salt licks back home, like unearthly creatures with mammoth tongues have been here."

They traversed along the river. Ralph heard a crack, ducked and yelled over his shoulder, "Stay back!" An icicle three feet ahead crashed down.

"You okay?" Peg cried anxiously.

"This might not be the best idea."

"Gotten faint-hearted on me?"

"I didn't have a wife who's expecting before." Ralph reached for Peg's hand.

Peg grasped it. "Thanks for bringing me here."

The only light filtered down from above; through the blue glow, they picked their way, taking care not to slip into the river.

"It's magical," Peg whispered completely awestruck by the beauty.

Ralph stopped and kissed her cheek. "Like you."

After leaving the cave, they rode northeast and heard a great roaring and splashing. As they rounded a bend, a mist enveloped them.

Peg gasped, "Look!" White water tumbled down the mountain to a lake, reflecting snow-covered peaks in its glassy waters.

Two tiers of water crashed onto the sandbar. "This must be what they call Nugget Falls," Ralph guessed.

Peg slid off. "Let's eat here!"

"Read my mind," Ralph confessed as he retrieved the saddlebags and looked at his watch. "Supper time, not lunch. No wonder I'm so hungry."

"This long summer sun fools me all the time, too." Peg plopped onto the beach, took off her shoes and dug her toes into the sand.

With full stomachs, they lay, relaxing in the sun. Peg fell asleep.

An hour later, Ralph shook her shoulder. "Wake up. Your face is getting sunburned."

Peg moaned and rolled up.

"Time to head back. It's almost eight. Only a few hours of daylight left."

They rode into town just as the sun slipped behind a peak, making the tops of the mountain blush.

CHAPTER 118

"The next morning over breakfast, Ralph proposed a plan. How 'bout we stop at Primrose on the way home?"

Peg took a bite of toast. "Where's that?"

"North of home a few hours, still on Kenai Peninsula. I want to see the salmon spawn."

"Which kind?"

"Sockeye, Coho, chum salmon, all spawn on Ptarmigan Lake near Primrose. Sundsby said it's the best place to watch the sockeye."

Peg jumped up and brushed the crumbs from her lap. "Let's do it!"

"Hang on. We have to go to Seward first. It's about 15 miles north." Ralph looked over the map. "You up for a couple days of hiking?"

"What do you think?"

By the time they arrived at the ocean shore, Peg lagged behind. *Boy! He acts half his age!* "This pregnancy must be slowing me down," she explained when Ralph kept looking over his shoulder.

They stopped where the sockeyes entered fresh water. Silvery blue hoards fighting upstream flashed beneath the water. "They'll have to smolt before they head upstream," Ralph said.

"Do what?"

"Smolt. Adjust from seawater back to fresh water," Ralph explained. "Let's camp here tonight." He stopped beneath two towering pines. "We'll follow the stream to the lake tomorrow."

Peg unpacked her pole. "Right. I'm hankering for fish dinner!"

Ralph cleared a tent spot and made a fire ring.

After dinner, they lay on the blanket. "We used to stargaze this time of night, but the sun hasn't even set yet!" Peg yawned. "I don't think I can wait until they come out."

Ralph stood and held out his hand. "We need a good rest. 'Nother big hike ahead tomorrow."

The next day, Ralph stopped and held one finger to his mouth. Playful grizzlies splashed through water, churned by thousands of salmon. The bears bit off the head and skin, letting the rest fall back into the water.

"Why are they wasting most of the fish?" Peg whispered.

"Skin and brain are the fattiest parts." They put down their packs and watched for over an hour. Then they followed the stream, threading its way to the sea. At noon, Peg suggested they eat. Ralph opened a can of beans with his pocketknife and Peg washed apples in the stream.

"Look! It's different fish!" she called back to Ralph. The stream swarmed with brilliant red bodies and green heads.

Ralph trotted over. "No, they change color after entering fresh water."

"What is that?" Peg pointed at a fish's large bottom jaw shaped like a hook.

"His kype. He uses it to nip at other males in his fight for females."

"It's sure ugly! When do they head back to the ocean?"

"They don't. They return back to their birthplace, spawn and die. But they provide food for other species, bear, eagles and other fish."

"Mother Earth's incredible."

"Yes," Ralph concurred. "Alyeska, The Great Land."

Peg watched a fish beating its tail rapidly in the steam's gravel. "Is that a female trying to attract a male?"

"No, she's digging a hole to lay her eggs in. Look over here." He led her upstream. Clusters of pink eggs hung among the rocks in the streambed. Parts of the river teemed with them, tinting the water. "Some people think the eggs are a delicacy, you know." Ralph's eyes twinkled and he smacked his lips.

"Horse feathers!"

His eyes widened. "Believe it. It's true."

"Show me. Eat some!" Peg challenged.

He scooped up a handful and swallowed.

CHAPTER 119

The next afternoon, Peg pushed herself from her sickbed to a sitting position. "Augh!" She reached for the can and deposited what was left of breakfast. Nothing helped—not ginger root, not keeping her stomach full—nothing. *I'm over three months. The nausea should have subsided! Hope my baby's getting enough nourishment.*

Outside, Ralph stoked the fire, then returned to the tent. "Peg?" he knelt next to her. She stared from sunken eyes.

"Where've you been?"

"Around. You're dehydrated." He held forth the rusty canteen, "Drink."

She shook her head. "I'll just heave it up."

He slipped his hand behind her neck and raised her head. "Think of the baby. Sip slowly."

She closed her eyes, took a sip and collapsed back into the pile of blankets.

Footsteps approached the tent. "Anyone home?"

Ralph flinched, reached for the gun, sprung up and poked his head out.

"Hope I didn't wake you," a tall stranger apologized.

"Nah, just checking on my wife." Ralph clambered out. He held the gun in plain sight as he walked closer and held out his hand. "Name's Ralph, Ralph Sparks. We need a doctor."

The man drew back in surprise. "Well . . . there's a survey crew for the bridge at Hurricane Gulch. I'll go get help." He craned his neck, trying to look in the tent.

"Appreciate it!" Ralph exhaled. "Don't dare leave her."

An hour later, the roar of an engine brought Ralph to his feet. A bulldozer dragged a flatbed through the meadow. His new friend waved. Ralph loped toward him. "How'd ya manage this?"

"Got connections. Get your blankets. I'll make 'er a bed." He flapped his hand. "Now go help yer wife."

Ralph gently shook Peg's shoulder. "Sweetheart, wake up. Your ride's here."

She rolled over and mumbled, "What ride?"

He pulled back the covers and jerked her clothes from the knapsack. "Come and see! Here," he dropped her clothes. "Put these on while we make you a bed."

Peg groaned, tugged on a shirt and pants and staggered out.

"Ta-da!" Ralph patted the blankets piled on the flatbed. "Hop up."

Confused, she looked about. "Where are we going?"

"To the doctor!" Ralph boosted her on the flatbed, climbed aboard and plopped next to her. He chatted with the sun-burned driver. "How's the bridge coming?"

"Pretty well. Should be ready for trains end of August." He swept his arm over the landscape. "Highest bridge in the whole U.S.," he boasted.

The flatbed jostled over a jarring dirt road. Diesel fumes floated back. Peg hung her head over the side. Ralph made her sip water, but she threw it up, twice. Two hours later, they jolted to a stop at Hurricane Gulch. Ralph shook his head as he surveyed the area.

The road held a tangle of trees and boulders that blocked their way. "Washed out. Now what?" he asked the driver.

The driver looked up. "See that platform up there on the cable? We use it to send tools back and forth. If you can get her to climb that ladder, we could take her across."

Peg shaded her eyes and peered up at the platform, swinging over the gulch. Three hundred feet below it, a river coursed through jagged rocks. She gulped.

"She'll do it," Ralph assured him. Turning to Peg, he put his arm around her. "Come on. I'll be right behind you."

Peg placed one foot on the ladder's first step, straining for a hold on the higher one while Ralph pushed from behind. She gritted her teeth and avoided looking down. Hand over hand, her knees shook as they gradually ascended. When they got to the platform, Ralph looked over the side and whistled, "Woo! Long way down!"

Peg collapsed, shut her eyes and clamped sweaty hands onto the cable car's side. The cable whined, and the car screeched as it swung slowly across the gulch.

After two weeks in the Anchorage hospital, Peg rose. "Let's go home. I'm afraid I'm a better nurse than patient."

Chapter 120

Mother Nature yawned. Cotton grass bowed sleepy heads in the wind, signaling the end of August. Even the pesky mosquitoes died. Flying squirrels chirped, barked and soared through trees, intent on their missions. Red squirrels dropped thousands of spruce cones and scurried about, storing the seeds in underground tunnels. Daylight lessened. Fog crept in often. By early October, fall reigned. Bright yellow and deep purple crawled over mountains while snow dusted their peaks. Russet, amber, scarlet leaves and shades of gold from birch and alder trees stood out among a backdrop of evergreens.

With winter coming, Peg spent every possible minute outdoors. Most days, she walked Miko to Amka's and looked forward to playing with little Karl. She trained Miko, an apt student, to pull the sled. He followed commands unless he spotted something to chase. When a pika scurried by, Miko shot off, deaf to Peg's commands, tipping her from the sled and barking furiously in pursuit. When the sled caught in the brush, Miko strained at the reins, and the pika escaped—almost. Just as it made it to a pile of rocks, a Golden Eagle dove snatching it. Peg hurried over, scolding, "Miko, you naughty boy!" and untangled the reins.

She meandered through dappled forest light. A cow moose, eating leaves and bark, raised its head at the sound of bulls. Their bellowing and crashing rang through the forest. "Rutting season," Peg murmured and tightened her hold on Miko's leash. The bulls pounded closer. Bloody velvet hung from one's antlers. They circled each other like boxers, pawing the ground, the bells of their necks wagging. They locked antlers. The victor forced his opponent to skate backwards into the undergrowth. Peg and even Miko watched transfixed. When the cow took off, the reigning bull followed. The losing contestant sank into the woods. Miko came back to life, barking, and straining at his leash. "Stay!" she commanded and waited until they couldn't hear the moose before continuing to Amka's.

That night, Peg related the incident to Ralph. "We'll keep a watch for moose antlers this winter," he commented.

"When do they lose them?"

"Middle of December into early spring—after rutting season. I've seen some that must a been six feet across." Ralph blew a circle of cigarette smoke, leaned back and watched it float above his head. "Not easy to find a clean set, though. Mice, squirrels and such gnaw 'em."

Peg raised her eyebrows. "They eat bone?"

"Yep."

Chapter 121

Winter blasted in with relentless winds and heavy snowfall. After the turmoil, Peg stepped outside. Snow smothered all life, and clouds erased the horizon. Yet, the valiant sun tried to push through. Complete silence reigned—no birds twittering, no leaves rustling. Glistening daggers grew along the bottom of a downed tree limb. Peg tensed her muscles, hugging herself against winter's biting teeth.

"There's beauty in death," she whispered to the hushed world. A wind kicked up, making the naked trees shiver and fling snow floating to the earth. She scurried inside and backed up to the wood stove. Time for a bath, but she was loath to take off any clothes in the drafty tent. Taking the bucket by the door, she dashed outside to gather snow and filled the big pot on the stove. She added wood to the fire and jumped back under bed covers, waiting for the snow to melt and heat.

When the water boiled, she gritted her teeth, forced herself up and put on a pot of coffee. Peeling off two layers, she looked at her swollen stomach, cupping her hands underneath. "Who are you, little one?" The baby kicked, making a bulge. Peg giggled. "So you heard me!" She scrubbed goose-pimpled skin above her bulging waist and pulled her shirt on before washing the lower half.

Since the weather turned, Peg didn't often venture to Amka's. She spent time keeping the stove stoked, replenishing the wood next to the tent, cooking, crocheting baby booties, sewing a layette and working with Miko. She read and reread Ralph's books on Alaska and learned facts, even he didn't know.

Late one afternoon, after returning from checking his traps, Ralph dragged in a wolverine. Peg looked askance. "What are you going to do with that?"

"Eat-un it," Ralph replied with a poker face.

"*I'm* not cooking it!"

"No, I'll have Amka help me skin it. It'll make a great conversation piece," he stated as he held it up proudly.

"I'll go with you. Let's hook up Miko to the sled," Peg suggested.

"Tomorrow. It's too late now. By the way, I heard from Sundsby today of a woman who will help us when it's time for the baby."

Relief flooded Peg. "Who?"

"Name's Norton—trained nurse from the navy—guess she graduated John Hopkins. Came ta doctor the Natives. Sundsby said he'd talk to her. She comes a couple of weeks before, just in case."

"Good."

"When you want her to come?"

She took a clothespin from the makeshift laundry line strung across the tent and grabbed a towel to wipe her hands on. "Well, I think the first part of February will work."

"I'll pass it on." He took the lid off the pot bubbling on the stove.

"That's not ready to eat yet," Peg warned. "Can I check the trapline with you tomorrow?"

"O-kaay," he hesitated, "I've a trap a couple of miles away."

CHAPTER 122

A milky moon still presided over the crystalline landscape at nine in the morning. While Ralph prepared the sled, Peg banked the fire. As she pulled the door open, smoke filled her lungs. She shrank back, coughing and rubbing her eyes and opened the damper. Smoke rose, allowing her to wrestle a couple more logs in.

As she kicked the last log, Ralph entered reproving, "Hey, you should wait for me. Quit lifting such heavy things!"

"It wasn't that heavy. What do you think we'll find in the trap?"

"Mmm . . . any number of animals: marten, fox—if we get lucky—a lynx!"

Peg strained to button her coat over her stomach. "I hope it's a red fox. That'd make a nice collar."

They entered the frozen wilderness. Miko sat waiting in front of the sled. Peg waddled up and patted his head.

Ralph held up the snowshoes. "Want these or the sled? Can ya stay on the runners? Don't want you to take a spill."

"Don't want to wobble on snowshoes," Peg stated as she climbed onto the sled.

He lifted a gun. "Well, don't go too far ahead. Put this in."

The hushed silence cracked as Peg called, "Hike!" Miko sprang forward, creating a spray of crystals in the dry snow. She looked over her shoulder, stopping periodically when she couldn't see Ralph.

"Whoa!" Miko slowed to a stop. Only the dog's panting broke the silence of the desolate landscape. Peg readjusted the scarf over her face and squeezed her hands inside her mittens, pulling her fingers and thumb into the warmth of the middle while waiting for him to catch up. It didn't take long for him to reappear, but this time she waited until he came alongside as she wasn't sure which way to turn.

Without stopping, he motioned to the left. She waited until he almost disappeared, then urged Miko forward. Finally, Ralph stopped and surveyed the landscape. "In that grove of trees," he directed and snowshoed toward them.

A gray shape in the distance told Peg they'd caught something. She stopped next to Ralph who waited for the gun. "A coyote?" she guessed.

"Nope, too small. Stay back. I'll make sure it's dead. Bring the knife when I drag it out. Needs to be gutted ASAP before it freezes." He headed to a clearing in the trees.

Peg staked Miko and dug through their pack for knives, then plodded through snow, wishing she'd thought to put in more snowshoes. "What is it?"

"Gray fox." He released the catch. "This won't take long, not too frozen yet. Why don't you keep an eye out?"

"For what?" Peg's eyes darted. "Aren't the bears hibernating?"

"For anything," he grunted.

A shadow slipped behind a tree. Peg stood and peered into the forest. Nothing moved. Maybe it was her imagination. She strained to hear something. Silence. The pre-dawn light started seeping in. She turned slowly ninety degrees and listened again. Nothing. Mentioning bears made her jumpy. She cocked her gun and walked toward the trees, noticing frozen berries still on the bush. The sky opened, giving birth to soft flakes. The dot-dash prints of an arctic hare filled with snow, erasing any sign of its passing.

Miko began barking. "Quiet, boy," she called, but he jerked at the rope and barked furiously. Slogging over as fast as possible, she reached him just as he pulled the stake from the ground. He jumped. She caught him. They both tumbled. Miko sprang up, overturned the sled and dumped its contents, dragging it as he darted toward Ralph. She pulled herself up to a chilling sight. A snarling cohort of wolves circled Ralph and the dead fox. One charged Miko. As dog and wolf fought, Peg groped in the snow for the gun. The animals rolled through the snow, preventing a clean shot, so she drew a bead on a wolf near Ralph and squeezed the trigger. It yelped, jumped and fell into the snow. The rest stalked Ralph and the food they needed.

Peg moved closer; growling increased. She put another bullet in the chamber. Boom! The rest ran into the forest. She returned to the fighting pair. Blood-stained snow made her heart jump. "You dirty devil," she hissed, raised the barrel and watched for an opportunity. The lines from the sled tangled around Miko, hampering him. Boom! The wolf collapsed. Peg started for Miko.

"Hold up!" Ralph shouted. "Make sure it's safe!"

Peg waddled toward Miko. He lay still in the snow, eyes closed. "Miko?" Peg sobbed. Ralph gently turned the dog over. "He's still alive. Untangle the lines. I'll load him." While Peg worked at the lines, Ralph retrieved the gray fox; he loaded it and Miko in the sled. He placed himself in the lines and called to Peg, "Can you get the snowshoes and walk out?"

"Yes." She strained over her stomach, fumbling with buckles. They started the slow pull home. The walk and emotion left Peg drained. She put snow on to melt, retrieved her medical kit, sewed up three large gashes on Miko, applied ointment and wrapped the wounds. Miko lay quietly, only whimpering a little when she cleaned the deepest cut. Ralph made Miko a bed by the door. "Too warm," he explained when Peg raised her eyebrows. "We can step over him."

During the night, Peg's back ached. *Did too much today.* She fidgeted while Ralph snored softly. She rubbed her back suffering in silence. *I should check on Miko.* Covers slipped from her shoulder; she slithered closer to Ralph. A strong wind kicked up. It started as a moan and worked itself into a keening howl, undulating the tent's walls. *How does he sleep through this? I need to use the bedpan.*

He yawned and pulled her back. "Where ya off to?"

"Got to go!" she pushed off his chest.

He rose. "So do I. Better check my trap line 'fore that storm brewing comes in."

"I'll go with you." Peg offered half-heartedly.

"You stay here where it's warm."

"OK," she agreed immediately. After checking on Miko, she crawled under the covers.

Ralph stoked the fire, pulled on his coat and fought his way out the tent door.

When Miko stirred and whined, Peg sat up. "Coming, boy. Let's get you some food."

The wind subsided. After dressing Miko's wounds, she grabbed her back. *This baby's coming early.* She scribbled Ralph a note, dressed and wrangled the rowboat into the cove. Halfway down the island, a southwest storm shoved the boat back, raising swells over the sides. At Beluga Spit, she gave up, pulled the boat ashore and started home. By the time she arrived, 30-foot tides crashed in. There'd be no leaving now. Adding to her worry, Ralph still hadn't returned.

She checked Miko, gave him water, lay down and started timing the pains—thirty minutes. She boiled water, gathered clean towels and sterilized their sharpest knife. The next pain doubled her over. She glanced at her watch—ten minutes apart. She lay down, going over everything she remembered about childbirth. Someone kicked snow from boots on the porch. When Ralph entered, tears started.

He rushed to her side. "What's wrong?"

"I'm having the baby," she sniffed, squared her shoulders and wiped her face on the sheet.

"No way to get out of the cove. Colossal swells out there, but we'll manage. You've helped deliver babies, and I've birthed animals. Can't be that different."

Two hours later, Peg held a baby girl in her arms. Ralph cleaned up and sank into a chair. "What shall we name her?"

"Peggy Joy. Peggy after me, and Joy 'cause I know she'll be one her whole life."

Ralph groaned, "Drat! I've got a couple of martens to skin. You okay? I'll be right outside if you need me."

Peg kissed the fuzzy little head nestled in her arm. "Go ahead. We'll be fine."

CHAPTER 123

23 February 1922

Dear Family,

I'm a mother! On February 8th, I had a beautiful little girl, Peggy Joy Sparks. She has dark hair, brown eyes like mine and a little round face. She's living up to her name—truly a joy! Mom, I missed having you here, but Ralph and I did fine. Had a giant storm, and no one could get in or out of the cove. I'm grateful for the times I went with you on those midwife visits!

We have a couple of doctors not far from here. They're brothers. One's a doctor and one a dentist. They raise blue and silver foxes. The doctor had planned to work in some hunting and fishing with Ralph and be around for the delivery, but the baby came early during a monstrous storm! Also, Mrs. Norton was going to come. She's been here this week helping, though, and things are going well. I feel great, but of course, don't go out—too cold for a new baby!

We stay close to the fire. I read, sew and crochet. I'm knitting Peggy some little mittens. Thanks for teaching me to do handwork. It keeps me from going crazy.

When cabin fever strikes, Ralph sits with the baby, and I visit my friend, Amka, or take our dog, Miko, out. I worked with him all summer, and he's turned into a good sled dog.

Do you think you could come for a visit after breakup next year? I miss you all terribly and am so anxious to show off my little girl! Don't know when I'll be able to get this letter out. Hoping The Kid pulls in soon with the mail.

My love to all,

Peg

Ralph stepped outside. "Peg! Come out and look at this," he called urgently.

"Coming," she lay the baby down and held her finger over her lips. "The baby's sleep—," she stopped, her attention drawn to the sky. "What is **that**?"

A bright ball of fire filled the horizon, flanked by two shimmering half suns, all connected by a halo of light.

"They're called Sun Dogs."

"Feels like we're on another planet," Peg whispered in awe.

Ralph put his arm around her. "Beautiful, but the Natives fear them. They think they're evil stars, trying to kill the sun, so they make all kinds of noise to scare them away."

Where'd they come from?

"Ice crystals in the atmosphere that reflect light."

Peg snuggled in under his arm. "It's for the three of us, you, me and little Peg."

Unladylike Peg

*Tarbet Family on front porch of their home in
Penrith, Washington about 1907*

Left to right
Back Row: John Burt, Mary Luemma, Lelah Zoe Tarbet Amsbaugh,
Inez Vivian Tarbet Lickly, Jesse Eugene, George Wilbur,
Freda Marie Tarbet Fox
Front Row: Lester Mervyn (Mud) , Gladys Irene (Peg),
and Edwin Bertelle Tarbet

Great Northern Railroad station, Newport, Washington, 1920s

Peg about 1920

Lester Mervyn Tarbet, "Mud," Peg's closest sibling

Ed Tarbet, oldest of the Tarbet children and "The Wrestler."
The contest in the book did occur, but I created the details.

On their honeymoon: Ralph Sparks,
Stanley Park, Vancouver, British Columbia, July 1920

Peg in Alaska, 1920

Herring saltires in Alaska

Ralph's 120-pound halibut

Peg with dog sleds

*When Peg became dehydrated from nausea,
she used this cable car to get to the hospital
(http://www.alaskarails.org/historical/nore/3/index.html).*

Peg's Mother, Mary Luemma Long Tarbet

Acknowledgments

My heartfelt thanks to all those who have supported me in writing this book:

My loving husband who believes in my dreams.

My editor, Linda Kay Kurtenbach, the best cheerleader and editor, who works tirelessly until she's satisfied everything is perfect!

My dear sisters in heaven, Linda and Kathy, who have joined our grandmother in the next great adventure.

My saintly departed mother after whom I modeled Peg's mother, Mary.

And of course, my adventurous, fun and optimistic grandmother, Peg.

Great thanks to familysearch.org and ancestry.com for helping me discover and preserve my family history.

About the Author
Nikki Freestone Sorensen

Nikki Freestone Sorensen, a family history enthusiast and teacher, has been researching and preserving family stories for over forty years.

She finds this African proverb inspiring: "When an old man (or woman) dies, a library burns to the ground."

Nikki believes connecting with ancestors provides us with a sense of identity. We learn new perspectives and gain insights from them. Family stories inspire and strengthen us to meet life's challenges.

For people with a difficult family history, consider the advice of George Bernard Shaw: "If you cannot get rid of the family skeleton, you may as well make it dance."

She recommends visiting the following to help you find and preserve your own family history:

familysearch.org   storycorps.com
ancestry.com   rootstech.org

To learn more about the author and read the first chapter in the second book of this series, visit
www.unladylikebook.com
or scan the QR code on the back of the book.

Nikki would love to hear from you.
Contact her at nikkidear4@gmail.com.

CPSIA information can be obtained
at www.ICGtesting.com
Printed in the USA
BVHW031054020721
611052BV00001B/206

9 781737 042327